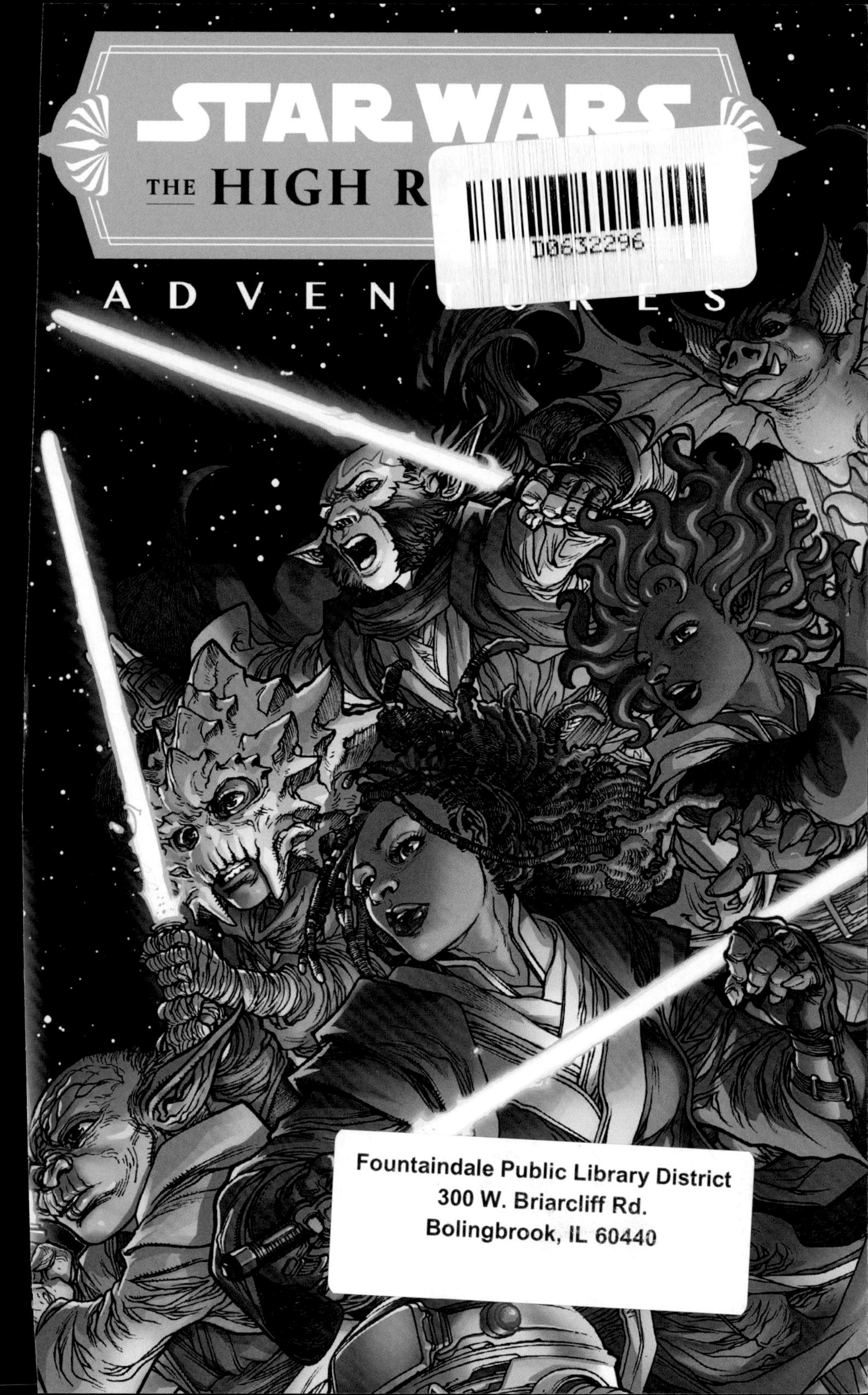
STAR WARS
THE HIGH R
ADVEN

Facebook: **facebook.com/idwpublishing**
Twitter: **@idwpublishing**
YouTube: **youtube.com/idwpublishing**
Instagram: **@idwpublishing**

ISBN: 978-1-68405-879-2   25 24 23 22   1 2 3 4

Cover Art by
Nick Brokenshire

Series Edits by
Heather Antos

Series Assistant Edits by
Riley Farmer

Collection Edits by
Alonzo Simon and
Zac Boone

Collection Design by
Nathan Widick

STAR WARS: THE HIGH REPUBLIC ADVENTURES, VOLUME 2. FEBRUARY 2022. FIRST PRINTING. © 2022 LUCASFILM LTD. & ® OR ™ WHERE INDICATED. All Rights Reserved. The IDW Logo is registered in the U.S. Patent and Trademark Office. IDW Publishing, a division of Idea and Design Works, LLC. Editorial offices: 2765 Truxtun Road, San Diego, CA 92106. Any similarities to persons living or dead are purely coincidental. With the exception of artwork used for review purposes, none of the contents of this publication may be reprinted without permission of Idea and Design Works, LLC. IDW Publishing does not read or accept unsolicited submissions of ideas, stories, or artwork. Printed in Canada.

Originally published as STAR WARS: THE HIGH REPUBLIC ADVENTURES FREE COMIC BOOK DAY 2021, STAR WARS: THE HIGH REPUBLIC ADVENTURES issues #6–8, and STAR WARS: THE HIGH REPUBLIC ADVENTURES ANNUAL 2021.

Lucasfilm Credits:

Senior Editor
Robert Simpson

Creative Director
Michael Siglain

Art Director
Troy Alders

Creative Art Manager
Phil Szostak

Story Group
Matt Martin, Pablo Hidalgo, Emily Shkoukani, and **Jason D. Stein**

Nachie Marsham, Publisher
Blake Kobashigawa, VP of Sales
Tara McCrillis, VP Publishing Operations
John Barber, Editor-in-Chief
Mark Doyle, Editorial Director, Originals
Erika Turner, Executive Editor
Scott Dunbier, Director, Special Projects
Lauren LePera, Managing Editor
Joe Hughes, Director, Talent Relations
Anna Morrow, Sr. Marketing Director
Alexandra Hargett, Book & Mass Market Sales Director
Keith Davidsen, Director, Marketing & PR
Topher Alford, Sr. Digital Marketing Manager
Shauna Monteforte, Sr. Director of Manufacturing Operations
Jamie Miller, Sr. Operations Manager
Nathan Widick, Sr. Art Director, Head of Design
Neil Uyetake, Sr. Art Director, Design & Production
Shawn Lee, Art Director, Design & Production
Jack Rivera, Art Director, Marketing

Ted Adams and Robbie Robbins, IDW Founders

ATTACK ON THE REPUBLIC FAIR

WRITTEN BY DANIEL JOSÉ OLDER
ART BY NICK BROKENSHIRE
COLORS BY REBECCA NALTY
LETTERS BY JAKE M. WOOD

MISSION TO BILBOUSA

WRITTEN BY DANIEL JOSÉ OLDER
ART BY HARVEY TOLIBAO OF MAGNUS ARTS
AND POW RODRIX OF MAGNUS ARTS
COLORS BY REBECCA NALTY
LETTERS BY JAKE M. WOOD

BACK TOGETHER AND AWAY AGAIN

WRITTEN BY DANIEL JOSÉ OLDER
ART BY TONI BRUNO
COLORS BY REBECCA NALTY
LETTERS BY JAKE M. WOOD

SET FOR LIFE

WRITTEN BY CHARLES SOULE
ART & COLORS BY SAM BECK
LETTERS BY JOHANNA NATTALIE

NO STONE UNTURNED

WRITTEN BY CLAUDIA GRAY
ART BY JASON LOO
COLORS BY MEGAN HUANG
LETTERS BY NEIL UYETAKE

FIRST MISSION

WRITTEN BY JUSTINA IRELAND
ART & COLORS BY YAEL NATHAN
LETTERS BY NEIL UYETAKE

CRASH AND THE CREW DO WHAT THEY DO

WRITTEN BY DANIEL JOSÉ OLDER
ART & COLORS BY JESSE LONERGAN
LETTERS BY JAKE M. WOOD

THE HAUL

WRITTEN BY CAVAN SCOTT
ART & COLORS BY STEFANO SIMEONE
LETTERS BY NATHAN WIDICK

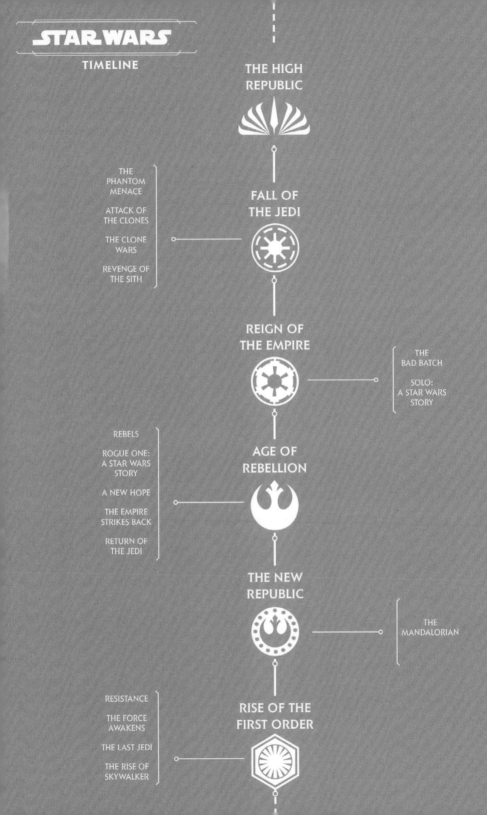

STAR WARS
TIMELINE

THE HIGH REPUBLIC

THE PHANTOM MENACE

ATTACK OF THE CLONES

THE CLONE WARS

REVENGE OF THE SITH

FALL OF THE JEDI

REIGN OF THE EMPIRE

THE BAD BATCH

SOLO: A STAR WARS STORY

REBELS

ROGUE ONE: A STAR WARS STORY

A NEW HOPE

THE EMPIRE STRIKES BACK

RETURN OF THE JEDI

AGE OF REBELLION

THE NEW REPUBLIC

THE MANDALORIAN

RESISTANCE

THE FORCE AWAKENS

THE LAST JEDI

THE RISE OF SKYWALKER

RISE OF THE FIRST ORDER

STAR WARS
THE HIGH REPUBLIC

The galaxy celebrates. With the dark days of the hyperspace disaster behind them, Chancellor Lina Soh pushes ahead with the latest of her GREAT WORKS. The Republic Fair will be her finest hour, a celebration of peace, unity, and hope on the frontier world of Valo.

But an insatiable horror appears on the horizon. One by one, planets fall as the carnivorous DRENGIR consume all life in their path. As Jedi Master AVAR KRISS leads the battle against this terror, Nihil forces gather in secret for the next stage of MARCHION RO'S diabolical plan.

Only the noble JEDI KNIGHTS stand in Ro's way, but even the protectors of light and life are not prepared for the terrible darkness that lies ahead. . . .

ATTACK ON THE REPUBLIC FAIR

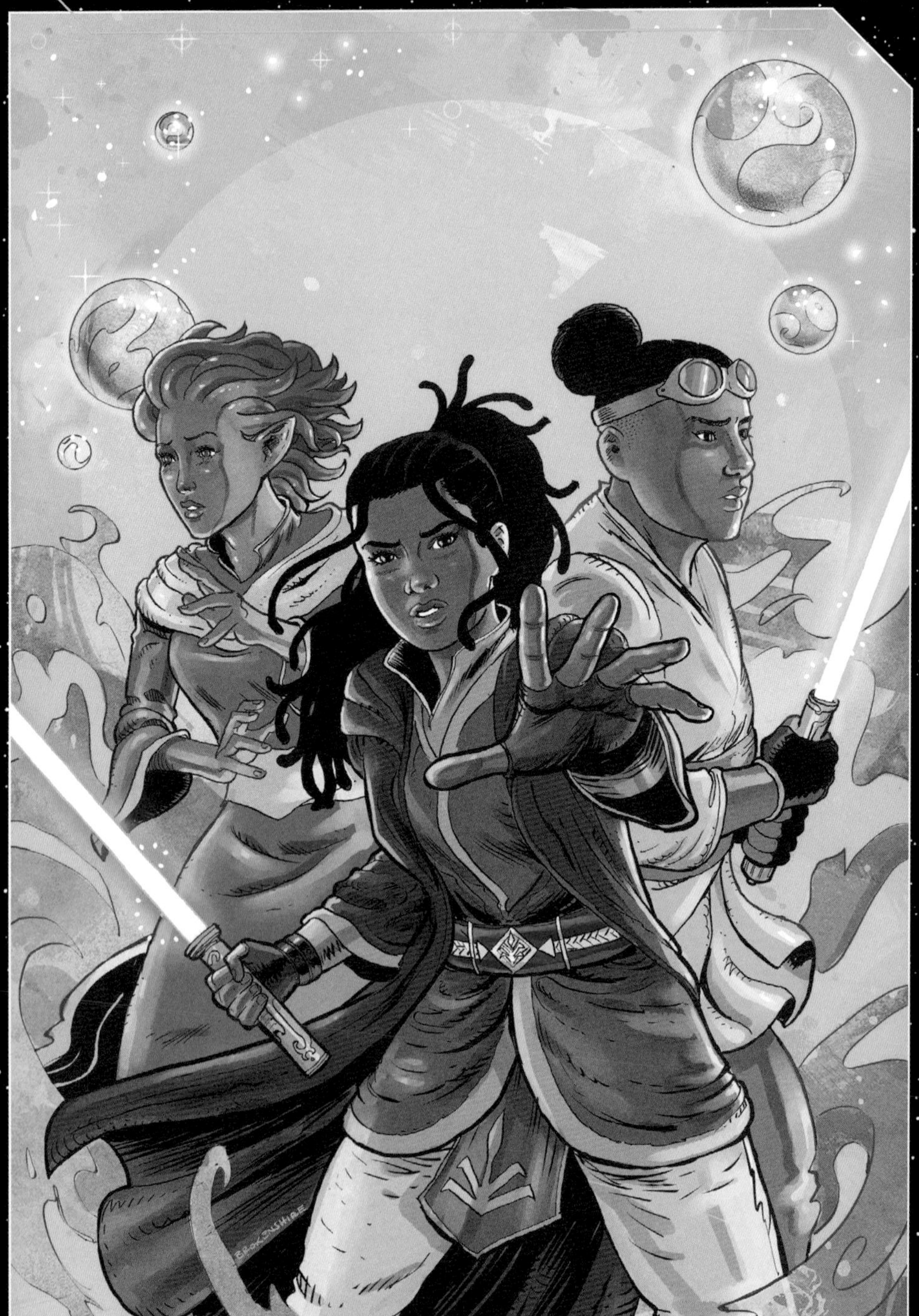

ART BY NICK BROKENSHIRE

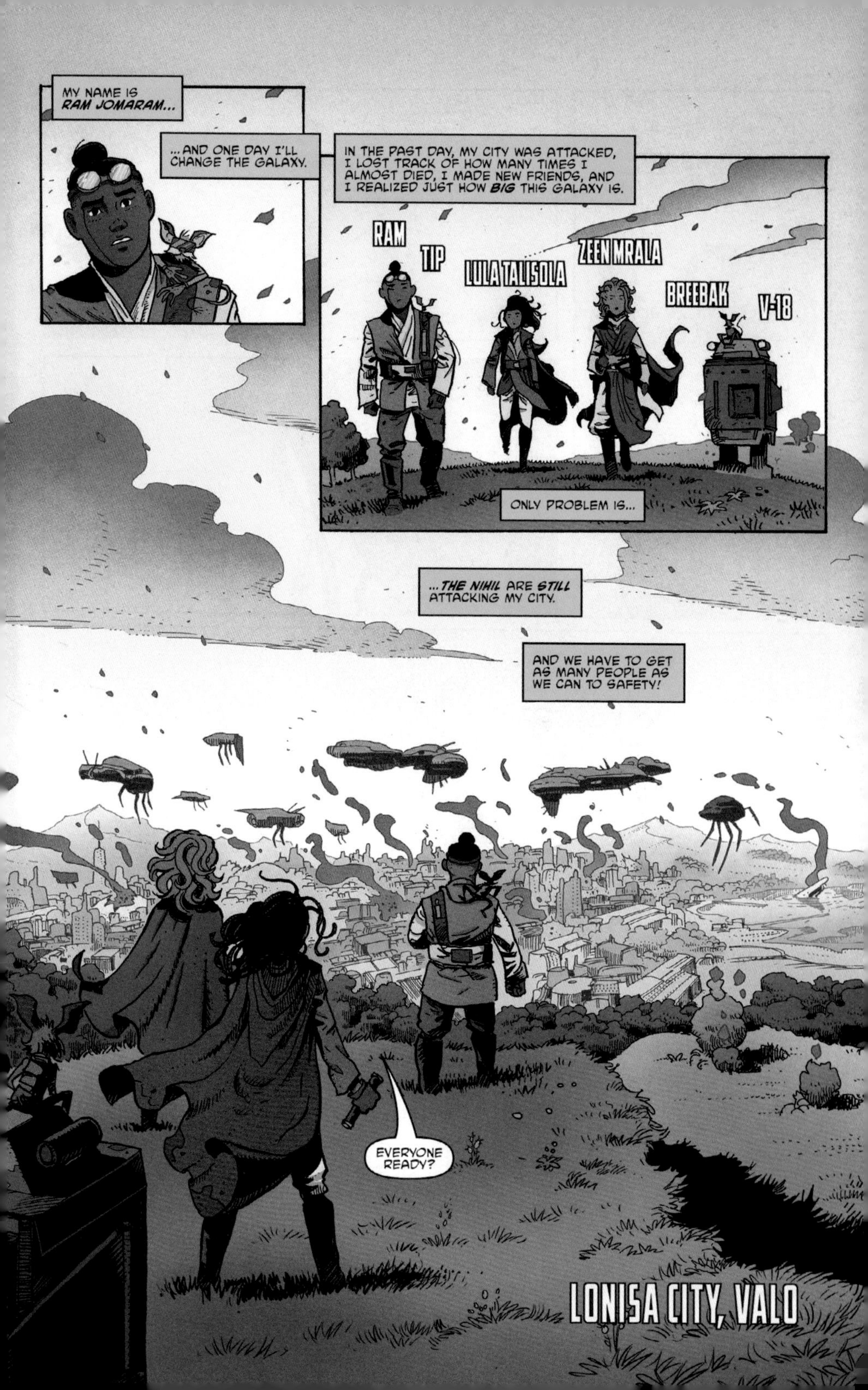
MY NAME IS RAM JOMARAM...
...AND ONE DAY I'LL CHANGE THE GALAXY.
IN THE PAST DAY, MY CITY WAS ATTACKED, I LOST TRACK OF HOW MANY TIMES I ALMOST DIED, I MADE NEW FRIENDS, AND I REALIZED JUST HOW BIG THIS GALAXY IS.
RAM
TIP
LULA TALISOLA
ZEEN MRALA
BREEBAK
V-18
ONLY PROBLEM IS...
...THE NIHIL ARE STILL ATTACKING MY CITY.
AND WE HAVE TO GET AS MANY PEOPLE AS WE CAN TO SAFETY!
EVERYONE READY?
LONISA CITY, VALO

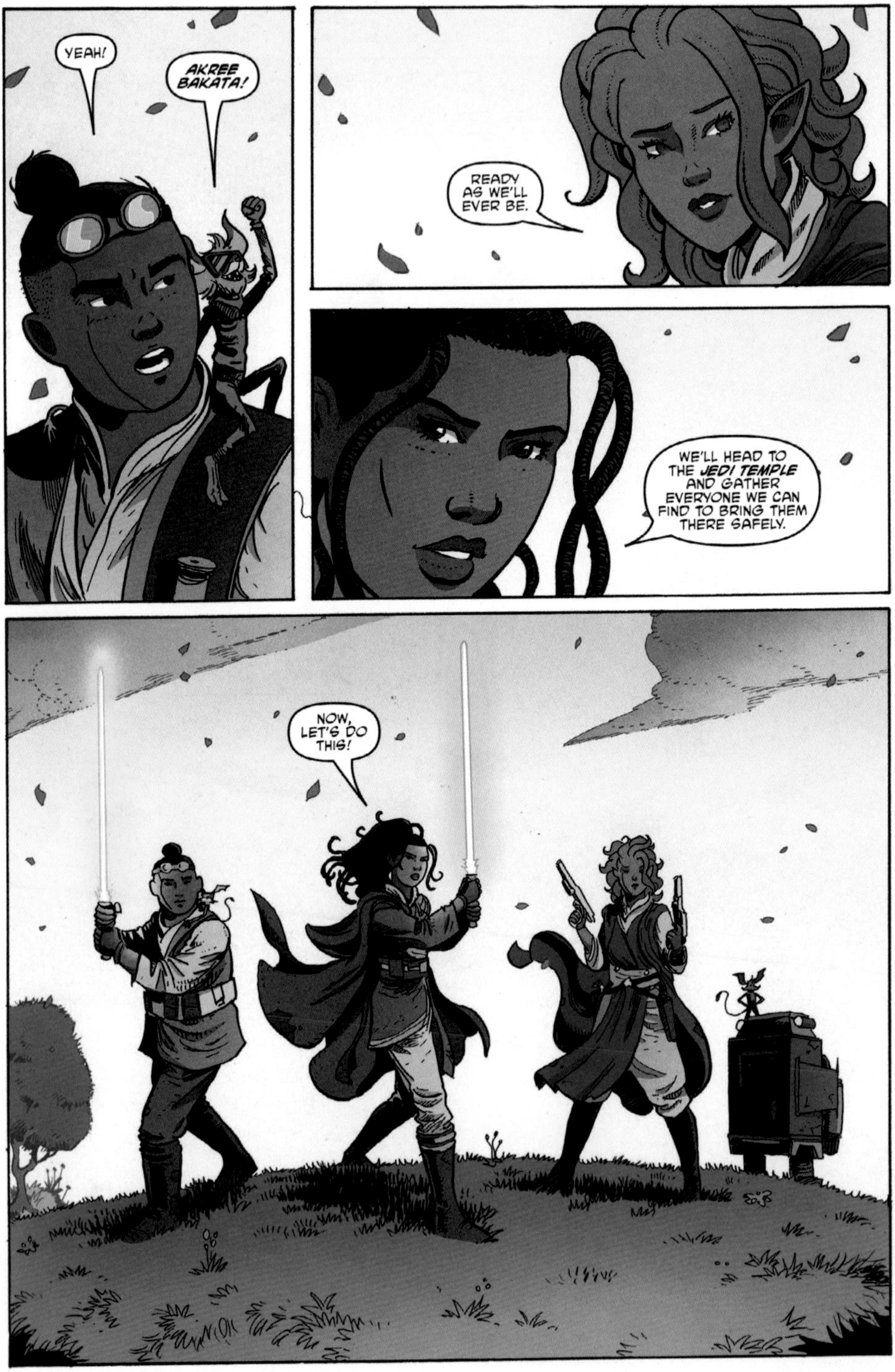
YEAH!
AKREE BAKATA!
READY AS WE'LL EVER BE.
WE'LL HEAD TO THE JEDI TEMPLE AND GATHER EVERYONE WE CAN FIND TO BRING THEM THERE SAFELY.
NOW, LET'S DO THIS!

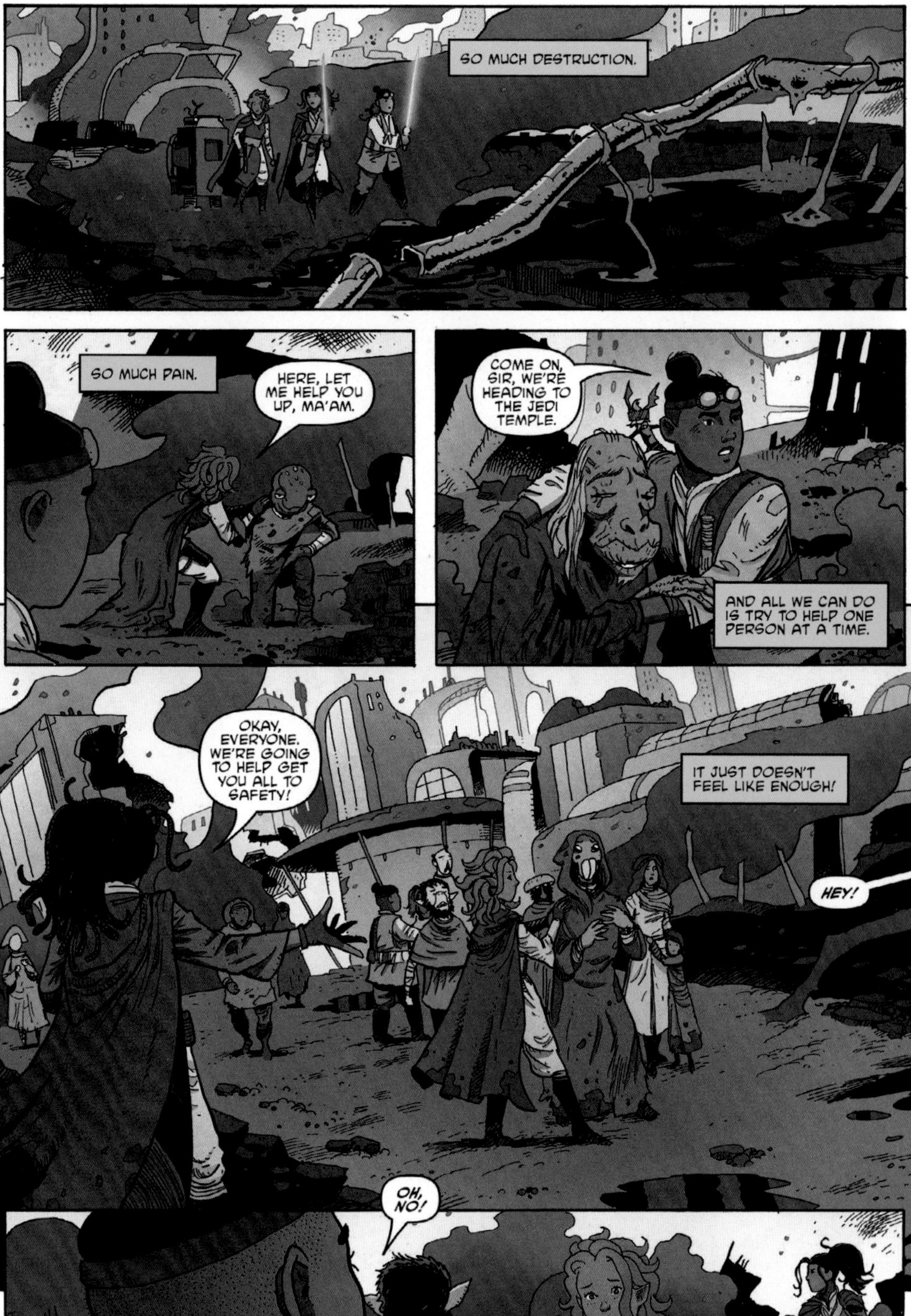
SO MUCH DESTRUCTION.
SO MUCH PAIN.
HERE, LET ME HELP YOU UP, MA'AM.
COME ON, SIR, WE'RE HEADING TO THE JEDI TEMPLE.
AND ALL WE CAN DO IS TRY TO HELP ONE PERSON AT A TIME.
OKAY, EVERYONE. WE'RE GOING TO HELP GET YOU ALL TO SAFETY!
IT JUST DOESN'T FEEL LIKE ENOUGH!
HEY!
OH, NO!

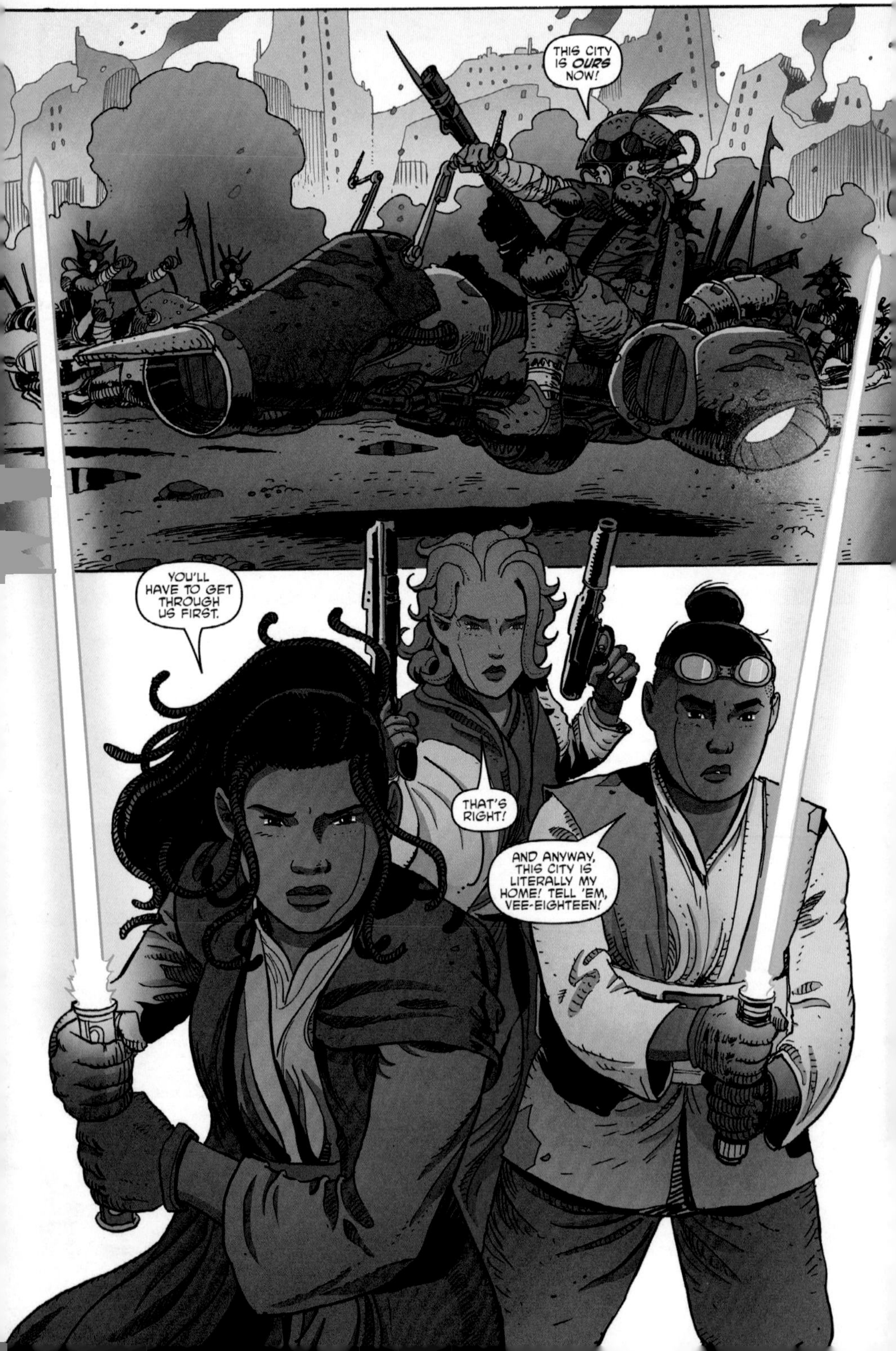
THIS CITY IS OURS NOW!
YOU'LL HAVE TO GET THROUGH US FIRST.
THAT'S RIGHT!
AND ANYWAY, THIS CITY IS LITERALLY MY HOME! TELL 'EM, VEE-EIGHTEEN!

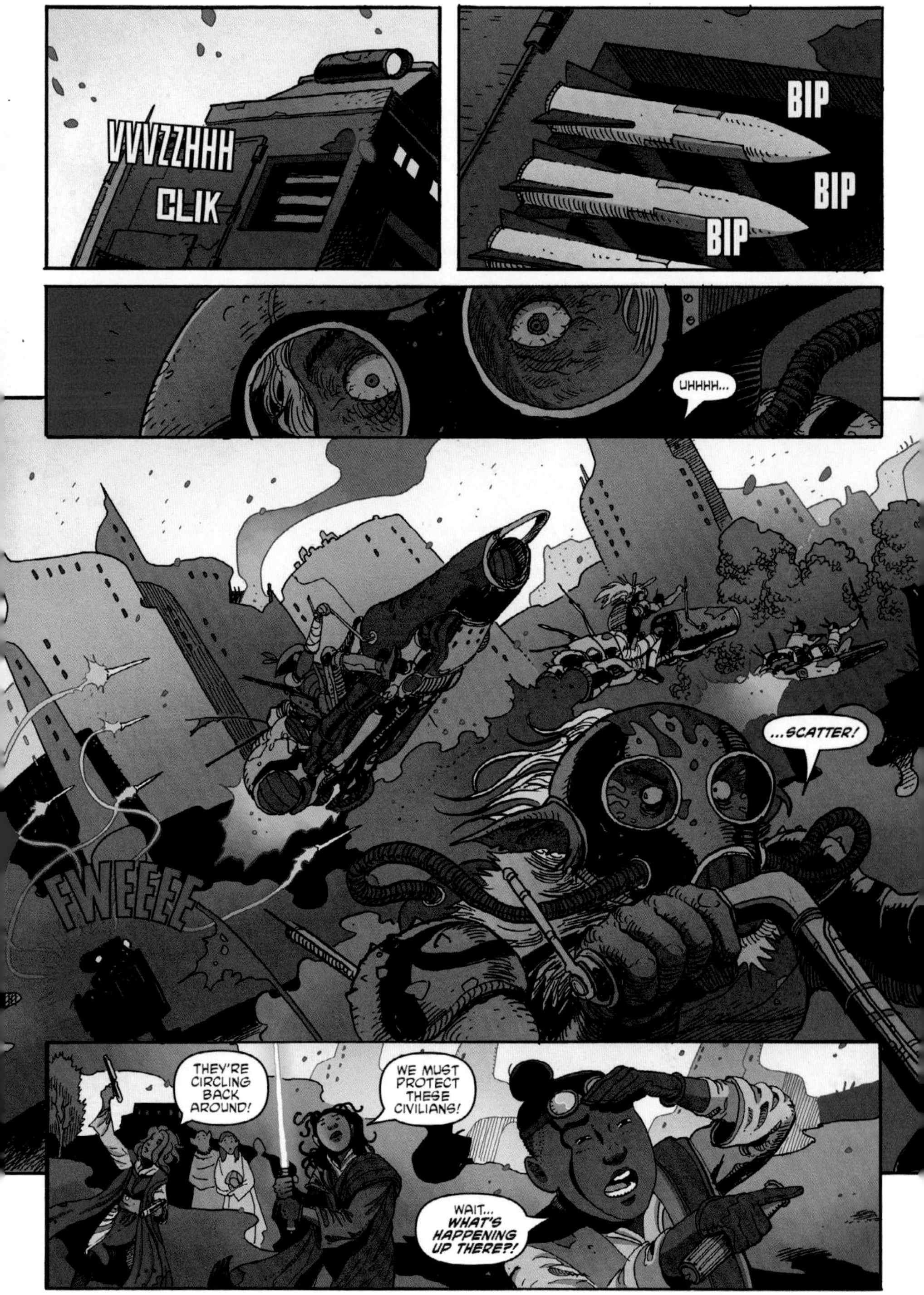
VVVZZHHH
CLIK
BIP
BIP
BIP
UHHHH...
...SCATTER!
FWEEEE
THEY'RE CIRCLING BACK AROUND!
WE MUST PROTECT THESE CIVILIANS!
WAIT... WHAT'S HAPPENING UP THERE?!

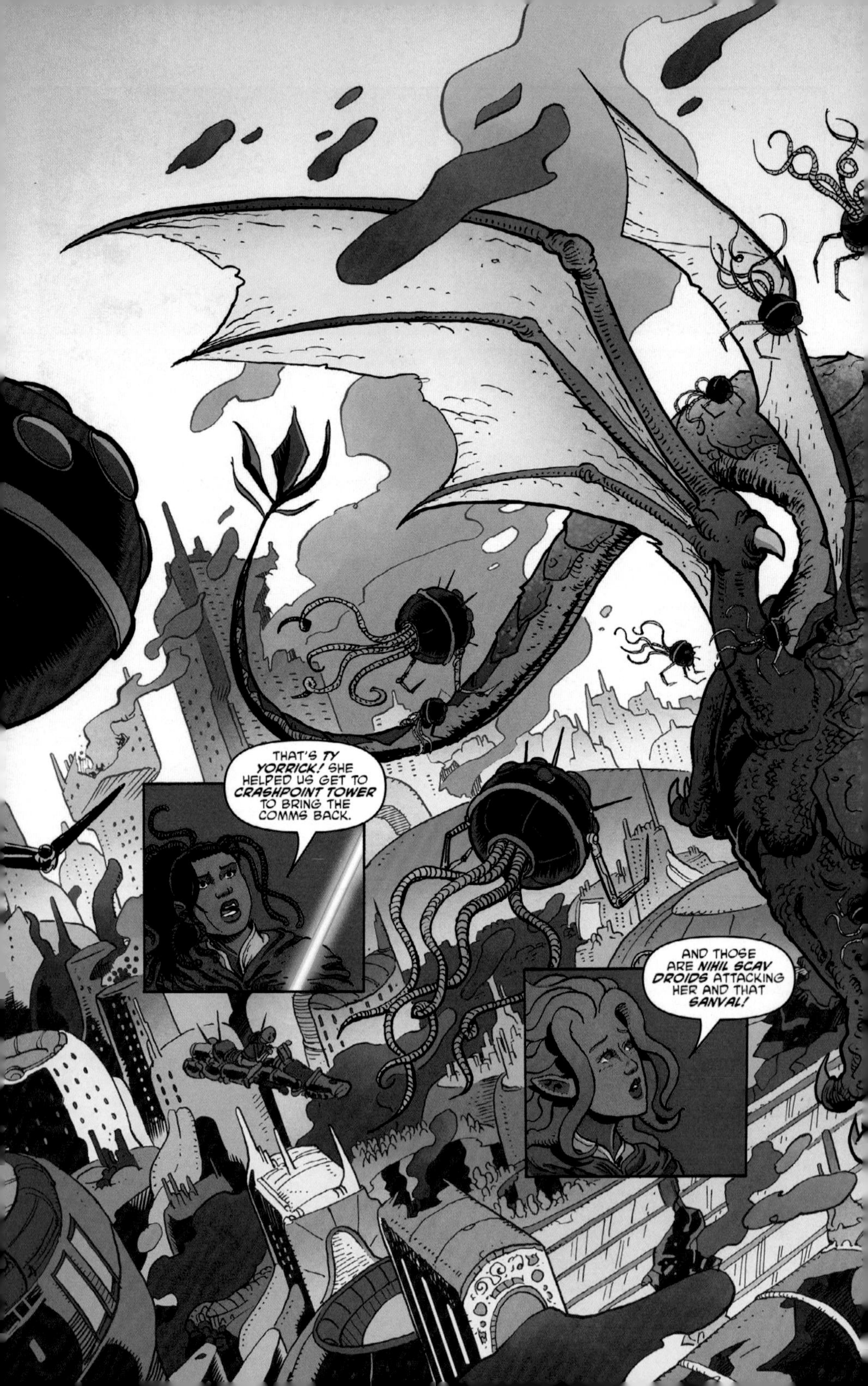
THAT'S TY YORRICK! SHE HELPED US GET TO CRASHPOINT TOWER TO BRING THE COMMS BACK.
AND THOSE ARE NIHIL SCAV DROIDS ATTACKING HER AND THAT SANVAL!

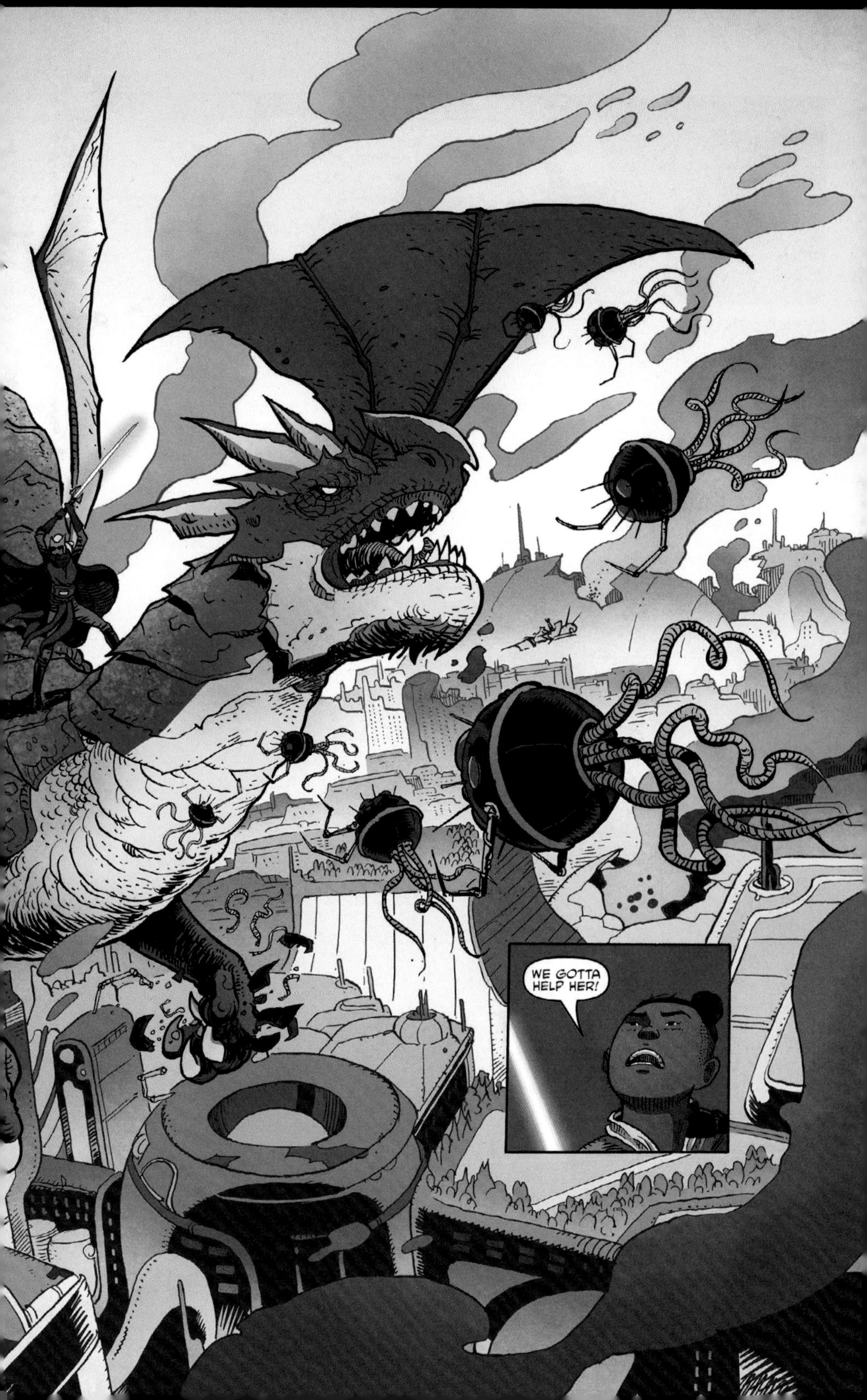
WE GOTTA HELP HER!

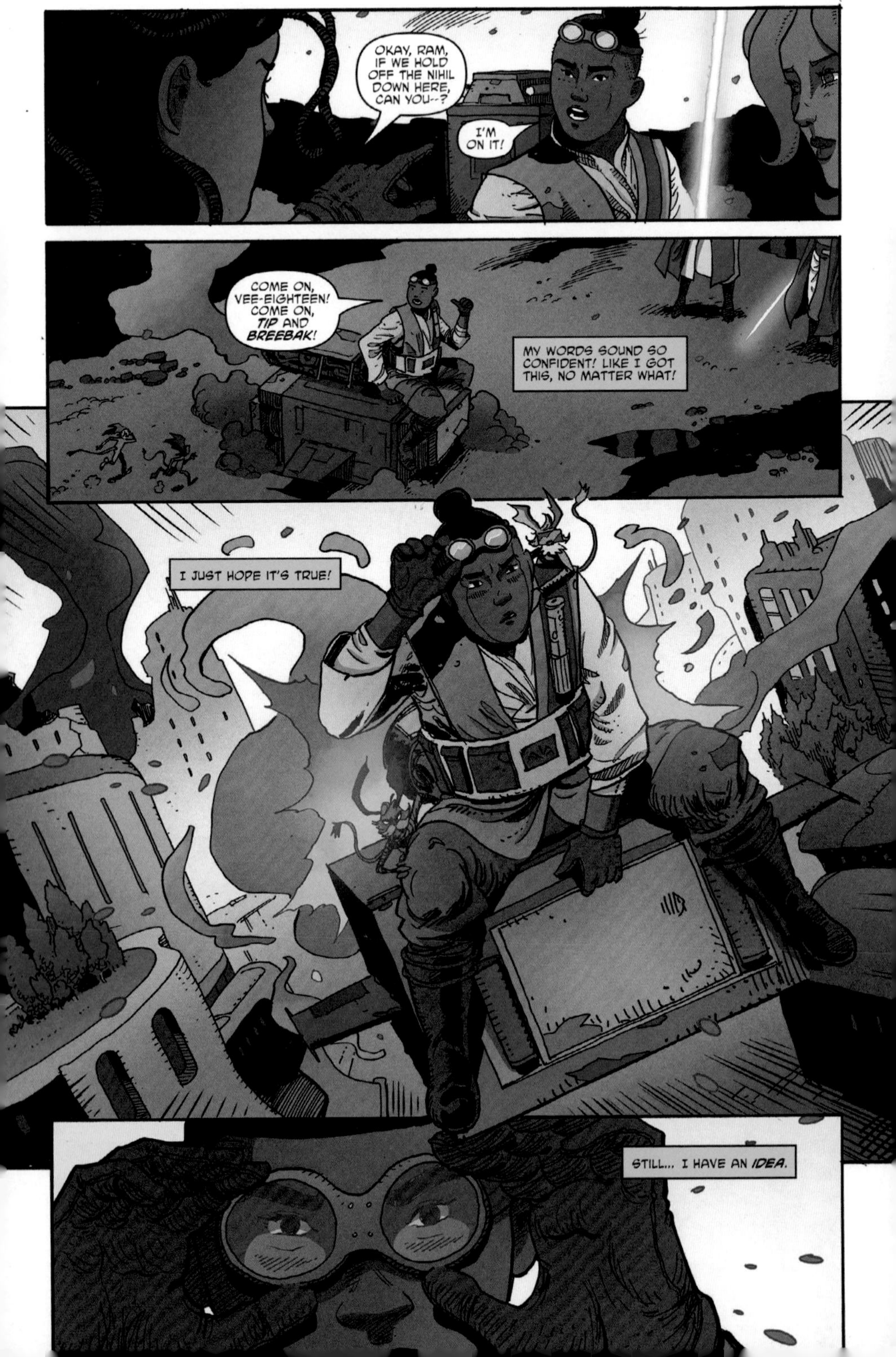
OKAY, RAM, IF WE HOLD OFF THE NIHIL DOWN HERE, CAN YOU--?
I'M ON IT!
COME ON, VEE-EIGHTEEN! COME ON, TIP AND BREEBAK!
MY WORDS SOUND SO CONFIDENT! LIKE I GOT THIS, NO MATTER WHAT!
I JUST HOPE IT'S TRUE!
STILL... I HAVE AN IDEA.

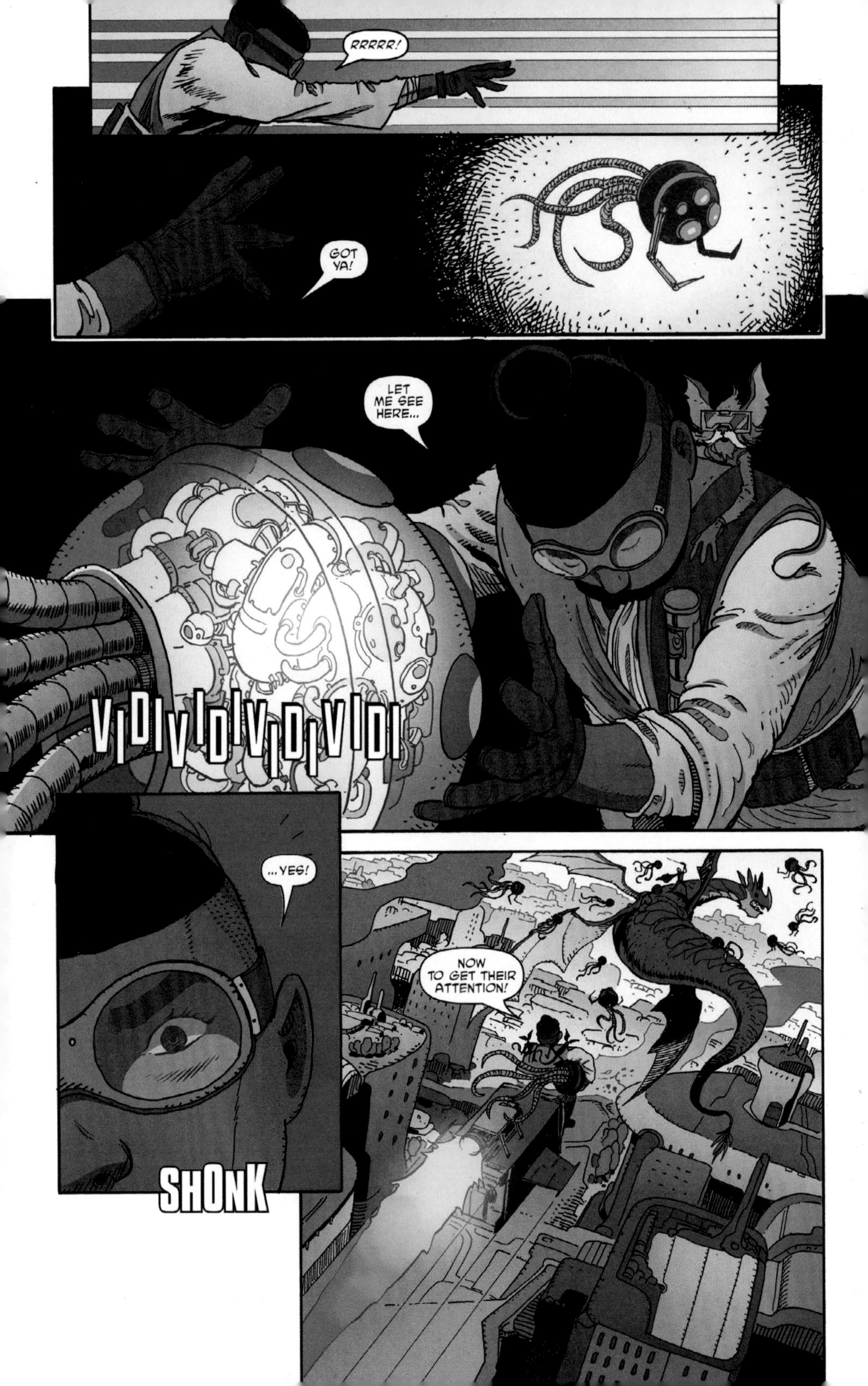
RRRRR!
GOT YA!
LET ME SEE HERE...
VIDIVIDIVIDIVIDI
...YES!
SHONK
NOW TO GET THEIR ATTENTION!

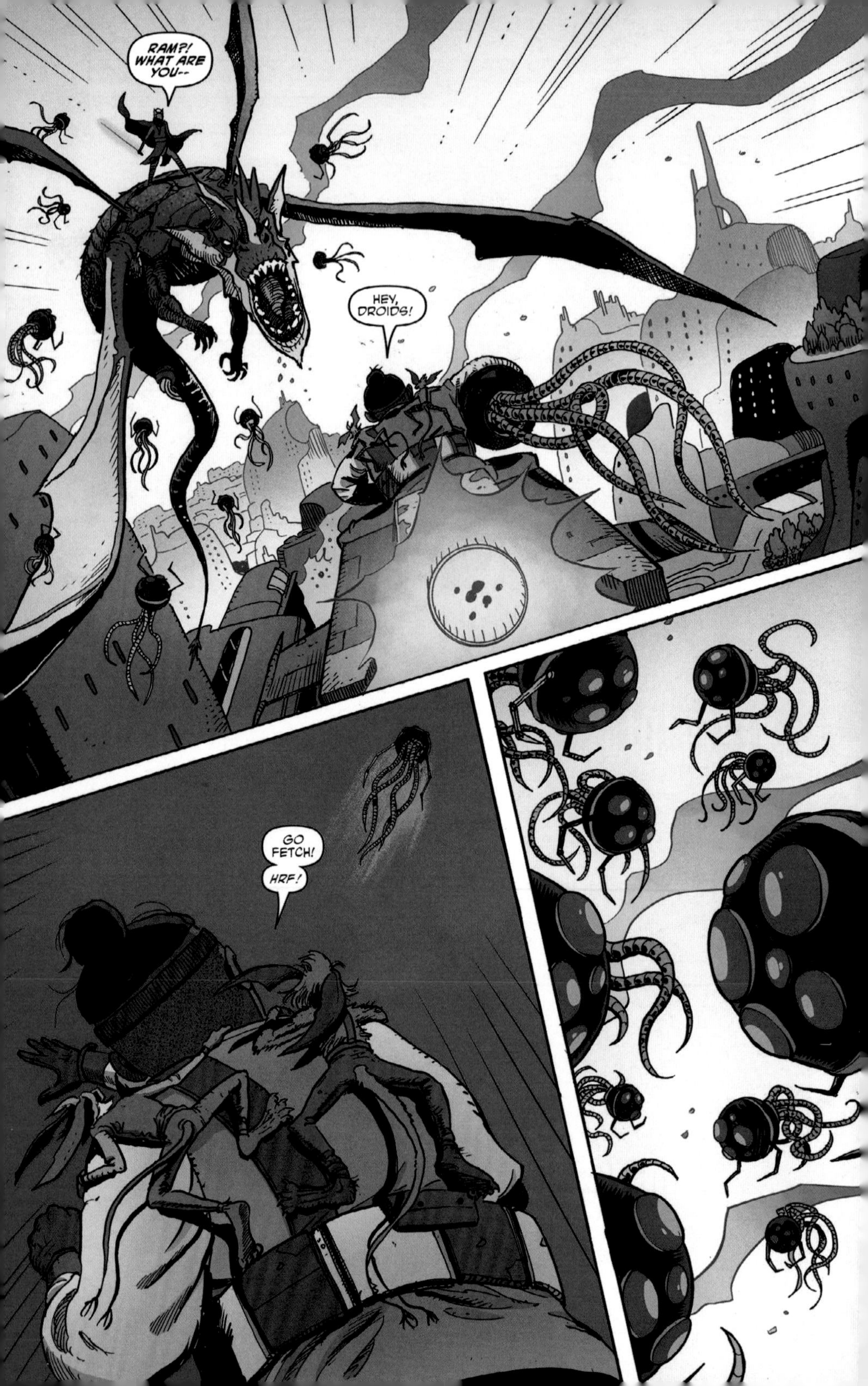
RAM?! WHAT ARE YOU--
HEY, DROIDS!
GO FETCH!
HRF!

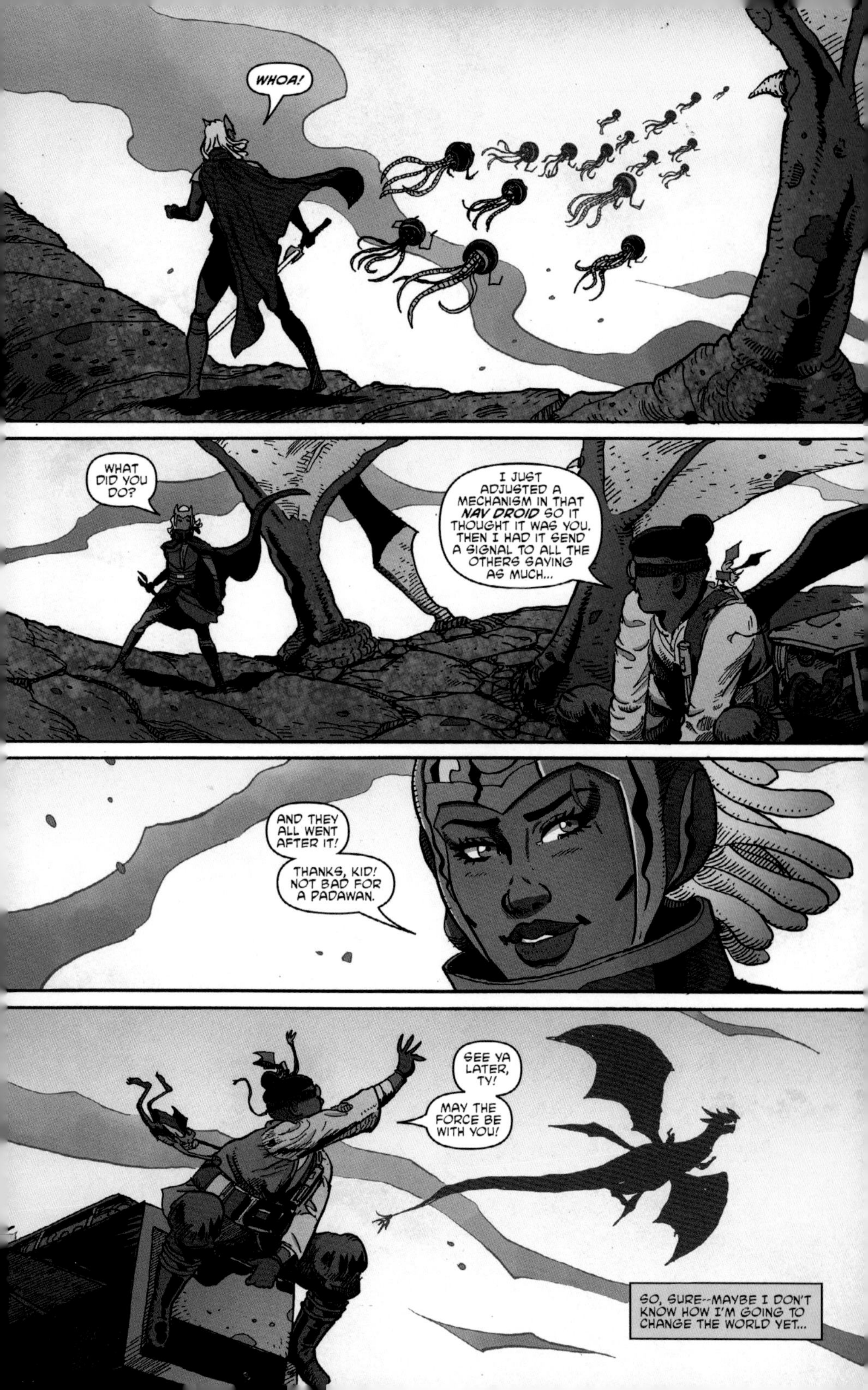
WHOA!
WHAT DID YOU DO?
I JUST ADJUSTED A MECHANISM IN THAT NAV DROID SO IT THOUGHT IT WAS YOU. THEN I HAD IT SEND A SIGNAL TO ALL THE OTHERS SAYING AS MUCH...
AND THEY ALL WENT AFTER IT!
THANKS, KID! NOT BAD FOR A PADAWAN.
SEE YA LATER, TY!
MAY THE FORCE BE WITH YOU!
SO, SURE--MAYBE I DON'T KNOW HOW I'M GOING TO CHANGE THE WORLD YET...

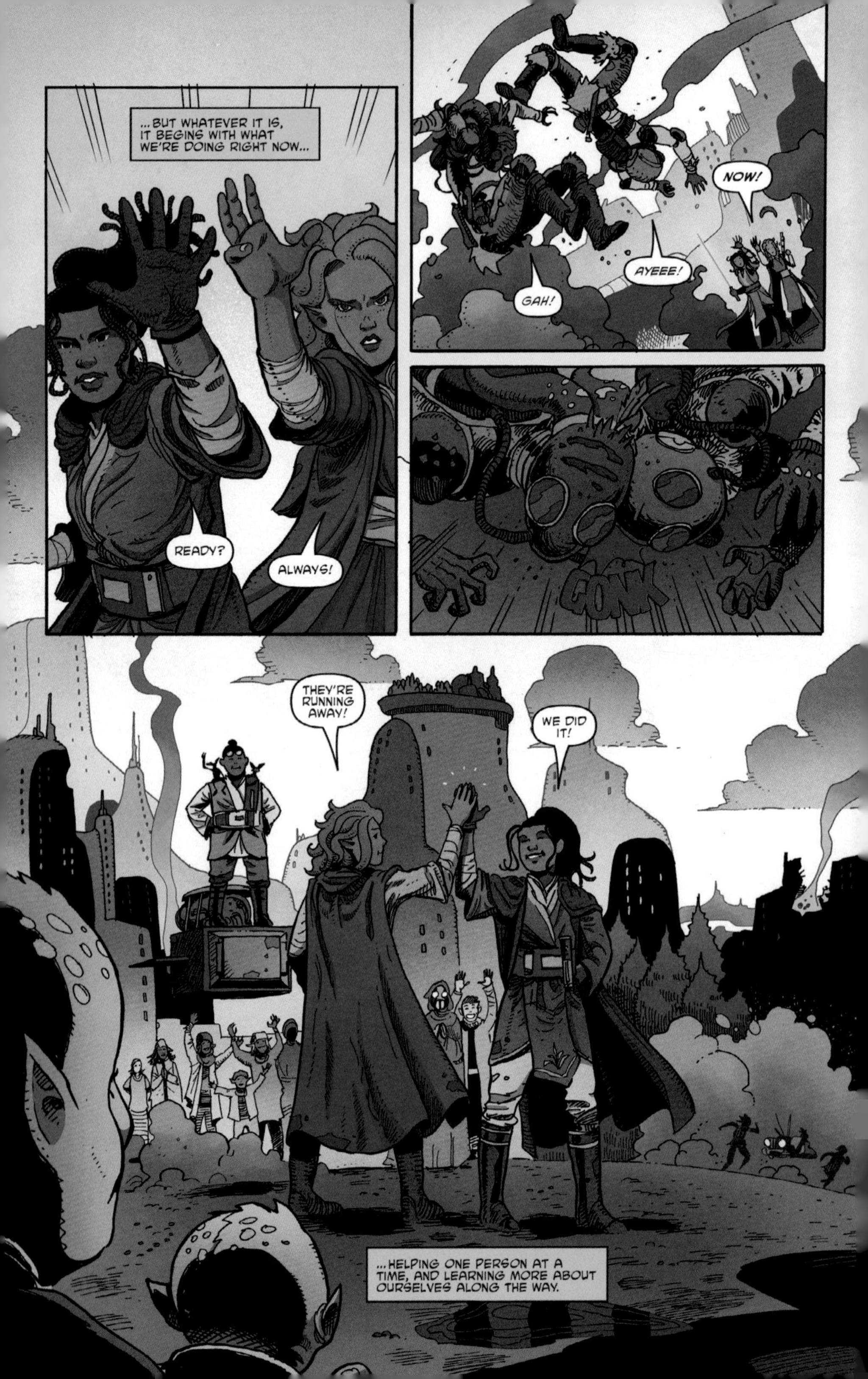
...BUT WHATEVER IT IS, IT BEGINS WITH WHAT WE'RE DOING RIGHT NOW...
READY?
ALWAYS!
NOW!
AYEEE!
GAH!
GONK
THEY'RE RUNNING AWAY!
WE DID IT!
...HELPING ONE PERSON AT A TIME, AND LEARNING MORE ABOUT OURSELVES ALONG THE WAY.

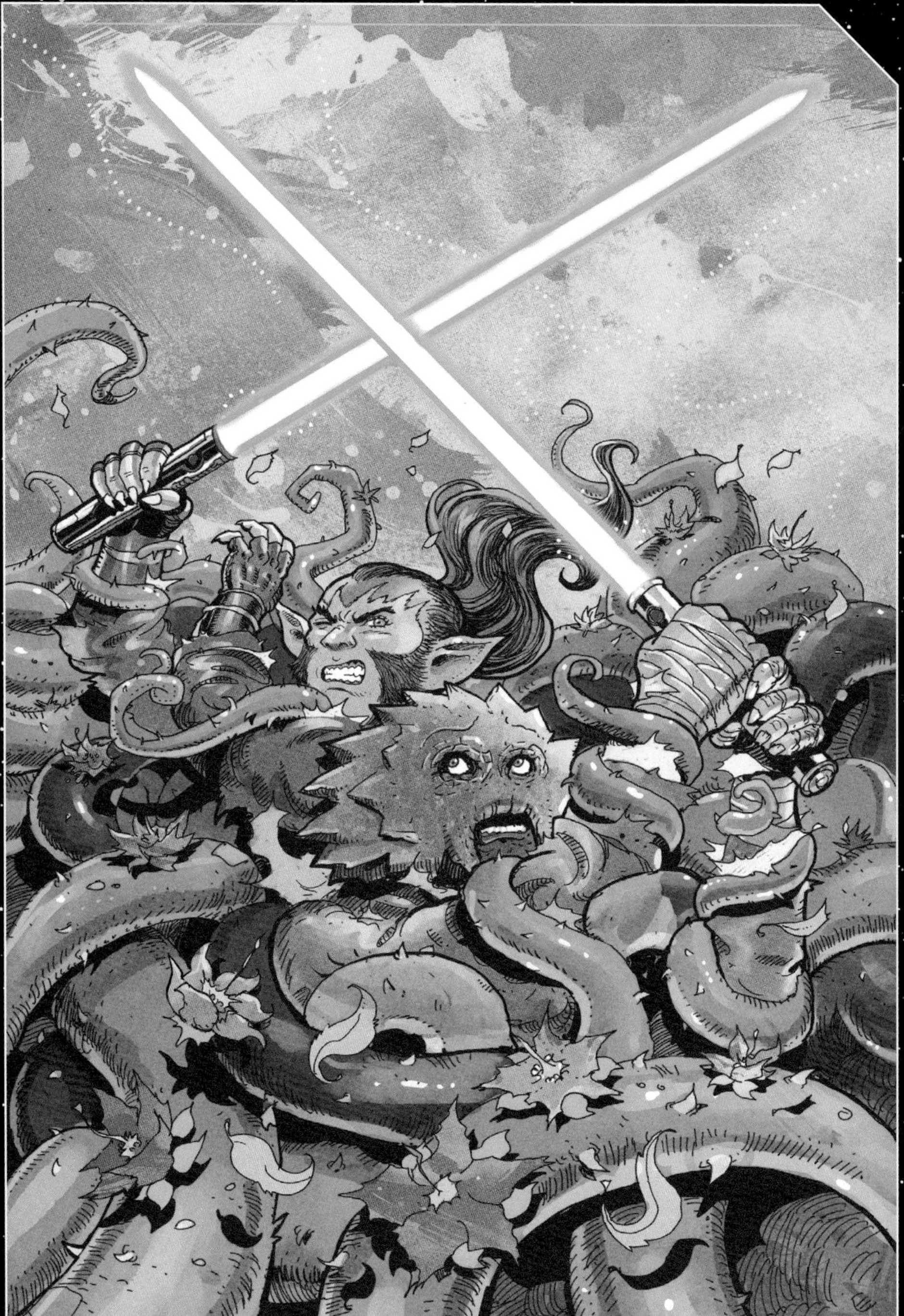

ART BY NICK BROKENSHIRE

MISSION TO BILBOUSA, PART I

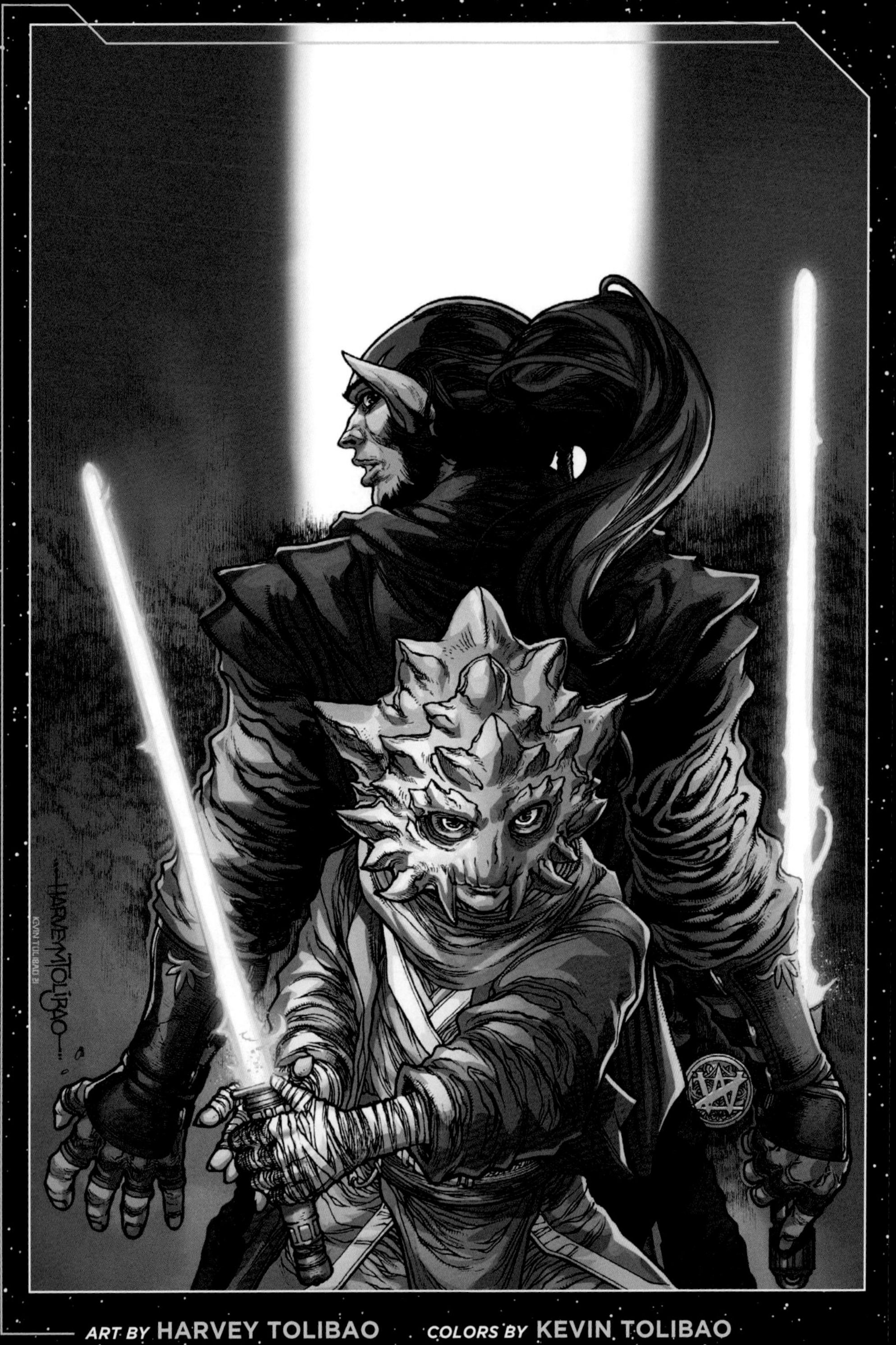

ART BY **HARVEY TOLIBAO** *COLORS BY* **KEVIN TOLIBAO**

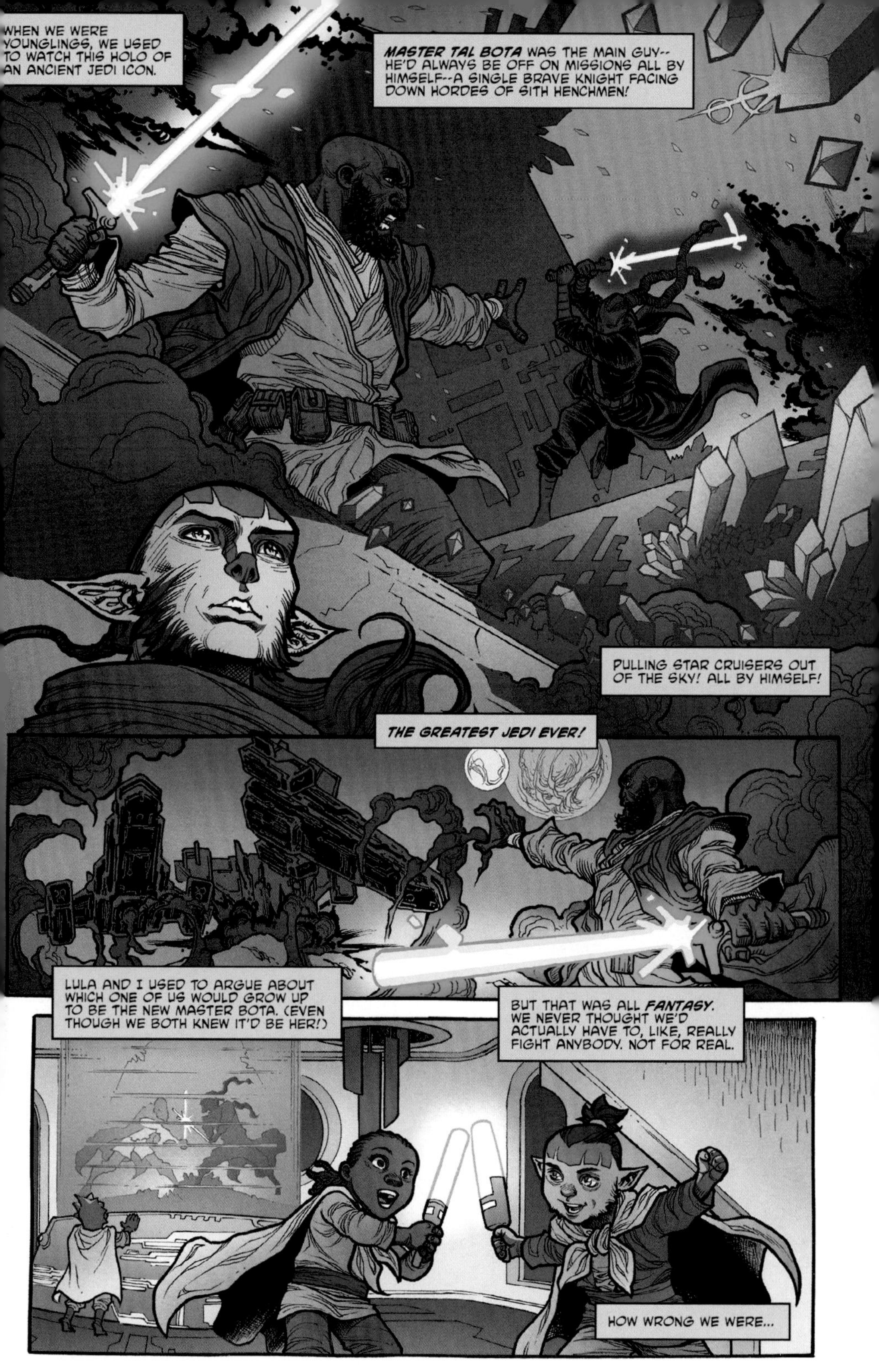
WHEN WE WERE YOUNGLINGS, WE USED TO WATCH THIS HOLO OF AN ANCIENT JEDI ICON.
MASTER TAL BOTA WAS THE MAIN GUY-- HE'D ALWAYS BE OFF ON MISSIONS ALL BY HIMSELF--A SINGLE BRAVE KNIGHT FACING DOWN HORDES OF SITH HENCHMEN!
PULLING STAR CRUISERS OUT OF THE SKY! ALL BY HIMSELF!
THE GREATEST JEDI EVER!
LULA AND I USED TO ARGUE ABOUT WHICH ONE OF US WOULD GROW UP TO BE THE NEW MASTER BOTA. (EVEN THOUGH WE BOTH KNEW IT'D BE HER!)
BUT THAT WAS ALL FANTASY. WE NEVER THOUGHT WE'D ACTUALLY HAVE TO, LIKE, REALLY FIGHT ANYBODY. NOT FOR REAL.
HOW WRONG WE WERE...

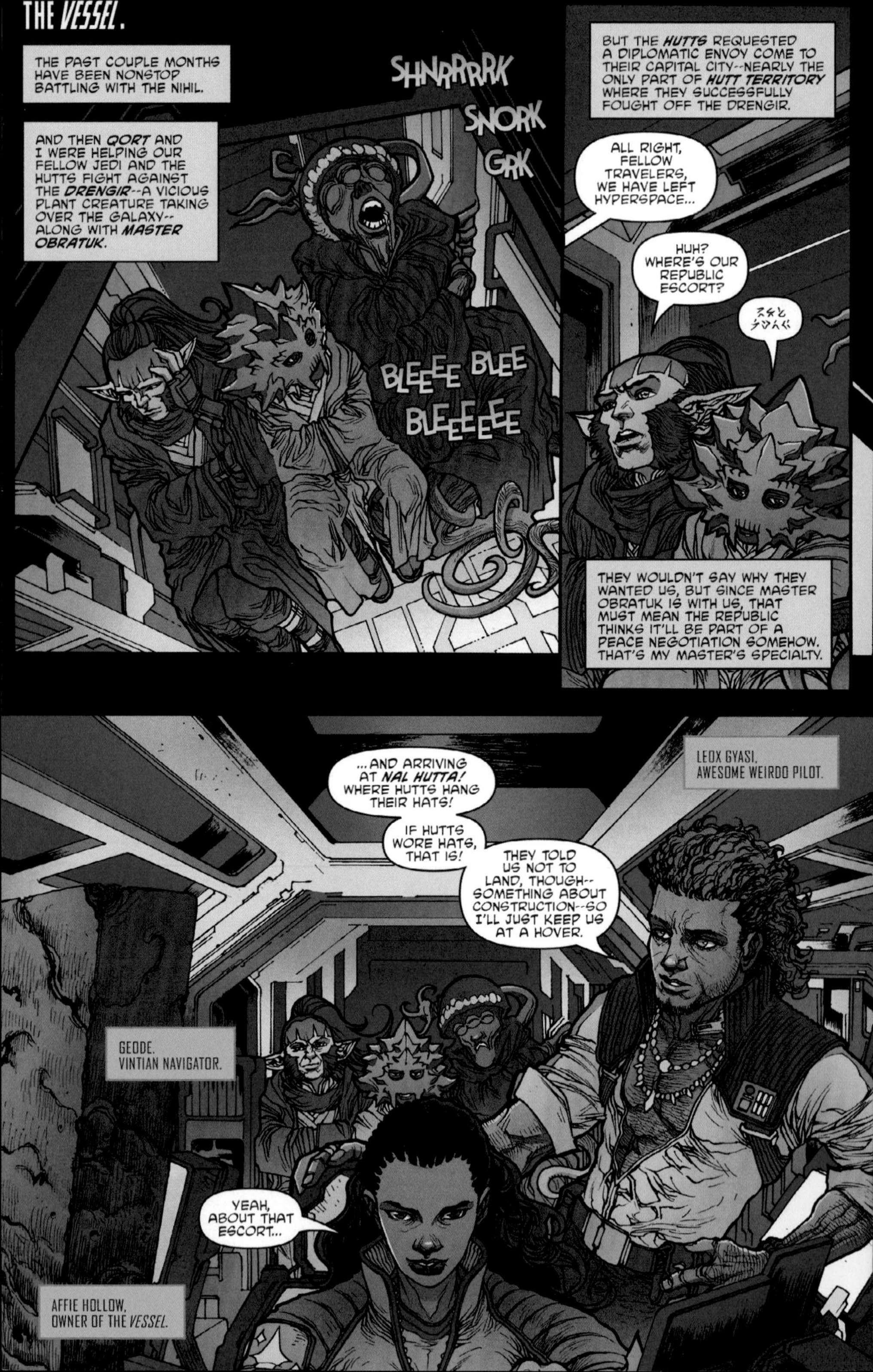

THE VESSEL.
THE PAST COUPLE MONTHS HAVE BEEN NONSTOP BATTLING WITH THE NIHIL.
AND THEN QORT AND I WERE HELPING OUR FELLOW JEDI AND THE HUTTS FIGHT AGAINST THE DRENGIR--A VICIOUS PLANT CREATURE TAKING OVER THE GALAXY--ALONG WITH MASTER OBRATUK.
SHNRRRRK
SNORK
GRK
BLEEEE BLEE
BLEEEEEE
BUT THE HUTTS REQUESTED A DIPLOMATIC ENVOY COME TO THEIR CAPITAL CITY--NEARLY THE ONLY PART OF HUTT TERRITORY WHERE THEY SUCCESSFULLY FOUGHT OFF THE DRENGIR.
ALL RIGHT, FELLOW TRAVELERS, WE HAVE LEFT HYPERSPACE...
HUH? WHERE'S OUR REPUBLIC ESCORT?
THEY WOULDN'T SAY WHY THEY WANTED US, BUT SINCE MASTER OBRATUK IS WITH US, THAT MUST MEAN THE REPUBLIC THINKS IT'LL BE PART OF A PEACE NEGOTIATION SOMEHOW. THAT'S MY MASTER'S SPECIALTY.
LEOX GYASI, AWESOME WEIRDO PILOT.
...AND ARRIVING AT NAL HUTTA! WHERE HUTTS HANG THEIR HATS!
IF HUTTS WORE HATS, THAT IS!
THEY TOLD US NOT TO LAND, THOUGH--SOMETHING ABOUT CONSTRUCTION--SO I'LL JUST KEEP US AT A HOVER.
GEODE. VINTIAN NAVIGATOR.
YEAH, ABOUT THAT ESCORT...
AFFIE HOLLOW, OWNER OF THE VESSEL.

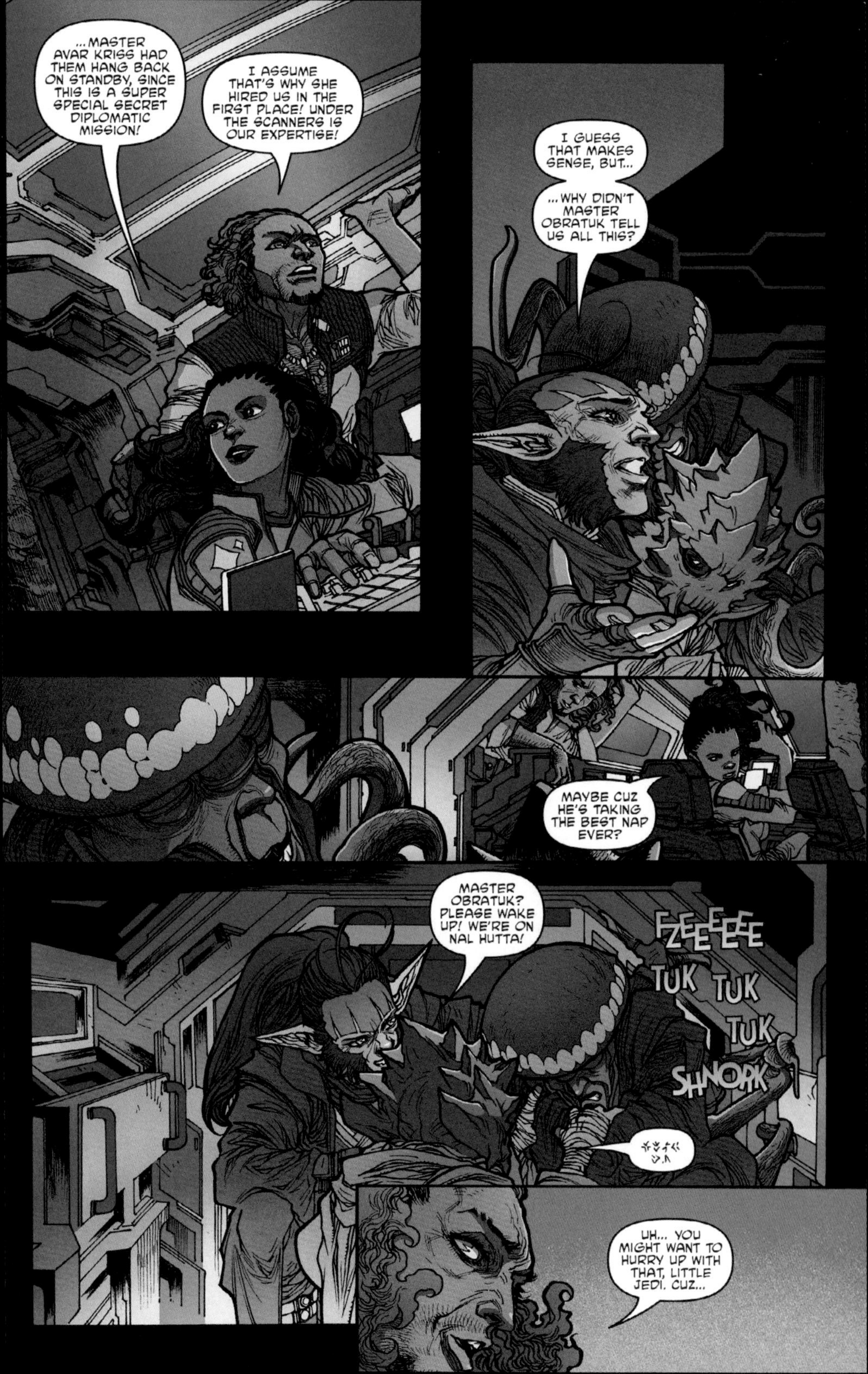
...MASTER AVAR KRISS HAD THEM HANG BACK ON STANDBY, SINCE THIS IS A SUPER SPECIAL SECRET DIPLOMATIC MISSION!
I ASSUME THAT'S WHY SHE HIRED US IN THE FIRST PLACE! UNDER THE SCANNERS IS OUR EXPERTISE!
I GUESS THAT MAKES SENSE, BUT...
...WHY DIDN'T MASTER OBRATUK TELL US ALL THIS?
MAYBE CUZ HE'S TAKING THE BEST NAP EVER?
MASTER OBRATUK? PLEASE WAKE UP! WE'RE ON NAL HUTTA!
FZEEEEEE
TUK TUK TUK
SHNORK
UH... YOU MIGHT WANT TO HURRY UP WITH THAT, LITTLE JEDI. CUZ...

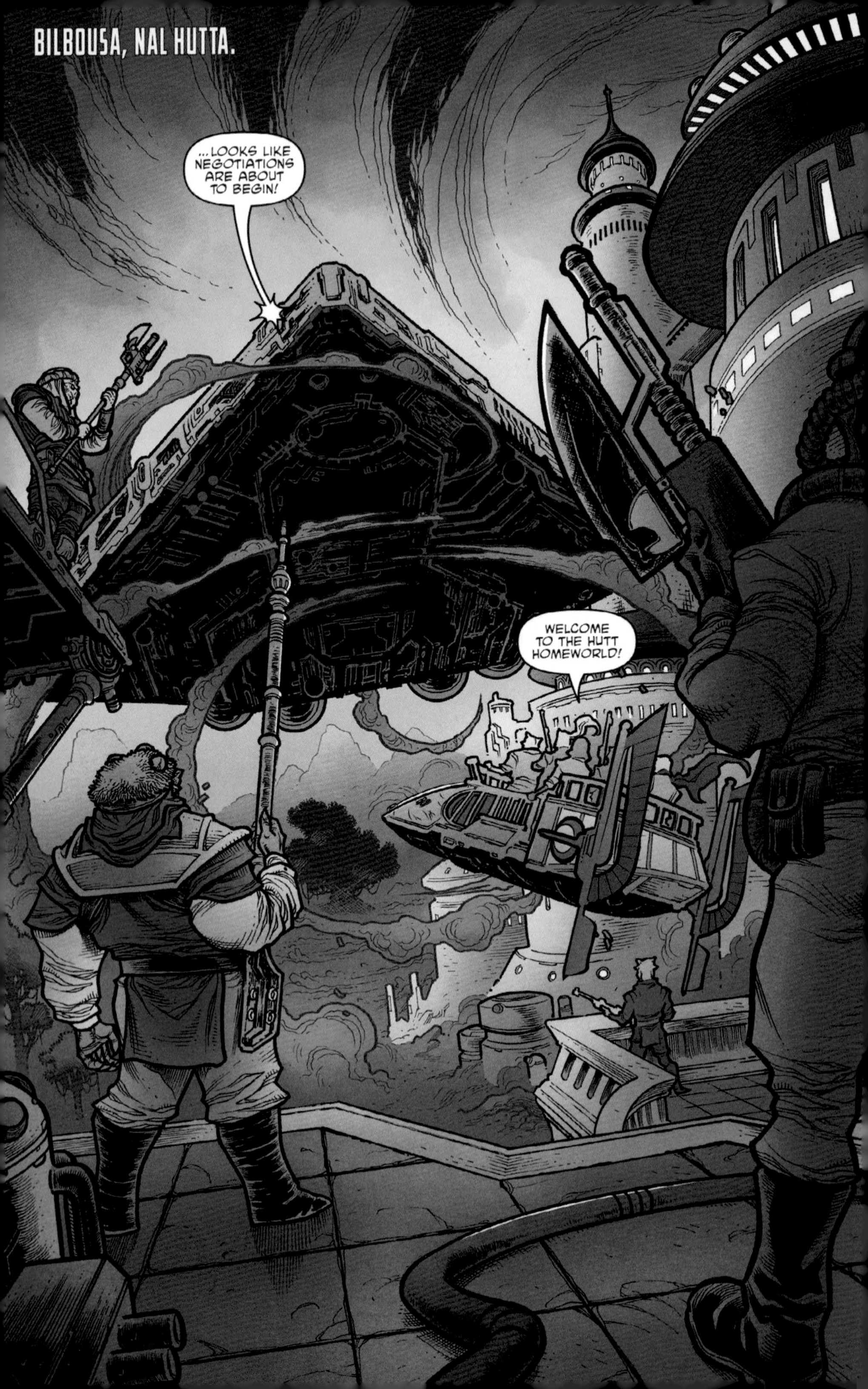
BILBOUSA, NAL HUTTA.
...LOOKS LIKE NEGOTIATIONS ARE ABOUT TO BEGIN!
WELCOME TO THE HUTT HOMEWORLD!

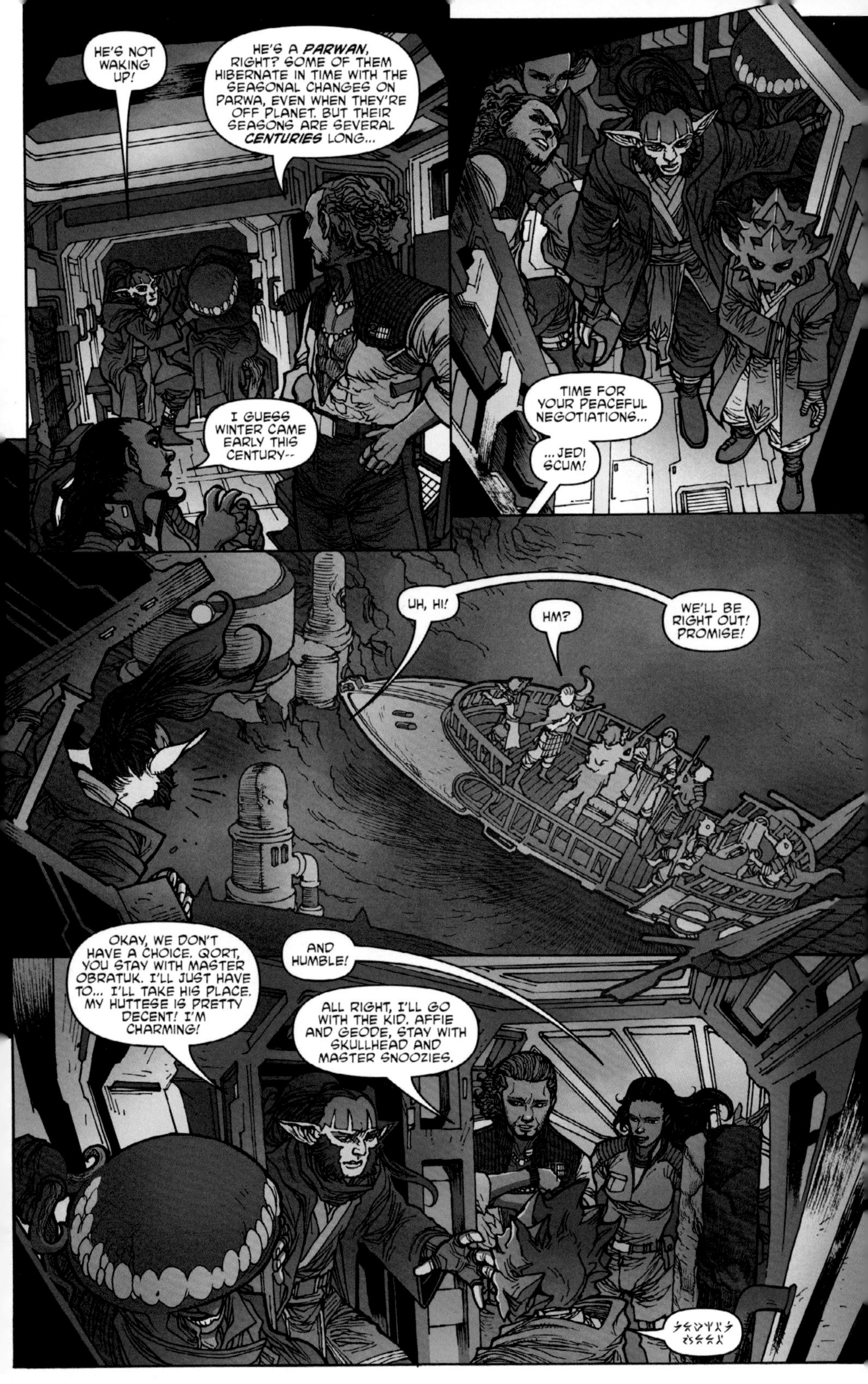
HE'S NOT WAKING UP!
HE'S A *PARWAN*, RIGHT? SOME OF THEM HIBERNATE IN TIME WITH THE SEASONAL CHANGES ON PARWA, EVEN WHEN THEY'RE OFF PLANET. BUT THEIR SEASONS ARE SEVERAL *CENTURIES* LONG...
I GUESS WINTER CAME EARLY THIS CENTURY--
TIME FOR YOUR PEACEFUL NEGOTIATIONS...
...JEDI SCUM!
UH, HI!
HM?
WE'LL BE RIGHT OUT! PROMISE!
OKAY, WE DON'T HAVE A CHOICE. QORT, YOU STAY WITH MASTER OBRATUK. I'LL JUST HAVE TO... I'LL TAKE HIS PLACE. MY HUTTESE IS PRETTY DECENT! I'M CHARMING!
AND HUMBLE!
ALL RIGHT, I'LL GO WITH THE KID. AFFIE AND GEODE, STAY WITH SKULLHEAD AND MASTER SNOOZIES.

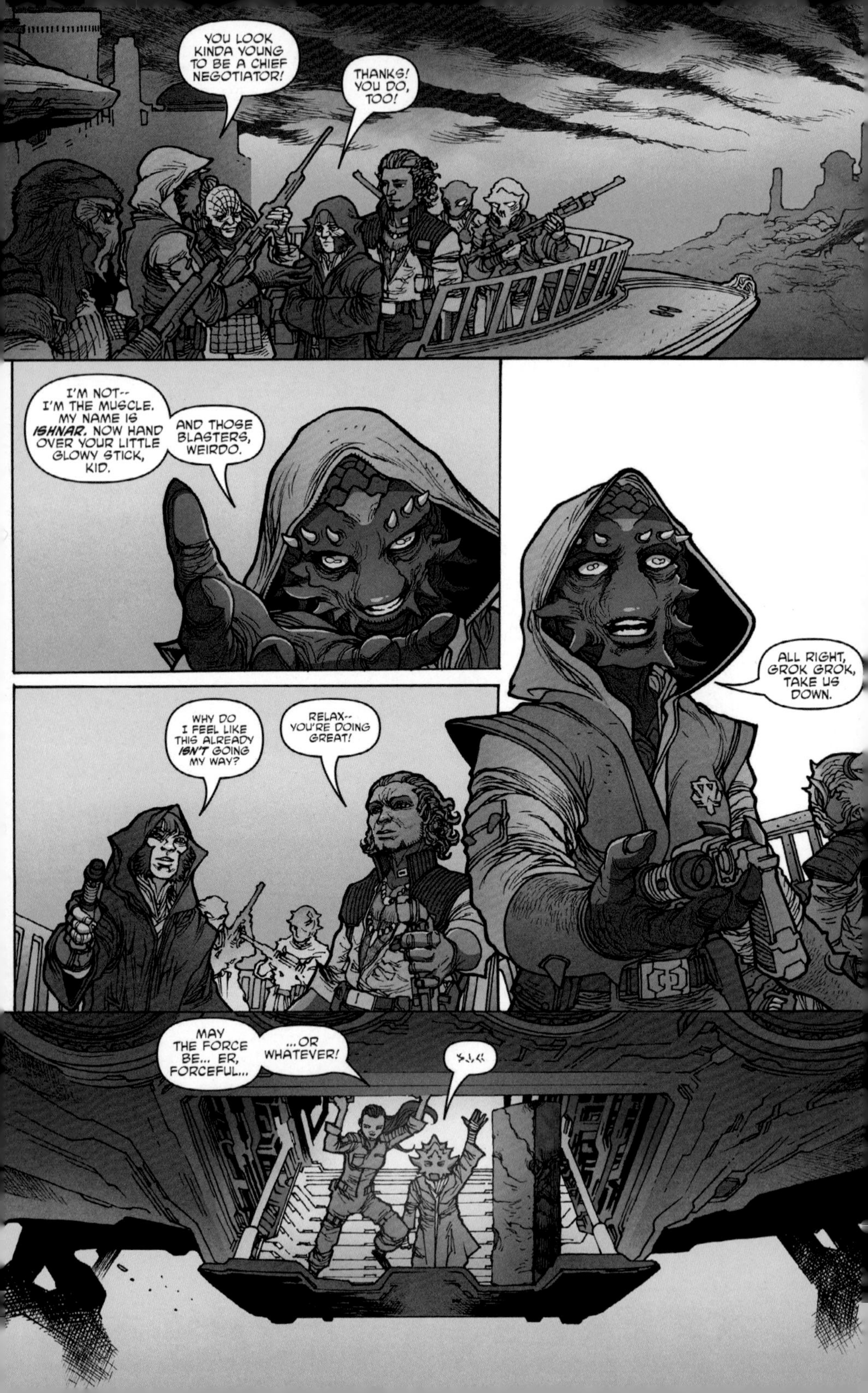
YOU LOOK KINDA YOUNG TO BE A CHIEF NEGOTIATOR!
THANKS! YOU DO, TOO!
I'M NOT-- I'M THE MUSCLE. MY NAME IS ISHNAR. NOW HAND OVER YOUR LITTLE GLOWY STICK, KID.
AND THOSE BLASTERS, WEIRDO.
WHY DO I FEEL LIKE THIS ALREADY ISN'T GOING MY WAY?
RELAX-- YOU'RE DOING GREAT!
ALL RIGHT, GROK GROK, TAKE US DOWN.
MAY THE FORCE BE... ER, FORCEFUL...
...OR WHATEVER!

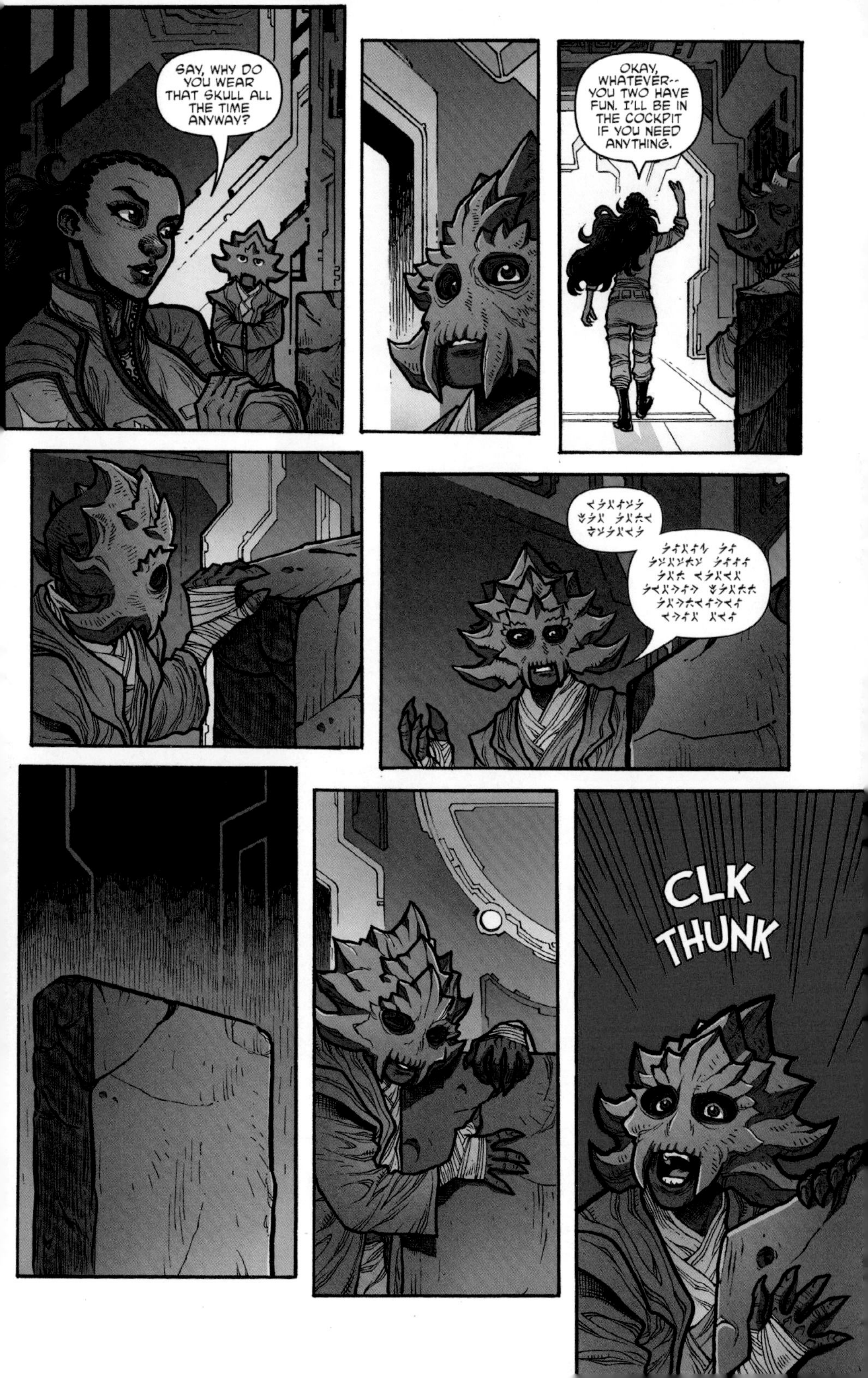

SAY, WHY DO YOU WEAR THAT SKULL ALL THE TIME ANYWAY?
OKAY, WHATEVER-- YOU TWO HAVE FUN. I'LL BE IN THE COCKPIT IF YOU NEED ANYTHING.
CLK
THUNK

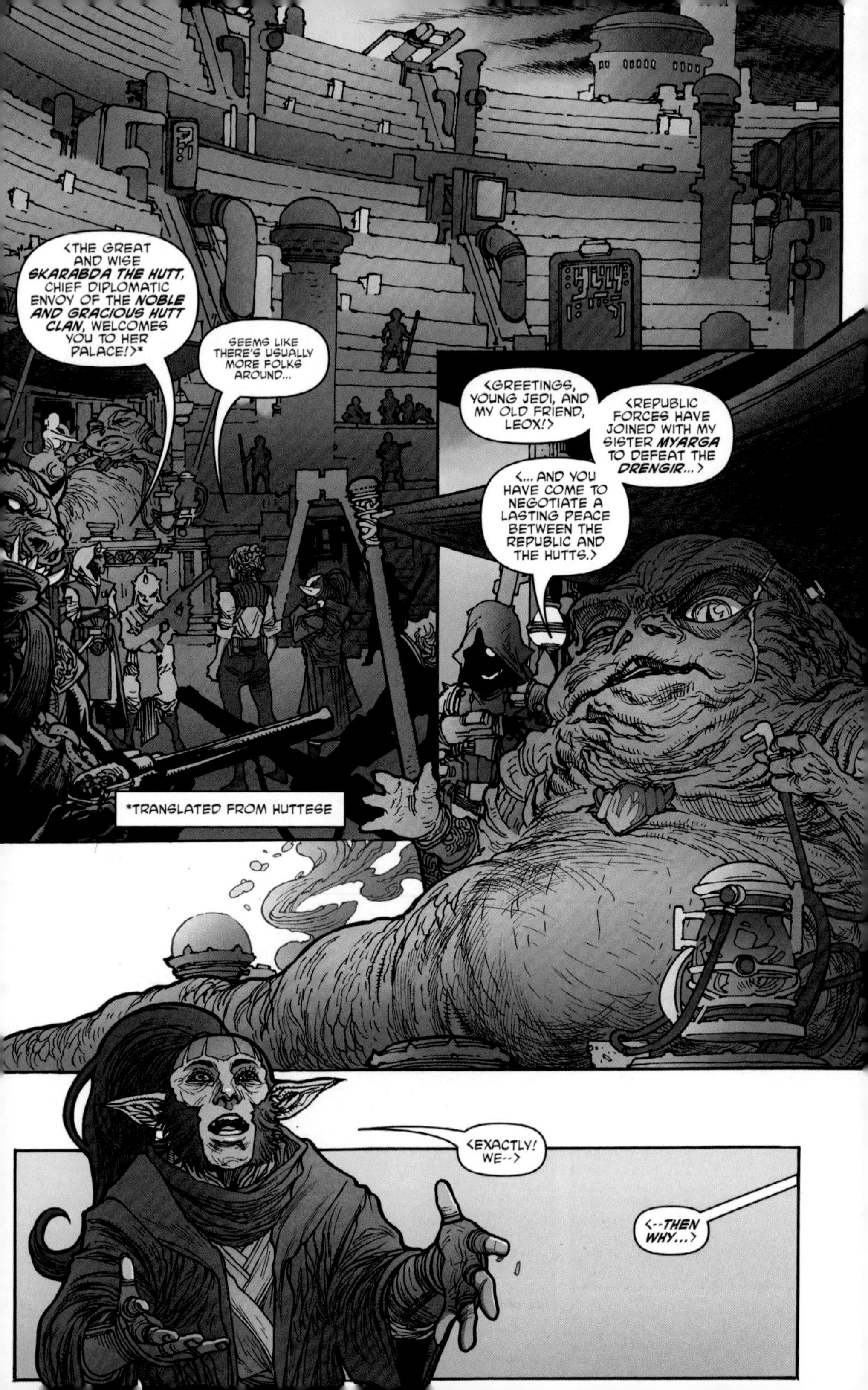
<THE GREAT AND WISE SKARABDA THE HUTT, CHIEF DIPLOMATIC ENVOY OF THE NOBLE AND GRACIOUS HUTT CLAN, WELCOMES YOU TO HER PALACE!>*
SEEMS LIKE THERE'S USUALLY MORE FOLKS AROUND...
<GREETINGS, YOUNG JEDI, AND MY OLD FRIEND, LEOX!>
<REPUBLIC FORCES HAVE JOINED WITH MY SISTER MYARGA TO DEFEAT THE DRENGIR...>
<...AND YOU HAVE COME TO NEGOTIATE A LASTING PEACE BETWEEN THE REPUBLIC AND THE HUTTS.>
*TRANSLATED FROM HUTTESE
<EXACTLY! WE-->
<--THEN WHY...>

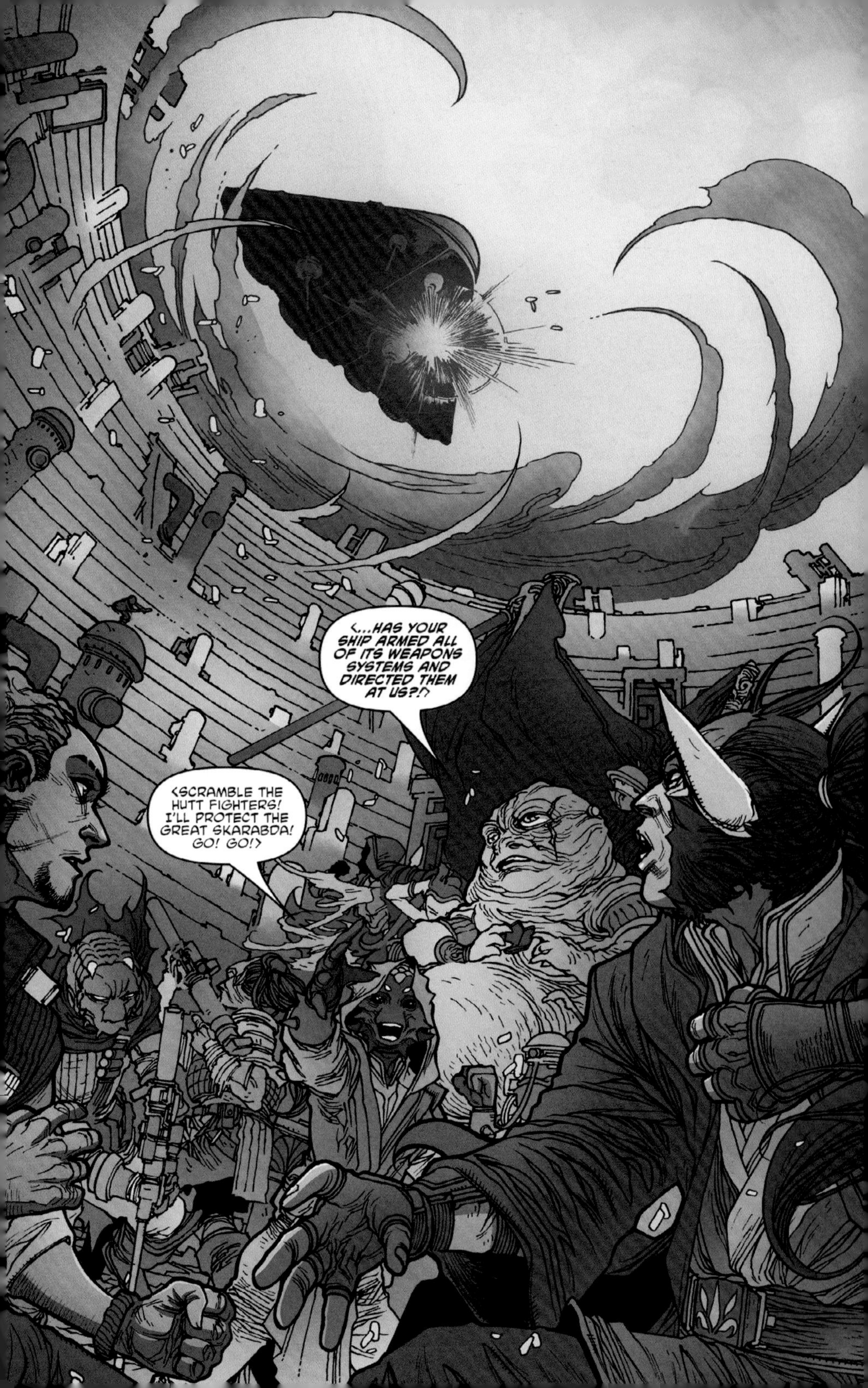
<...HAS YOUR SHIP ARMED ALL OF ITS WEAPONS SYSTEMS AND DIRECTED THEM AT US?!>
<SCRAMBLE THE HUTT FIGHTERS! I'LL PROTECT THE GREAT SKARABDA! GO! GO!>

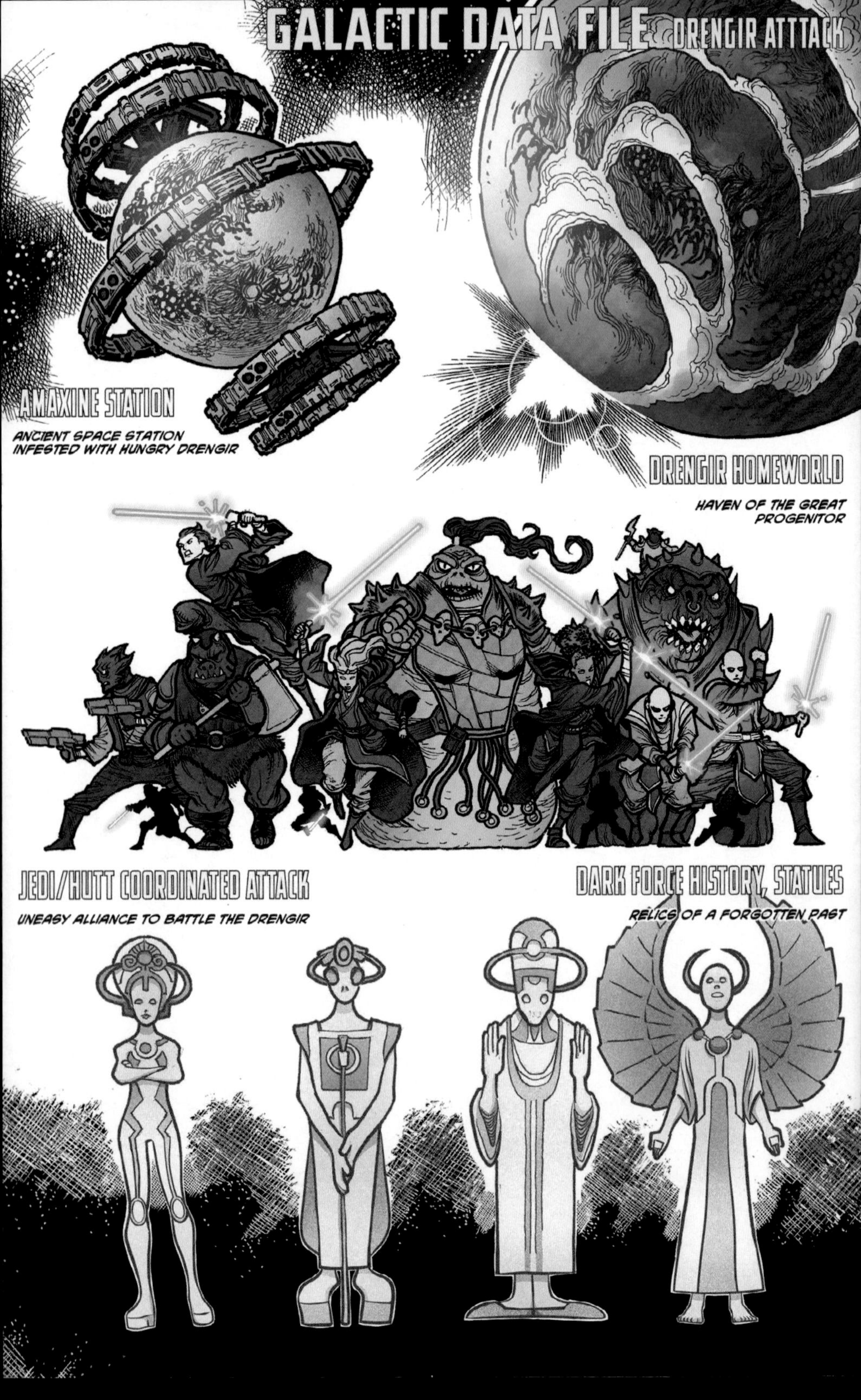
GALACTIC DATA FILE DRENGIR ATTTACK
AMAXINE STATION
ANCIENT SPACE STATION INFESTED WITH HUNGRY DRENGIR
DRENGIR HOMEWORLD
HAVEN OF THE GREAT PROGENITOR
JEDI/HUTT COORDINATED ATTACK
UNEASY ALLIANCE TO BATTLE THE DRENGIR
DARK FORCE HISTORY, STATUES
RELICS OF A FORGOTTEN PAST

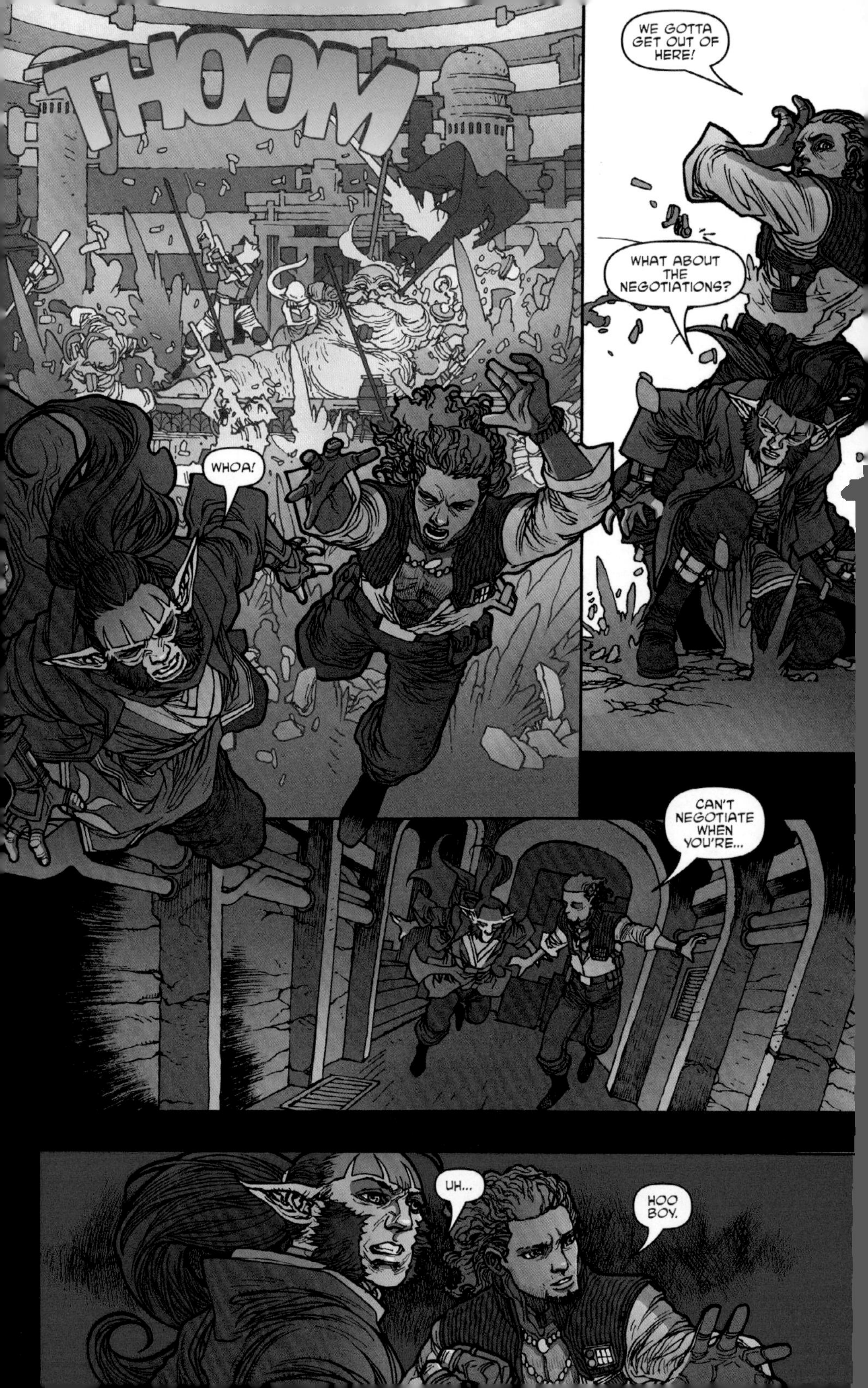
THOOM
WE GOTTA GET OUT OF HERE!
WHAT ABOUT THE NEGOTIATIONS?
WHOA!
CAN'T NEGOTIATE WHEN YOU'RE...
UH...
HOO BOY.

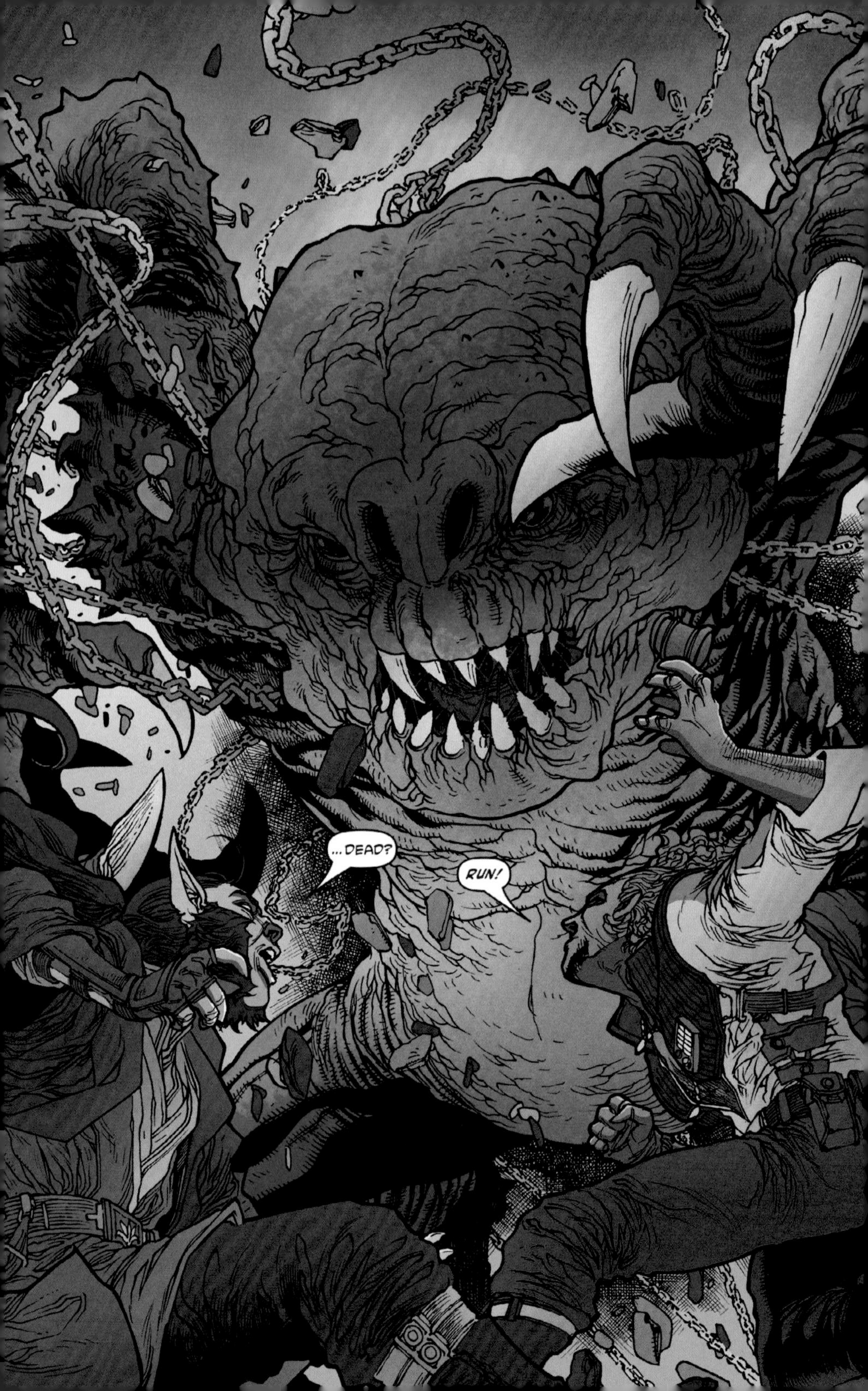
...DEAD?
RUN!

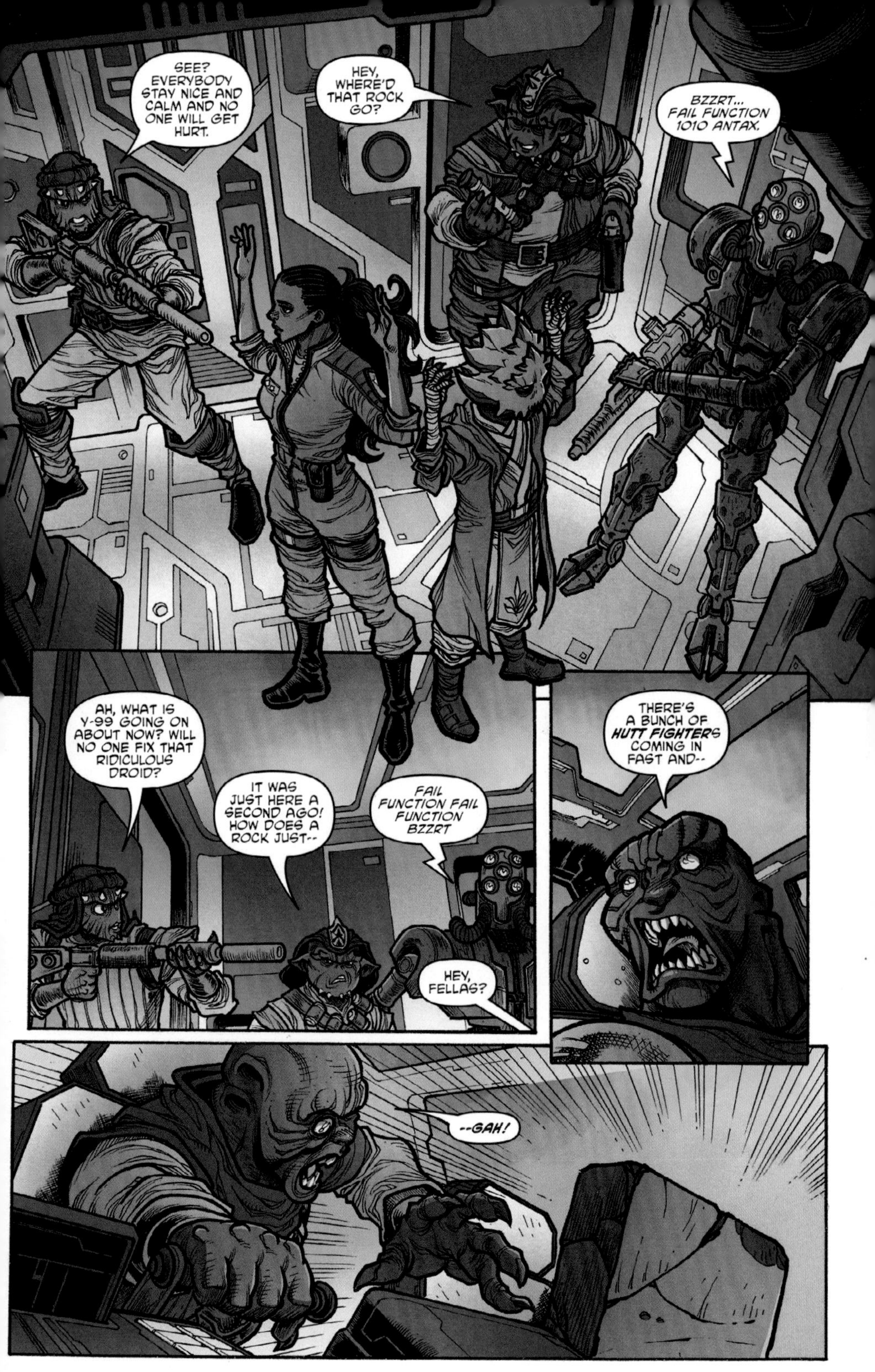
SEE? EVERYBODY STAY NICE AND CALM AND NO ONE WILL GET HURT.
HEY, WHERE'D THAT ROCK GO?
BZZRT... FAIL FUNCTION 1010 ANTAX.
AH, WHAT IS Y-99 GOING ON ABOUT NOW? WILL NO ONE FIX THAT RIDICULOUS DROID?
IT WAS JUST HERE A SECOND AGO! HOW DOES A ROCK JUST--
FAIL FUNCTION FAIL FUNCTION BZZRT
HEY, FELLAS?
THERE'S A BUNCH OF HUTT FIGHTERS COMING IN FAST AND--
--GAH!

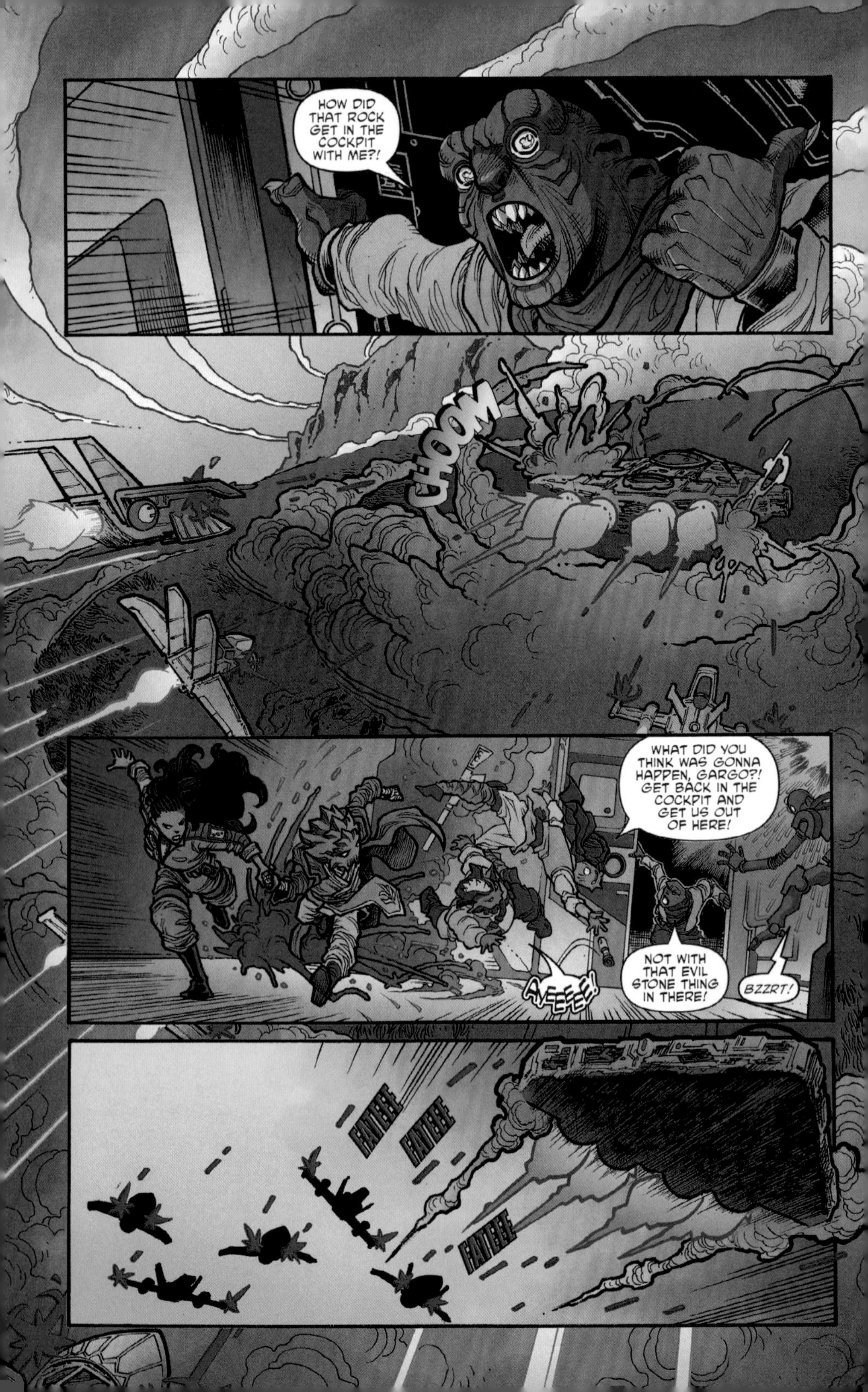
HOW DID THAT ROCK GET IN THE COCKPIT WITH ME?!
CHOOM
WHAT DID YOU THINK WAS GONNA HAPPEN, GARGO?! GET BACK IN THE COCKPIT AND GET US OUT OF HERE!
AYEEEEE!
NOT WITH THAT EVIL STONE THING IN THERE!
BZZRT!
FEATEEEE
FEATEEEE
FEATEEEE

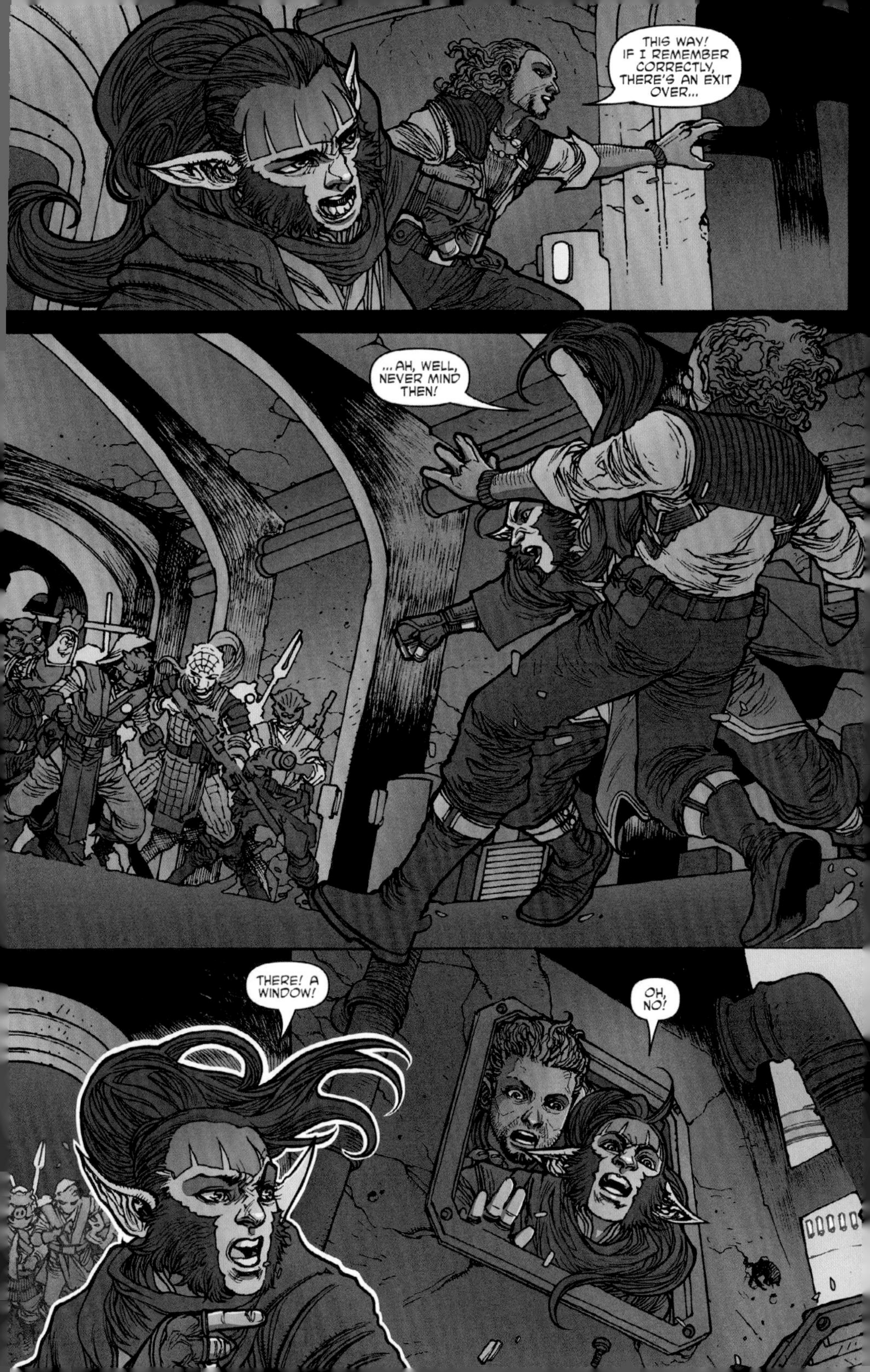
THIS WAY! IF I REMEMBER CORRECTLY, THERE'S AN EXIT OVER...
...AH, WELL, NEVER MIND THEN!
THERE! A WINDOW!
OH, NO!

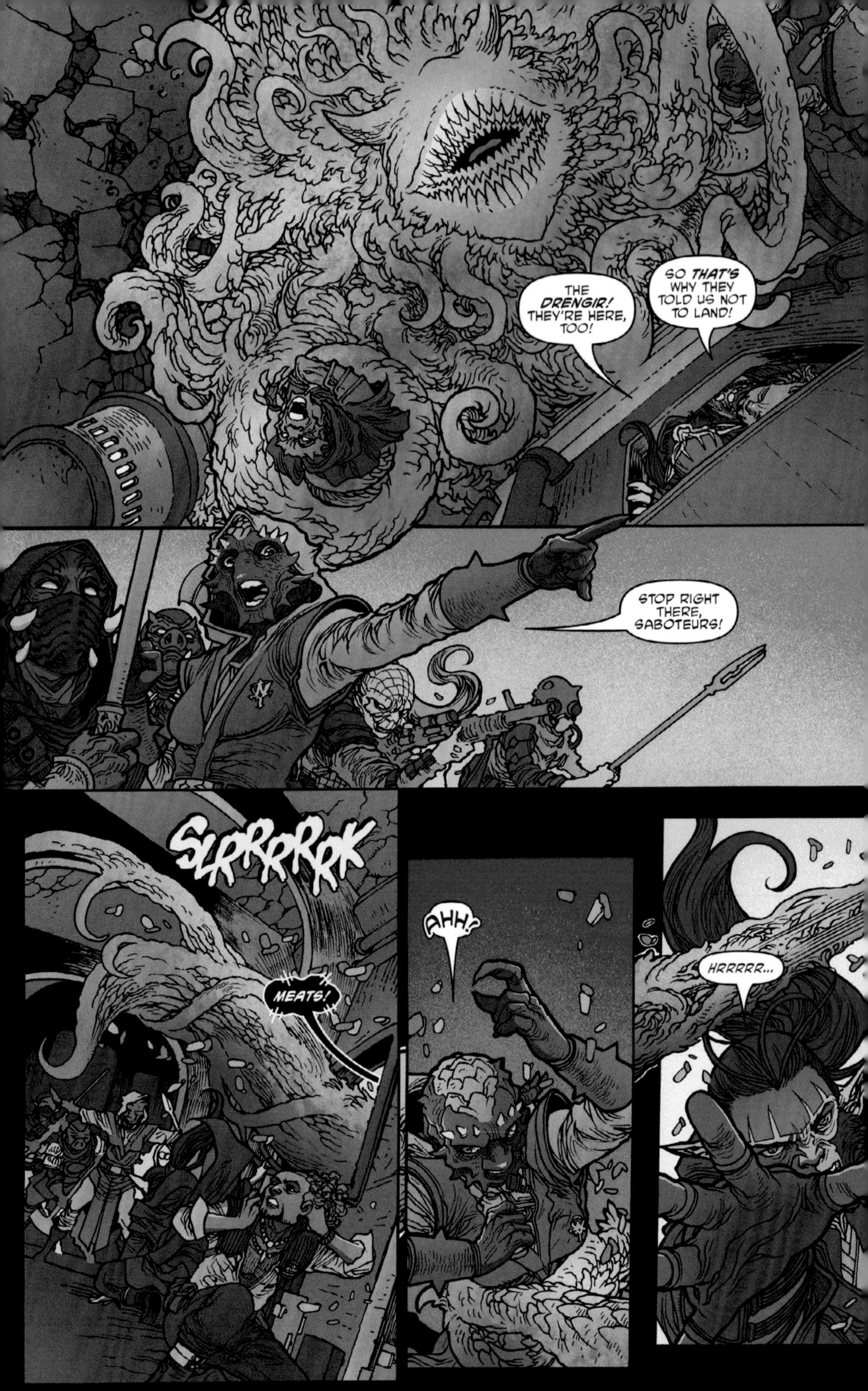
THE *DRENGIR!* THEY'RE HERE, TOO!
SO *THAT'S* WHY THEY TOLD US NOT TO LAND!
STOP RIGHT THERE, SABOTEURS!
SLRRRRRK
MEATS!
AHH!
HRRRRR...

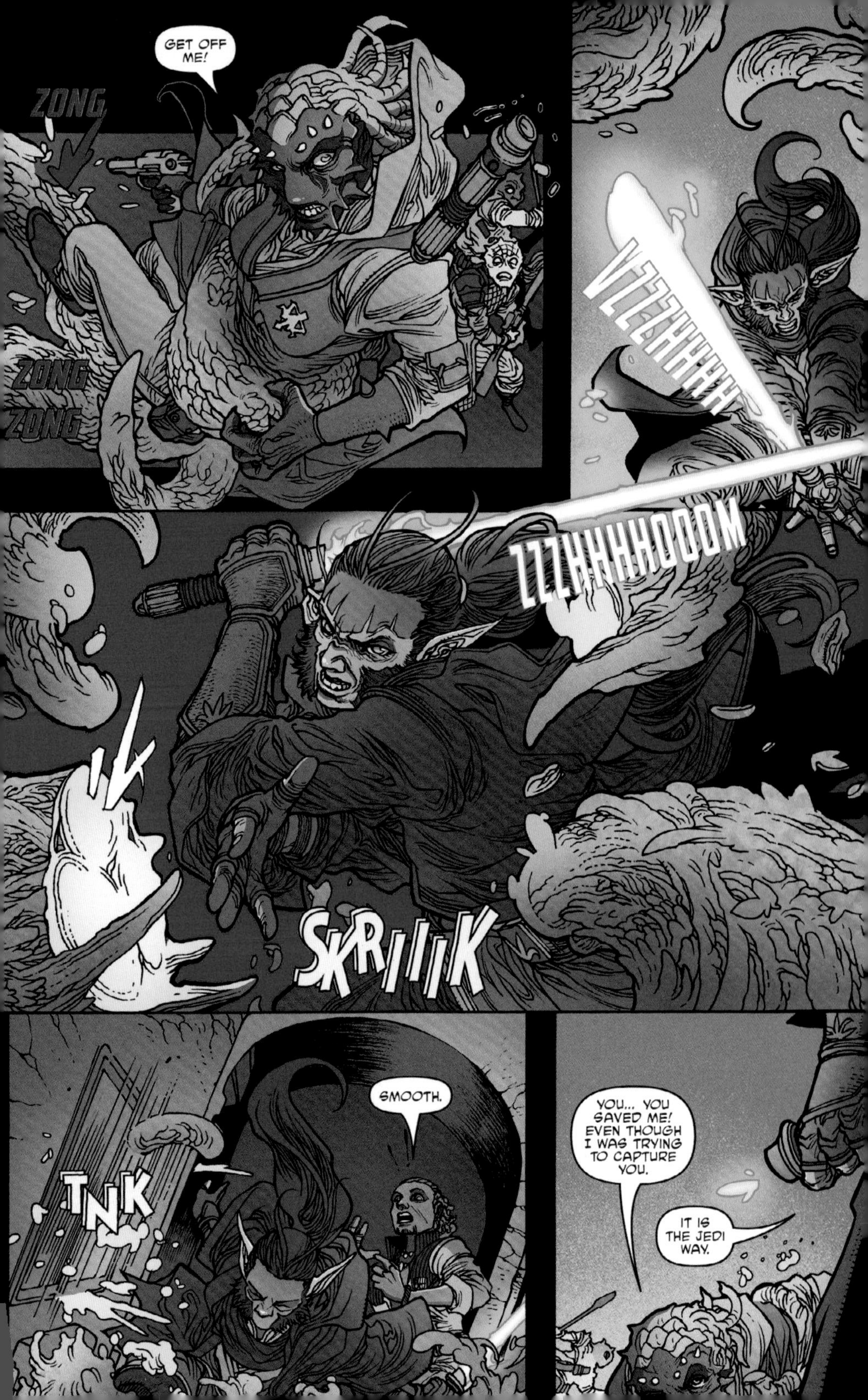
GET OFF ME!
ZONG
ZONG
ZONG
VZZHHHHHH
ZZZHHHHOOOM
SKRIIIIK
TNK
SMOOTH.
YOU... YOU SAVED ME! EVEN THOUGH I WAS TRYING TO CAPTURE YOU.
IT IS THE JEDI WAY.

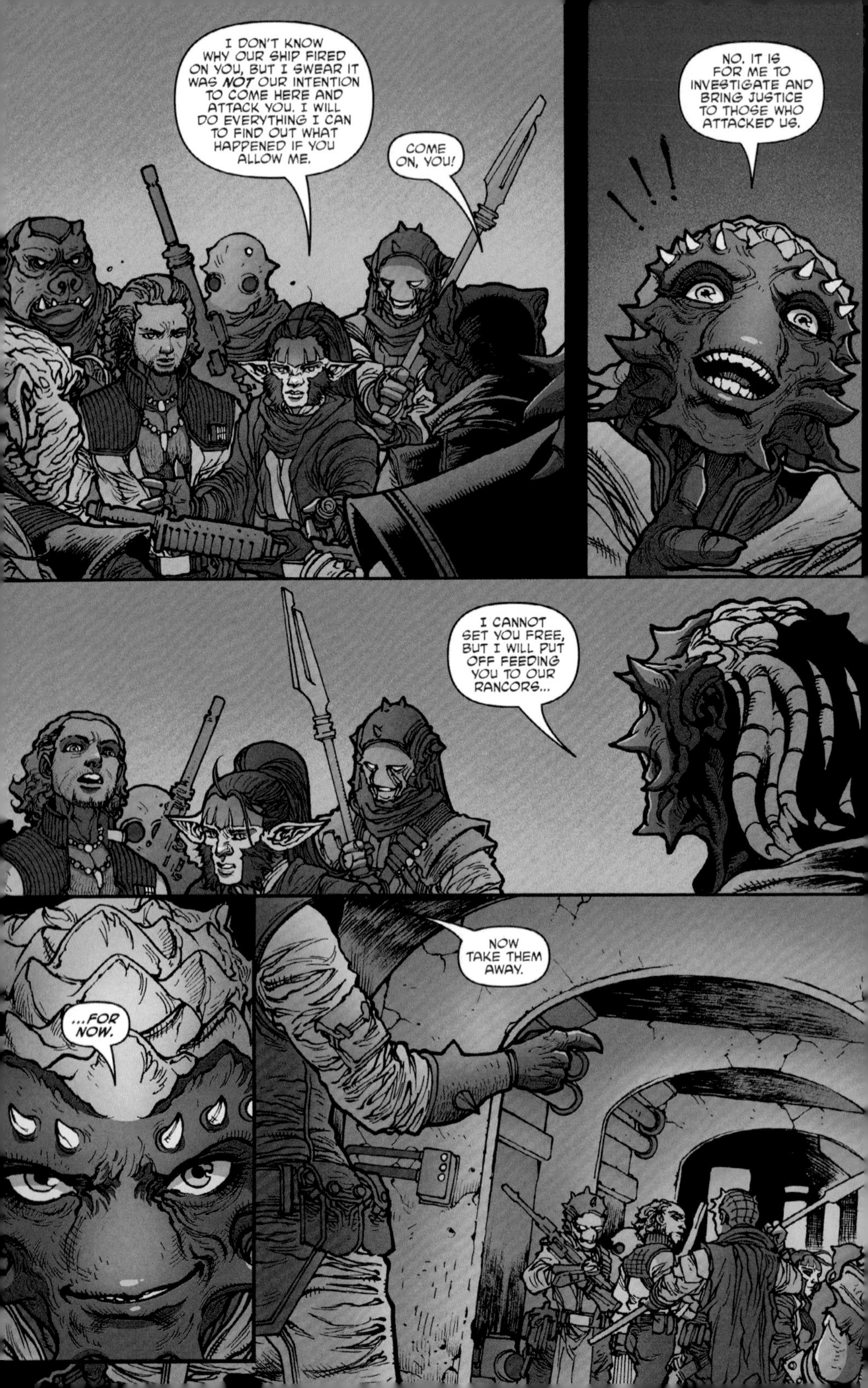
I DON'T KNOW WHY OUR SHIP FIRED ON YOU, BUT I SWEAR IT WAS *NOT* OUR INTENTION TO COME HERE AND ATTACK YOU. I WILL DO EVERYTHING I CAN TO FIND OUT WHAT HAPPENED IF YOU ALLOW ME.
COME ON, YOU!
NO. IT IS FOR ME TO INVESTIGATE AND BRING JUSTICE TO THOSE WHO ATTACKED US.
!!!
I CANNOT SET YOU FREE, BUT I WILL PUT OFF FEEDING YOU TO OUR RANCORS...
...FOR NOW.
NOW TAKE THEM AWAY.

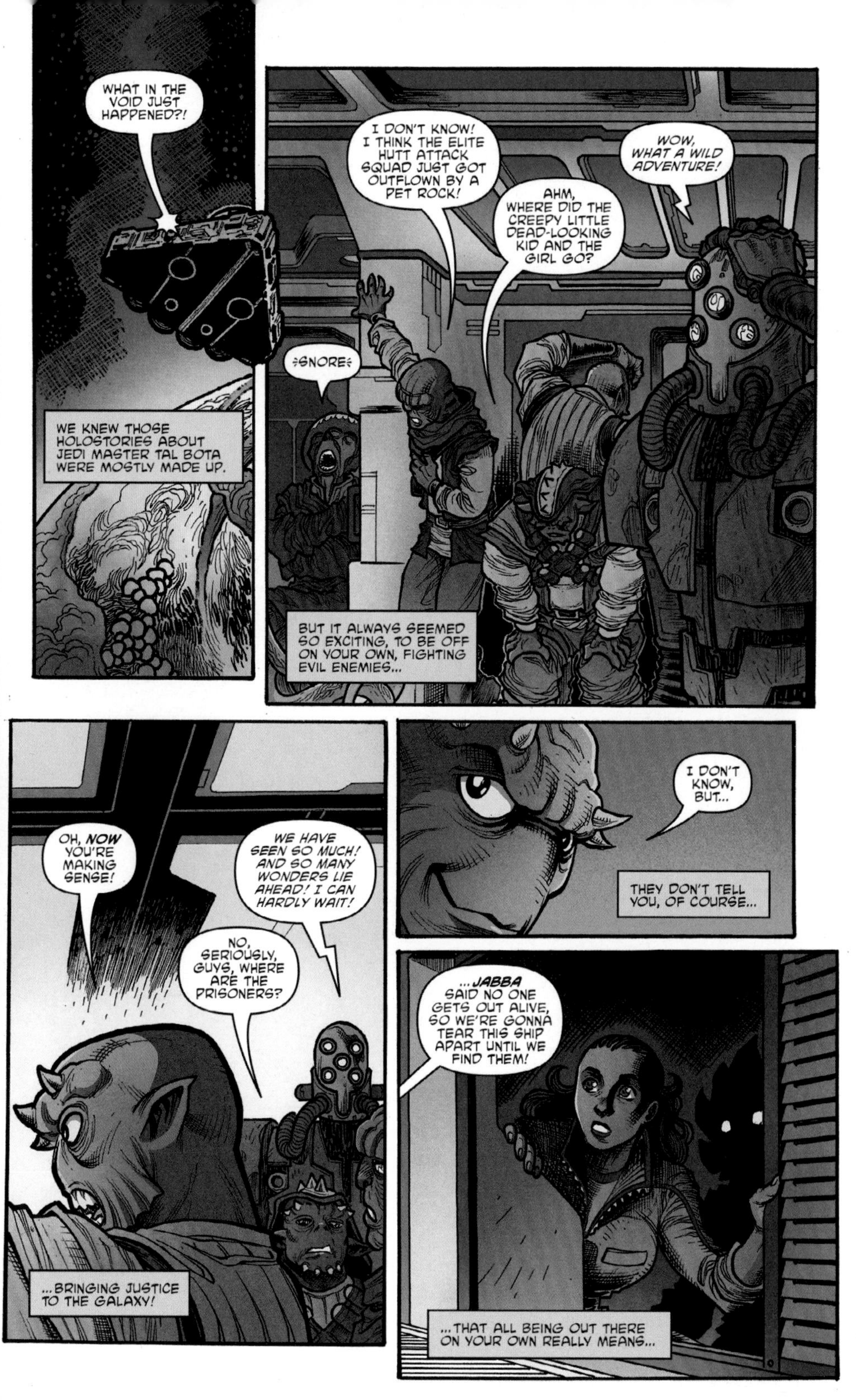
WHAT IN THE VOID JUST HAPPENED?!
WE KNEW THOSE HOLOSTORIES ABOUT JEDI MASTER TAL BOTA WERE MOSTLY MADE UP.
I DON'T KNOW! I THINK THE ELITE HUTT ATTACK SQUAD JUST GOT OUTFLOWN BY A PET ROCK!
WOW, WHAT A WILD ADVENTURE!
AHM, WHERE DID THE CREEPY LITTLE DEAD-LOOKING KID AND THE GIRL GO?
SNORE
BUT IT ALWAYS SEEMED SO EXCITING, TO BE OFF ON YOUR OWN, FIGHTING EVIL ENEMIES...
OH, NOW YOU'RE MAKING SENSE!
WE HAVE SEEN SO MUCH! AND SO MANY WONDERS LIE AHEAD! I CAN HARDLY WAIT!
NO, SERIOUSLY, GUYS, WHERE ARE THE PRISONERS?
...BRINGING JUSTICE TO THE GALAXY!
I DON'T KNOW, BUT...
THEY DON'T TELL YOU, OF COURSE...
...JABBA SAID NO ONE GETS OUT ALIVE, SO WE'RE GONNA TEAR THIS SHIP APART UNTIL WE FIND THEM!
...THAT ALL BEING OUT THERE ON YOUR OWN REALLY MEANS...

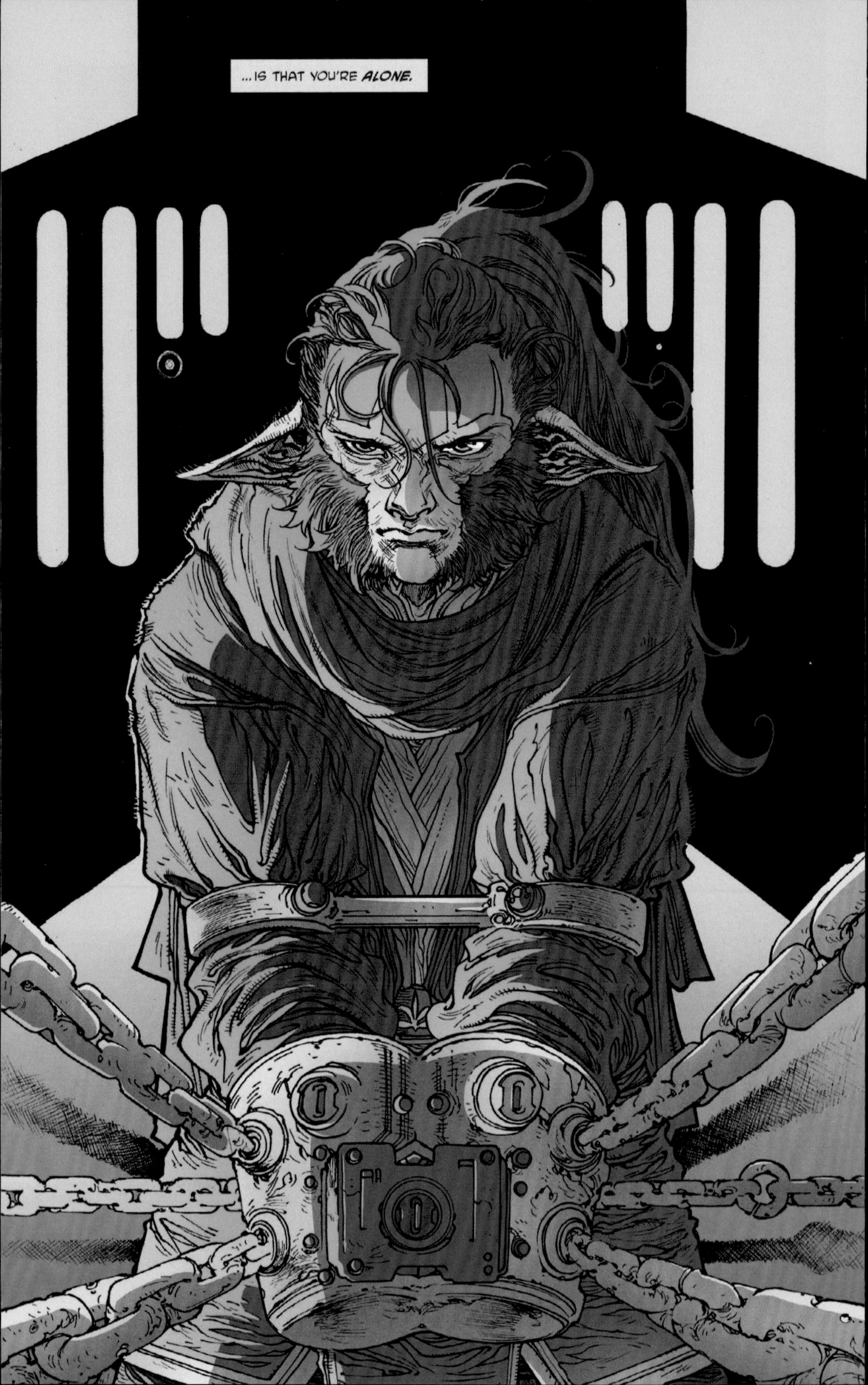
...IS THAT YOU'RE *ALONE.*

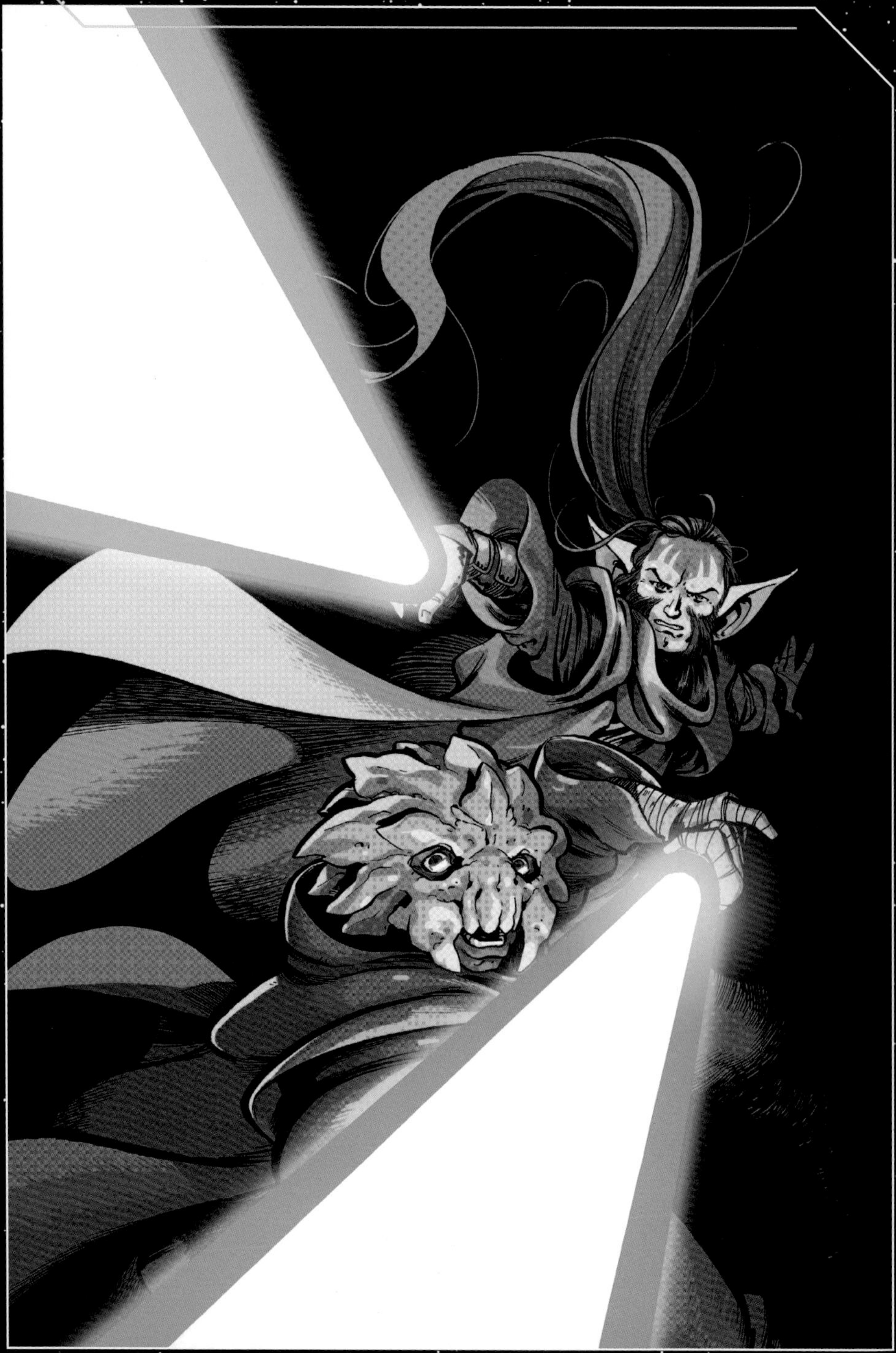

ART BY ILIAS KYRIAZIS

MISSION TO BILBOUSA, PART II

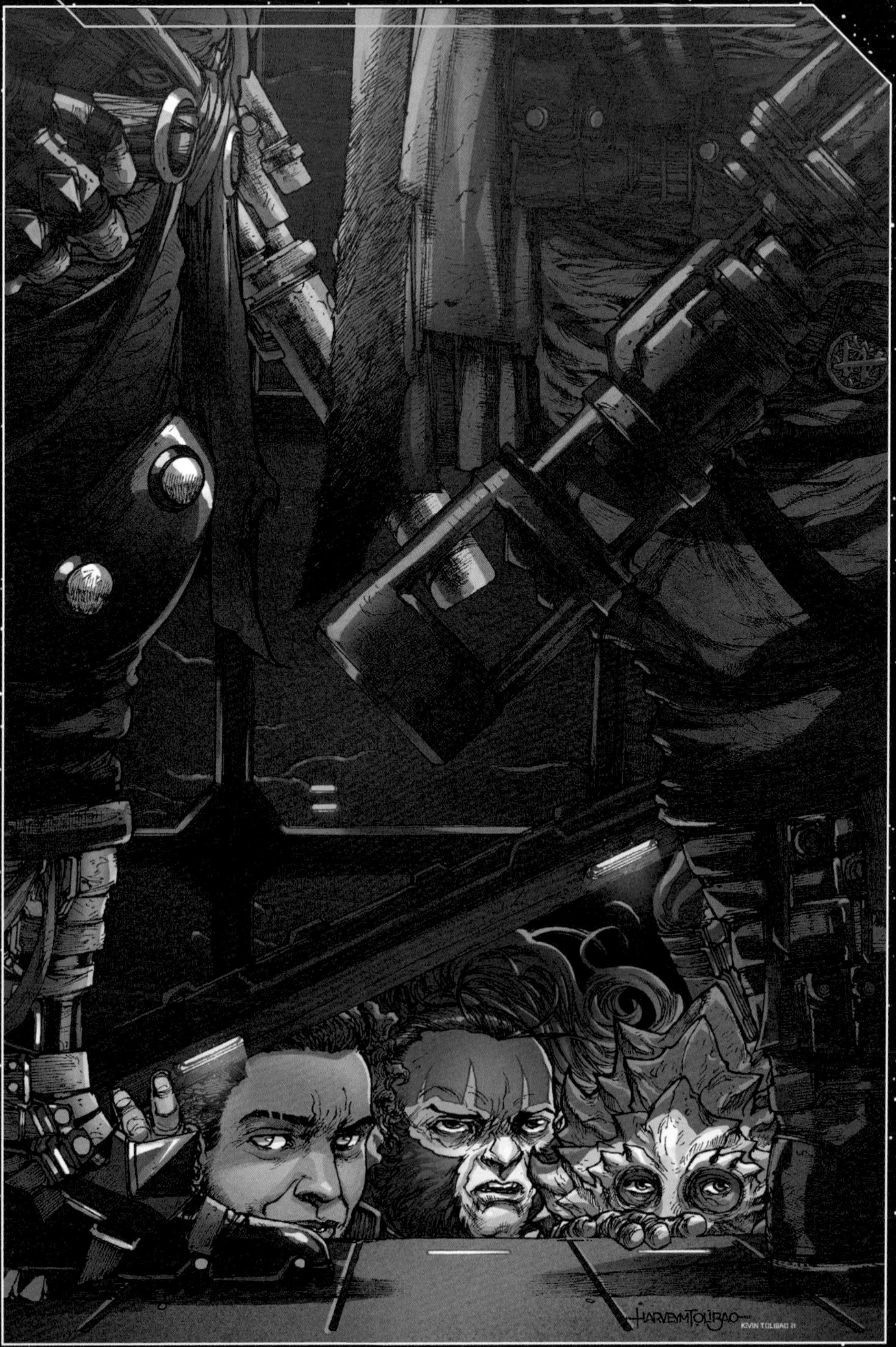
HARVEYMTOLIBAO
KEVIN TOLIBAO 21

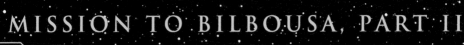

ART BY **HARVEY TOLIBAO** *COLORS BY* **KEVIN TOLIBAO**

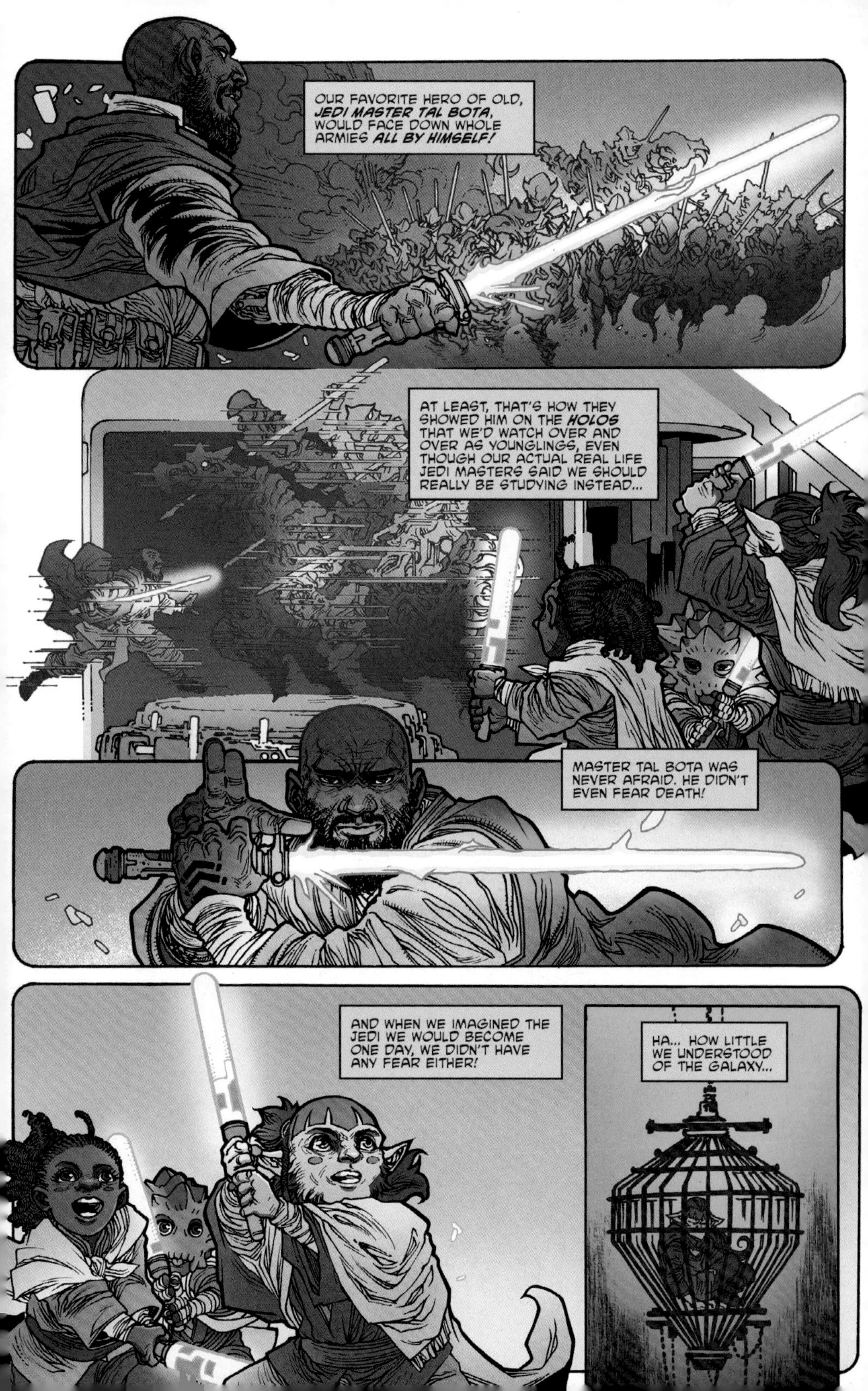
OUR FAVORITE HERO OF OLD, JEDI MASTER TAL BOTA, WOULD FACE DOWN WHOLE ARMIES ALL BY HIMSELF!
AT LEAST, THAT'S HOW THEY SHOWED HIM ON THE HOLOS THAT WE'D WATCH OVER AND OVER AS YOUNGLINGS, EVEN THOUGH OUR ACTUAL REAL LIFE JEDI MASTERS SAID WE SHOULD REALLY BE STUDYING INSTEAD...
MASTER TAL BOTA WAS NEVER AFRAID. HE DIDN'T EVEN FEAR DEATH!
AND WHEN WE IMAGINED THE JEDI WE WOULD BECOME ONE DAY, WE DIDN'T HAVE ANY FEAR EITHER!
HA... HOW LITTLE WE UNDERSTOOD OF THE GALAXY...

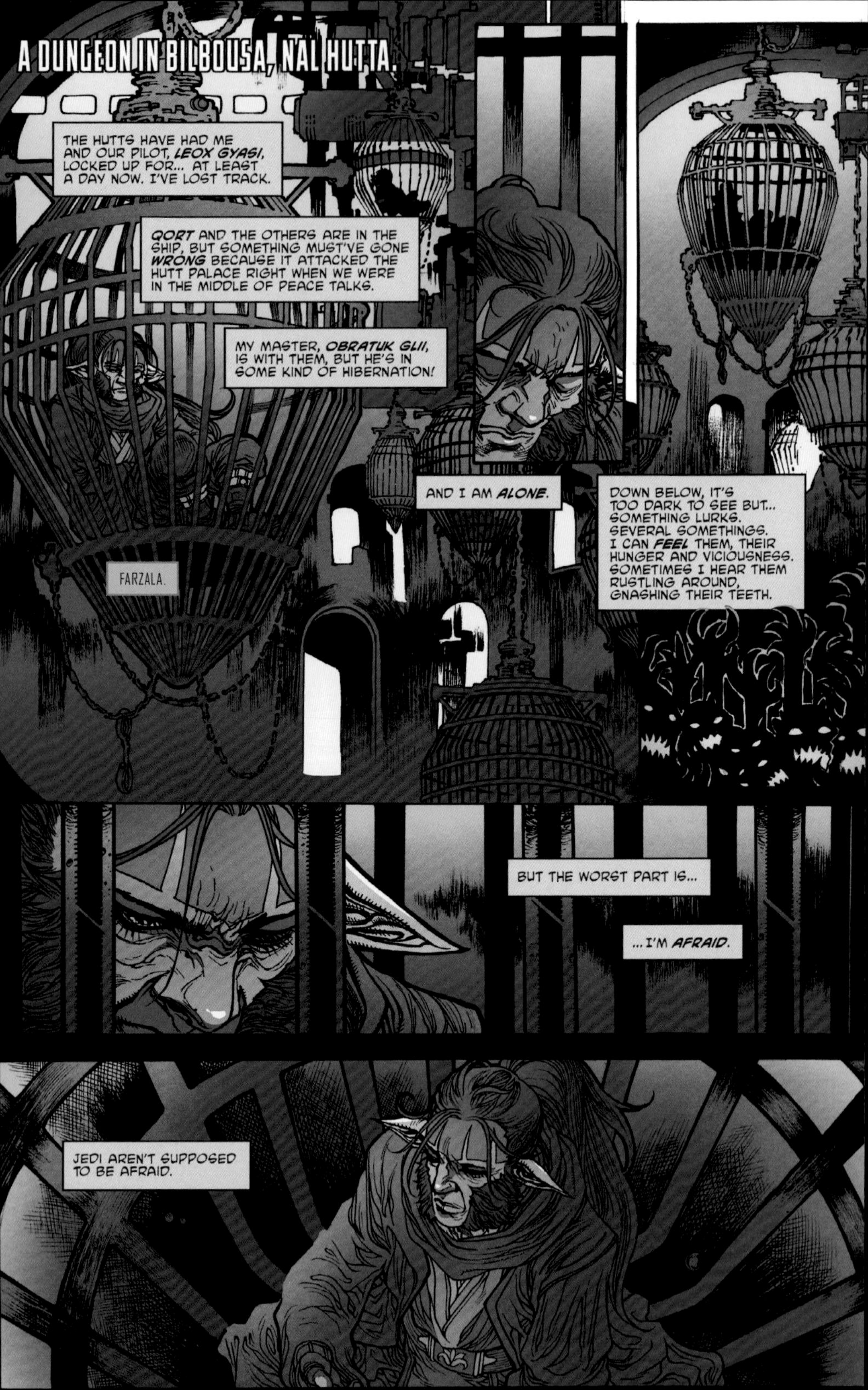
A DUNGEON IN BILBOUSA, NAL HUTTA.
THE HUTTS HAVE HAD ME AND OUR PILOT, LEOX GYASI, LOCKED UP FOR... AT LEAST A DAY NOW. I'VE LOST TRACK.
QORT AND THE OTHERS ARE IN THE SHIP, BUT SOMETHING MUST'VE GONE WRONG BECAUSE IT ATTACKED THE HUTT PALACE RIGHT WHEN WE WERE IN THE MIDDLE OF PEACE TALKS.
MY MASTER, OBRATUK GLII, IS WITH THEM, BUT HE'S IN SOME KIND OF HIBERNATION!
FARZALA.
AND I AM ALONE.
DOWN BELOW, IT'S TOO DARK TO SEE BUT... SOMETHING LURKS. SEVERAL SOMETHINGS. I CAN FEEL THEM, THEIR HUNGER AND VICIOUSNESS. SOMETIMES I HEAR THEM RUSTLING AROUND, GNASHING THEIR TEETH.
BUT THE WORST PART IS...
...I'M AFRAID.
JEDI AREN'T SUPPOSED TO BE AFRAID.

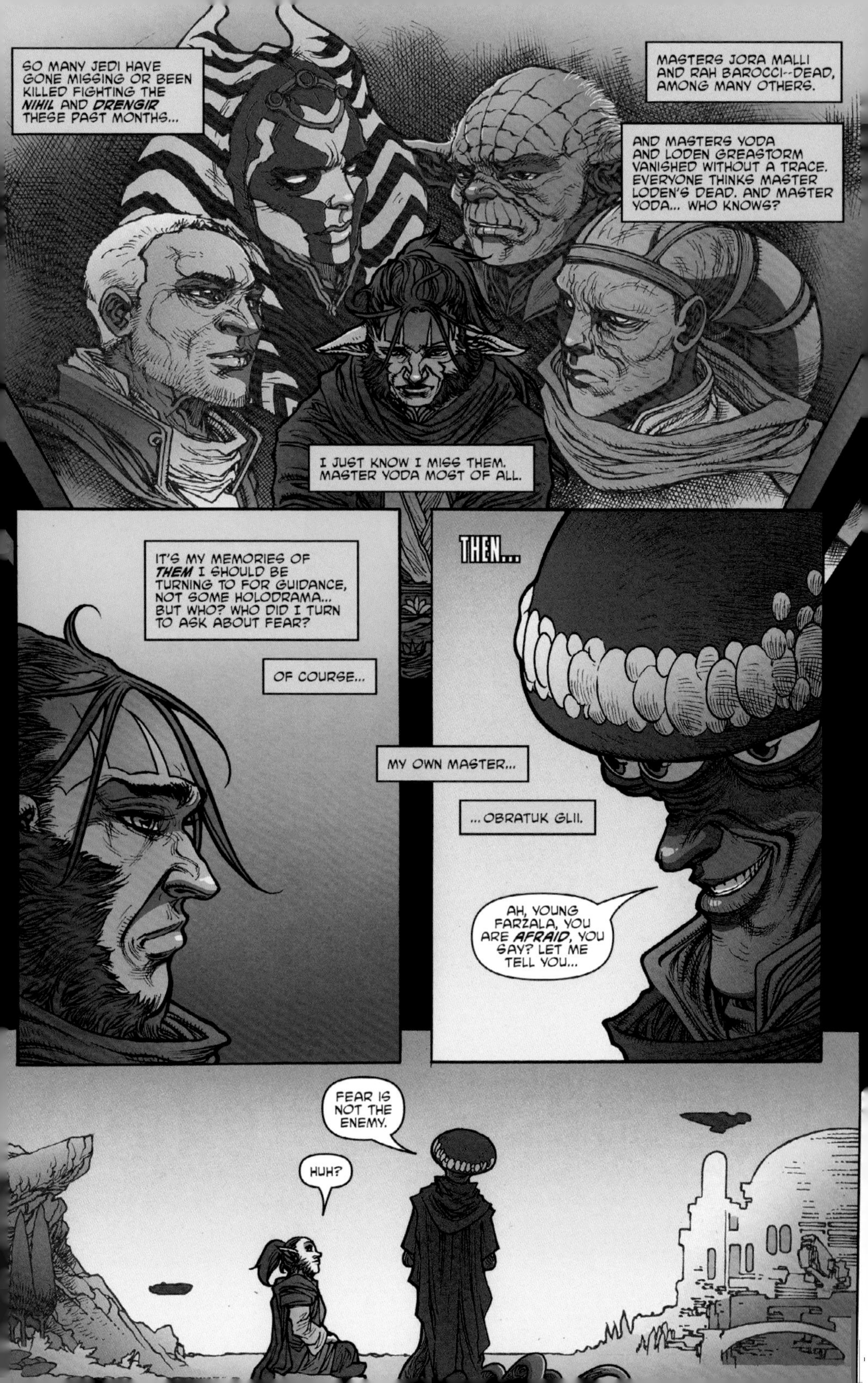
SO MANY JEDI HAVE GONE MISSING OR BEEN KILLED FIGHTING THE *NIHIL* AND *DRENGIR* THESE PAST MONTHS...
MASTERS JORA MALLI AND RAH BAROCCI--DEAD, AMONG MANY OTHERS.
AND MASTERS YODA AND LODEN GREASTORM VANISHED WITHOUT A TRACE. EVERYONE THINKS MASTER LODEN'S DEAD. AND MASTER YODA... WHO KNOWS?
I JUST KNOW I MISS THEM. MASTER YODA MOST OF ALL.
IT'S MY MEMORIES OF *THEM* I SHOULD BE TURNING TO FOR GUIDANCE, NOT SOME HOLODRAMA... BUT WHO? WHO DID I TURN TO ASK ABOUT FEAR?
OF COURSE...
THEN...
MY OWN MASTER...
...OBRATUK GLII.
AH, YOUNG FARZALA, YOU ARE *AFRAID*, YOU SAY? LET ME TELL YOU...
FEAR IS NOT THE ENEMY.
HUH?

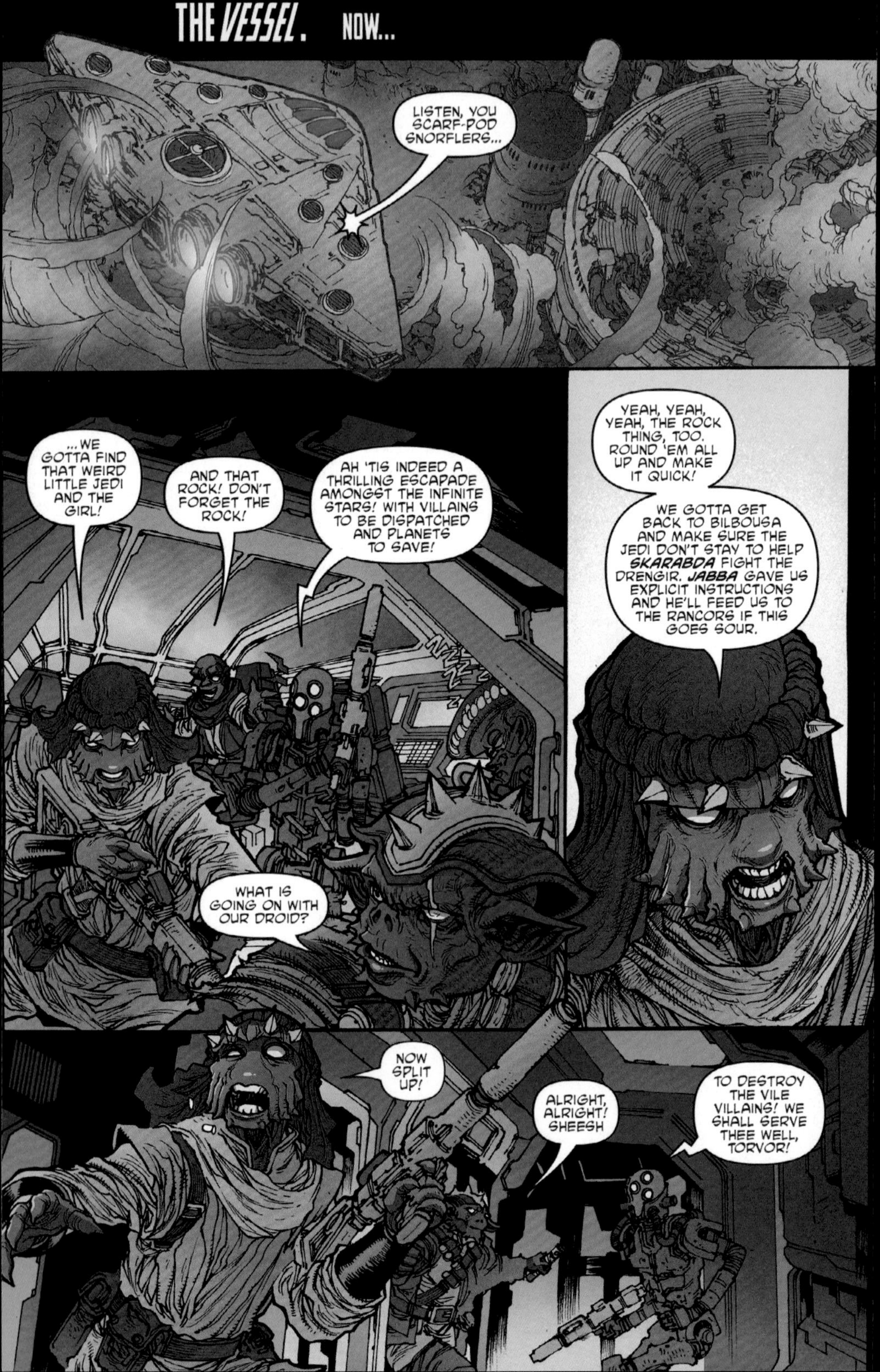
THE VESSEL. NOW...
LISTEN, YOU SCARF-POD SNORFLERS...
...WE GOTTA FIND THAT WEIRD LITTLE JEDI AND THE GIRL!
AND THAT ROCK! DON'T FORGET THE ROCK!
AH 'TIS INDEED A THRILLING ESCAPADE AMONGST THE INFINITE STARS! WITH VILLAINS TO BE DISPATCHED AND PLANETS TO SAVE!
YEAH, YEAH, YEAH, THE ROCK THING, TOO. ROUND 'EM ALL UP AND MAKE IT QUICK!
WE GOTTA GET BACK TO BILBOUSA AND MAKE SURE THE JEDI DON'T STAY TO HELP SKARABDA FIGHT THE DRENGIR. JABBA GAVE US EXPLICIT INSTRUCTIONS AND HE'LL FEED US TO THE RANCORS IF THIS GOES SOUR.
WHAT IS GOING ON WITH OUR DROID?
NOW SPLIT UP!
ALRIGHT, ALRIGHT! SHEESH
TO DESTROY THE VILE VILLAINS! WE SHALL SERVE THEE WELL, TORVOR!

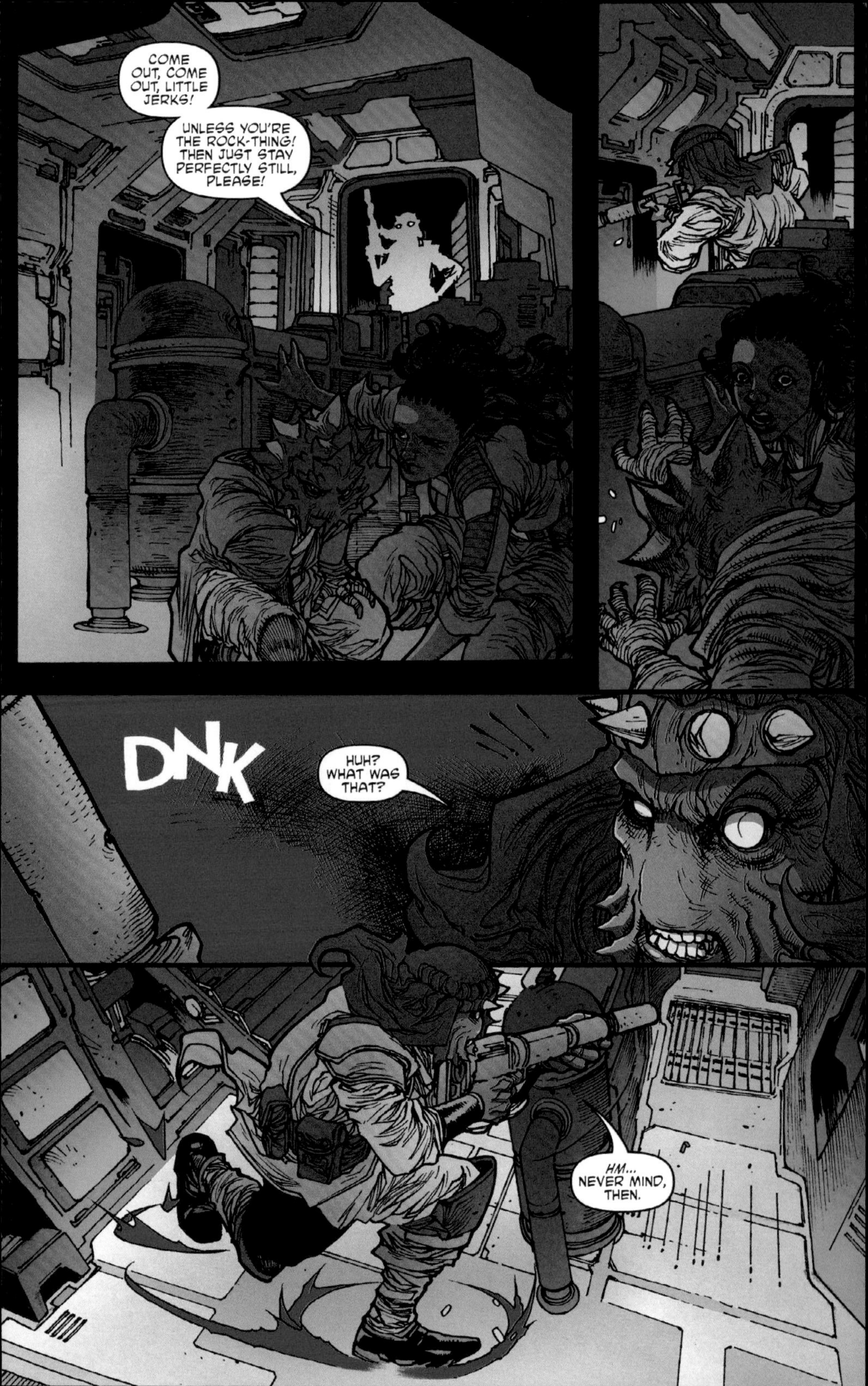
COME OUT, COME OUT, LITTLE JERKS!
UNLESS YOU'RE THE ROCK-THING! THEN JUST STAY PERFECTLY STILL, PLEASE!
DNK
HUH? WHAT WAS THAT?
HM... NEVER MIND, THEN.

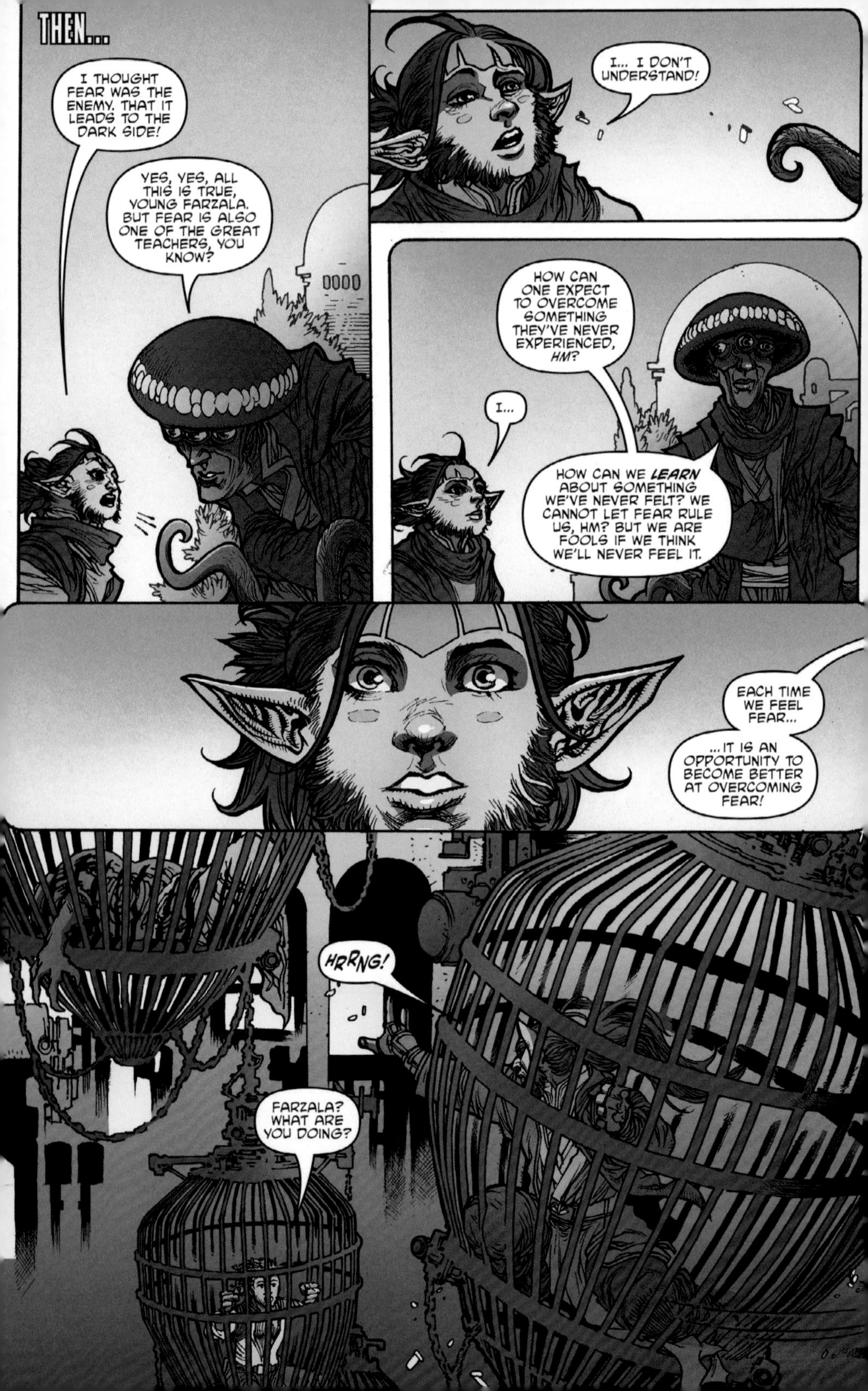
THEN...
I THOUGHT FEAR WAS THE ENEMY. THAT IT LEADS TO THE DARK SIDE!
YES, YES, ALL THIS IS TRUE, YOUNG FARZALA. BUT FEAR IS ALSO ONE OF THE GREAT TEACHERS, YOU KNOW?
I... I DON'T UNDERSTAND!
HOW CAN ONE EXPECT TO OVERCOME SOMETHING THEY'VE NEVER EXPERIENCED, HM?
I...
HOW CAN WE LEARN ABOUT SOMETHING WE'VE NEVER FELT? WE CANNOT LET FEAR RULE US, HM? BUT WE ARE FOOLS IF WE THINK WE'LL NEVER FEEL IT.
EACH TIME WE FEEL FEAR...
...IT IS AN OPPORTUNITY TO BECOME BETTER AT OVERCOMING FEAR!
HRRNG!
FARZALA? WHAT ARE YOU DOING?

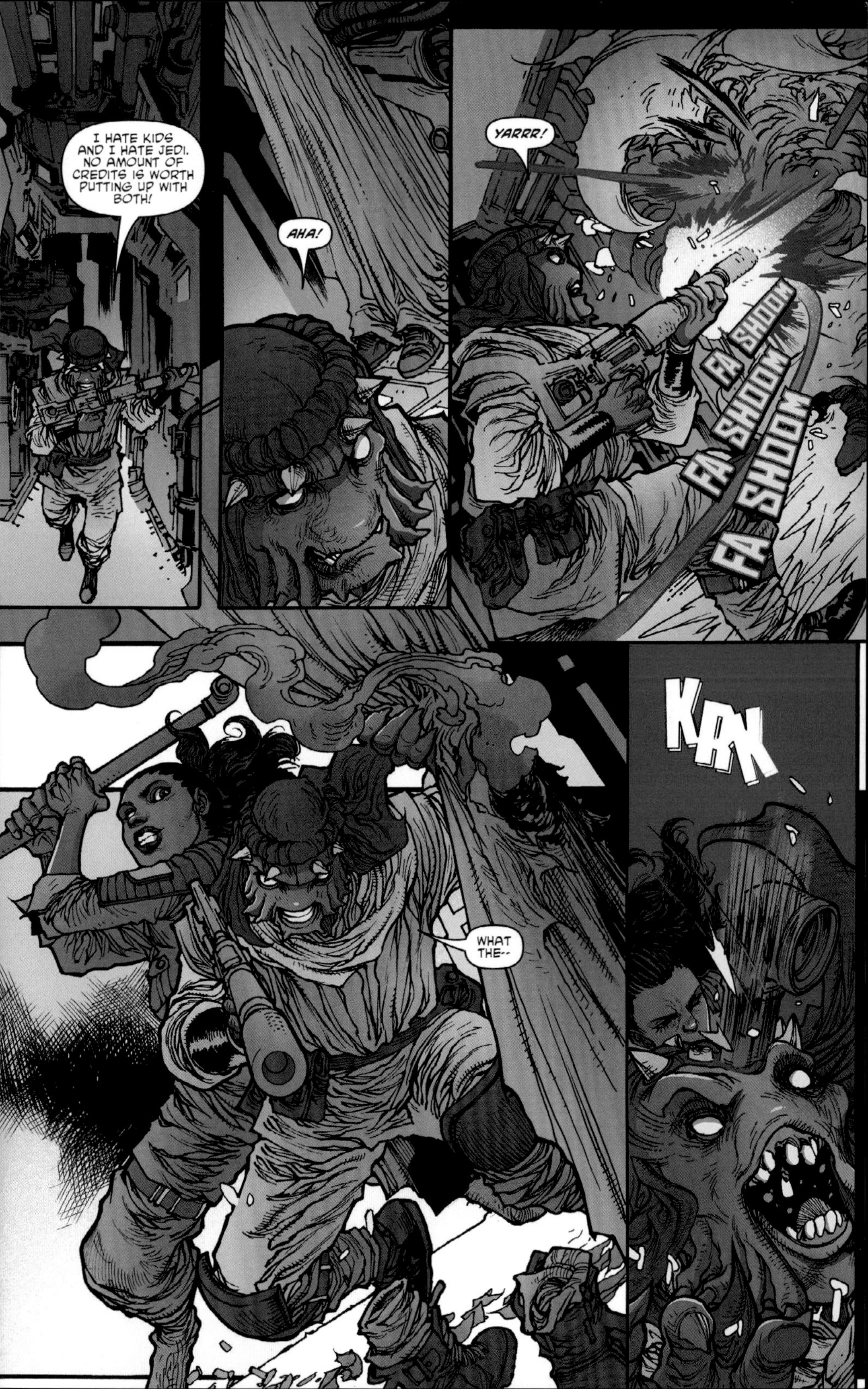
I HATE KIDS AND I HATE JEDI. NO AMOUNT OF CREDITS IS WORTH PUTTING UP WITH BOTH!
AHA!
YARRR!
FA SHOOM
FA SHOOM
FA SHOOM
WHAT THE--
KRAK

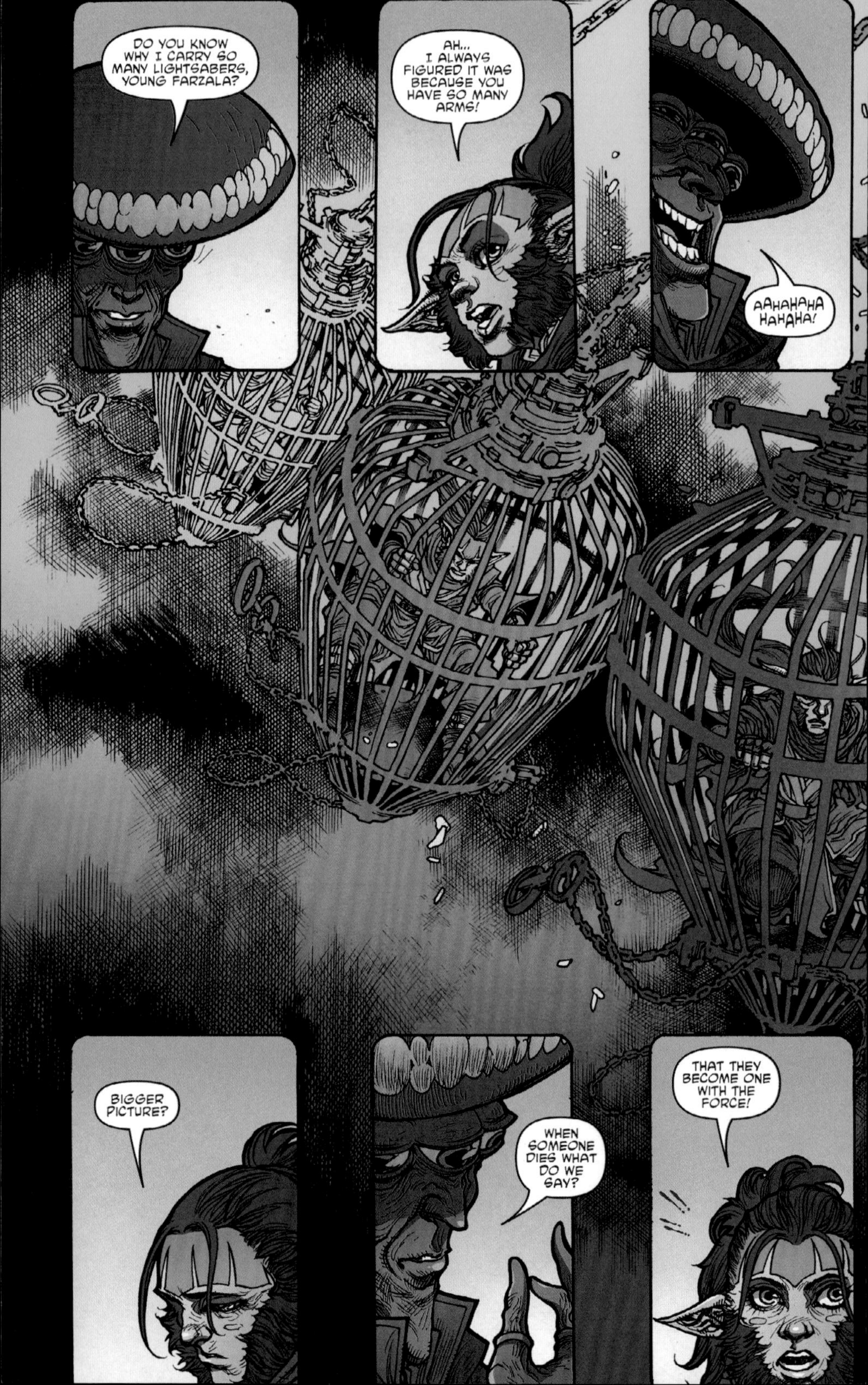
DO YOU KNOW WHY I CARRY SO MANY LIGHTSABERS, YOUNG FARZALA?
AH... I ALWAYS FIGURED IT WAS BECAUSE YOU HAVE SO MANY ARMS!
AAHAHAHA HAHAHA!
BIGGER PICTURE?
WHEN SOMEONE DIES WHAT DO WE SAY?
THAT THEY BECOME ONE WITH THE FORCE!

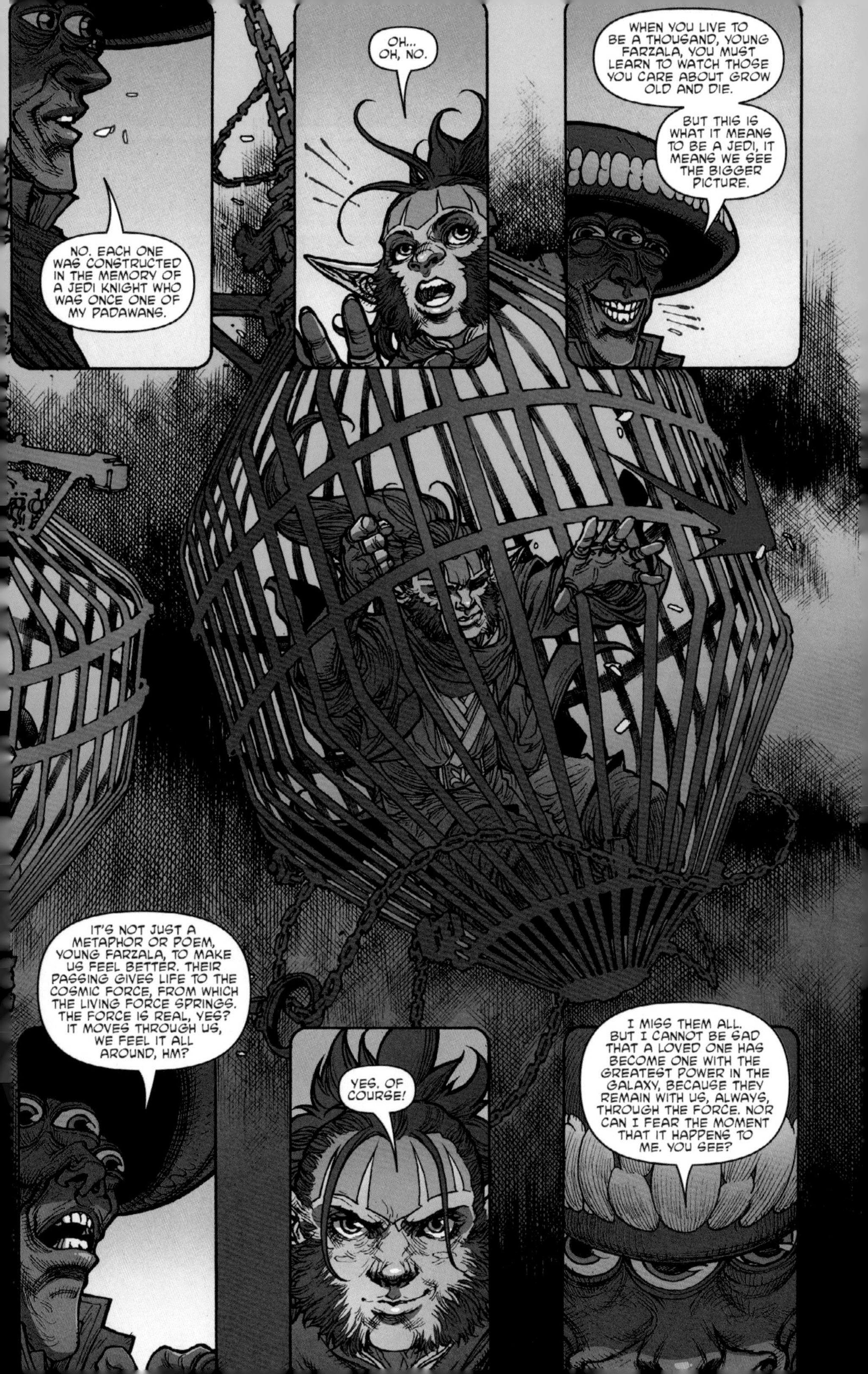
NO. EACH ONE WAS CONSTRUCTED IN THE MEMORY OF A JEDI KNIGHT WHO WAS ONCE ONE OF MY PADAWANS.
OH... OH, NO.
WHEN YOU LIVE TO BE A THOUSAND, YOUNG FARZALA, YOU MUST LEARN TO WATCH THOSE YOU CARE ABOUT GROW OLD AND DIE.
BUT THIS IS WHAT IT MEANS TO BE A JEDI, IT MEANS WE SEE THE BIGGER PICTURE.
IT'S NOT JUST A METAPHOR OR POEM, YOUNG FARZALA, TO MAKE US FEEL BETTER. THEIR PASSING GIVES LIFE TO THE COSMIC FORCE, FROM WHICH THE LIVING FORCE SPRINGS. THE FORCE IS REAL, YES? IT MOVES THROUGH US, WE FEEL IT ALL AROUND, HM?
YES. OF COURSE!
I MISS THEM ALL. BUT I CANNOT BE SAD THAT A LOVED ONE HAS BECOME ONE WITH THE GREATEST POWER IN THE GALAXY, BECAUSE THEY REMAIN WITH US, ALWAYS, THROUGH THE FORCE. NOR CAN I FEAR THE MOMENT THAT IT HAPPENS TO ME. YOU SEE?

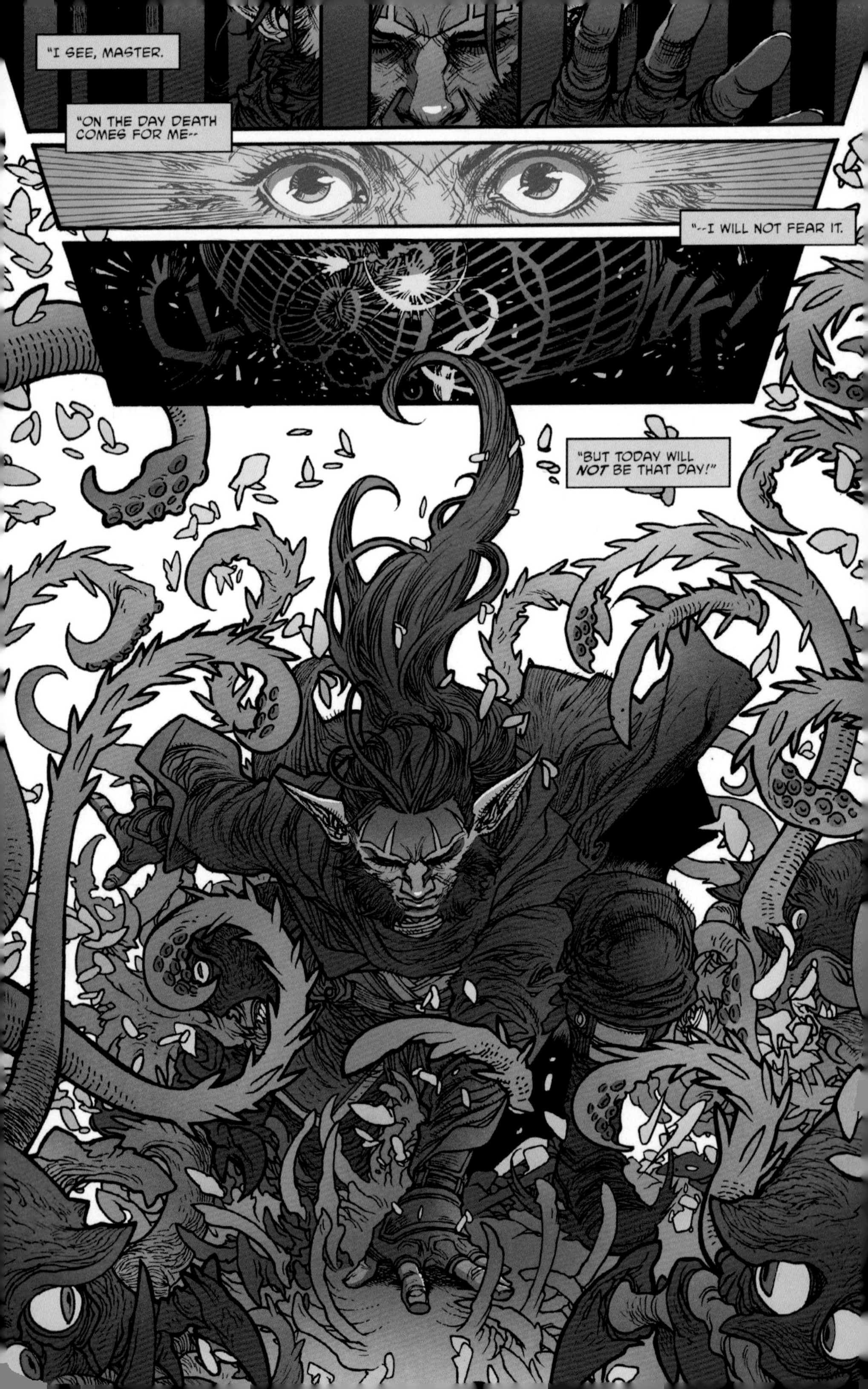
"I SEE, MASTER.
"ON THE DAY DEATH COMES FOR ME--
"--I WILL NOT FEAR IT.
"BUT TODAY WILL *NOT* BE THAT DAY!"

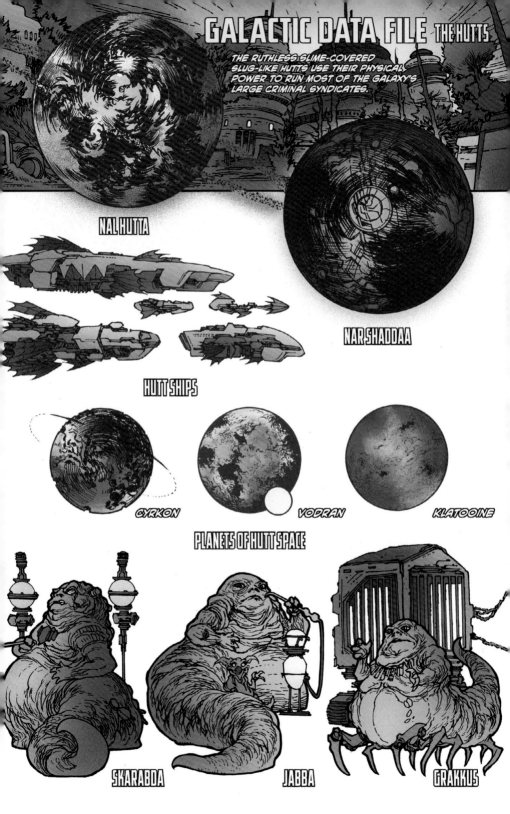

GALACTIC DATA FILE THE HUTTS

THE RUTHLESS SLIME-COVERED SLUG-LIKE HUTTS USE THEIR PHYSICAL POWER TO RUN MOST OF THE GALAXY'S LARGE CRIMINAL SYNDICATES.

NAL HUTTA

NAR SHADDAA

HUTT SHIPS

CYRKON

VODRAN

KLATOOINE

PLANETS OF HUTT SPACE

SKARABDA

JABBA

GRAKKUS

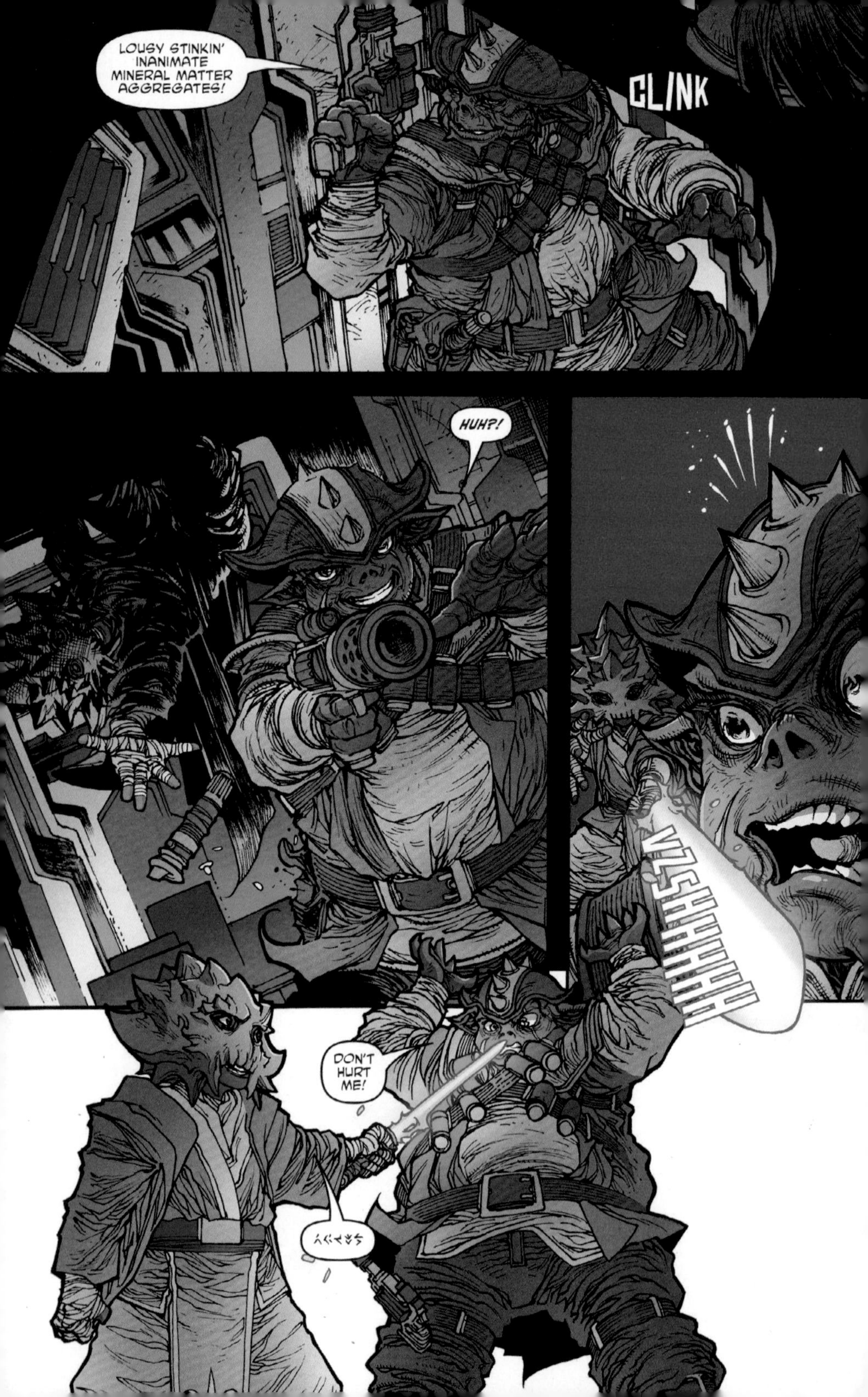
LOUSY STINKIN' INANIMATE MINERAL MATTER AGGREGATES!
CLINK
HUH?!
VZSHHHHH
DON'T HURT ME!

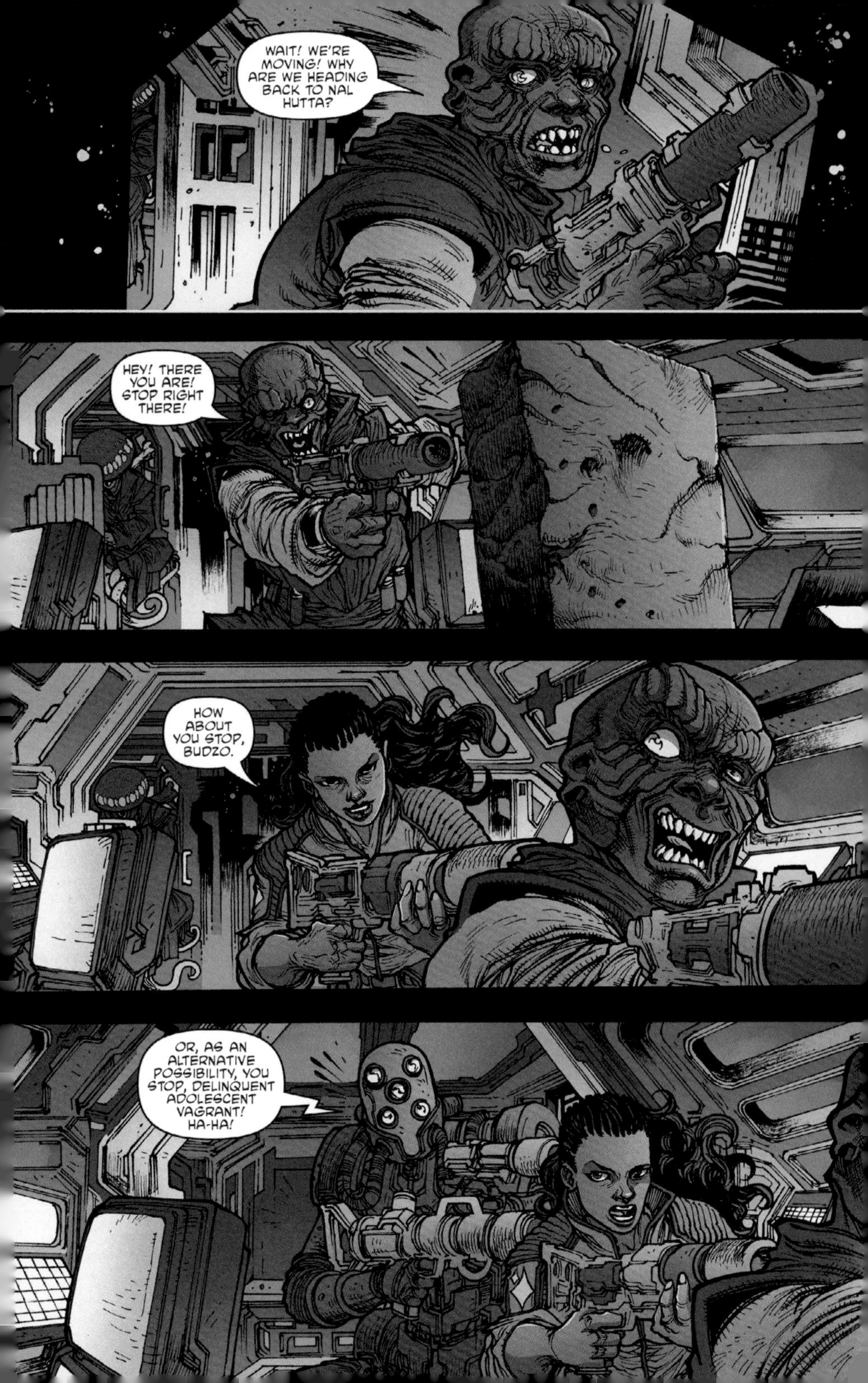
WAIT! WE'RE MOVING! WHY ARE WE HEADING BACK TO NAL HUTTA?
HEY! THERE YOU ARE! STOP RIGHT THERE!
HOW ABOUT YOU STOP, BUDZO.
OR, AS AN ALTERNATIVE POSSIBILITY, YOU STOP, DELINQUENT ADOLESCENT VAGRANT! HA-HA!

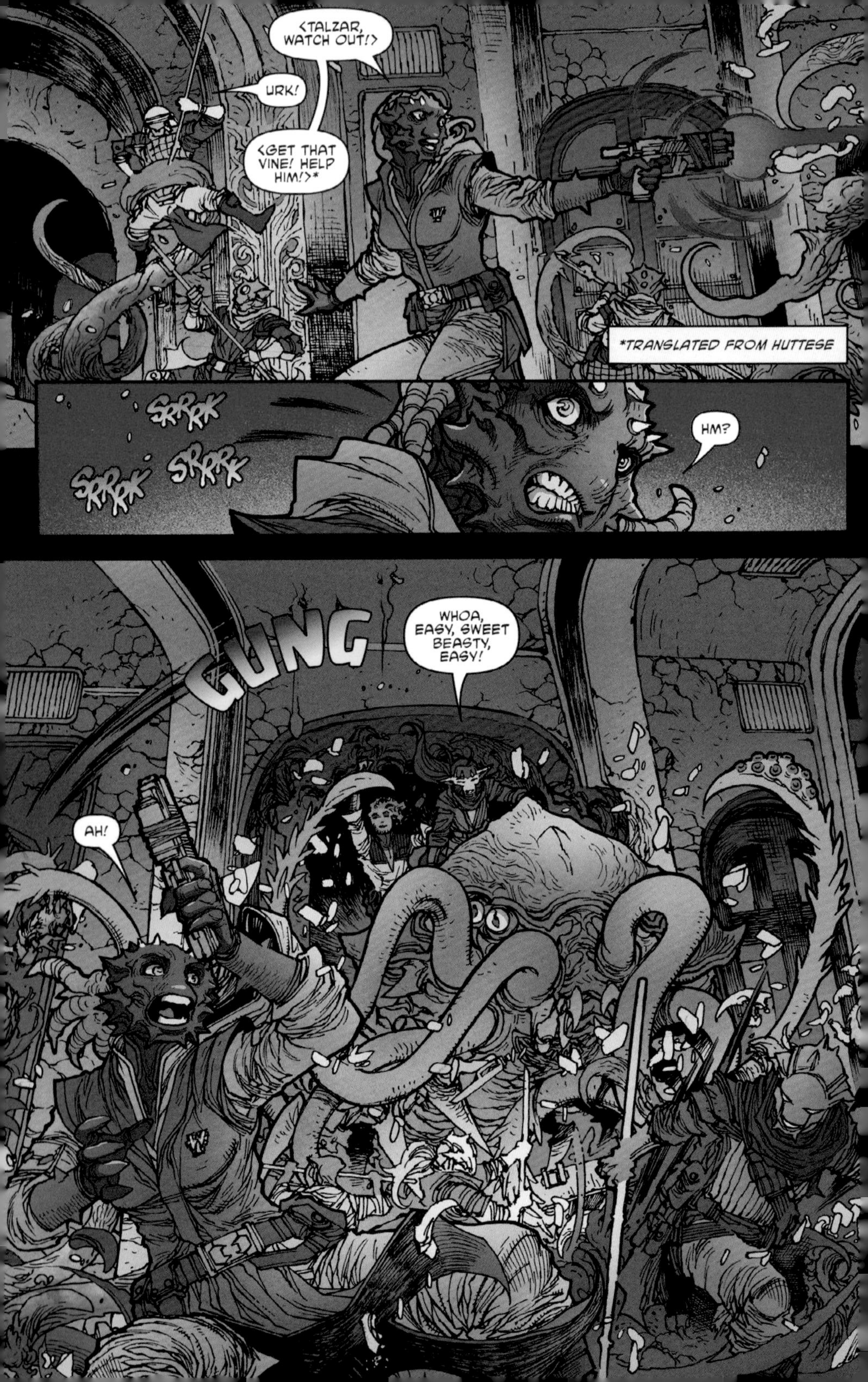

<TALZAR, WATCH OUT!>
URK!
<GET THAT VINE! HELP HIM!>*
*TRANSLATED FROM HUTTESE
SRRRK
SRRRK SRRRK
HM?
GUNG
WHOA, EASY, SWEET BEASTY, EASY!
AH!

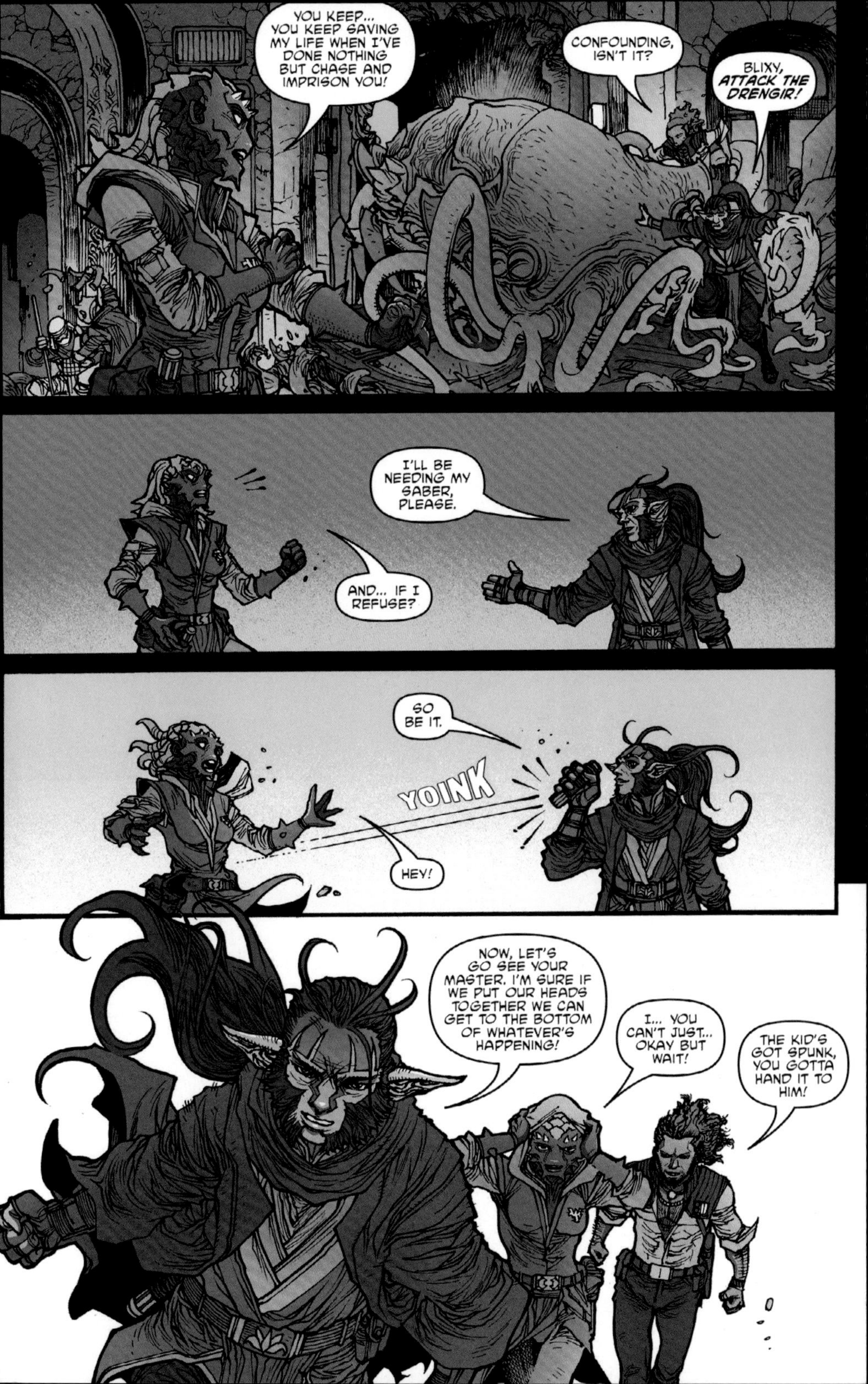
YOU KEEP... YOU KEEP SAVING MY LIFE WHEN I'VE DONE NOTHING BUT CHASE AND IMPRISON YOU!
CONFOUNDING, ISN'T IT?
BLIXY, ATTACK THE DRENGIR!
I'LL BE NEEDING MY SABER, PLEASE.
AND... IF I REFUSE?
SO BE IT.
YOINK
HEY!
NOW, LET'S GO SEE YOUR MASTER. I'M SURE IF WE PUT OUR HEADS TOGETHER WE CAN GET TO THE BOTTOM OF WHATEVER'S HAPPENING!
I... YOU CAN'T JUST... OKAY BUT WAIT!
THE KID'S GOT SPUNK, YOU GOTTA HAND IT TO HIM!

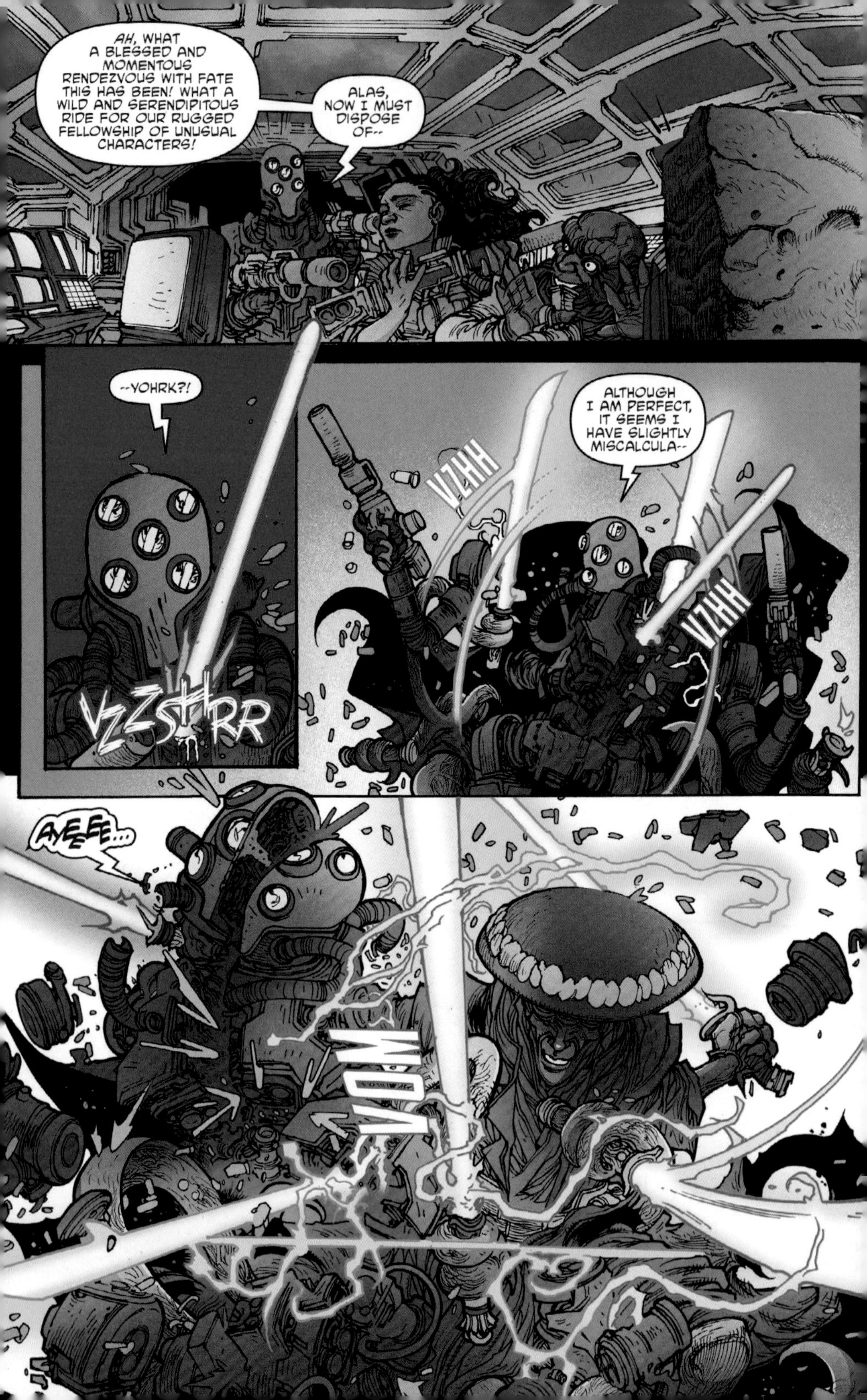
AH, WHAT A BLESSED AND MOMENTOUS RENDEZVOUS WITH FATE THIS HAS BEEN! WHAT A WILD AND SERENDIPITOUS RIDE FOR OUR RUGGED FELLOWSHIP OF UNUSUAL CHARACTERS!
ALAS, NOW I MUST DISPOSE OF--
--YOHRK?!
VZZSHRR
ALTHOUGH I AM PERFECT, IT SEEMS I HAVE SLIGHTLY MISCALCULA--
VZHH
VZHH
AYEEEEE...
VOM

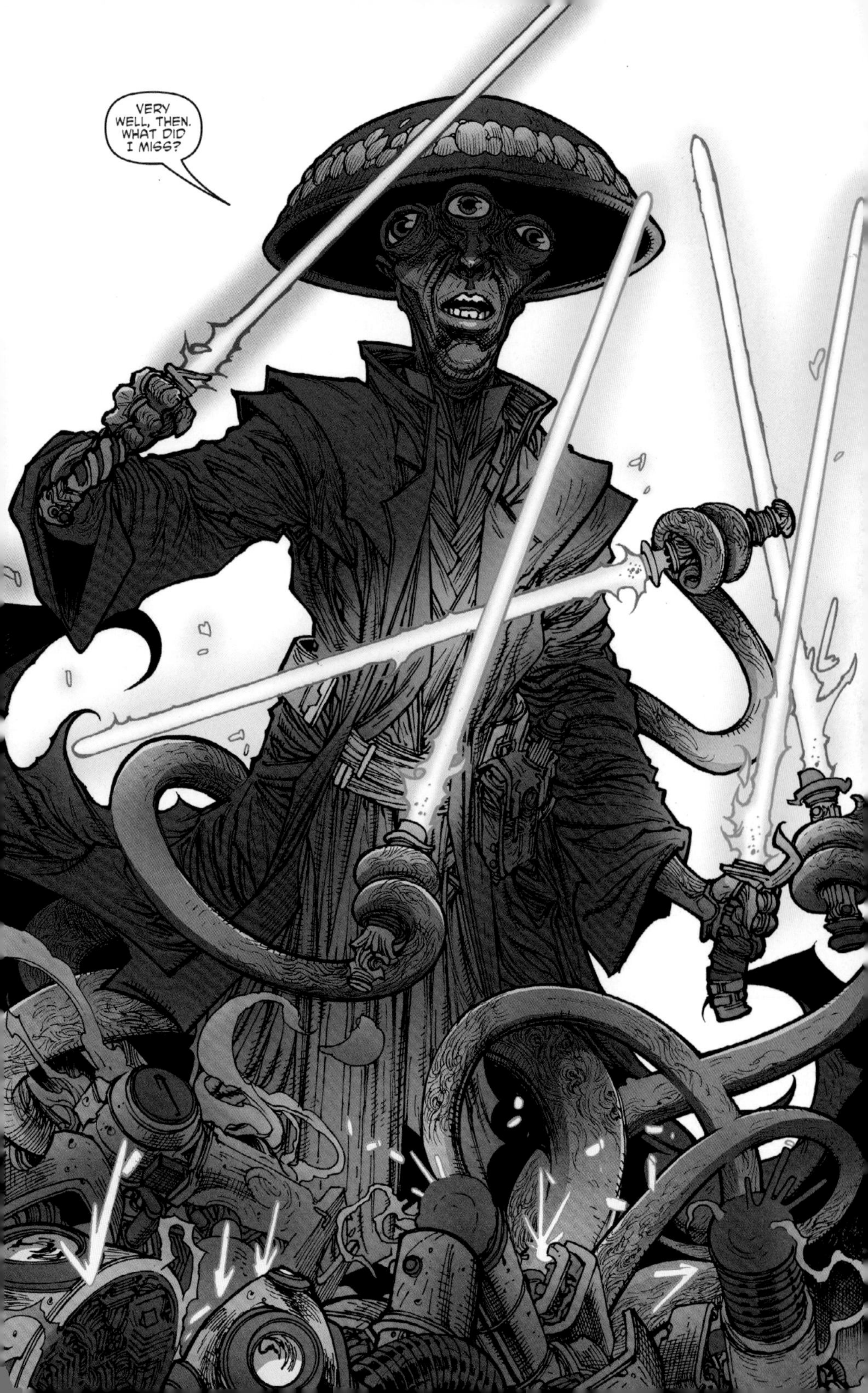
VERY WELL, THEN. WHAT DID I MISS?

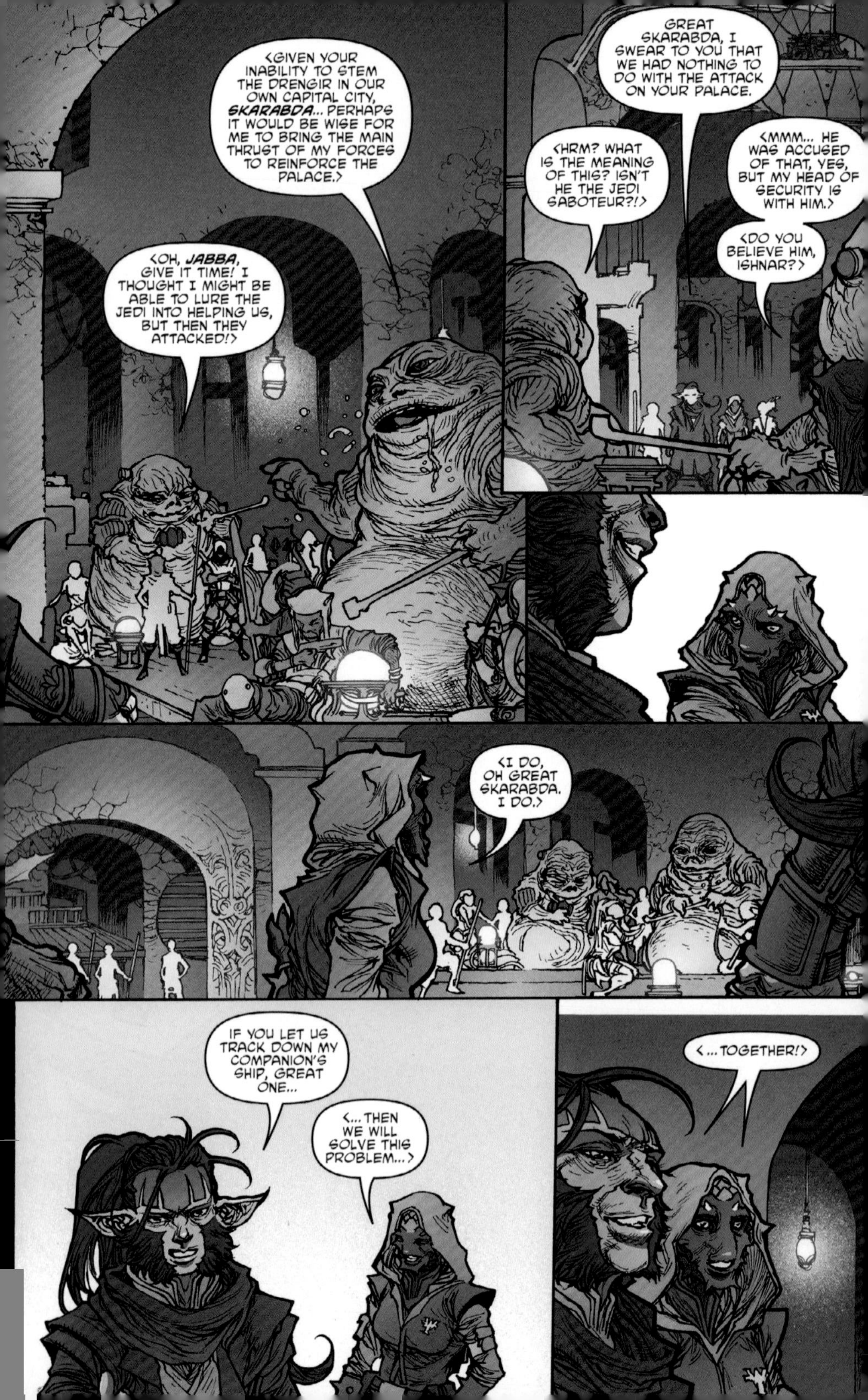
<GIVEN YOUR INABILITY TO STEM THE DRENGIR IN OUR OWN CAPITAL CITY, SKARABDA... PERHAPS IT WOULD BE WISE FOR ME TO BRING THE MAIN THRUST OF MY FORCES TO REINFORCE THE PALACE.>
<OH, JABBA, GIVE IT TIME! I THOUGHT I MIGHT BE ABLE TO LURE THE JEDI INTO HELPING US, BUT THEN THEY ATTACKED!>
GREAT SKARABDA, I SWEAR TO YOU THAT WE HAD NOTHING TO DO WITH THE ATTACK ON YOUR PALACE.
<HRM? WHAT IS THE MEANING OF THIS? ISN'T HE THE JEDI SABOTEUR?!>
<MMM... HE WAS ACCUSED OF THAT, YES, BUT MY HEAD OF SECURITY IS WITH HIM.>
<DO YOU BELIEVE HIM, ISHNAR?>
<I DO, OH GREAT SKARABDA. I DO.>
IF YOU LET US TRACK DOWN MY COMPANION'S SHIP, GREAT ONE...
<...THEN WE WILL SOLVE THIS PROBLEM...>
<...TOGETHER!>

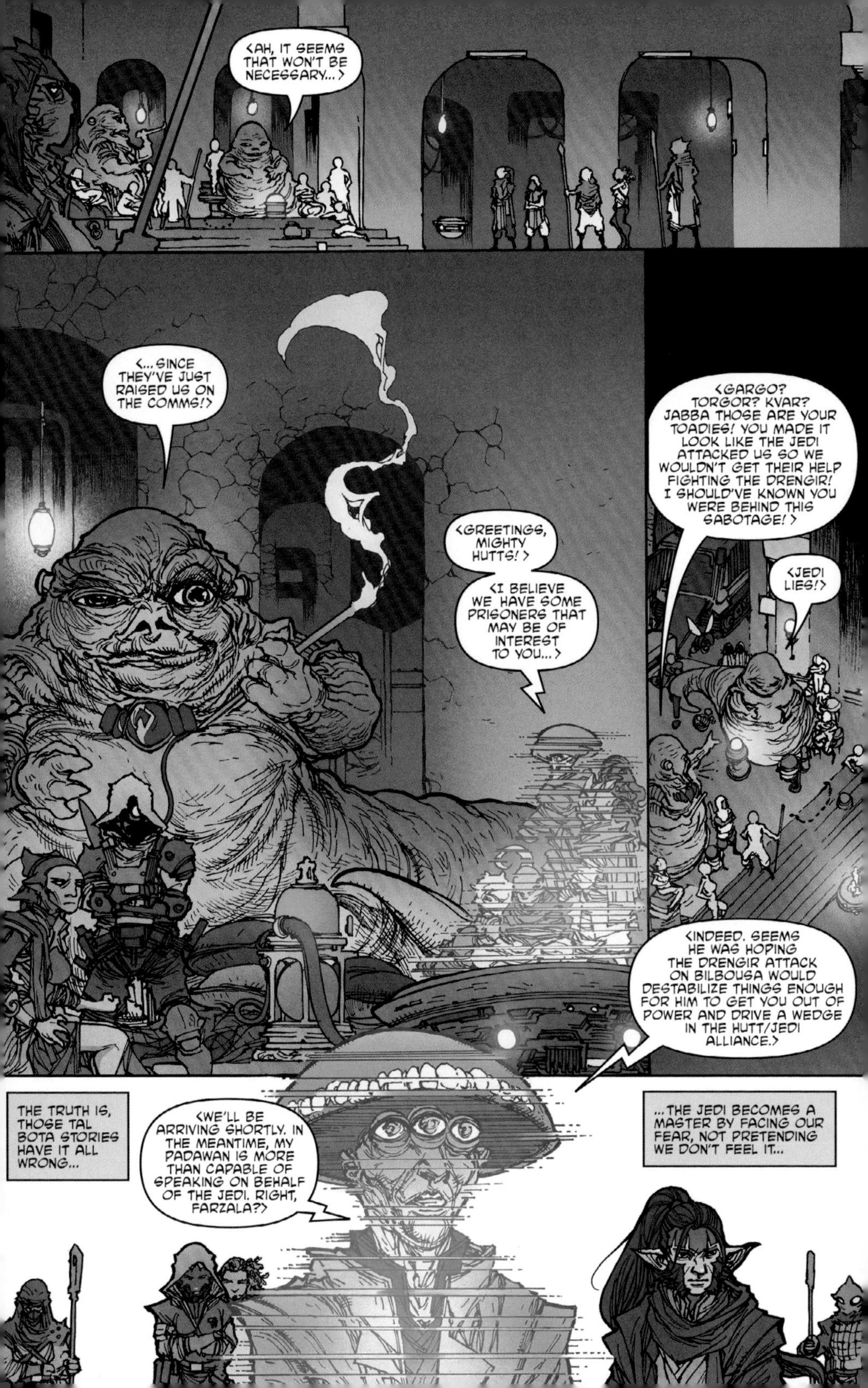
<AH, IT SEEMS THAT WON'T BE NECESSARY...>
<...SINCE THEY'VE JUST RAISED US ON THE COMMS!>
<GREETINGS, MIGHTY HUTTS!>
<I BELIEVE WE HAVE SOME PRISONERS THAT MAY BE OF INTEREST TO YOU...>
<GARGO? TORGOR? KVAR? JABBA THOSE ARE YOUR TOADIES! YOU MADE IT LOOK LIKE THE JEDI ATTACKED US SO WE WOULDN'T GET THEIR HELP FIGHTING THE DRENGIR! I SHOULD'VE KNOWN YOU WERE BEHIND THIS SABOTAGE!>
<JEDI LIES!>
<INDEED. SEEMS HE WAS HOPING THE DRENGIR ATTACK ON BILBOUSA WOULD DESTABILIZE THINGS ENOUGH FOR HIM TO GET YOU OUT OF POWER AND DRIVE A WEDGE IN THE HUTT/JEDI ALLIANCE.>
THE TRUTH IS, THOSE TAL BOTA STORIES HAVE IT ALL WRONG...
<WE'LL BE ARRIVING SHORTLY. IN THE MEANTIME, MY PADAWAN IS MORE THAN CAPABLE OF SPEAKING ON BEHALF OF THE JEDI. RIGHT, FARZALA?>
...THE JEDI BECOMES A MASTER BY FACING OUR FEAR, NOT PRETENDING WE DON'T FEEL IT...

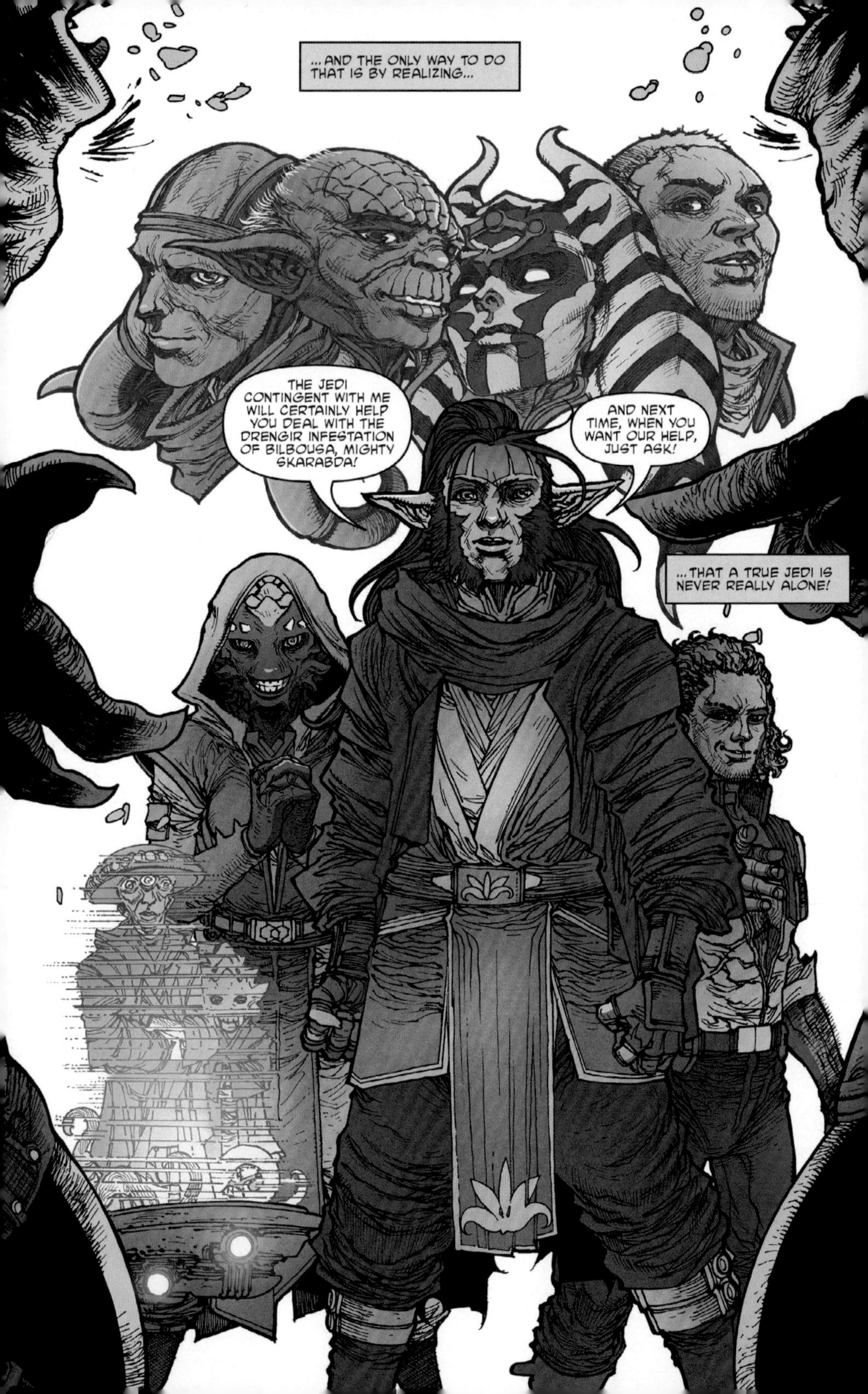
...AND THE ONLY WAY TO DO THAT IS BY REALIZING...
THE JEDI CONTINGENT WITH ME WILL CERTAINLY HELP YOU DEAL WITH THE DRENGIR INFESTATION OF BILBOUSA, MIGHTY SKARABDA!
AND NEXT TIME, WHEN YOU WANT OUR HELP, JUST ASK!
...THAT A TRUE JEDI IS NEVER REALLY ALONE!

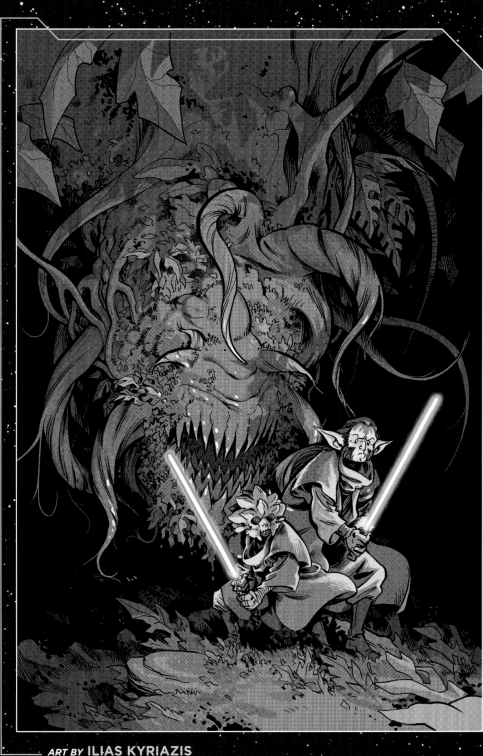

ART BY ILIAS KYRIAZIS

BACK TOGETHER AND AWAY AGAIN

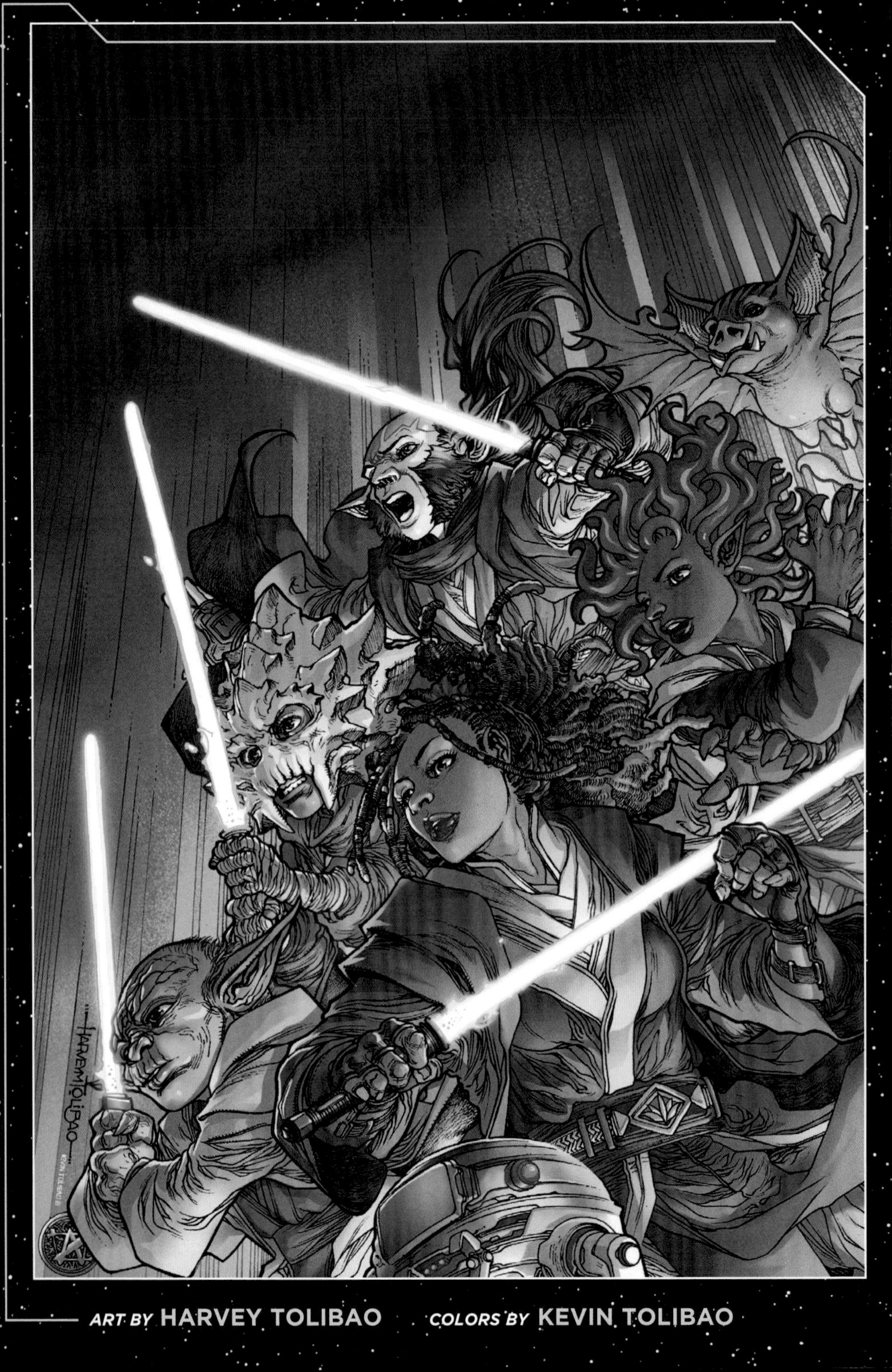

ART BY HARVEY TOLIBAO *COLORS BY* KEVIN TOLIBAO

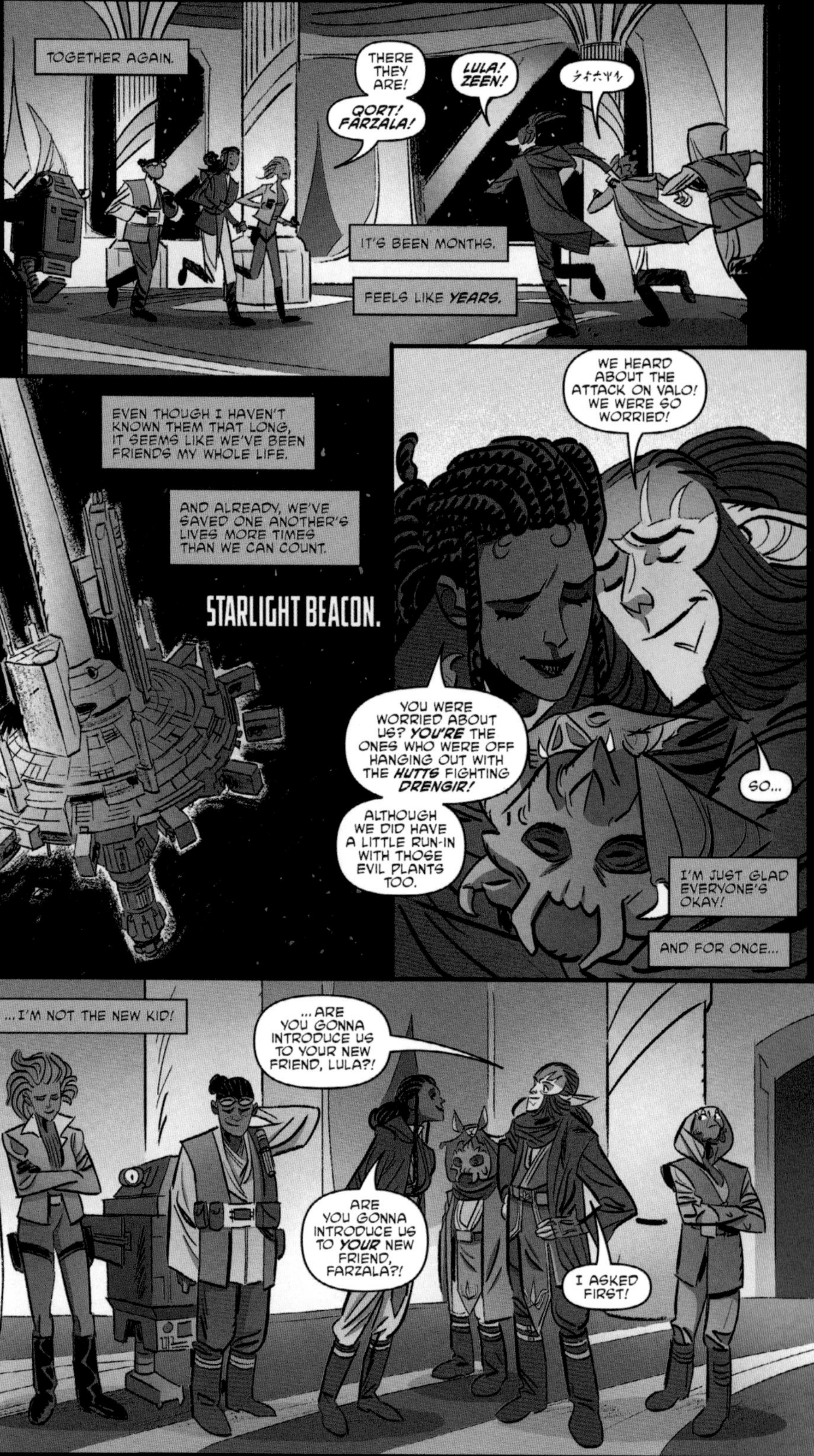
TOGETHER AGAIN.
THERE THEY ARE!
QORT! FARZALA!
LULA! ZEEN!
IT'S BEEN MONTHS.
FEELS LIKE YEARS.
EVEN THOUGH I HAVEN'T KNOWN THEM THAT LONG, IT SEEMS LIKE WE'VE BEEN FRIENDS MY WHOLE LIFE.
AND ALREADY, WE'VE SAVED ONE ANOTHER'S LIVES MORE TIMES THAN WE CAN COUNT.
STARLIGHT BEACON.
WE HEARD ABOUT THE ATTACK ON VALO! WE WERE SO WORRIED!
YOU WERE WORRIED ABOUT US? YOU'RE THE ONES WHO WERE OFF HANGING OUT WITH THE HUTTS FIGHTING DRENGIR!
ALTHOUGH WE DID HAVE A LITTLE RUN-IN WITH THOSE EVIL PLANTS TOO.
SO...
I'M JUST GLAD EVERYONE'S OKAY!
AND FOR ONCE...
...I'M NOT THE NEW KID!
...ARE YOU GONNA INTRODUCE US TO YOUR NEW FRIEND, LULA?!
ARE YOU GONNA INTRODUCE US TO YOUR NEW FRIEND, FARZALA?!
I ASKED FIRST!

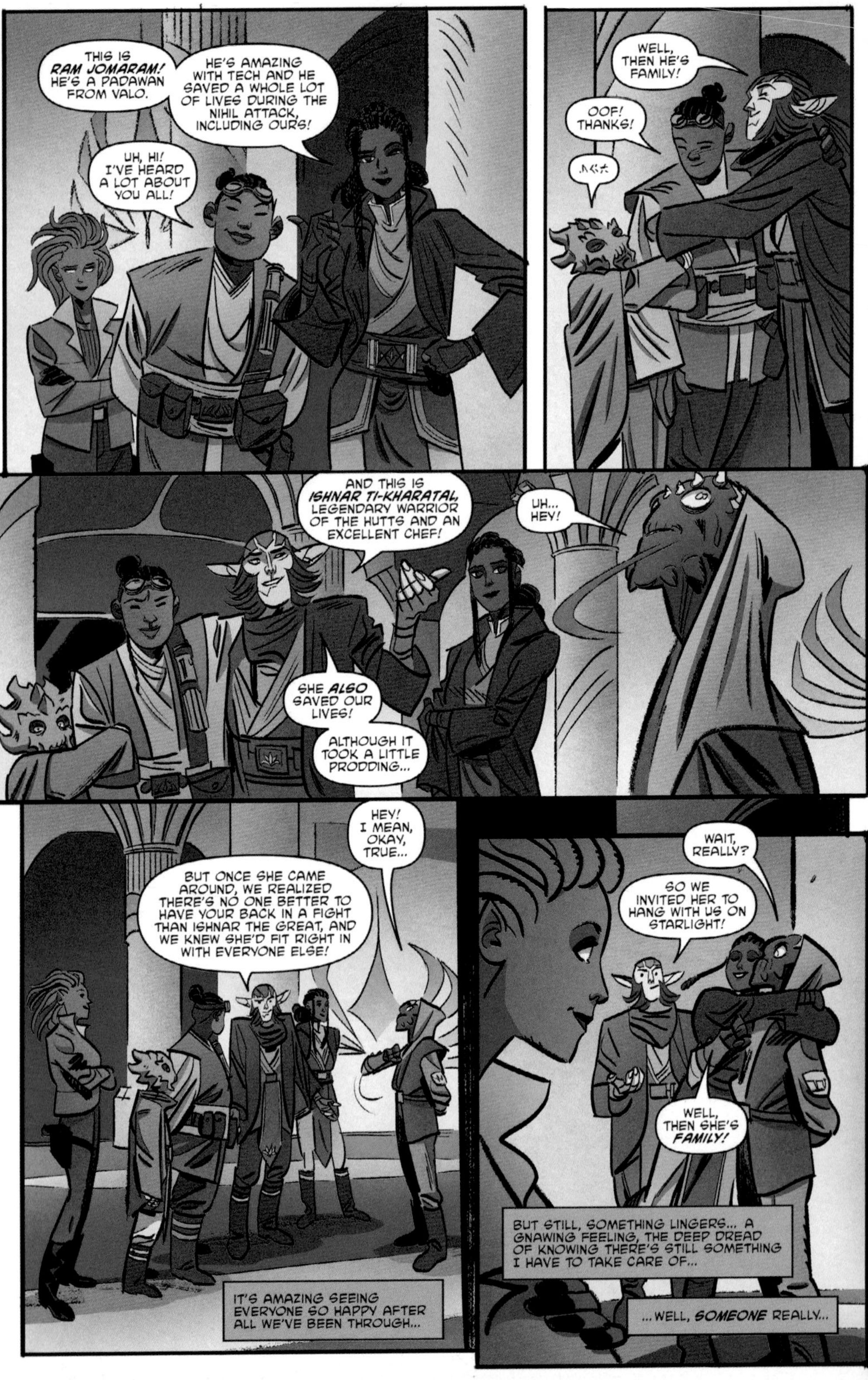
THIS IS RAM JOMARAM! HE'S A PADAWAN FROM VALO.
HE'S AMAZING WITH TECH AND HE SAVED A WHOLE LOT OF LIVES DURING THE NIHIL ATTACK, INCLUDING OURS!
UH, HI! I'VE HEARD A LOT ABOUT YOU ALL!
WELL, THEN HE'S FAMILY!
OOF! THANKS!
AND THIS IS ISHNAR TI-KHARATAL, LEGENDARY WARRIOR OF THE HUTTS AND AN EXCELLENT CHEF!
UH... HEY!
SHE ALSO SAVED OUR LIVES!
ALTHOUGH IT TOOK A LITTLE PRODDING...
HEY! I MEAN, OKAY, TRUE...
BUT ONCE SHE CAME AROUND, WE REALIZED THERE'S NO ONE BETTER TO HAVE YOUR BACK IN A FIGHT THAN ISHNAR THE GREAT, AND WE KNEW SHE'D FIT RIGHT IN WITH EVERYONE ELSE!
IT'S AMAZING SEEING EVERYONE SO HAPPY AFTER ALL WE'VE BEEN THROUGH...
WAIT, REALLY?
SO WE INVITED HER TO HANG WITH US ON STARLIGHT!
WELL, THEN SHE'S FAMILY!
BUT STILL, SOMETHING LINGERS... A GNAWING FEELING, THE DEEP DREAD OF KNOWING THERE'S STILL SOMETHING I HAVE TO TAKE CARE OF...
...WELL, SOMEONE REALLY...

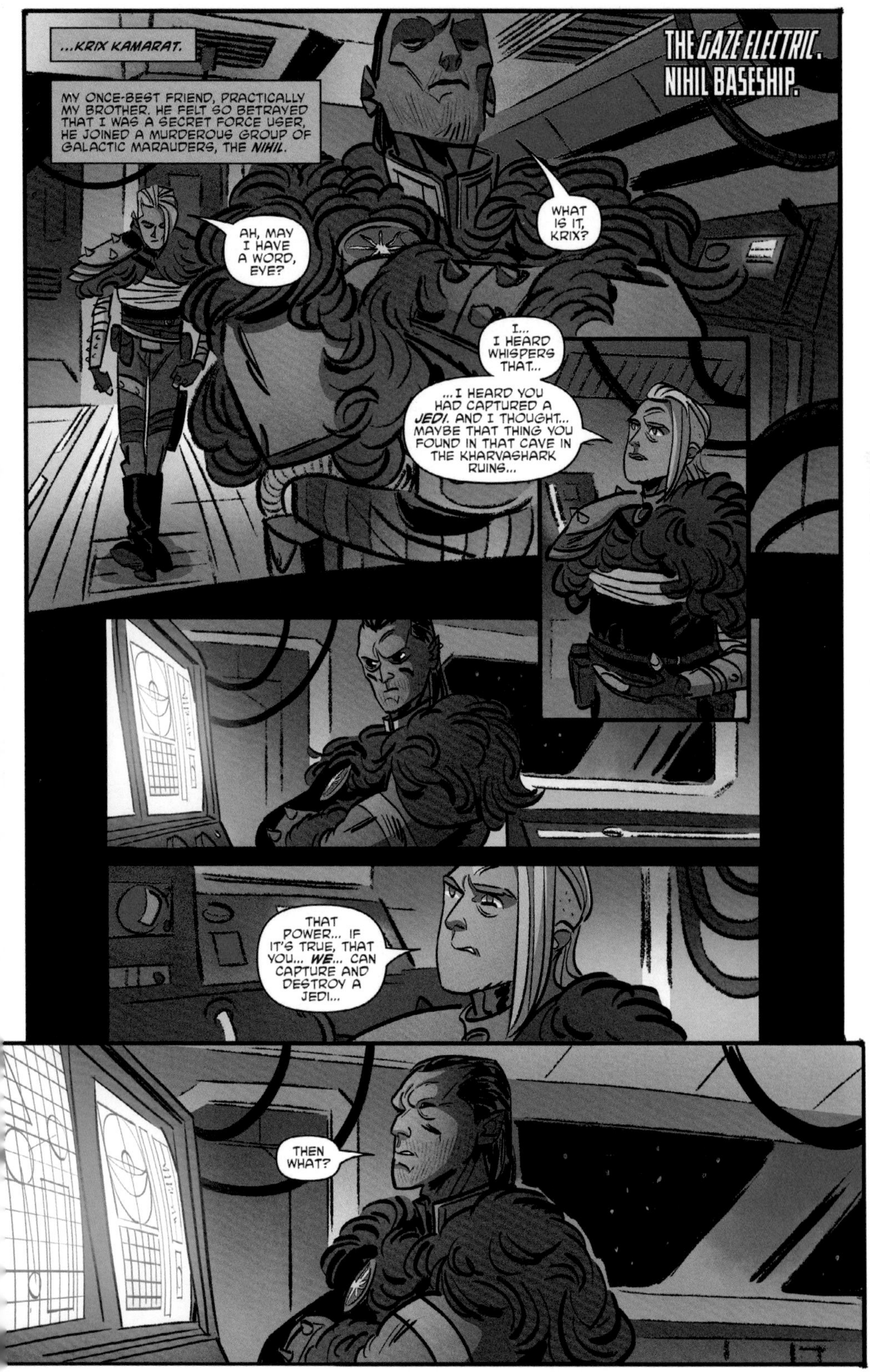
...KRIX KAMARAT.
THE GAZE ELECTRIC. NIHIL BASESHIP.
MY ONCE-BEST FRIEND, PRACTICALLY MY BROTHER. HE FELT SO BETRAYED THAT I WAS A SECRET FORCE USER, HE JOINED A MURDEROUS GROUP OF GALACTIC MARAUDERS, THE NIHIL.
AH, MAY I HAVE A WORD, EYE?
WHAT IS IT, KRIX?
I... I HEARD WHISPERS THAT...
...I HEARD YOU HAD CAPTURED A JEDI. AND I THOUGHT... MAYBE THAT THING YOU FOUND IN THAT CAVE IN THE KHARVASHARK RUINS...
THAT POWER... IF IT'S TRUE, THAT YOU... WE... CAN CAPTURE AND DESTROY A JEDI...
THEN WHAT?

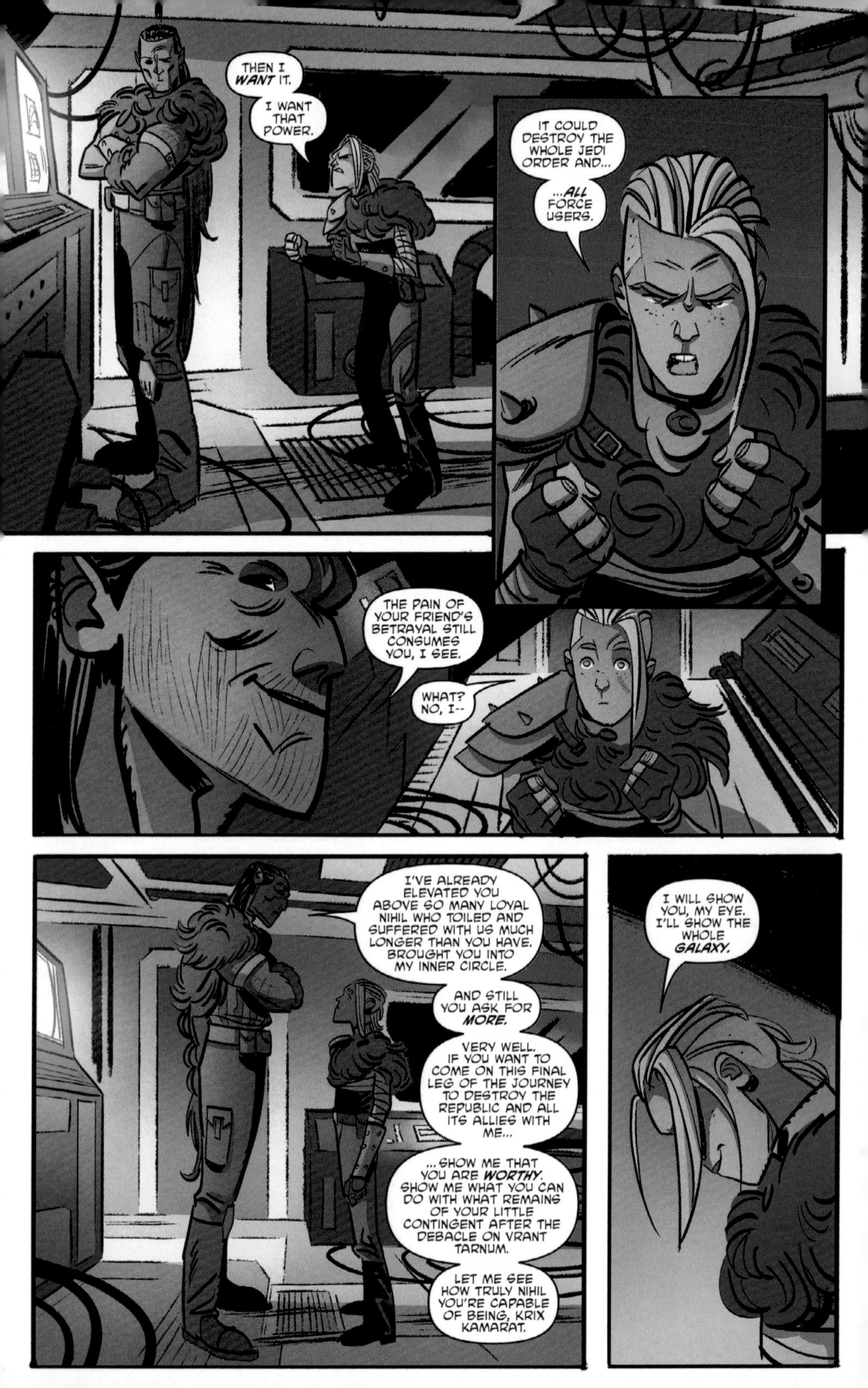
THEN I *WANT* IT.
I WANT THAT POWER.
IT COULD DESTROY THE WHOLE JEDI ORDER AND...
...*ALL* FORCE USERS.
THE PAIN OF YOUR FRIEND'S BETRAYAL STILL CONSUMES YOU, I SEE.
WHAT? NO, I--
I'VE ALREADY ELEVATED YOU ABOVE SO MANY LOYAL NIHIL WHO TOILED AND SUFFERED WITH US MUCH LONGER THAN YOU HAVE. BROUGHT YOU INTO MY INNER CIRCLE.
AND STILL YOU ASK FOR *MORE.*
VERY WELL. IF YOU WANT TO COME ON THIS FINAL LEG OF THE JOURNEY TO DESTROY THE REPUBLIC AND ALL ITS ALLIES WITH ME...
...SHOW ME THAT YOU ARE *WORTHY*. SHOW ME WHAT YOU CAN DO WITH WHAT REMAINS OF YOUR LITTLE CONTINGENT AFTER THE DEBACLE ON VRANT TARNUM.
LET ME SEE HOW TRULY NIHIL YOU'RE CAPABLE OF BEING, KRIX KAMARAT.
I WILL SHOW YOU, MY EYE. I'LL SHOW THE WHOLE *GALAXY.*

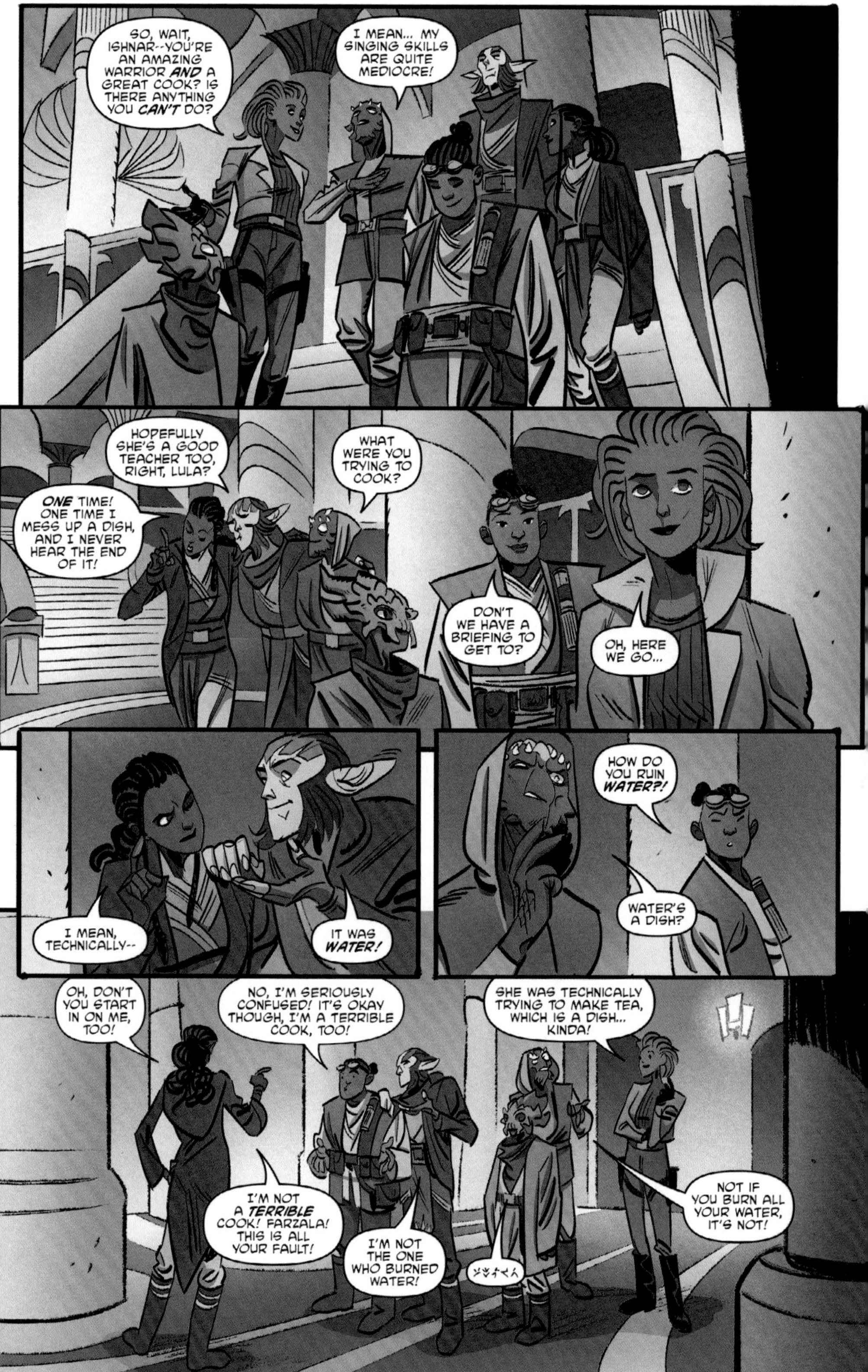
SO, WAIT, ISHNAR--YOU'RE AN AMAZING WARRIOR AND A GREAT COOK? IS THERE ANYTHING YOU CAN'T DO?
I MEAN... MY SINGING SKILLS ARE QUITE MEDIOCRE!
HOPEFULLY SHE'S A GOOD TEACHER TOO, RIGHT, LULA?
ONE TIME! ONE TIME I MESS UP A DISH, AND I NEVER HEAR THE END OF IT!
WHAT WERE YOU TRYING TO COOK?
DON'T WE HAVE A BRIEFING TO GET TO?
OH, HERE WE GO...
I MEAN, TECHNICALLY--
IT WAS WATER!
HOW DO YOU RUIN WATER?!
WATER'S A DISH?
OH, DON'T YOU START IN ON ME, TOO!
NO, I'M SERIOUSLY CONFUSED! IT'S OKAY THOUGH, I'M A TERRIBLE COOK, TOO!
SHE WAS TECHNICALLY TRYING TO MAKE TEA, WHICH IS A DISH... KINDA!
I'M NOT A TERRIBLE COOK! FARZALA! THIS IS ALL YOUR FAULT!
I'M NOT THE ONE WHO BURNED WATER!
NOT IF YOU BURN ALL YOUR WATER, IT'S NOT!

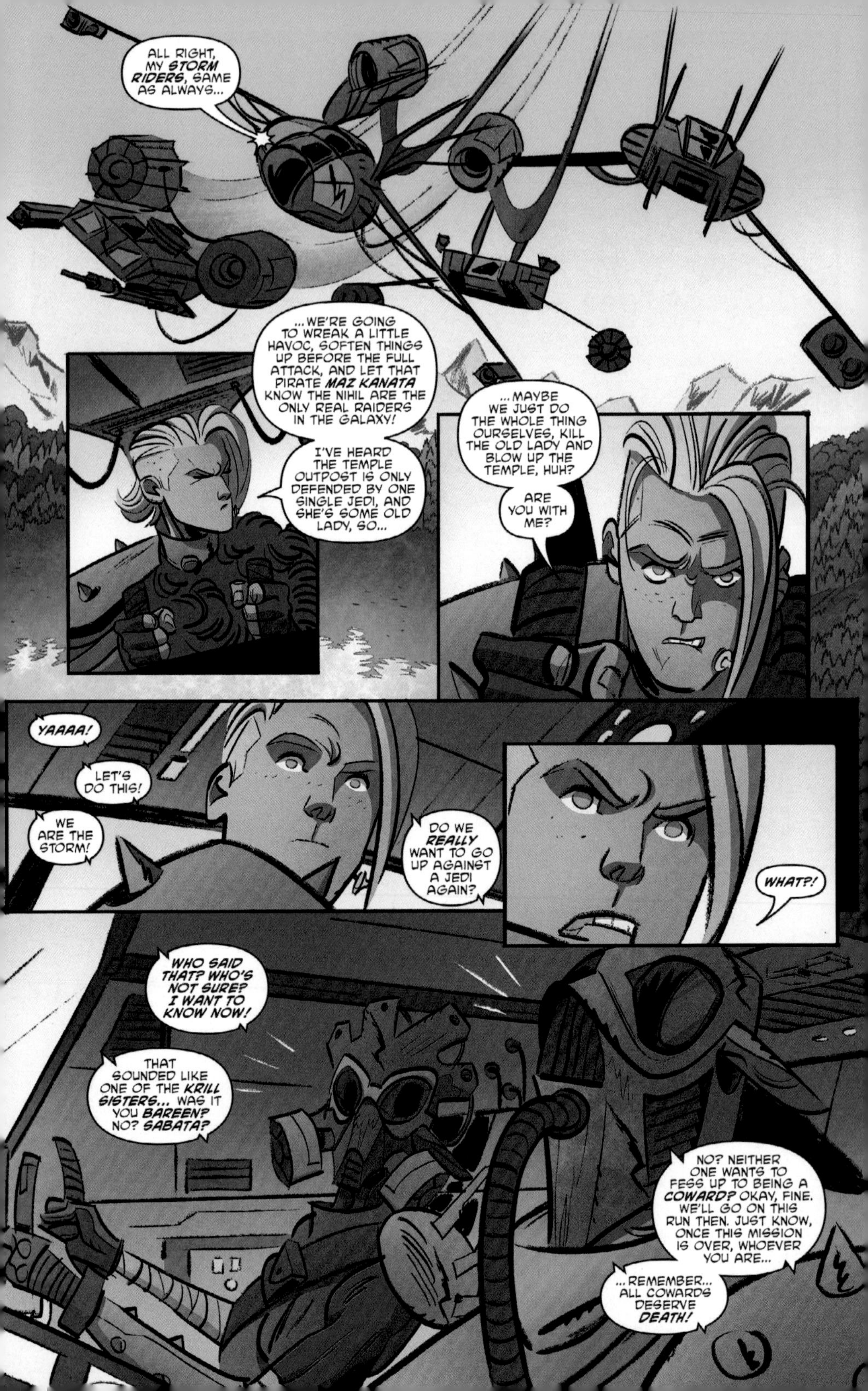
ALL RIGHT, MY STORM RIDERS, SAME AS ALWAYS...
...WE'RE GOING TO WREAK A LITTLE HAVOC, SOFTEN THINGS UP BEFORE THE FULL ATTACK, AND LET THAT PIRATE MAZ KANATA KNOW THE NIHIL ARE THE ONLY REAL RAIDERS IN THE GALAXY!
I'VE HEARD THE TEMPLE OUTPOST IS ONLY DEFENDED BY ONE SINGLE JEDI, AND SHE'S SOME OLD LADY, SO...
...MAYBE WE JUST DO THE WHOLE THING OURSELVES, KILL THE OLD LADY AND BLOW UP THE TEMPLE, HUH?
ARE YOU WITH ME?
YAAAA!
LET'S DO THIS!
WE ARE THE STORM!
DO WE REALLY WANT TO GO UP AGAINST A JEDI AGAIN?
WHAT?!
WHO SAID THAT? WHO'S NOT SURE? I WANT TO KNOW NOW!
THAT SOUNDED LIKE ONE OF THE KRILL SISTERS... WAS IT YOU BAREEN? NO? SABATA?
NO? NEITHER ONE WANTS TO FESS UP TO BEING A COWARD? OKAY, FINE. WE'LL GO ON THIS RUN THEN. JUST KNOW, ONCE THIS MISSION IS OVER, WHOEVER YOU ARE...
...REMEMBER... ALL COWARDS DESERVE DEATH!

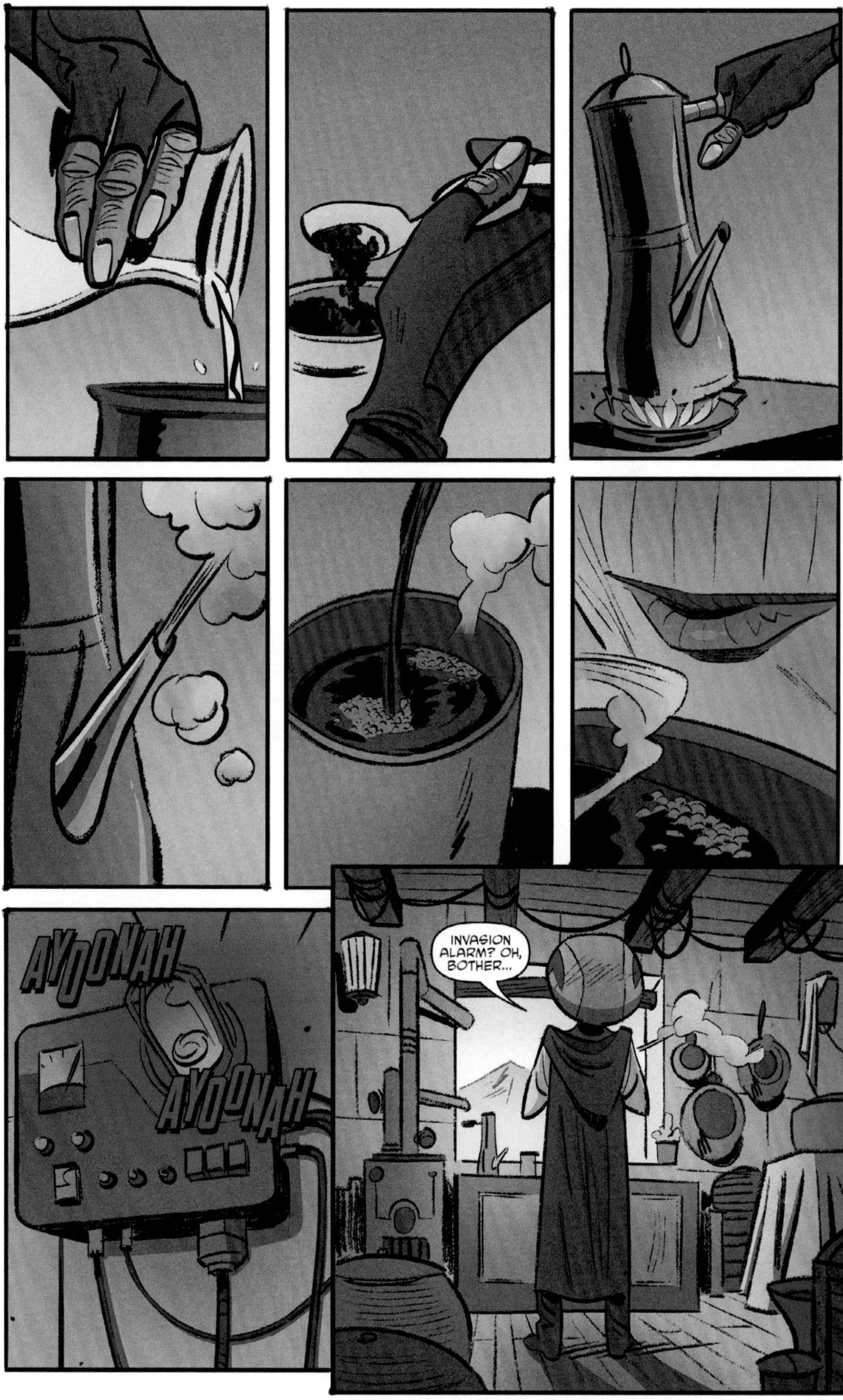
AYOONAH
AYOONAH
INVASION ALARM? OH, BOTHER...

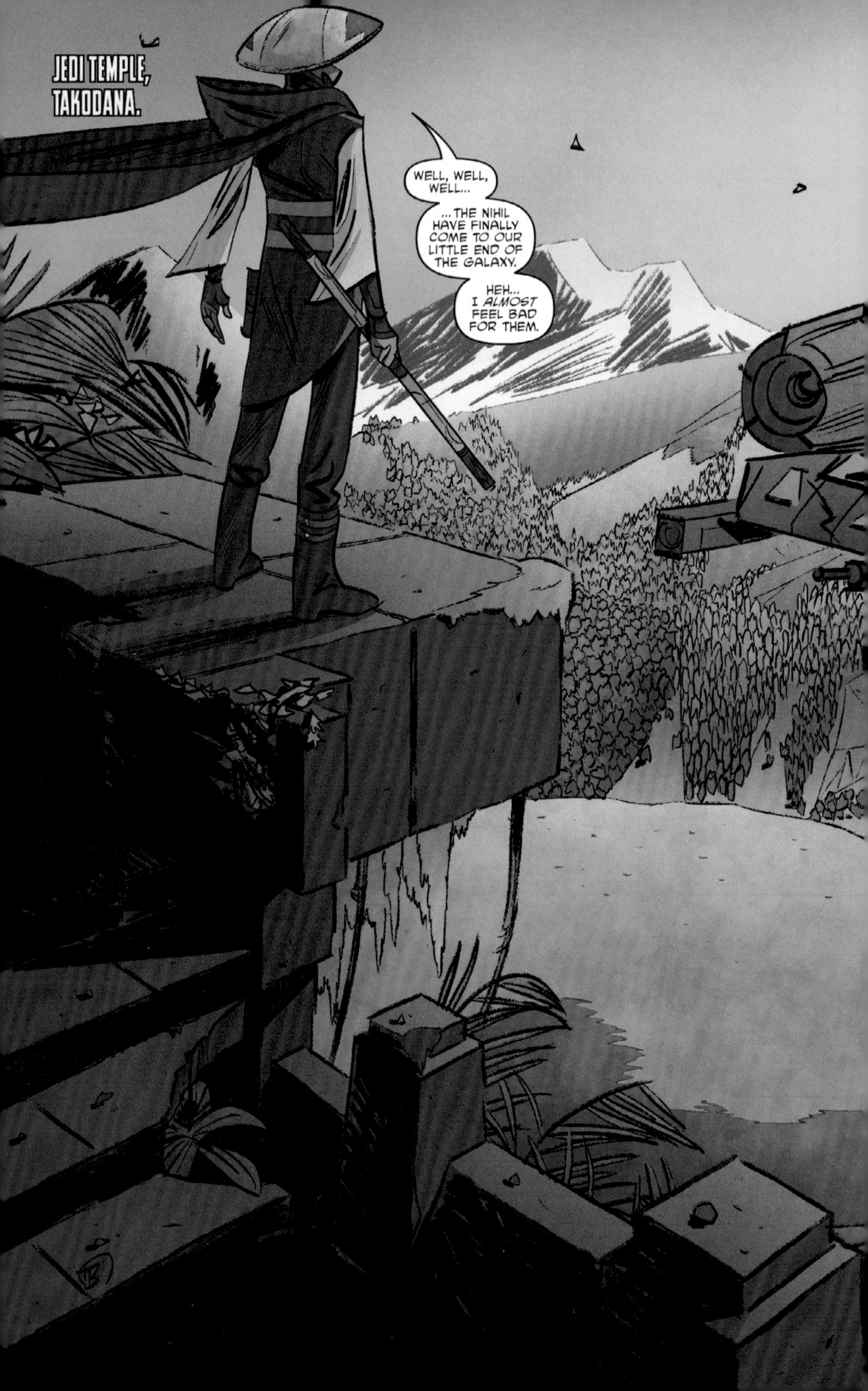
JEDI TEMPLE, TAKODANA.
WELL, WELL, WELL...
...THE NIHIL HAVE FINALLY COME TO OUR LITTLE END OF THE GALAXY.
HEH... I *ALMOST* FEEL BAD FOR THEM.

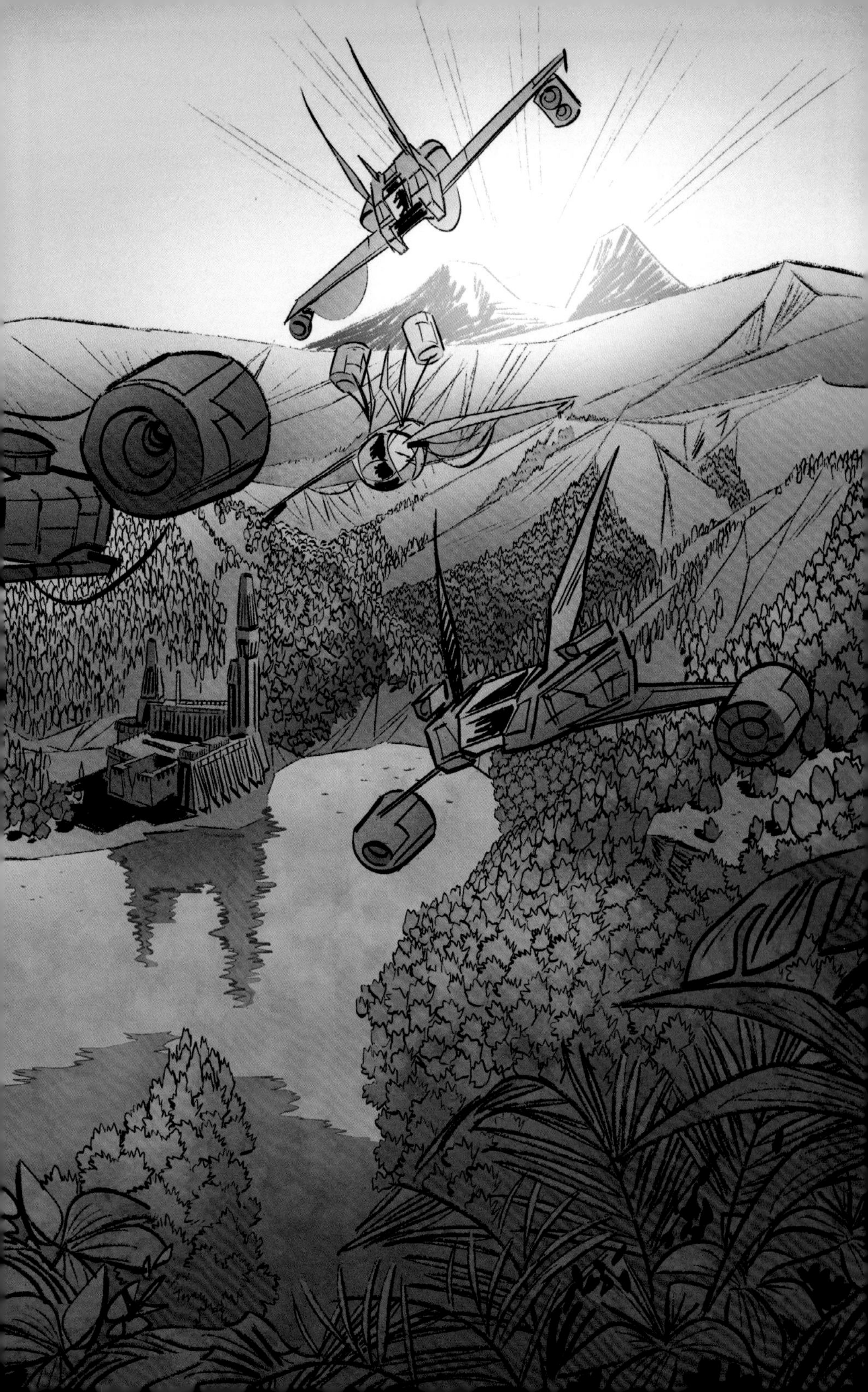

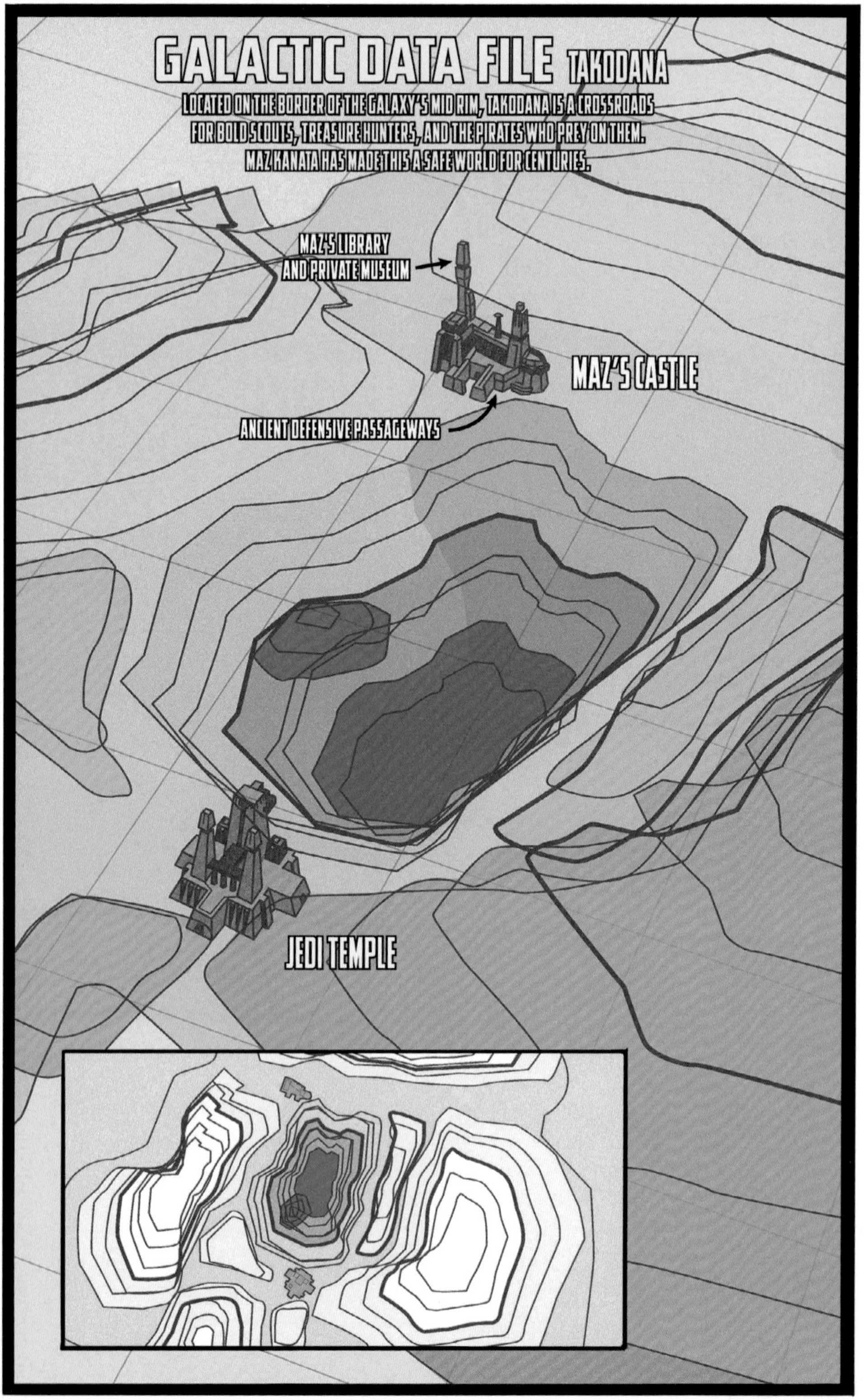
GALACTIC DATA FILE TAKODANA
LOCATED ON THE BORDER OF THE GALAXY'S MID RIM, TAKODANA IS A CROSSROADS FOR BOLD SCOUTS, TREASURE HUNTERS, AND THE PIRATES WHO PREY ON THEM. MAZ KANATA HAS MADE THIS A SAFE WORLD FOR CENTURIES.
MAZ'S LIBRARY AND PRIVATE MUSEUM
MAZ'S CASTLE
ANCIENT DEFENSIVE PASSAGEWAYS
JEDI TEMPLE

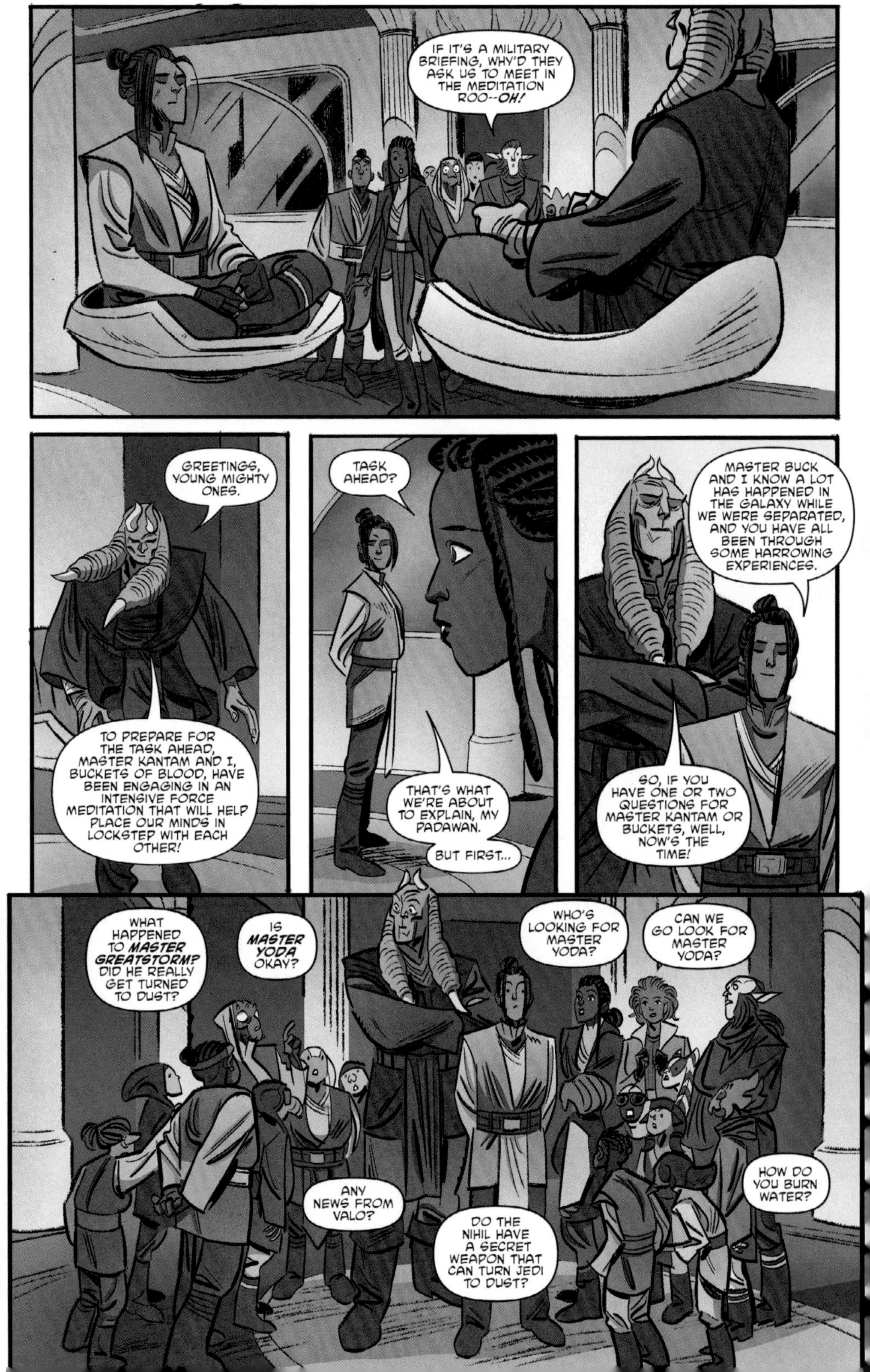
IF IT'S A MILITARY BRIEFING, WHY'D THEY ASK US TO MEET IN THE MEDITATION ROO--OH!
GREETINGS, YOUNG MIGHTY ONES.
TO PREPARE FOR THE TASK AHEAD, MASTER KANTAM AND I, BUCKETS OF BLOOD, HAVE BEEN ENGAGING IN AN INTENSIVE FORCE MEDITATION THAT WILL HELP PLACE OUR MINDS IN LOCKSTEP WITH EACH OTHER!
TASK AHEAD?
THAT'S WHAT WE'RE ABOUT TO EXPLAIN, MY PADAWAN.
BUT FIRST...
MASTER BUCK AND I KNOW A LOT HAS HAPPENED IN THE GALAXY WHILE WE WERE SEPARATED, AND YOU HAVE ALL BEEN THROUGH SOME HARROWING EXPERIENCES.
SO, IF YOU HAVE ONE OR TWO QUESTIONS FOR MASTER KANTAM OR BUCKETS, WELL, NOW'S THE TIME!
WHAT HAPPENED TO MASTER GREATSTORM? DID HE REALLY GET TURNED TO DUST?
IS MASTER YODA OKAY?
WHO'S LOOKING FOR MASTER YODA?
CAN WE GO LOOK FOR MASTER YODA?
ANY NEWS FROM VALO?
DO THE NIHIL HAVE A SECRET WEAPON THAT CAN TURN JEDI TO DUST?
HOW DO YOU BURN WATER?

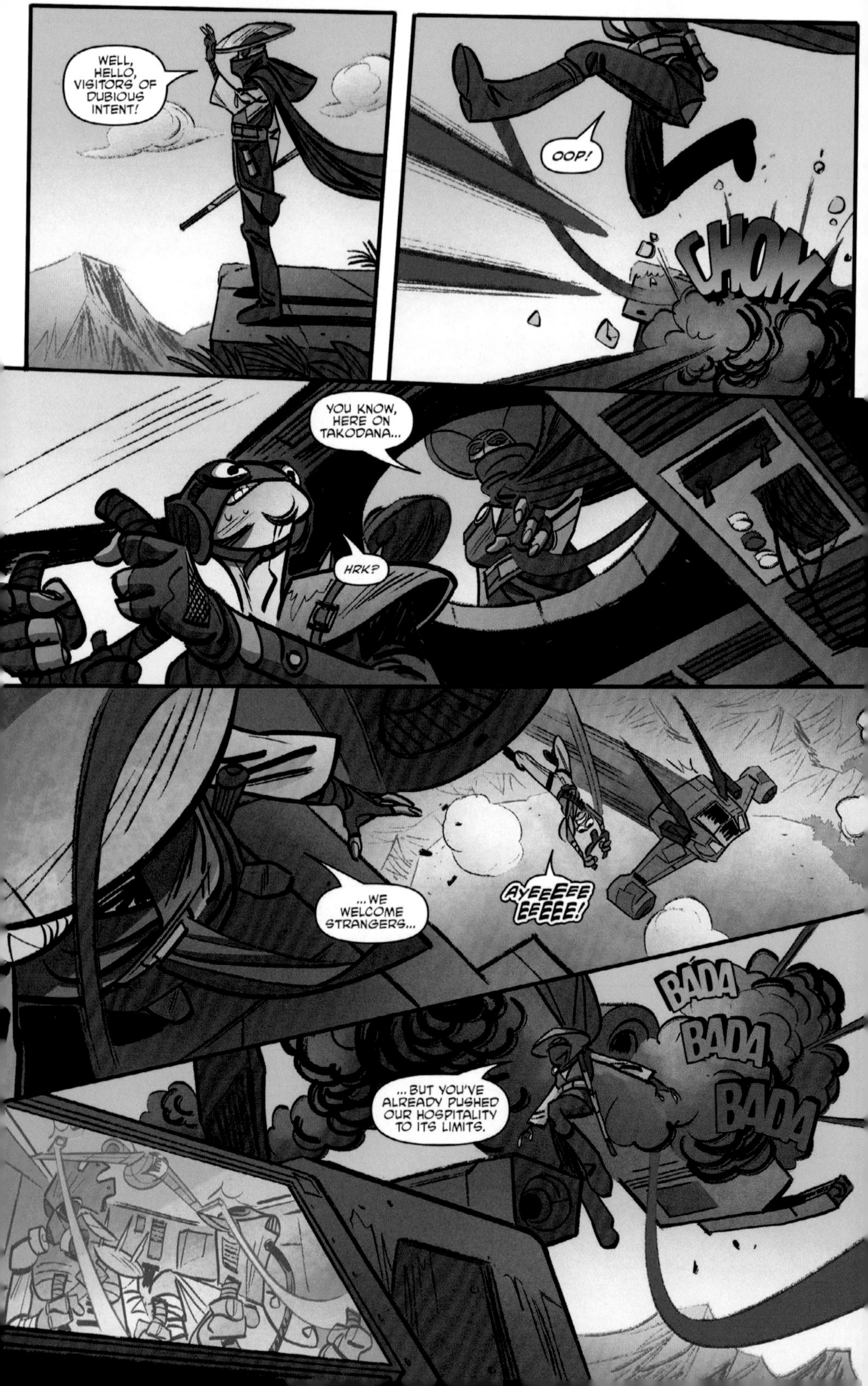
WELL, HELLO, VISITORS OF DUBIOUS INTENT!
OOP!
CHOM
YOU KNOW, HERE ON TAKODANA...
HRK?
...WE WELCOME STRANGERS...
AYEEEEE EEEEE!
BADA BADA BADA
...BUT YOU'VE ALREADY PUSHED OUR HOSPITALITY TO ITS LIMITS.

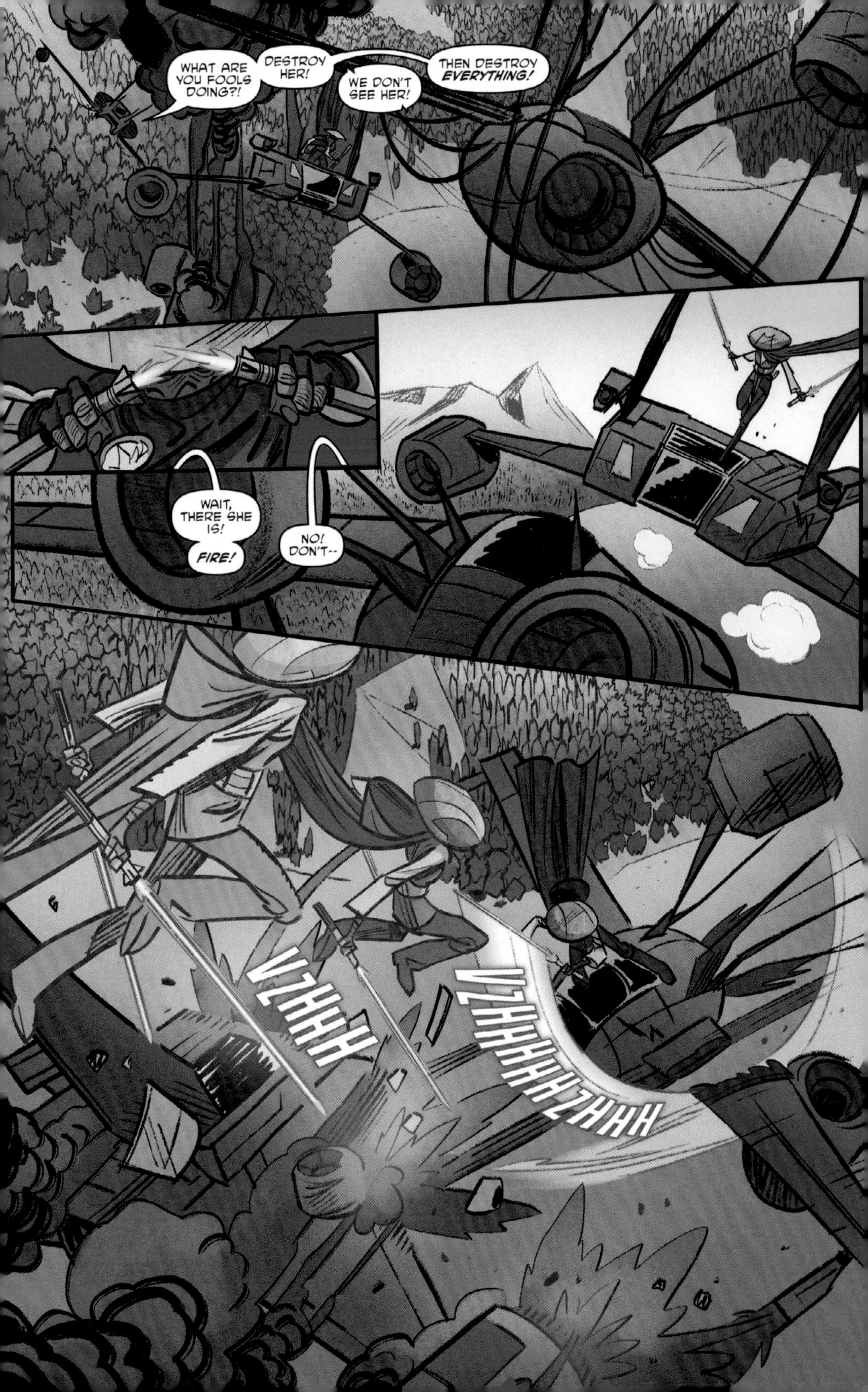
WHAT ARE YOU FOOLS DOING?!
DESTROY HER!
WE DON'T SEE HER!
THEN DESTROY *EVERYTHING!*
WAIT, THERE SHE IS! *FIRE!*
NO! DON'T--
VZHHH
VZHHHHHHHZHHH

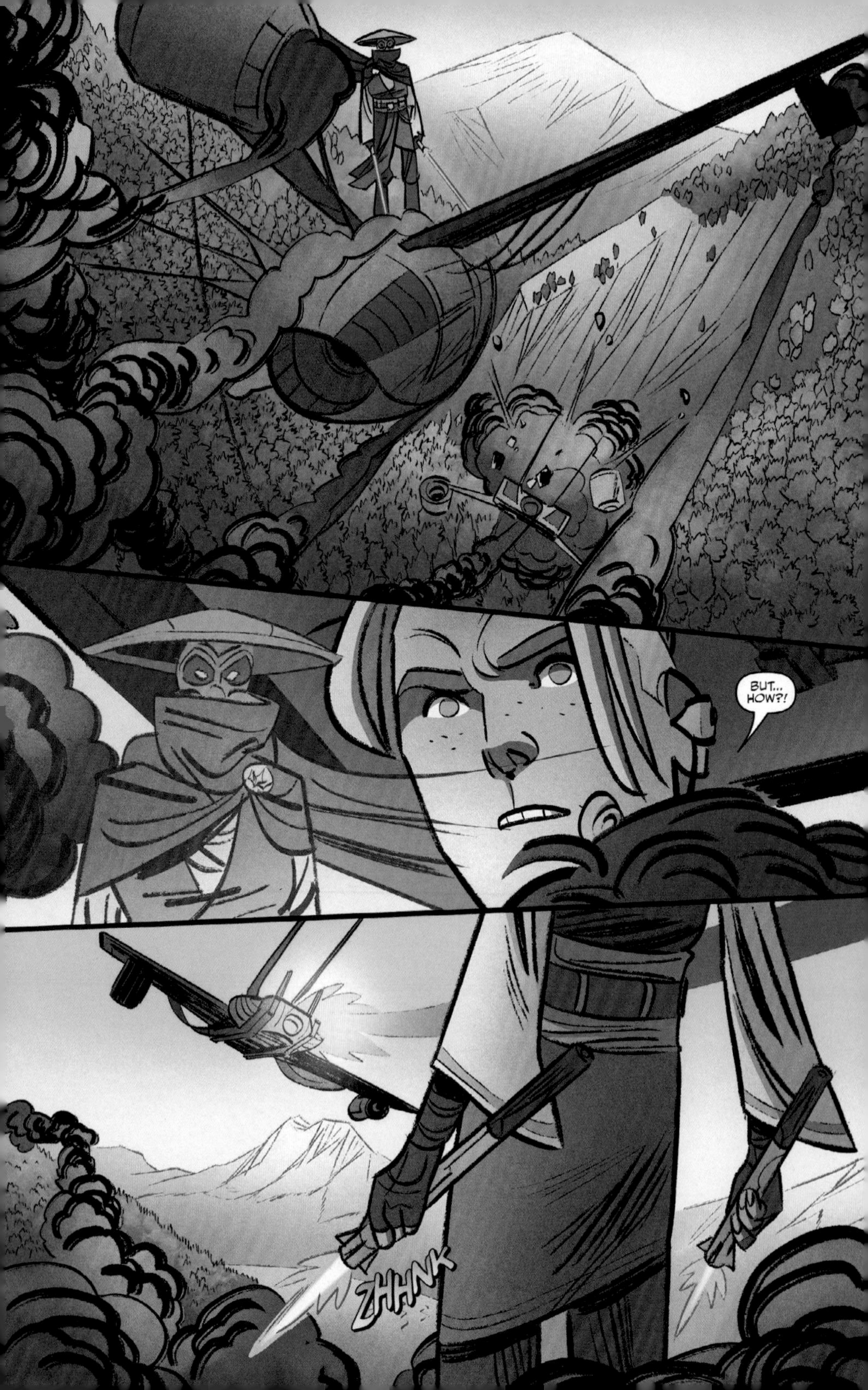
BUT... HOW?!
ZHHNK

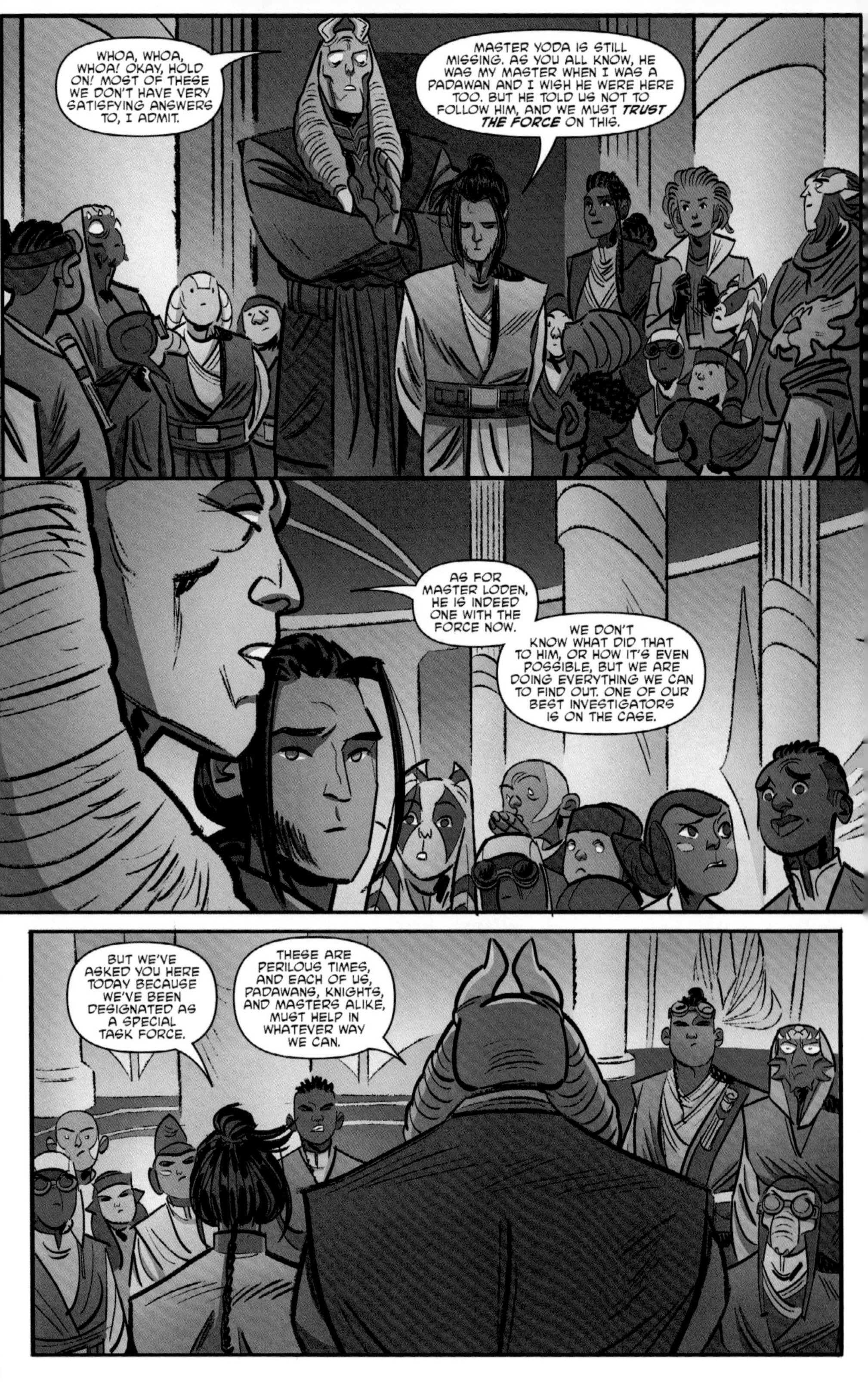
WHOA, WHOA, WHOA! OKAY, HOLD ON! MOST OF THESE WE DON'T HAVE VERY SATISFYING ANSWERS TO, I ADMIT.
MASTER YODA IS STILL MISSING. AS YOU ALL KNOW, HE WAS MY MASTER WHEN I WAS A PADAWAN AND I WISH HE WERE HERE TOO. BUT HE TOLD US NOT TO FOLLOW HIM, AND WE MUST ***TRUST THE FORCE*** ON THIS.
AS FOR MASTER LODEN, HE IS INDEED ONE WITH THE FORCE NOW.
WE DON'T KNOW WHAT DID THAT TO HIM, OR HOW IT'S EVEN POSSIBLE, BUT WE ARE DOING EVERYTHING WE CAN TO FIND OUT. ONE OF OUR BEST INVESTIGATORS IS ON THE CASE.
BUT WE'VE ASKED YOU HERE TODAY BECAUSE WE'VE BEEN DESIGNATED AS A SPECIAL TASK FORCE.
THESE ARE PERILOUS TIMES, AND EACH OF US, PADAWANS, KNIGHTS, AND MASTERS ALIKE, MUST HELP IN WHATEVER WAY WE CAN.

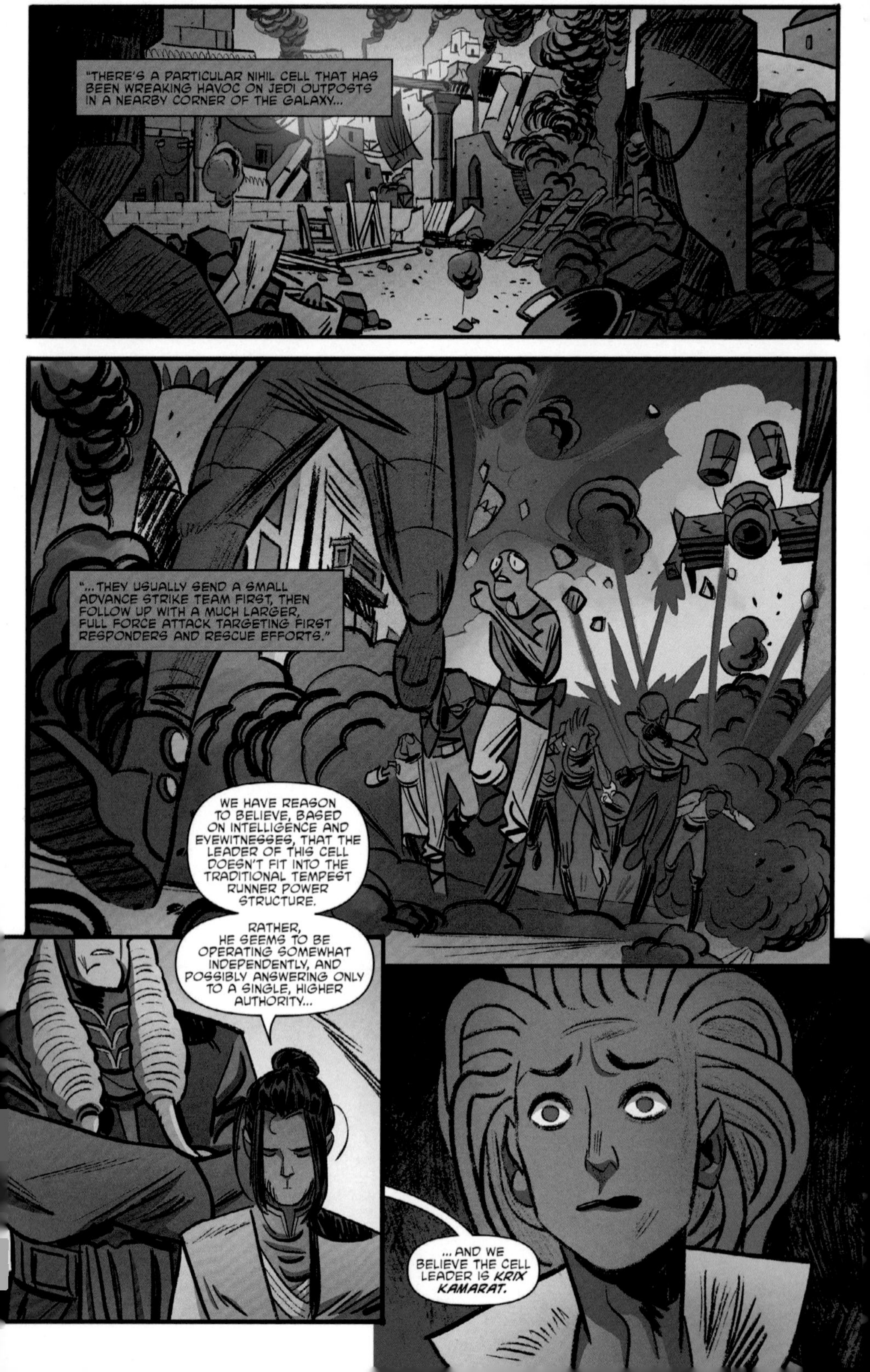
"THERE'S A PARTICULAR NIHIL CELL THAT HAS BEEN WREAKING HAVOC ON JEDI OUTPOSTS IN A NEARBY CORNER OF THE GALAXY...
"...THEY USUALLY SEND A SMALL ADVANCE STRIKE TEAM FIRST, THEN FOLLOW UP WITH A MUCH LARGER, FULL FORCE ATTACK TARGETING FIRST RESPONDERS AND RESCUE EFFORTS."
WE HAVE REASON TO BELIEVE, BASED ON INTELLIGENCE AND EYEWITNESSES, THAT THE LEADER OF THIS CELL DOESN'T FIT INTO THE TRADITIONAL TEMPEST RUNNER POWER STRUCTURE.
RATHER, HE SEEMS TO BE OPERATING SOMEWHAT INDEPENDENTLY, AND POSSIBLY ANSWERING ONLY TO A SINGLE, HIGHER AUTHORITY...
...AND WE BELIEVE THE CELL LEADER IS *KRIX KAMARAT.*

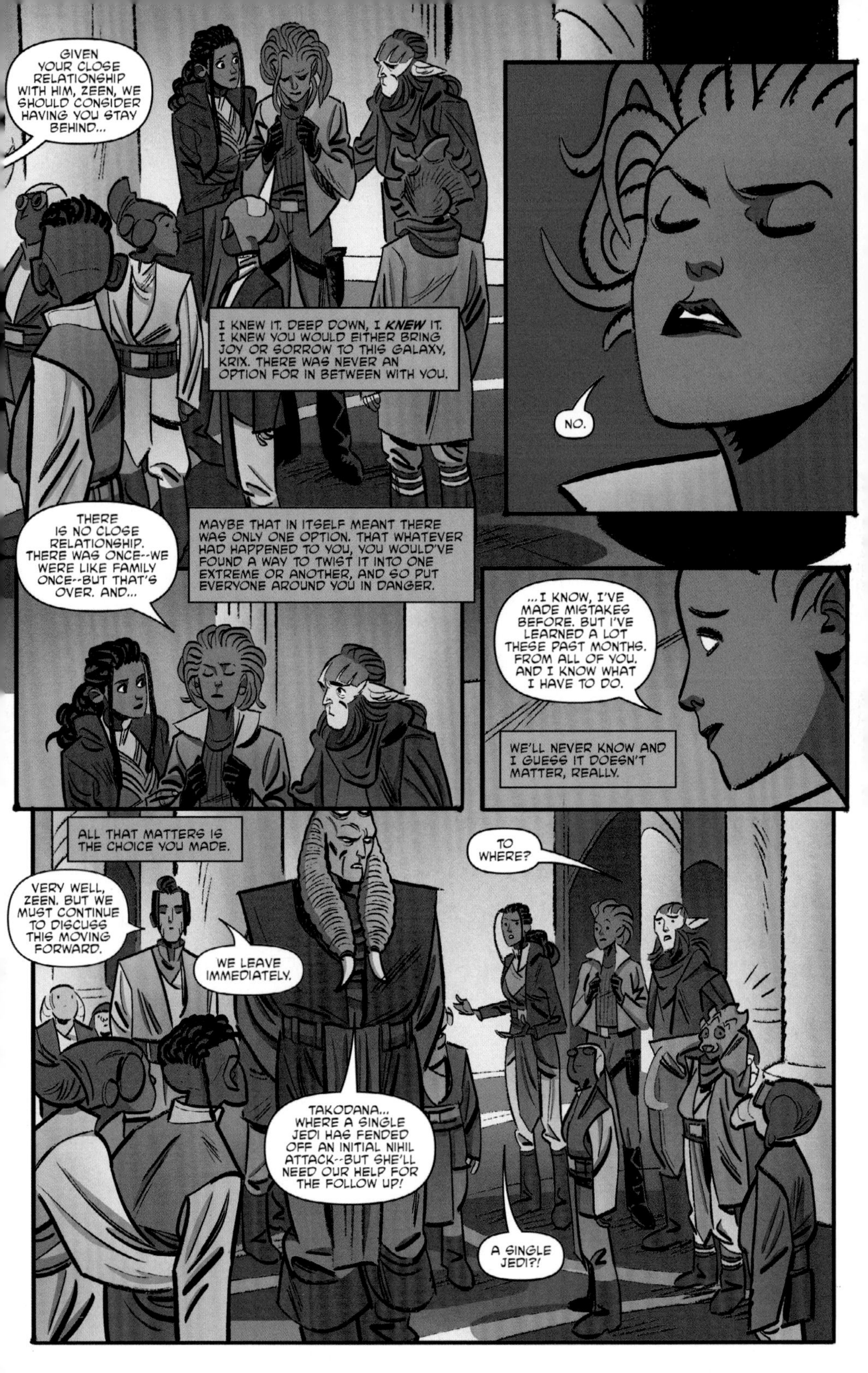
GIVEN YOUR CLOSE RELATIONSHIP WITH HIM, ZEEN, WE SHOULD CONSIDER HAVING YOU STAY BEHIND...
I KNEW IT. DEEP DOWN, I *KNEW* IT. I KNEW YOU WOULD EITHER BRING JOY OR SORROW TO THIS GALAXY, KRIX. THERE WAS NEVER AN OPTION FOR IN BETWEEN WITH YOU.
NO.
THERE IS NO CLOSE RELATIONSHIP. THERE WAS ONCE--WE WERE LIKE FAMILY ONCE--BUT THAT'S OVER. AND...
MAYBE THAT IN ITSELF MEANT THERE WAS ONLY ONE OPTION. THAT WHATEVER HAD HAPPENED TO YOU, YOU WOULD'VE FOUND A WAY TO TWIST IT INTO ONE EXTREME OR ANOTHER, AND SO PUT EVERYONE AROUND YOU IN DANGER.
...I KNOW, I'VE MADE MISTAKES BEFORE. BUT I'VE LEARNED A LOT THESE PAST MONTHS. FROM ALL OF YOU. AND I KNOW WHAT I HAVE TO DO.
WE'LL NEVER KNOW AND I GUESS IT DOESN'T MATTER, REALLY.
ALL THAT MATTERS IS THE CHOICE YOU MADE.
VERY WELL, ZEEN. BUT WE MUST CONTINUE TO DISCUSS THIS MOVING FORWARD.
WE LEAVE IMMEDIATELY.
TO WHERE?
TAKODANA... WHERE A SINGLE JEDI HAS FENDED OFF AN INITIAL NIHIL ATTACK--BUT SHE'LL NEED OUR HELP FOR THE FOLLOW UP!
A SINGLE JEDI?!

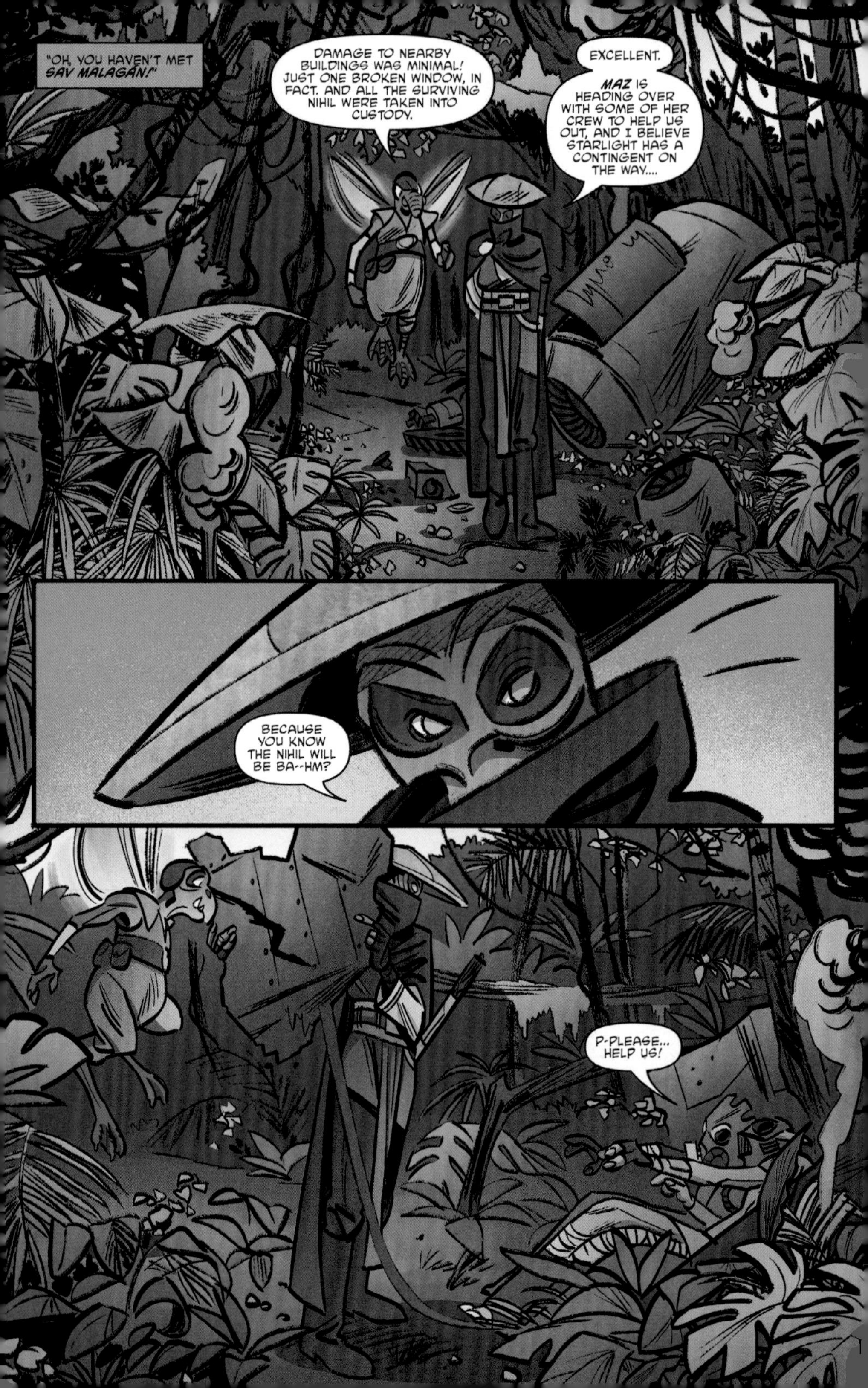
"OH, YOU HAVEN'T MET SAV MALAGAN!"
DAMAGE TO NEARBY BUILDINGS WAS MINIMAL! JUST ONE BROKEN WINDOW, IN FACT. AND ALL THE SURVIVING NIHIL WERE TAKEN INTO CUSTODY.
EXCELLENT.
MAZ IS HEADING OVER WITH SOME OF HER CREW TO HELP US OUT, AND I BELIEVE STARLIGHT HAS A CONTINGENT ON THE WAY....
BECAUSE YOU KNOW THE NIHIL WILL BE BA--HM?
P-PLEASE... HELP US!

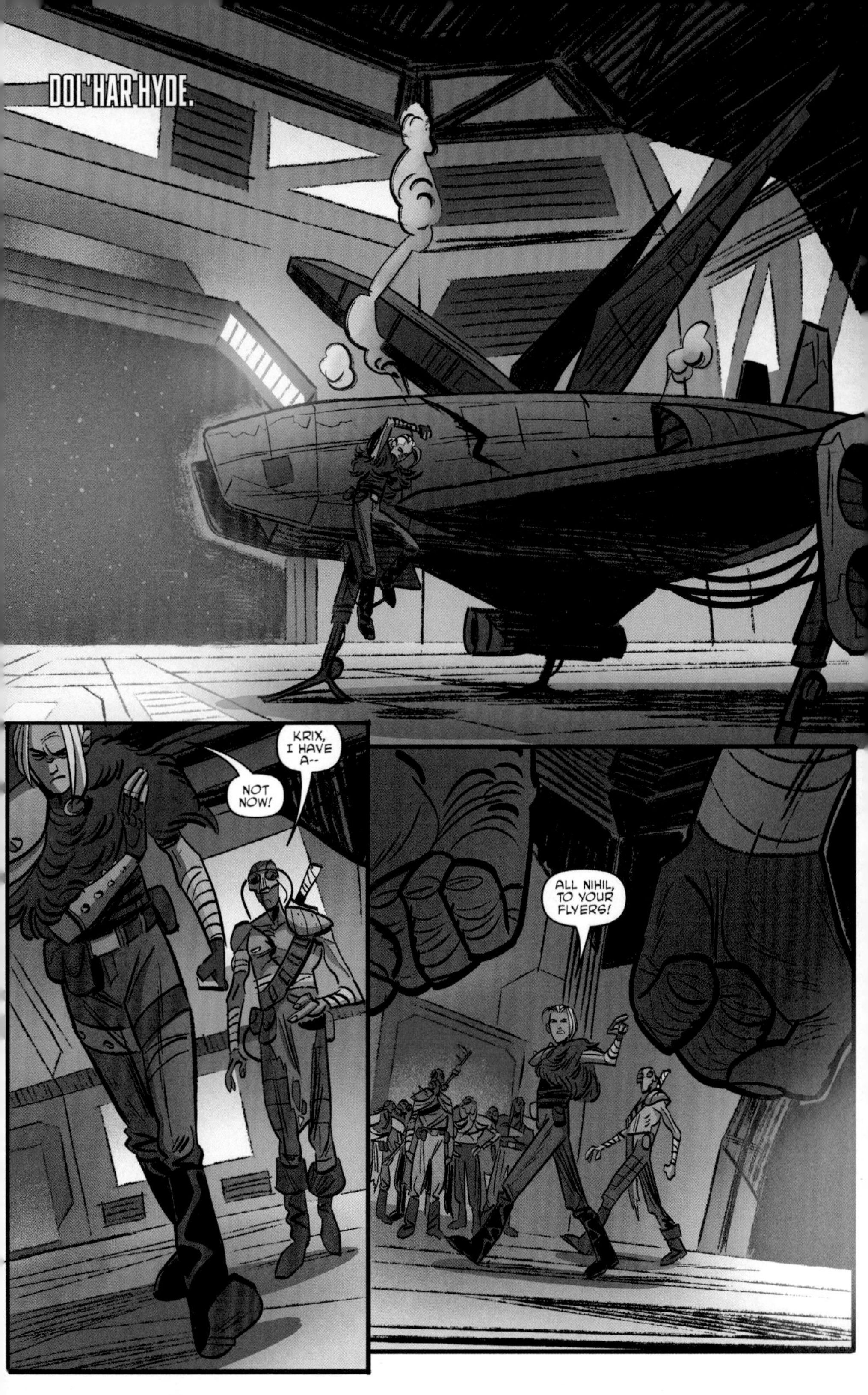
DOL'HAR HYDE.
KRIX, I HAVE A--
NOT NOW!
ALL NIHIL, TO YOUR FLYERS!

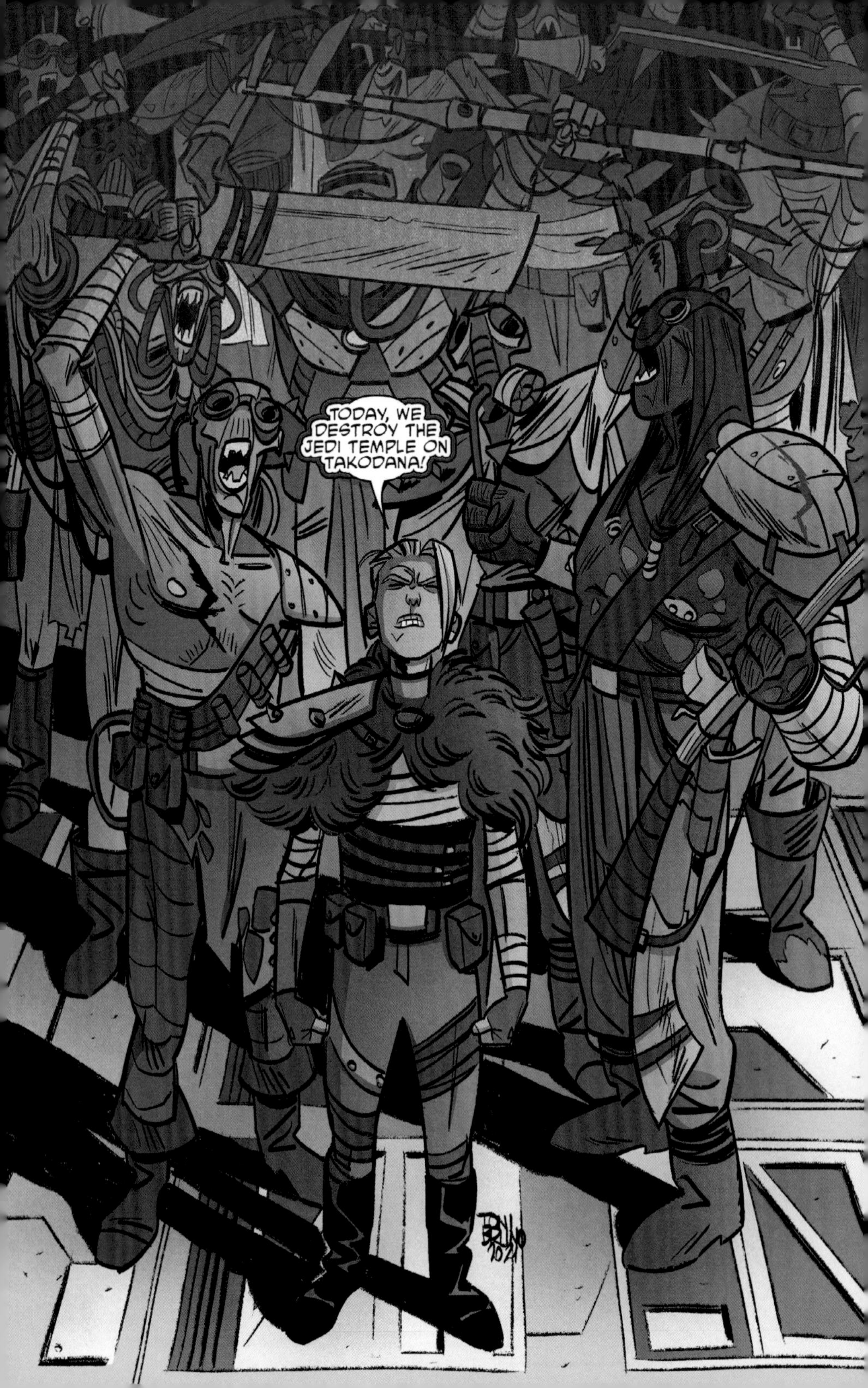
TODAY, WE DESTROY THE JEDI TEMPLE ON TAKODANA!

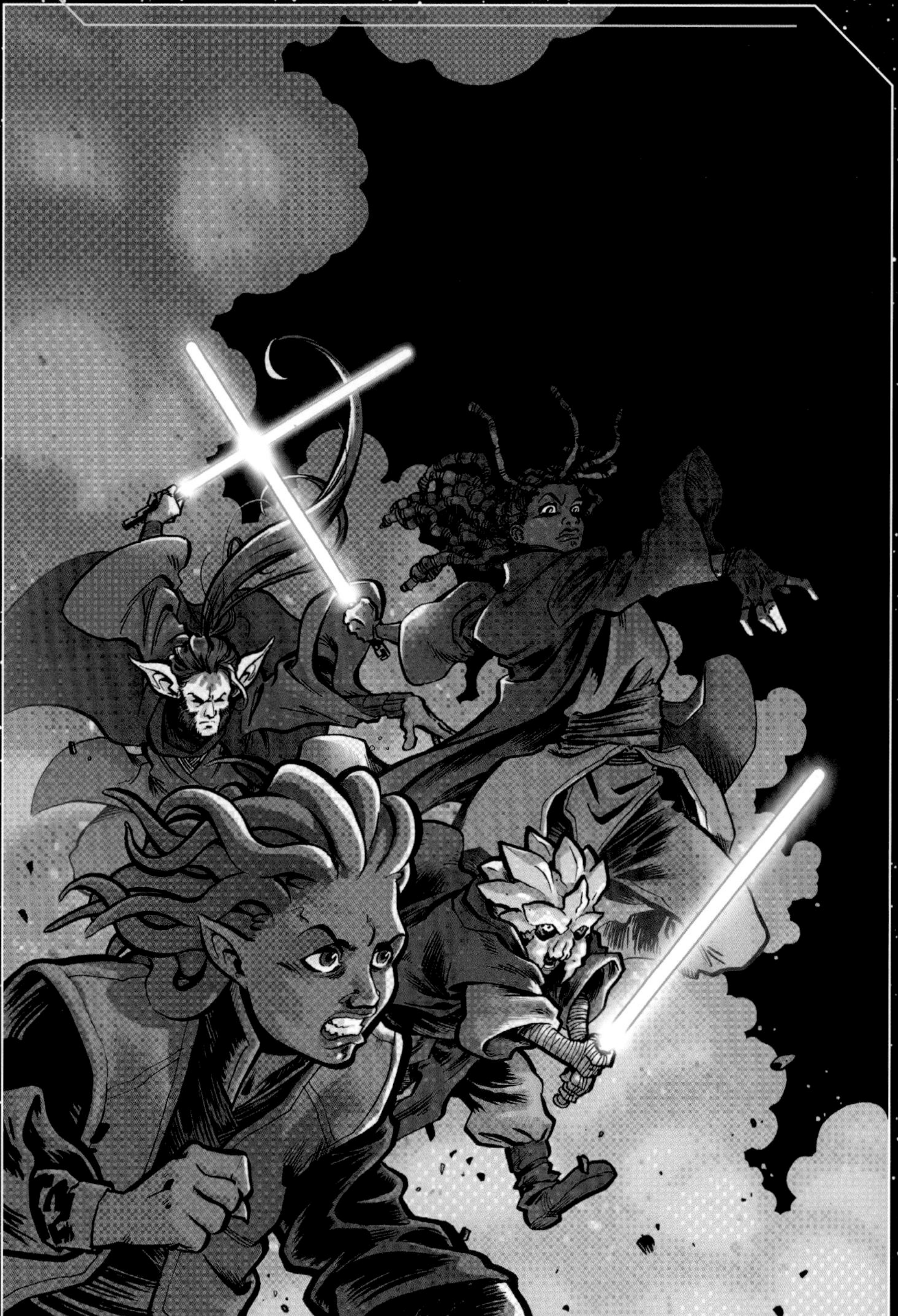

ART BY **ILIAS KYRIAZIS**

HIGH REPUBLIC ADVENTURES ANNUAL 2021

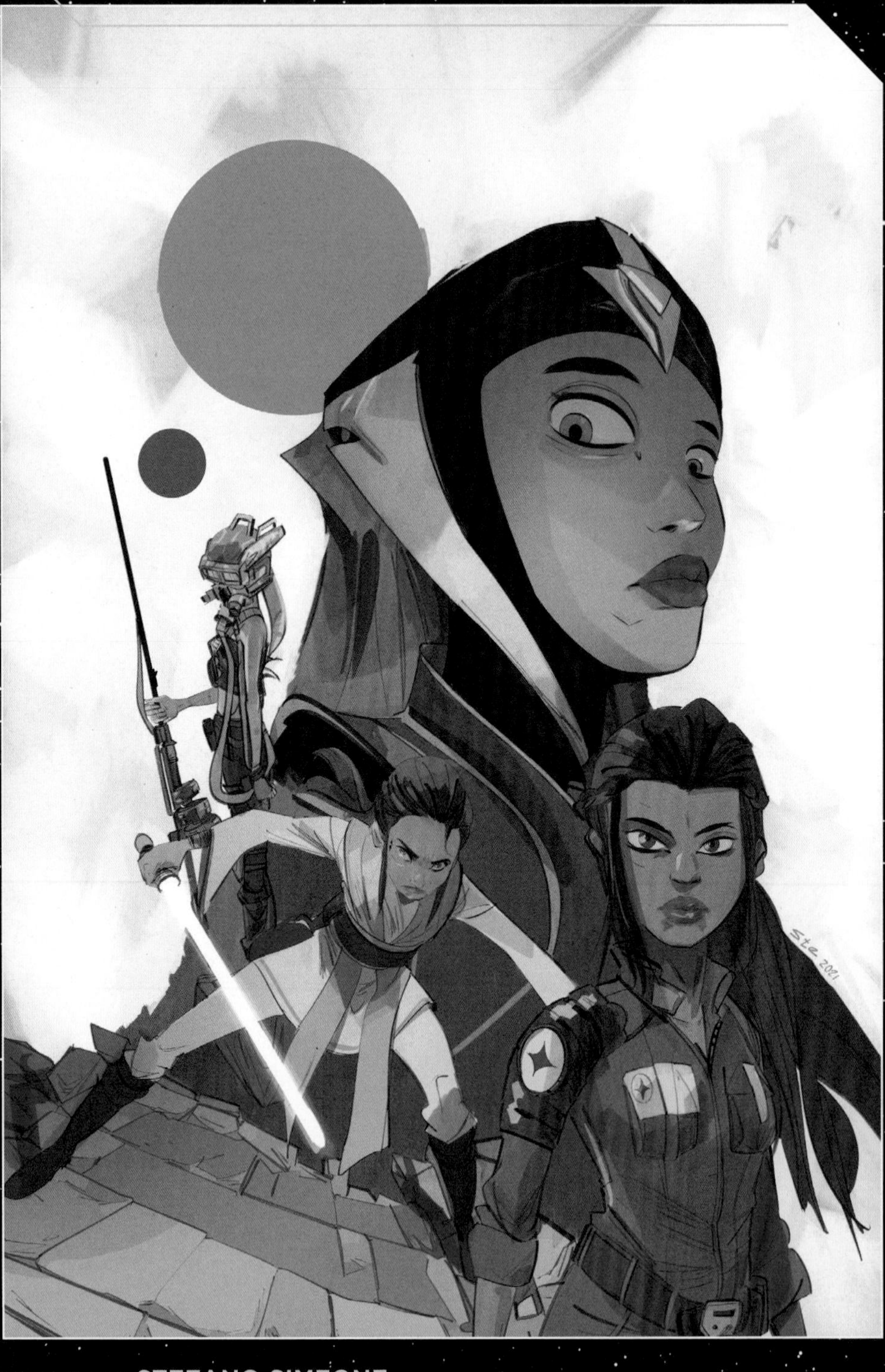
Ste 2021

ART BY STEFANO SIMEONE

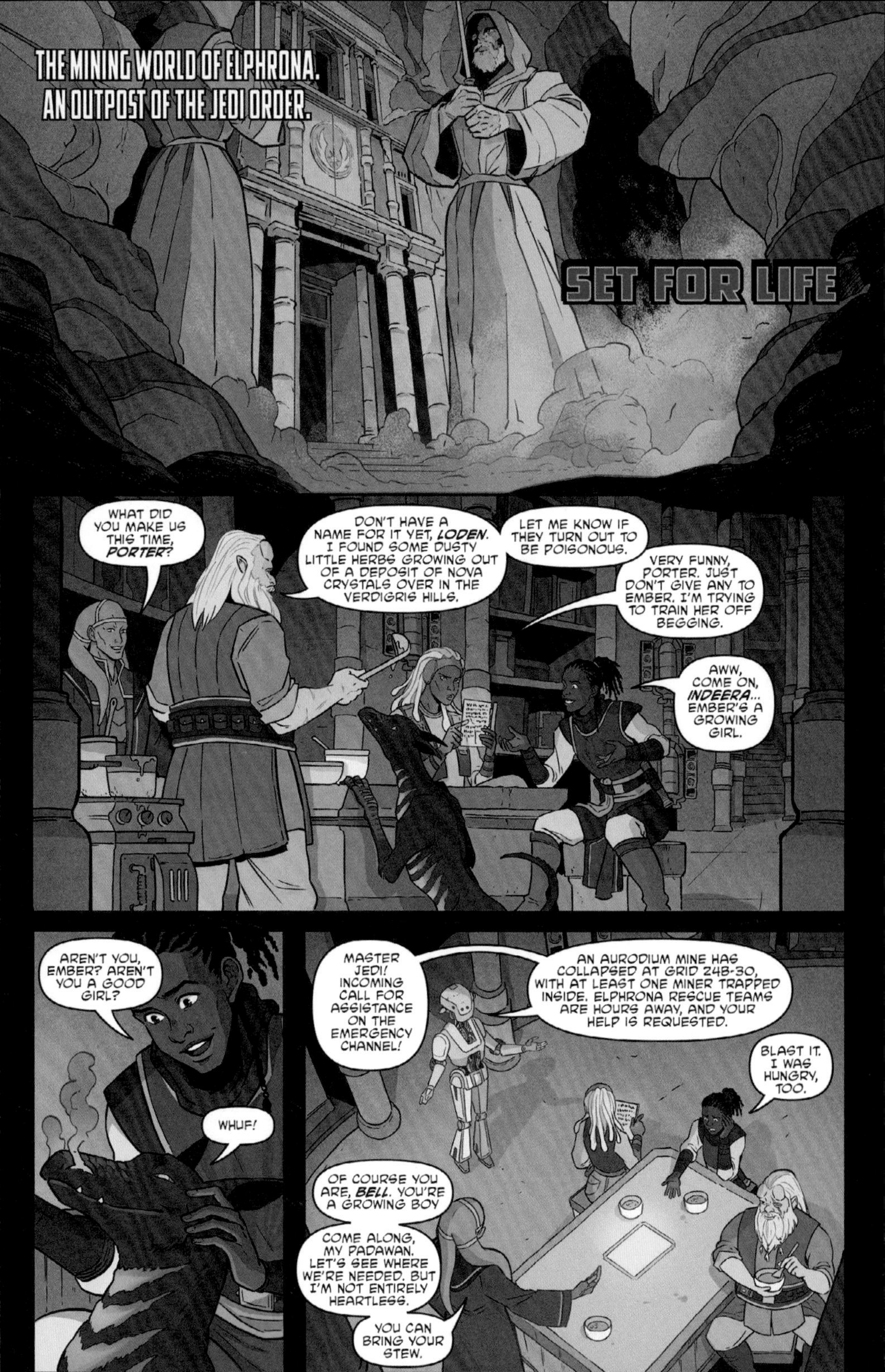
THE MINING WORLD OF ELPHRONA. AN OUTPOST OF THE JEDI ORDER.
SET FOR LIFE
WHAT DID YOU MAKE US THIS TIME, PORTER?
DON'T HAVE A NAME FOR IT YET, LODEN. I FOUND SOME DUSTY LITTLE HERBS GROWING OUT OF A DEPOSIT OF NOVA CRYSTALS OVER IN THE VERDIGRIS HILLS.
LET ME KNOW IF THEY TURN OUT TO BE POISONOUS.
VERY FUNNY, PORTER. JUST DON'T GIVE ANY TO EMBER. I'M TRYING TO TRAIN HER OFF BEGGING.
AWW, COME ON, INDEERA... EMBER'S A GROWING GIRL.
AREN'T YOU, EMBER? AREN'T YOU A GOOD GIRL?
WHUF!
MASTER JEDI! INCOMING CALL FOR ASSISTANCE ON THE EMERGENCY CHANNEL!
AN AURODIUM MINE HAS COLLAPSED AT GRID 24B-30, WITH AT LEAST ONE MINER TRAPPED INSIDE. ELPHRONA RESCUE TEAMS ARE HOURS AWAY, AND YOUR HELP IS REQUESTED.
BLAST IT. I WAS HUNGRY, TOO.
OF COURSE YOU ARE, BELL. YOU'RE A GROWING BOY
COME ALONG, MY PADAWAN. LET'S SEE WHERE WE'RE NEEDED. BUT I'M NOT ENTIRELY HEARTLESS.
YOU CAN BRING YOUR STEW.

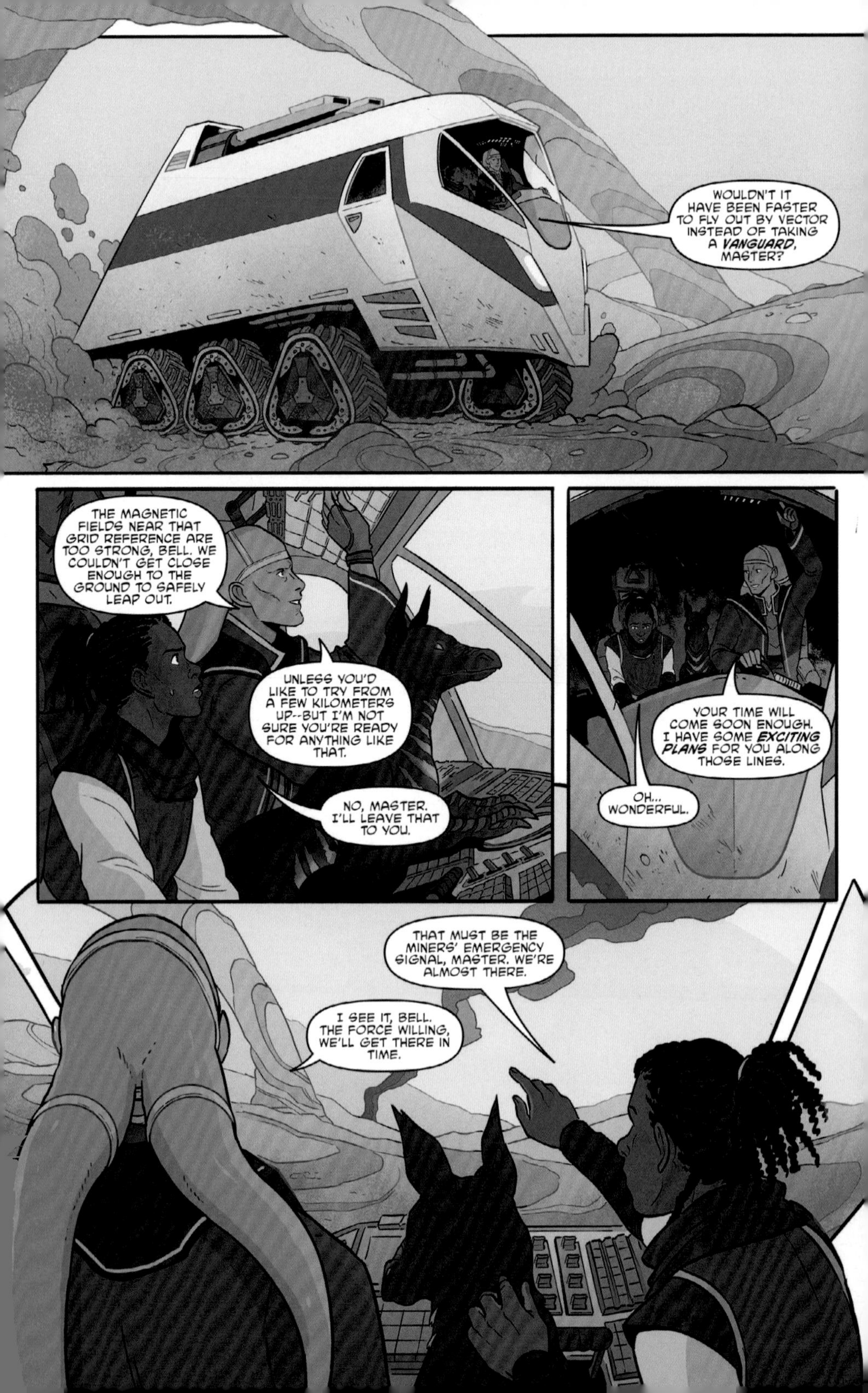
WOULDN'T IT HAVE BEEN FASTER TO FLY OUT BY VECTOR INSTEAD OF TAKING A *VANGUARD,* MASTER?
THE MAGNETIC FIELDS NEAR THAT GRID REFERENCE ARE TOO STRONG, BELL. WE COULDN'T GET CLOSE ENOUGH TO THE GROUND TO SAFELY LEAP OUT.
UNLESS YOU'D LIKE TO TRY FROM A FEW KILOMETERS UP--BUT I'M NOT SURE YOU'RE READY FOR ANYTHING LIKE THAT.
NO, MASTER. I'LL LEAVE THAT TO YOU.
YOUR TIME WILL COME SOON ENOUGH. I HAVE SOME *EXCITING PLANS* FOR YOU ALONG THOSE LINES.
OH... WONDERFUL.
THAT MUST BE THE MINERS' EMERGENCY SIGNAL, MASTER. WE'RE ALMOST THERE.
I SEE IT, BELL. THE FORCE WILLING, WE'LL GET THERE IN TIME.

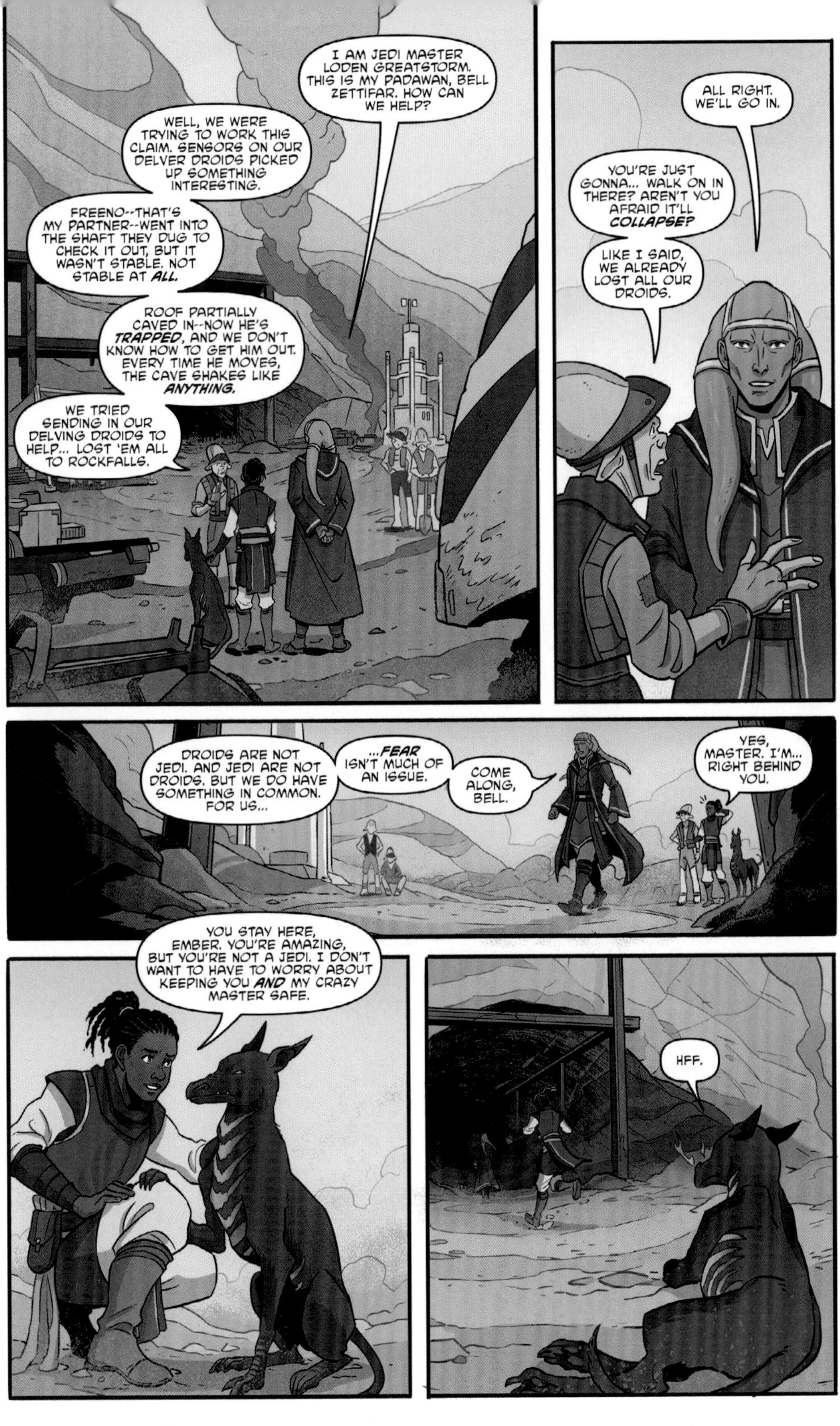
I AM JEDI MASTER LODEN GREATSTORM. THIS IS MY PADAWAN, BELL ZETTIFAR. HOW CAN WE HELP?
WELL, WE WERE TRYING TO WORK THIS CLAIM. SENSORS ON OUR DELVER DROIDS PICKED UP SOMETHING INTERESTING.
FREENO--THAT'S MY PARTNER--WENT INTO THE SHAFT THEY DUG TO CHECK IT OUT, BUT IT WASN'T STABLE. NOT STABLE AT ALL.
ROOF PARTIALLY CAVED IN--NOW HE'S TRAPPED, AND WE DON'T KNOW HOW TO GET HIM OUT. EVERY TIME HE MOVES, THE CAVE SHAKES LIKE ANYTHING.
WE TRIED SENDING IN OUR DELVING DROIDS TO HELP... LOST 'EM ALL TO ROCKFALLS.
ALL RIGHT. WE'LL GO IN.
YOU'RE JUST GONNA... WALK ON IN THERE? AREN'T YOU AFRAID IT'LL COLLAPSE?
LIKE I SAID, WE ALREADY LOST ALL OUR DROIDS.
DROIDS ARE NOT JEDI. AND JEDI ARE NOT DROIDS. BUT WE DO HAVE SOMETHING IN COMMON. FOR US...
...FEAR ISN'T MUCH OF AN ISSUE.
COME ALONG, BELL.
YES, MASTER. I'M... RIGHT BEHIND YOU.
YOU STAY HERE, EMBER. YOU'RE AMAZING, BUT YOU'RE NOT A JEDI. I DON'T WANT TO HAVE TO WORRY ABOUT KEEPING YOU AND MY CRAZY MASTER SAFE.
HFF.

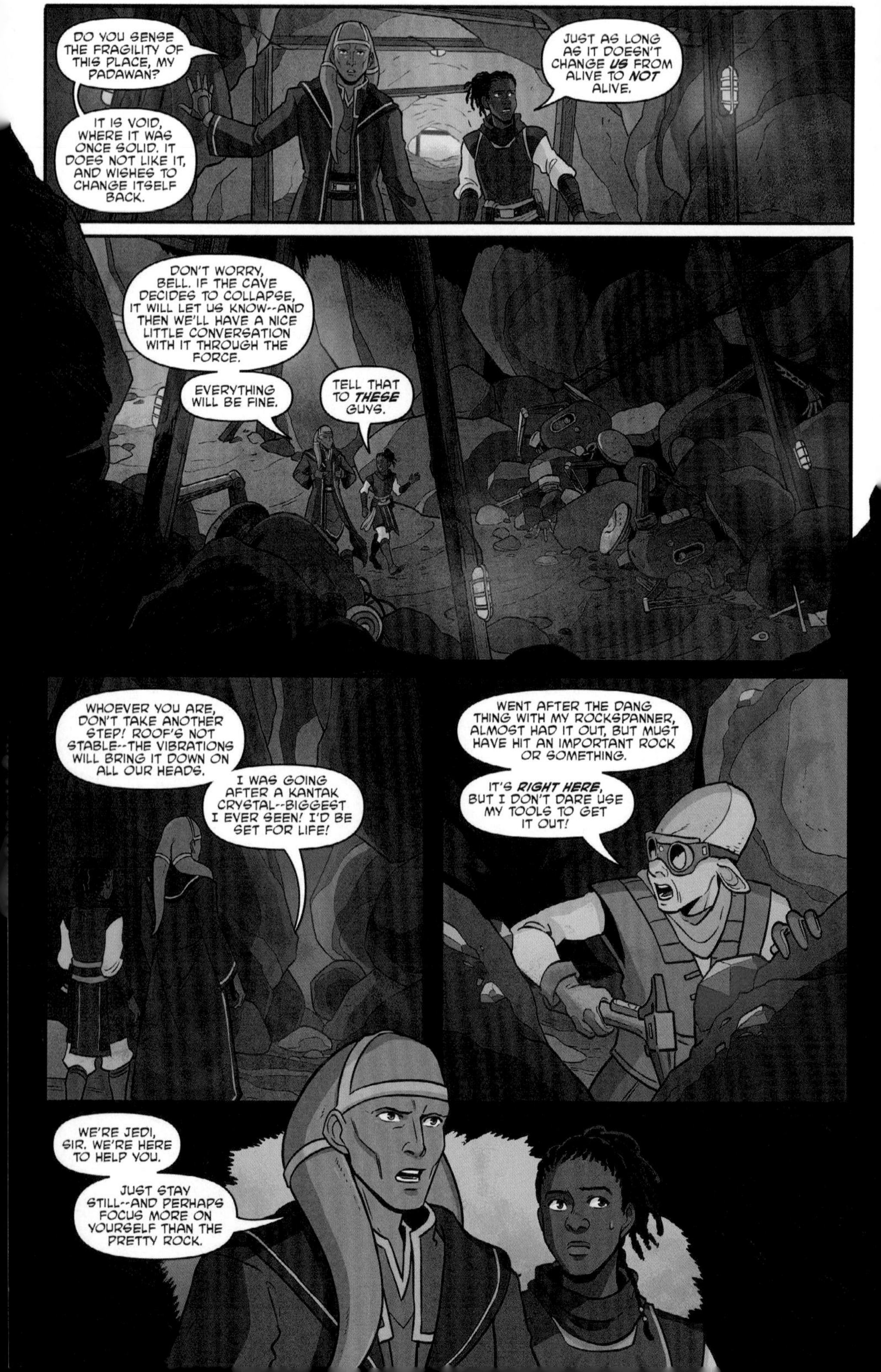

DO YOU SENSE THE FRAGILITY OF THIS PLACE, MY PADAWAN?
IT IS VOID, WHERE IT WAS ONCE SOLID. IT DOES NOT LIKE IT, AND WISHES TO CHANGE ITSELF BACK.
JUST AS LONG AS IT DOESN'T CHANGE *US* FROM ALIVE TO *NOT* ALIVE.
DON'T WORRY, BELL. IF THE CAVE DECIDES TO COLLAPSE, IT WILL LET US KNOW--AND THEN WE'LL HAVE A NICE LITTLE CONVERSATION WITH IT THROUGH THE FORCE.
EVERYTHING WILL BE FINE.
TELL THAT TO *THESE* GUYS.
WHOEVER YOU ARE, DON'T TAKE ANOTHER STEP! ROOF'S NOT STABLE--THE VIBRATIONS WILL BRING IT DOWN ON ALL OUR HEADS.
I WAS GOING AFTER A KANTAK CRYSTAL--BIGGEST I EVER SEEN! I'D BE SET FOR LIFE!
WENT AFTER THE DANG THING WITH MY ROCKSPANNER, ALMOST HAD IT OUT, BUT MUST HAVE HIT AN IMPORTANT ROCK OR SOMETHING.
IT'S *RIGHT HERE*, BUT I DON'T DARE USE MY TOOLS TO GET IT OUT!
WE'RE JEDI, SIR. WE'RE HERE TO HELP YOU.
JUST STAY STILL--AND PERHAPS FOCUS MORE ON YOURSELF THAN THE PRETTY ROCK.

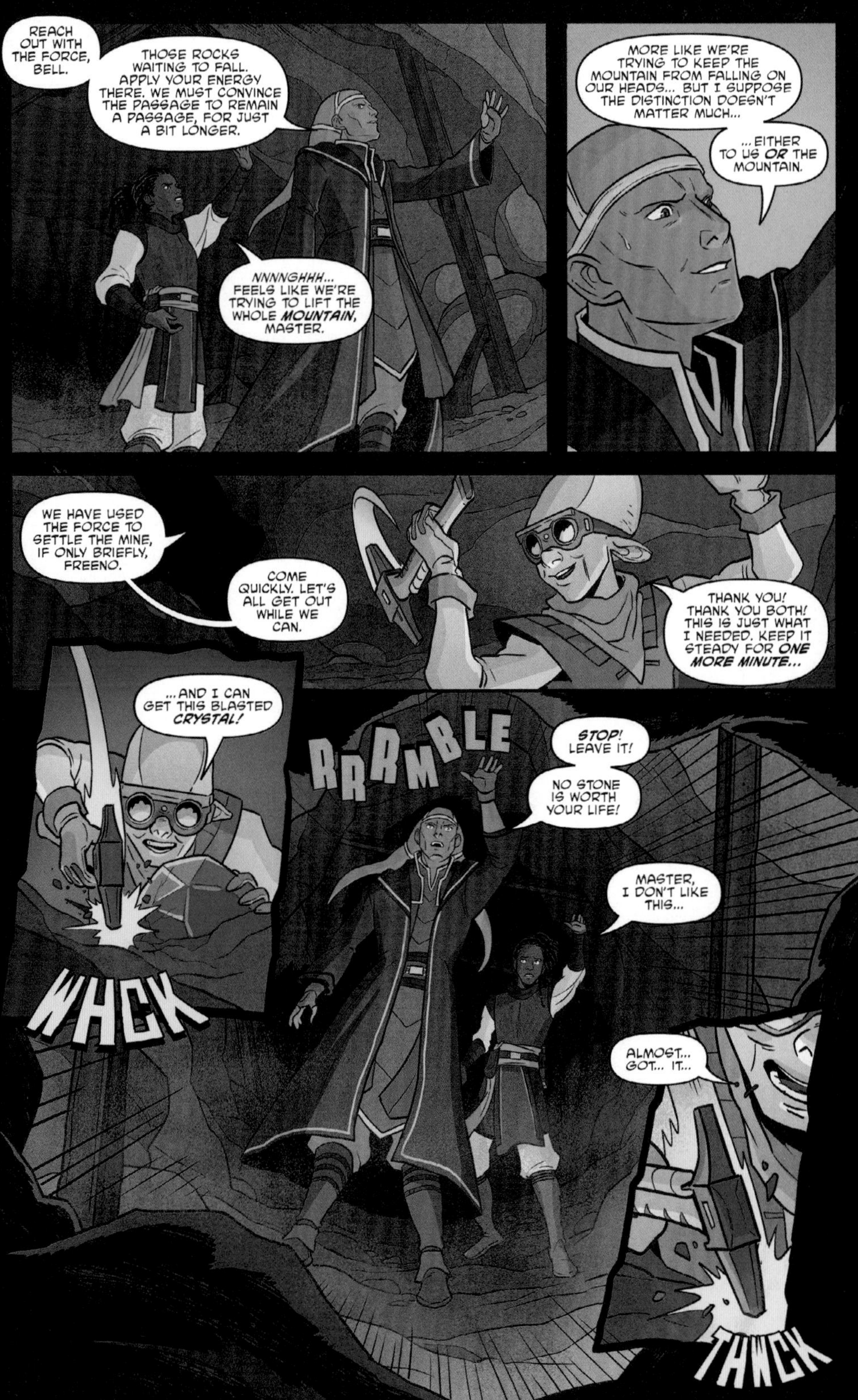
REACH OUT WITH THE FORCE, BELL.
THOSE ROCKS WAITING TO FALL. APPLY YOUR ENERGY THERE. WE MUST CONVINCE THE PASSAGE TO REMAIN A PASSAGE, FOR JUST A BIT LONGER.
NNNNGHHH... FEELS LIKE WE'RE TRYING TO LIFT THE WHOLE MOUNTAIN, MASTER.
MORE LIKE WE'RE TRYING TO KEEP THE MOUNTAIN FROM FALLING ON OUR HEADS... BUT I SUPPOSE THE DISTINCTION DOESN'T MATTER MUCH...
...EITHER TO US OR THE MOUNTAIN.
WE HAVE USED THE FORCE TO SETTLE THE MINE, IF ONLY BRIEFLY, FREENO.
COME QUICKLY. LET'S ALL GET OUT WHILE WE CAN.
THANK YOU! THANK YOU BOTH! THIS IS JUST WHAT I NEEDED. KEEP IT STEADY FOR ONE MORE MINUTE...
...AND I CAN GET THIS BLASTED CRYSTAL!
WHCK
RRRMBLE
STOP! LEAVE IT!
NO STONE IS WORTH YOUR LIFE!
MASTER, I DON'T LIKE THIS...
ALMOST... GOT... IT...
THWCK

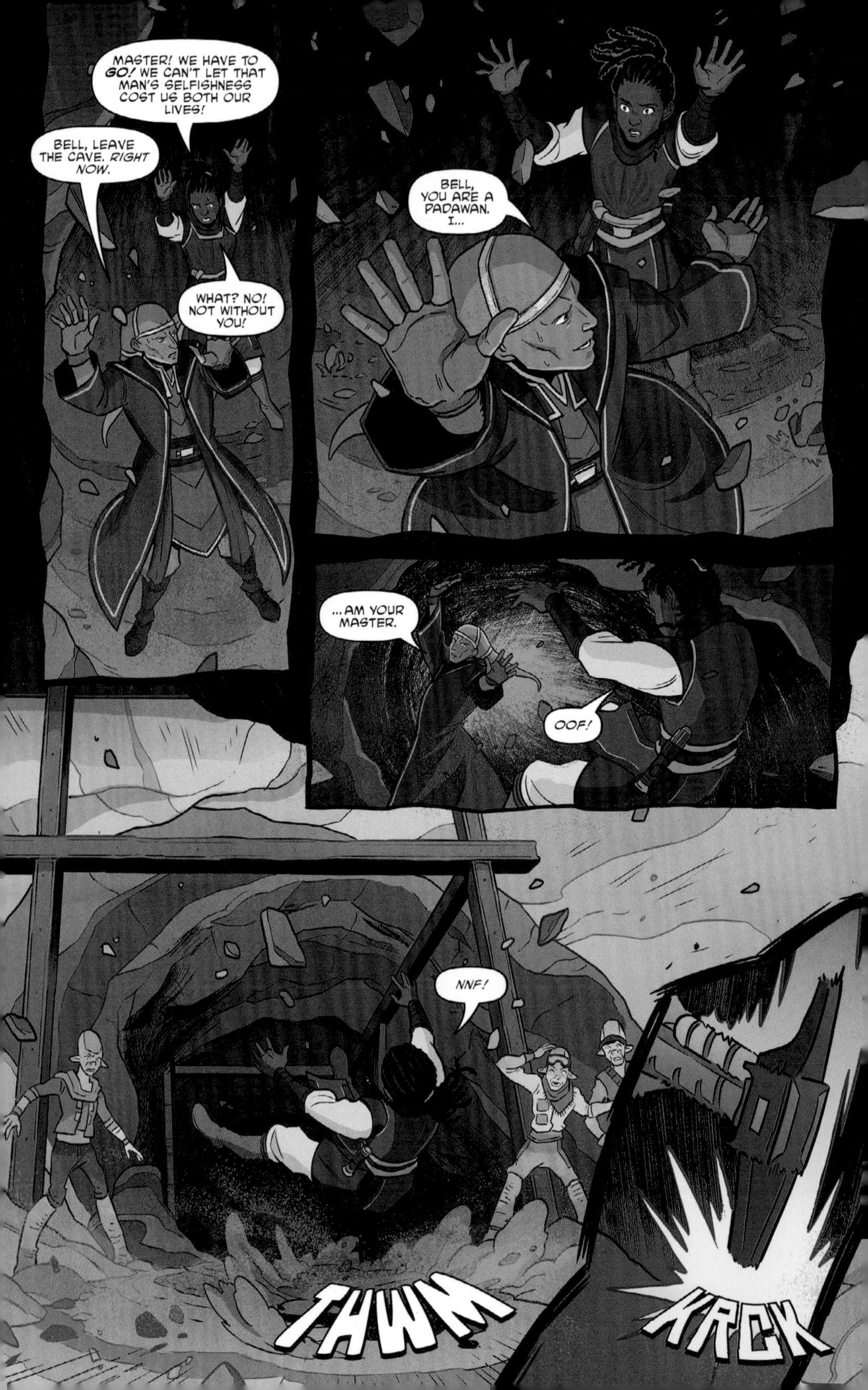
MASTER! WE HAVE TO GO! WE CAN'T LET THAT MAN'S SELFISHNESS COST US BOTH OUR LIVES!
BELL, LEAVE THE CAVE. RIGHT NOW.
WHAT? NO! NOT WITHOUT YOU!
BELL, YOU ARE A PADAWAN. I...
...AM YOUR MASTER.
OOF!
NNF!
THWM
KRCK

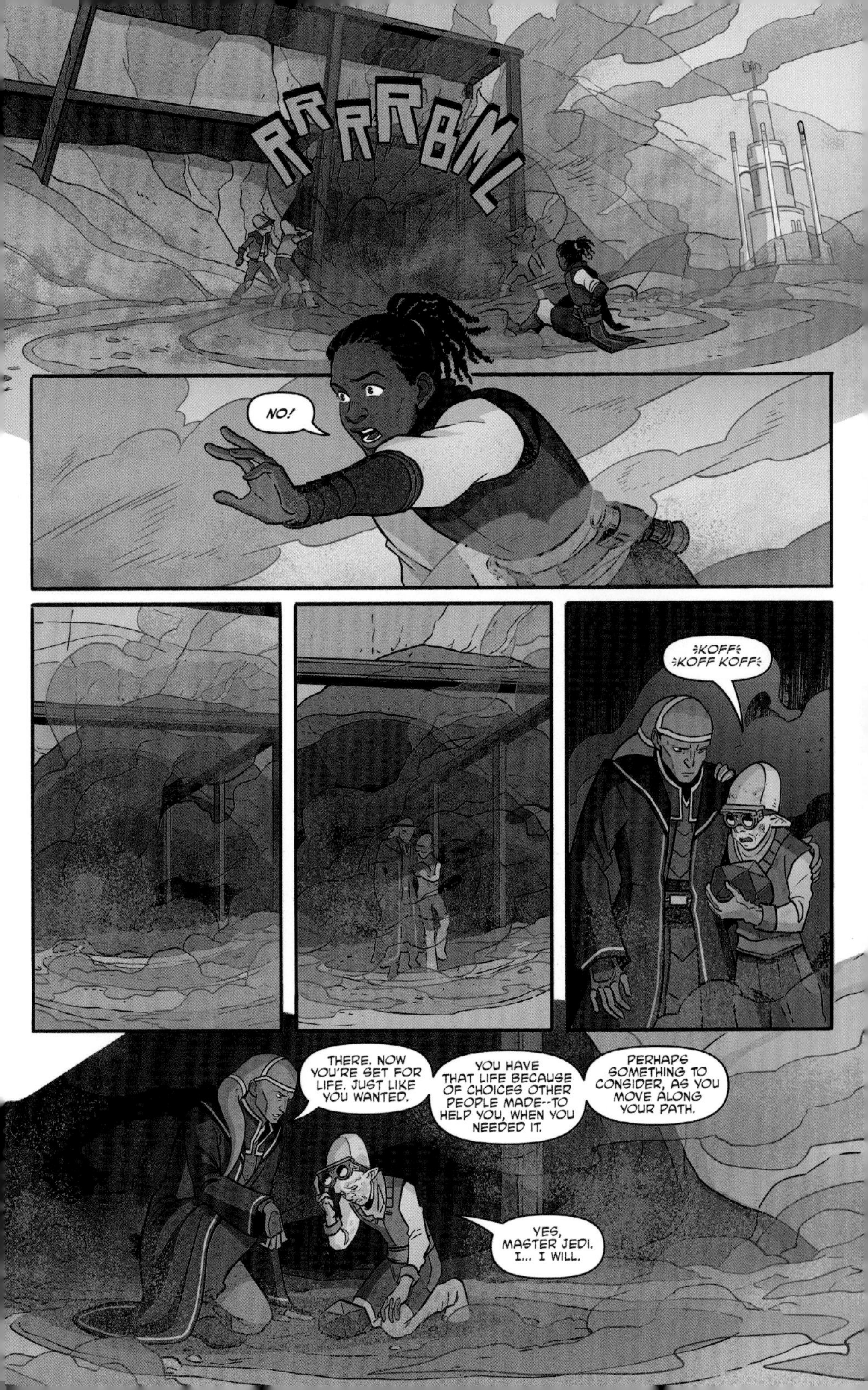
RRRRBML
NO!
KOFF KOFF KOFF
THERE. NOW YOU'RE SET FOR LIFE. JUST LIKE YOU WANTED.
YOU HAVE THAT LIFE BECAUSE OF CHOICES OTHER PEOPLE MADE--TO HELP YOU, WHEN YOU NEEDED IT.
PERHAPS SOMETHING TO CONSIDER, AS YOU MOVE ALONG YOUR PATH.
YES, MASTER JEDI. I... I WILL.

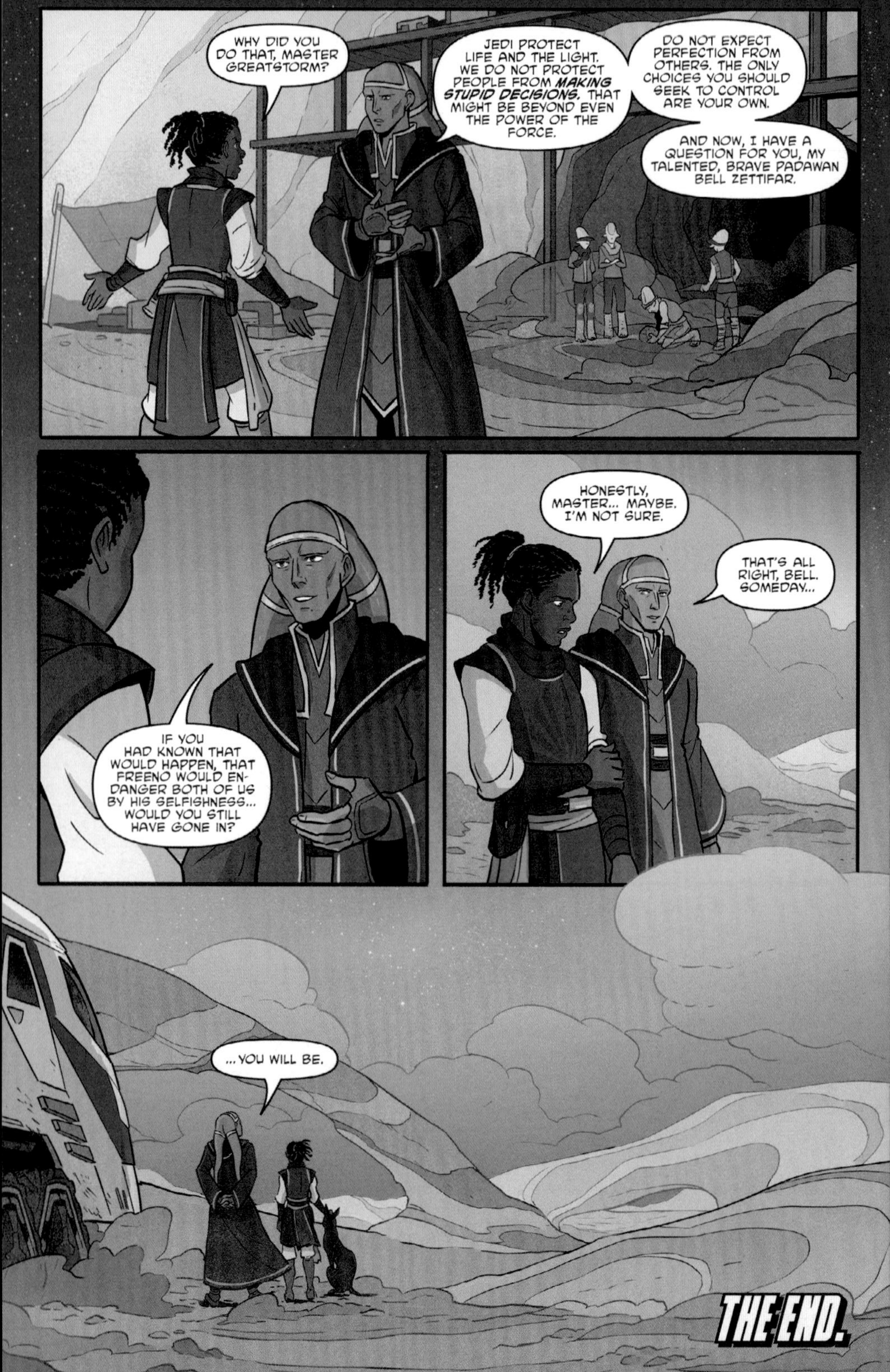
WHY DID YOU DO THAT, MASTER GREATSTORM?
JEDI PROTECT LIFE AND THE LIGHT. WE DO NOT PROTECT PEOPLE FROM MAKING STUPID DECISIONS. THAT MIGHT BE BEYOND EVEN THE POWER OF THE FORCE.
DO NOT EXPECT PERFECTION FROM OTHERS. THE ONLY CHOICES YOU SHOULD SEEK TO CONTROL ARE YOUR OWN.
AND NOW, I HAVE A QUESTION FOR YOU, MY TALENTED, BRAVE PADAWAN BELL ZETTIFAR.
IF YOU HAD KNOWN THAT WOULD HAPPEN, THAT FREENO WOULD ENDANGER BOTH OF US BY HIS SELFISHNESS... WOULD YOU STILL HAVE GONE IN?
HONESTLY, MASTER... MAYBE. I'M NOT SURE.
THAT'S ALL RIGHT, BELL. SOMEDAY...
...YOU WILL BE.
THE END.

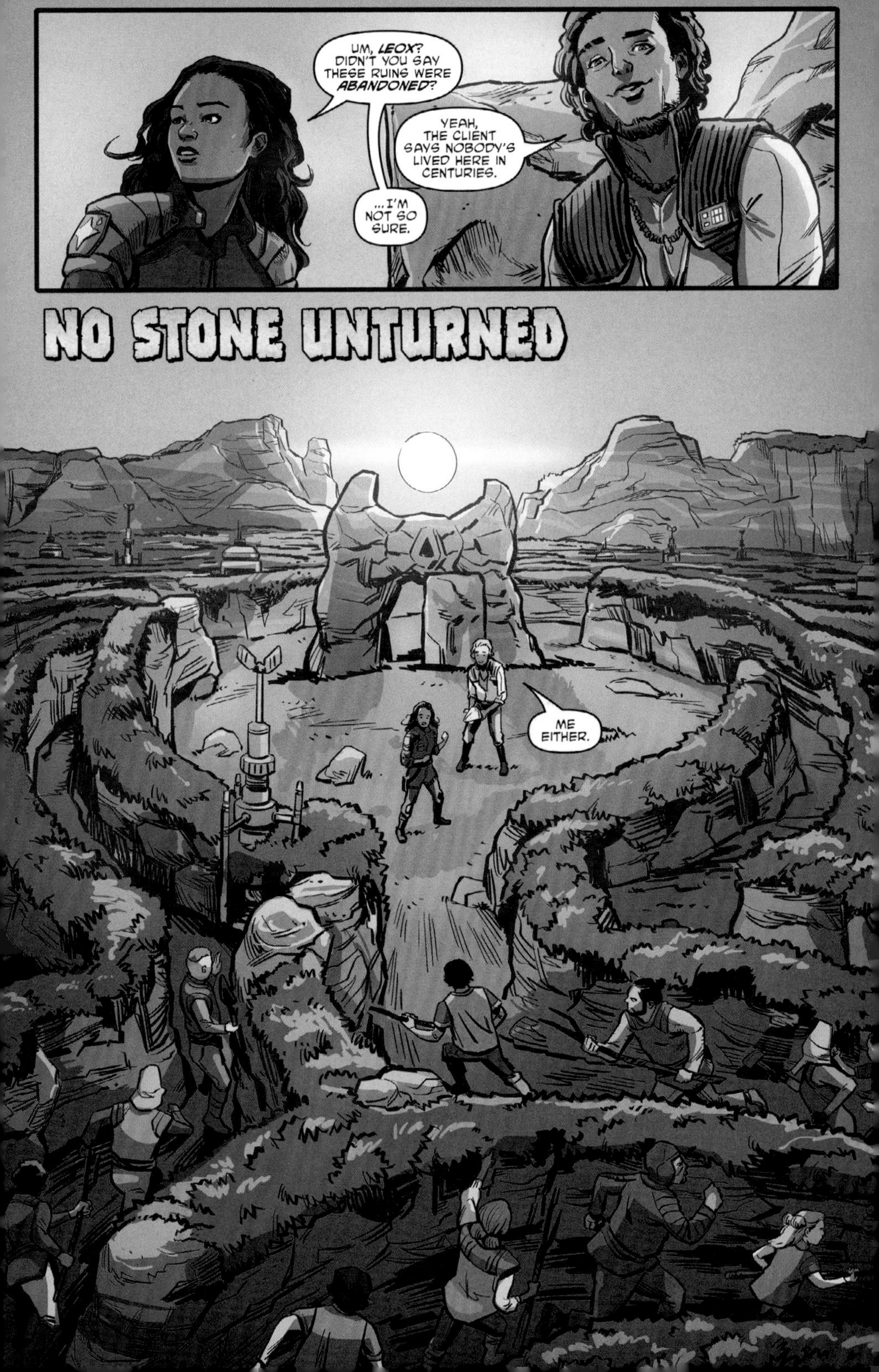
UM, *LEOX*? DIDN'T YOU SAY THESE RUINS WERE *ABANDONED*?
YEAH, THE CLIENT SAYS NOBODY'S LIVED HERE IN CENTURIES.
...I'M NOT SO SURE.
NO STONE UNTURNED
ME EITHER.

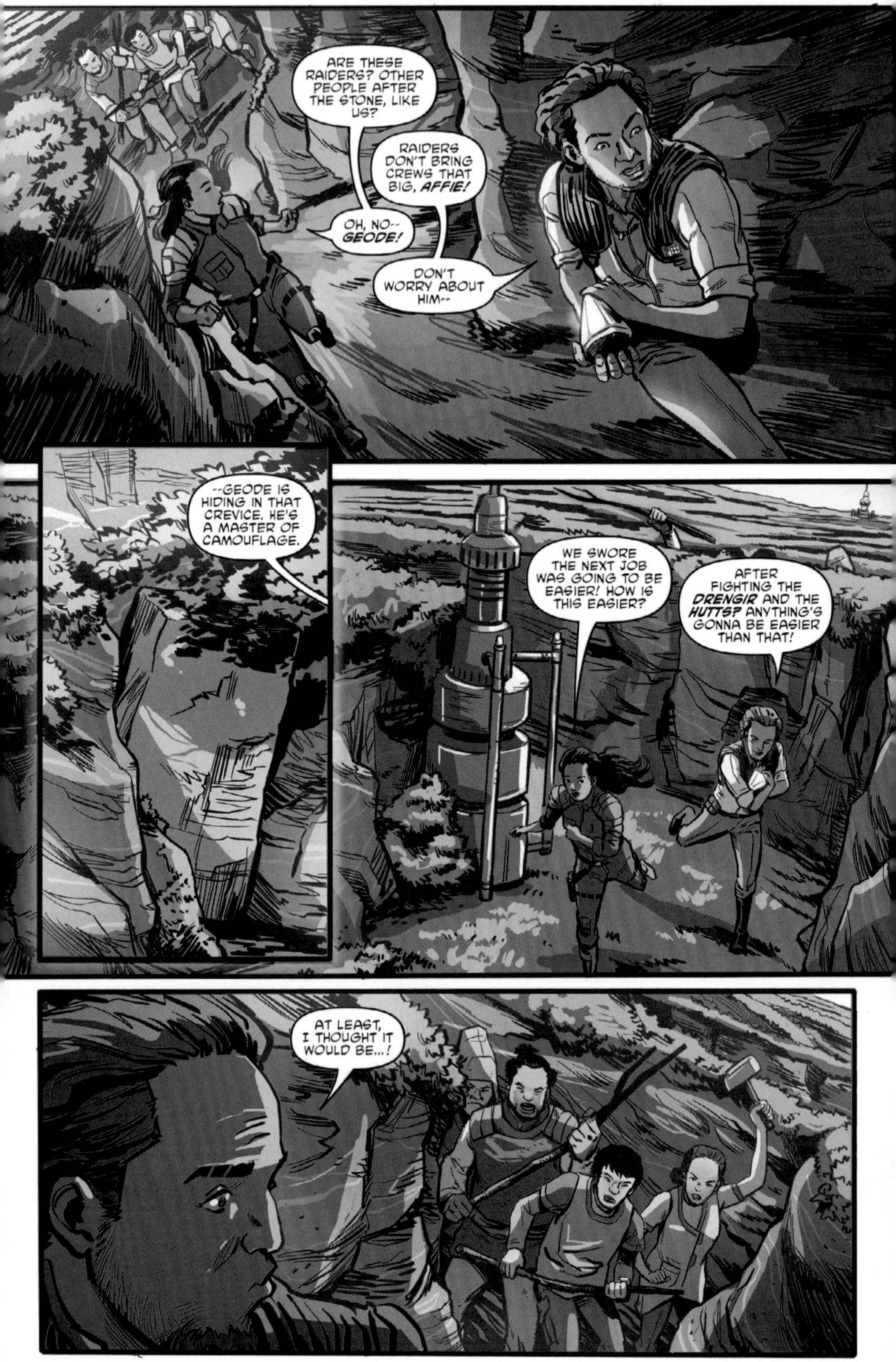
ARE THESE RAIDERS? OTHER PEOPLE AFTER THE STONE, LIKE US?
RAIDERS DON'T BRING CREWS THAT BIG, AFFIE!
OH, NO-- GEODE!
DON'T WORRY ABOUT HIM--
--GEODE IS HIDING IN THAT CREVICE. HE'S A MASTER OF CAMOUFLAGE.
WE SWORE THE NEXT JOB WAS GOING TO BE EASIER! HOW IS THIS EASIER?
AFTER FIGHTING THE DRENGIR AND THE HUTTS? ANYTHING'S GONNA BE EASIER THAN THAT!
AT LEAST, I THOUGHT IT WOULD BE...!

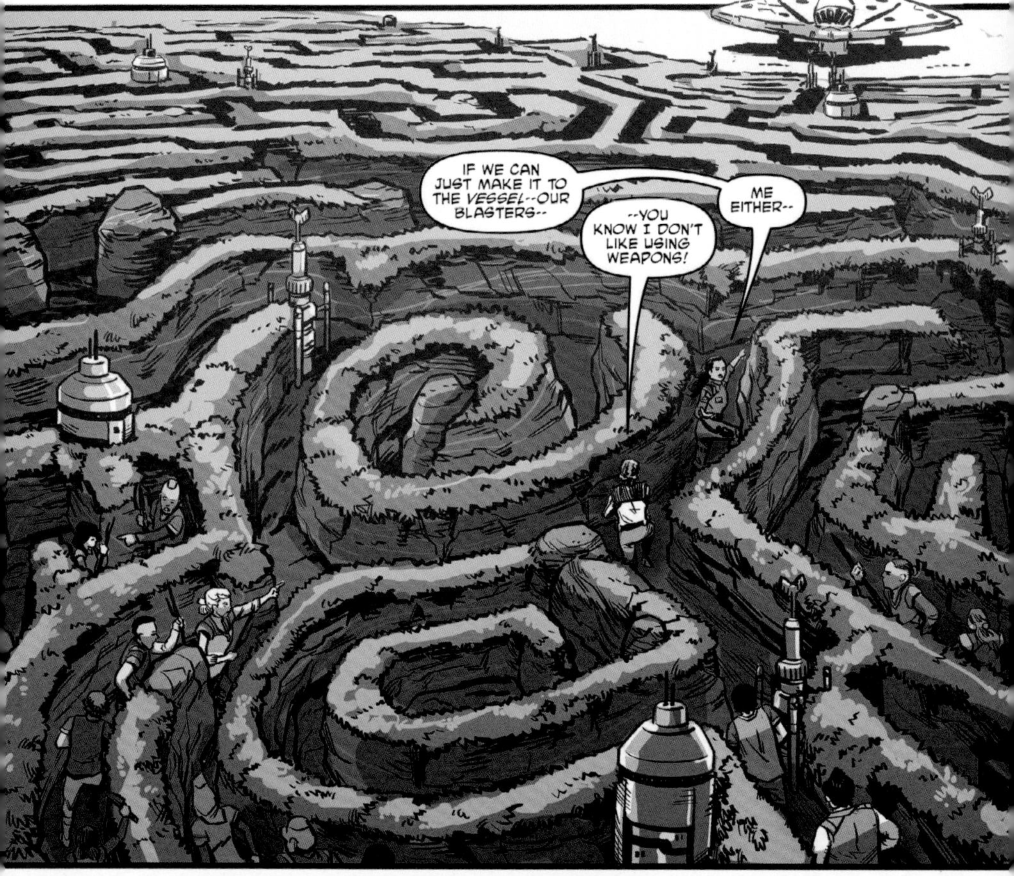
IF WE CAN JUST MAKE IT TO THE VESSEL--OUR BLASTERS--
--YOU KNOW I DON'T LIKE USING WEAPONS!
ME EITHER--

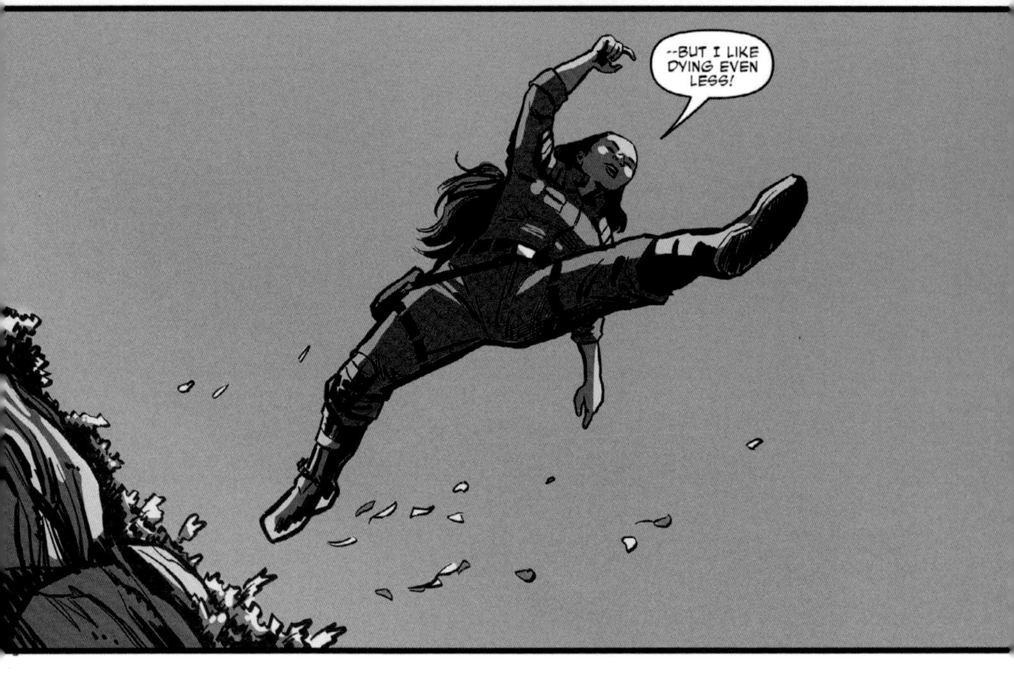
--BUT I LIKE DYING EVEN LESS!

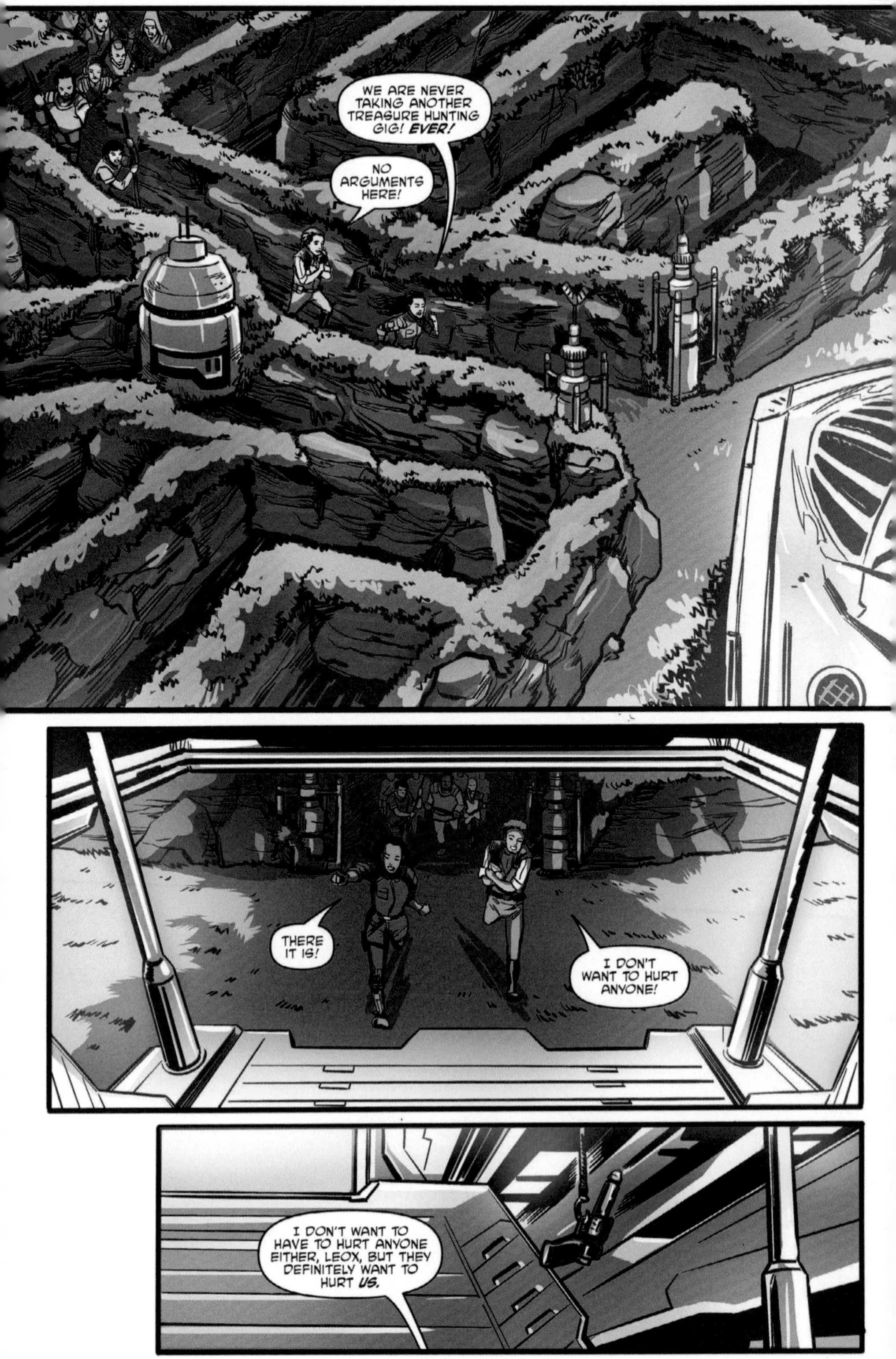
WE ARE NEVER TAKING ANOTHER TREASURE HUNTING GIG! EVER!
NO ARGUMENTS HERE!
THERE IT IS!
I DON'T WANT TO HURT ANYONE!
I DON'T WANT TO HAVE TO HURT ANYONE EITHER, LEOX, BUT THEY DEFINITELY WANT TO HURT US.

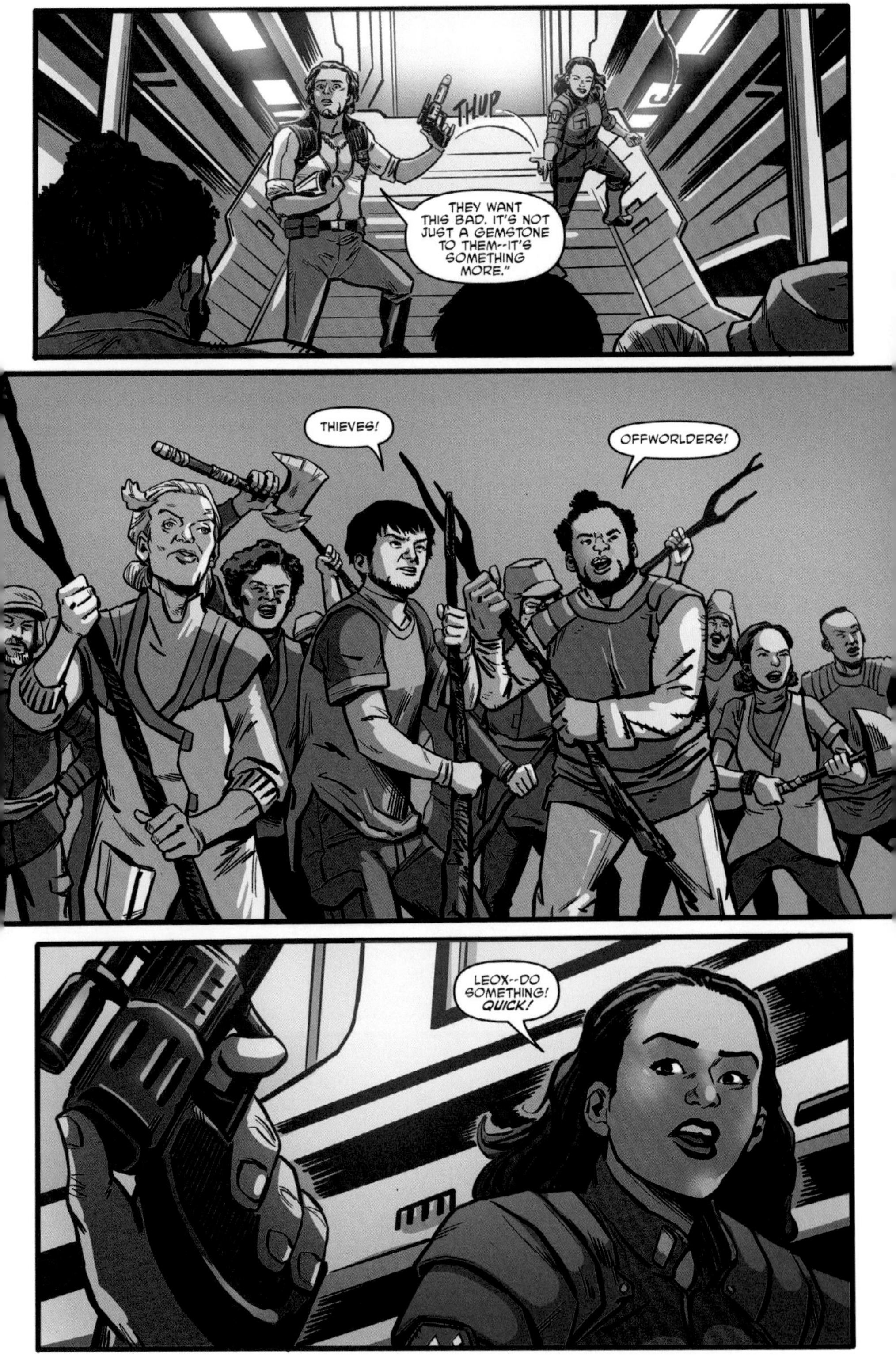
THUP
THEY WANT THIS BAD. IT'S NOT JUST A GEMSTONE TO THEM--IT'S SOMETHING MORE."
THIEVES!
OFFWORLDERS!
LEOX--DO SOMETHING! QUICK!

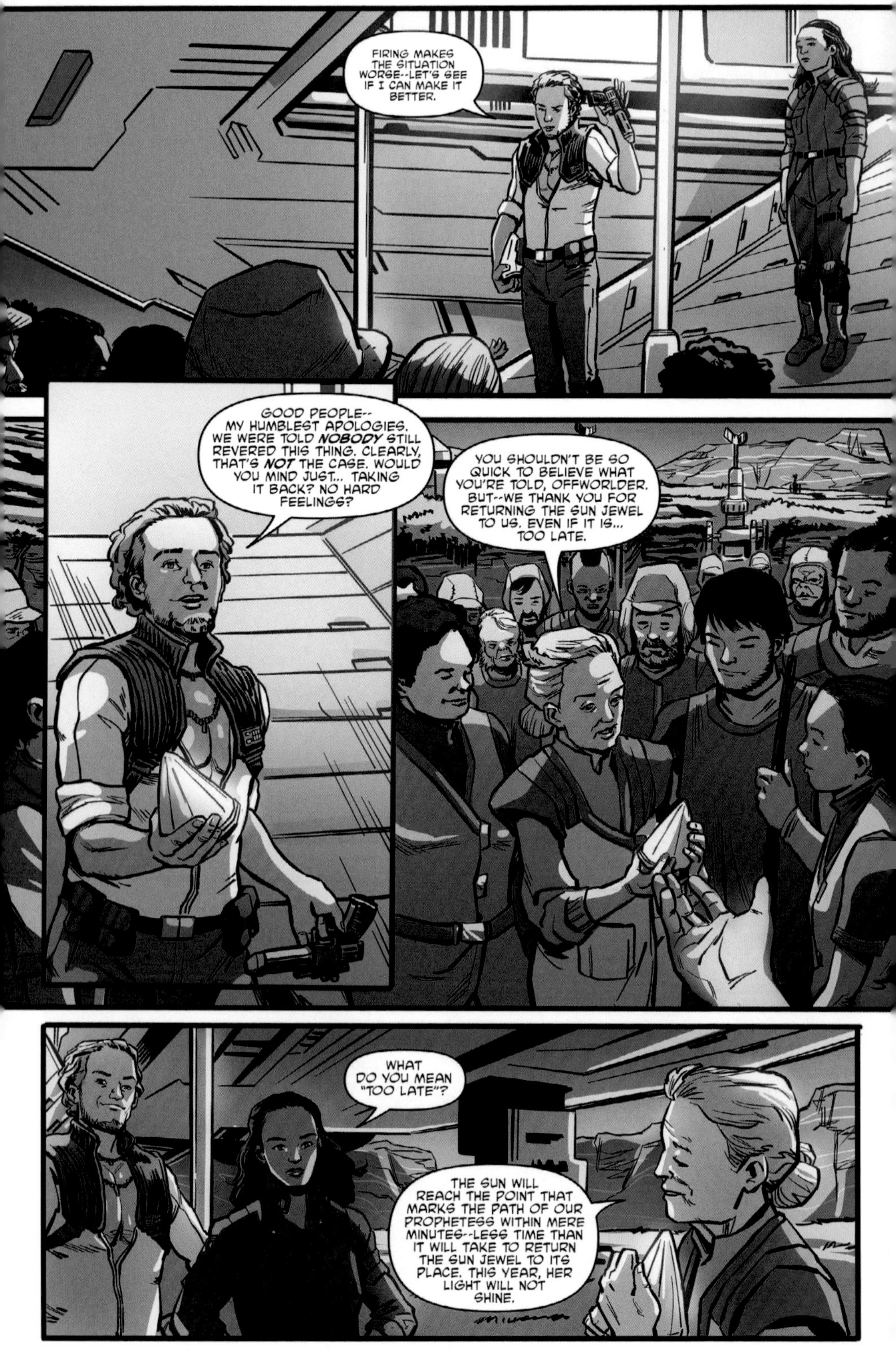
FIRING MAKES THE SITUATION WORSE--LET'S SEE IF I CAN MAKE IT BETTER.
GOOD PEOPLE-- MY HUMBLEST APOLOGIES. WE WERE TOLD NOBODY STILL REVERED THIS THING. CLEARLY, THAT'S NOT THE CASE. WOULD YOU MIND JUST... TAKING IT BACK? NO HARD FEELINGS?
YOU SHOULDN'T BE SO QUICK TO BELIEVE WHAT YOU'RE TOLD, OFFWORLDER. BUT--WE THANK YOU FOR RETURNING THE SUN JEWEL TO US. EVEN IF IT IS... TOO LATE.
WHAT DO YOU MEAN "TOO LATE"?
THE SUN WILL REACH THE POINT THAT MARKS THE PATH OF OUR PROPHETESS WITHIN MERE MINUTES--LESS TIME THAN IT WILL TAKE TO RETURN THE SUN JEWEL TO ITS PLACE. THIS YEAR, HER LIGHT WILL NOT SHINE.

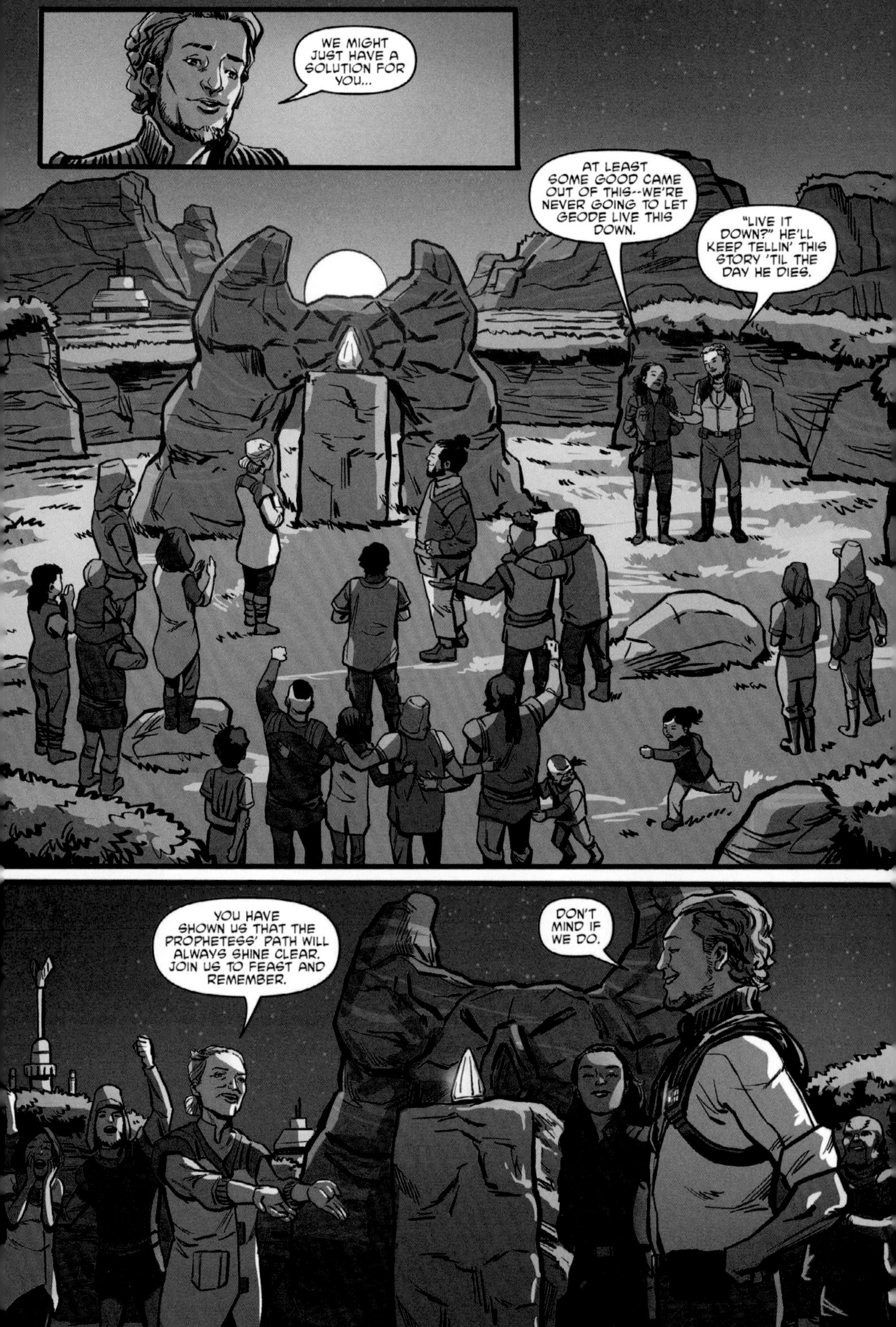
WE MIGHT JUST HAVE A SOLUTION FOR YOU...
AT LEAST SOME GOOD CAME OUT OF THIS--WE'RE NEVER GOING TO LET GEODE LIVE THIS DOWN.
"LIVE IT DOWN?" HE'LL KEEP TELLIN' THIS STORY 'TIL THE DAY HE DIES.
YOU HAVE SHOWN US THAT THE PROPHETESS' PATH WILL ALWAYS SHINE CLEAR. JOIN US TO FEAST AND REMEMBER.
DON'T MIND IF WE DO.

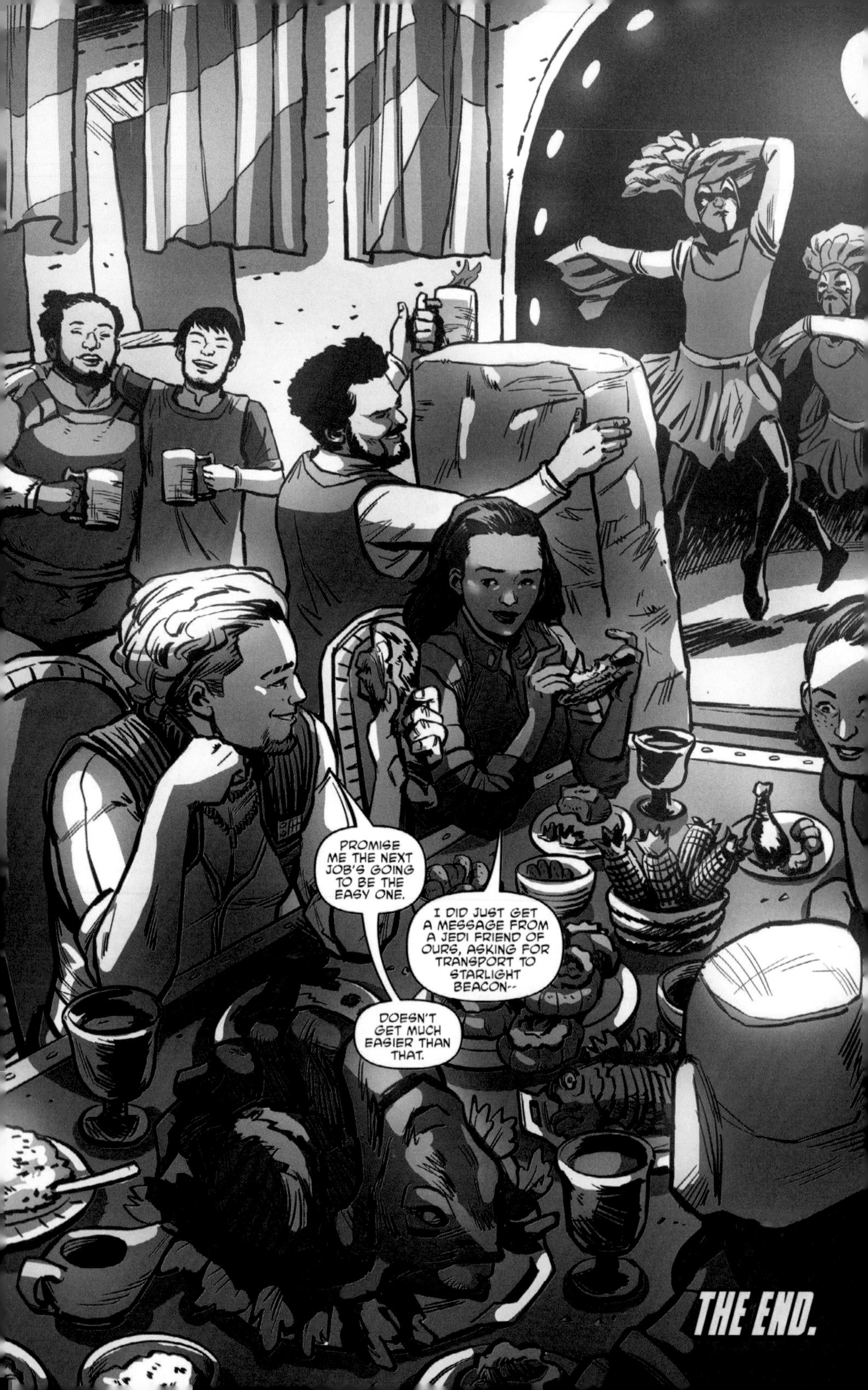
PROMISE ME THE NEXT JOB'S GOING TO BE THE EASY ONE.
I DID JUST GET A MESSAGE FROM A JEDI FRIEND OF OURS, ASKING FOR TRANSPORT TO STARLIGHT BEACON--
DOESN'T GET MUCH EASIER THAN THAT.
THE END.

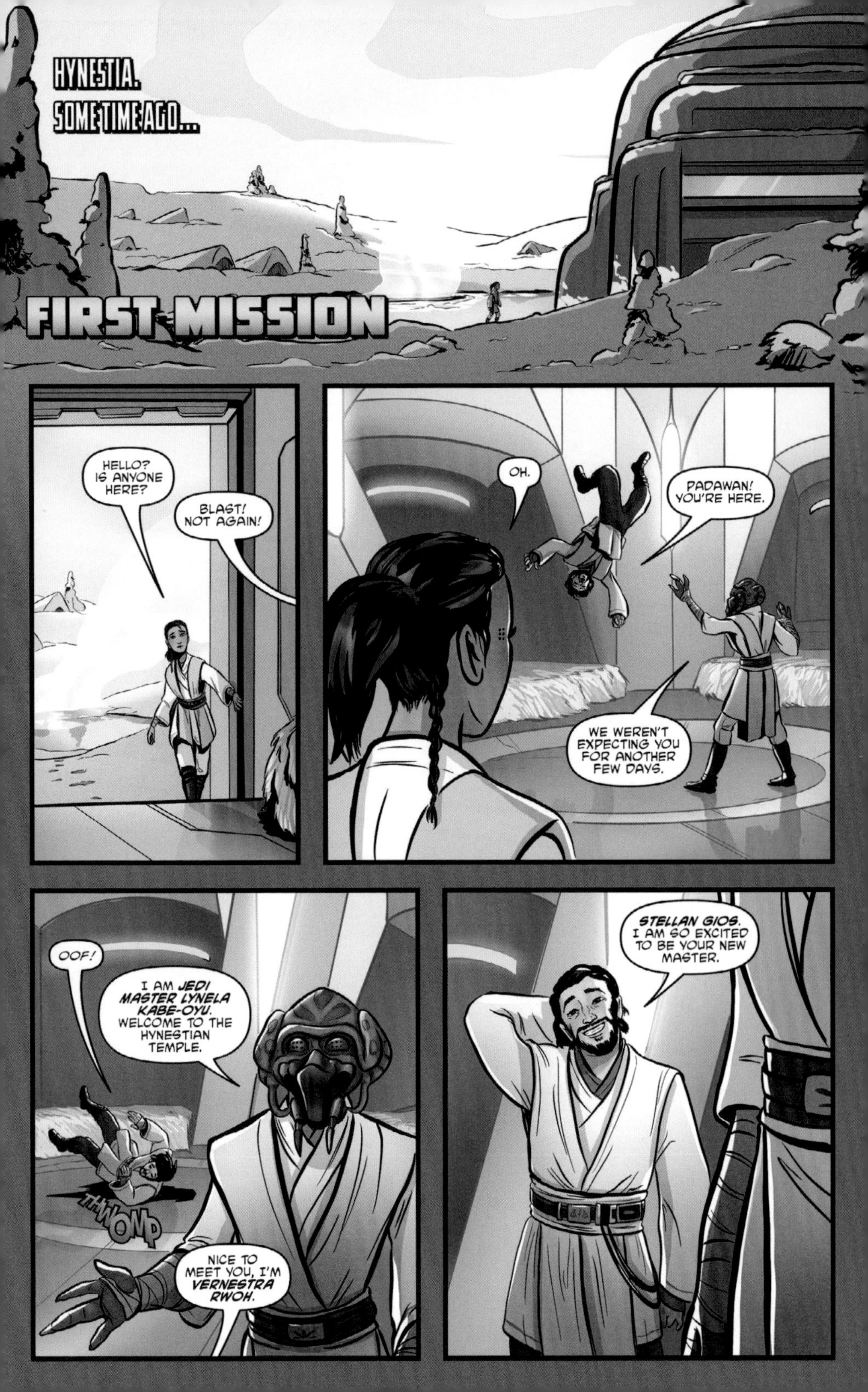
HYNESTIA.
SOME TIME AGO...
FIRST MISSION
HELLO? IS ANYONE HERE?
BLAST! NOT AGAIN!
OH.
PADAWAN! YOU'RE HERE.
WE WEREN'T EXPECTING YOU FOR ANOTHER FEW DAYS.
OOF!
THWOMP
I AM JEDI MASTER LYNELA KABE-OYU. WELCOME TO THE HYNESTIAN TEMPLE.
NICE TO MEET YOU, I'M VERNESTRA RWOH.
STELLAN GIOS. I AM SO EXCITED TO BE YOUR NEW MASTER.

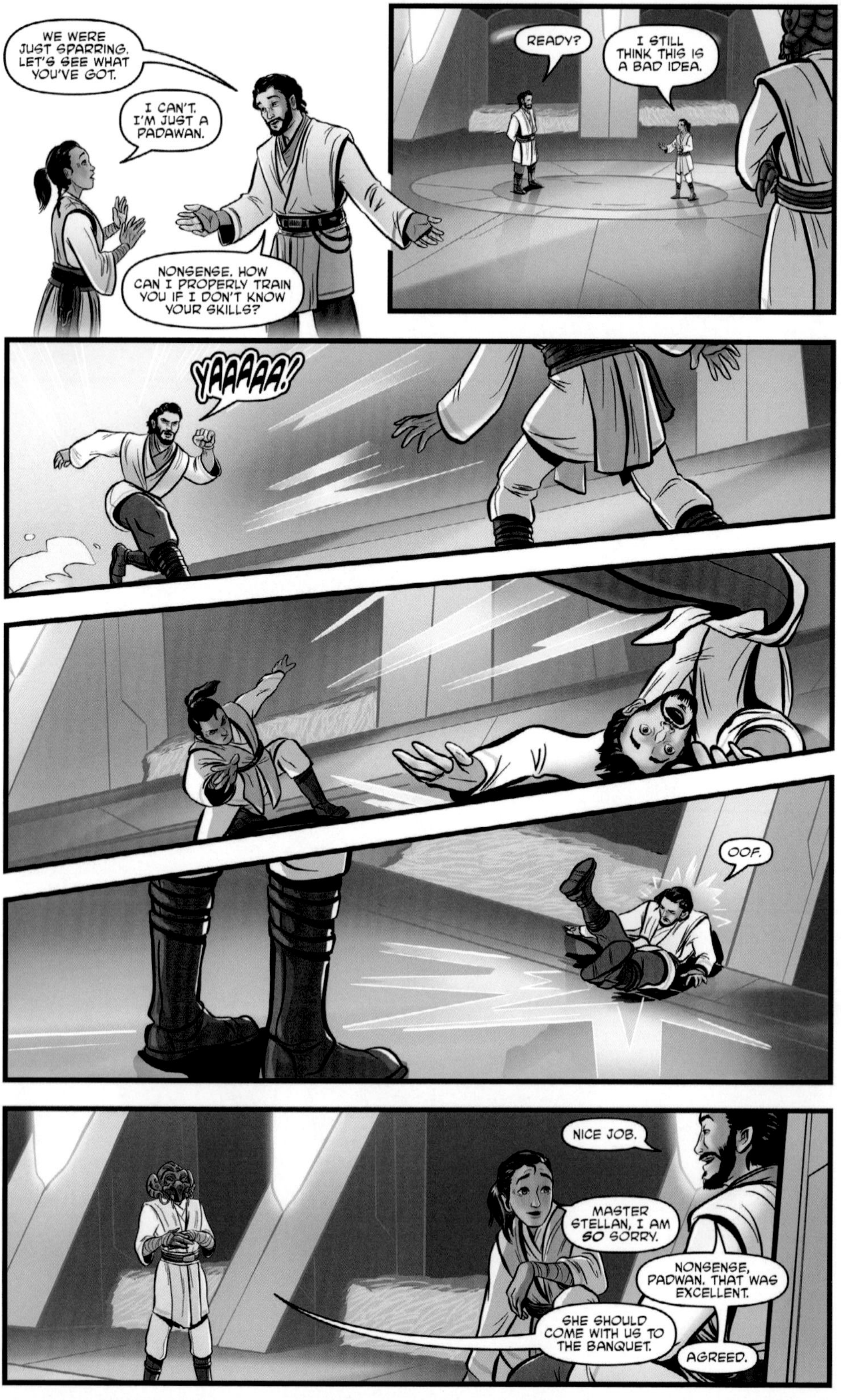
WE WERE JUST SPARRING. LET'S SEE WHAT YOU'VE GOT.
I CAN'T. I'M JUST A PADAWAN.
NONSENSE. HOW CAN I PROPERLY TRAIN YOU IF I DON'T KNOW YOUR SKILLS?
READY?
I STILL THINK THIS IS A BAD IDEA.
YAAAAA!
OOF.
NICE JOB.
MASTER STELLAN, I AM SO SORRY.
NONSENSE, PADAWAN. THAT WAS EXCELLENT.
SHE SHOULD COME WITH US TO THE BANQUET.
AGREED.

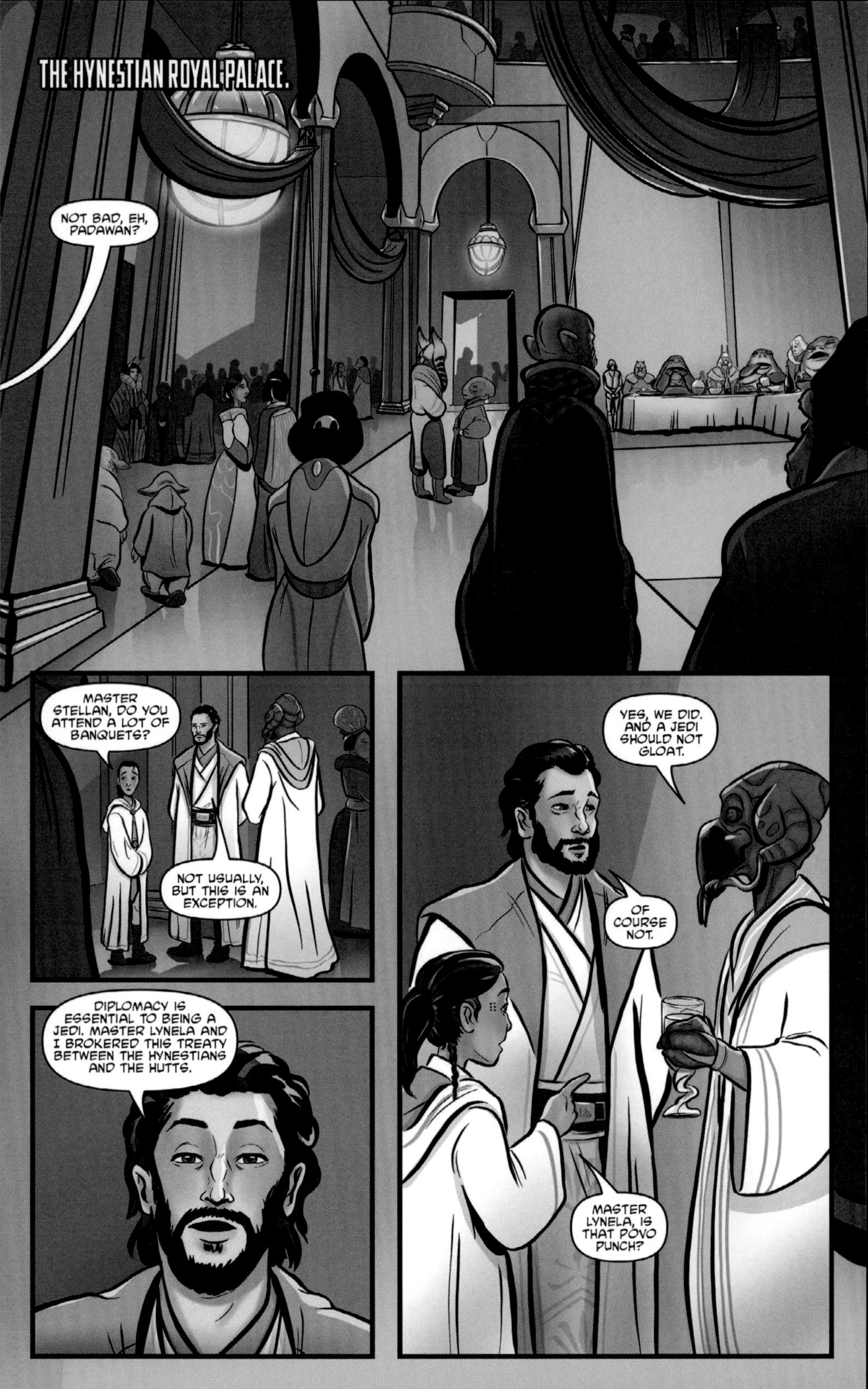
THE HYNESTIAN ROYAL PALACE.
NOT BAD, EH, PADAWAN?
MASTER STELLAN, DO YOU ATTEND A LOT OF BANQUETS?
NOT USUALLY, BUT THIS IS AN EXCEPTION.
DIPLOMACY IS ESSENTIAL TO BEING A JEDI. MASTER LYNELA AND I BROKERED THIS TREATY BETWEEN THE HYNESTIANS AND THE HUTTS.
YES, WE DID. AND A JEDI SHOULD NOT GLOAT.
OF COURSE NOT.
MASTER LYNELA, IS THAT POVO PUNCH?

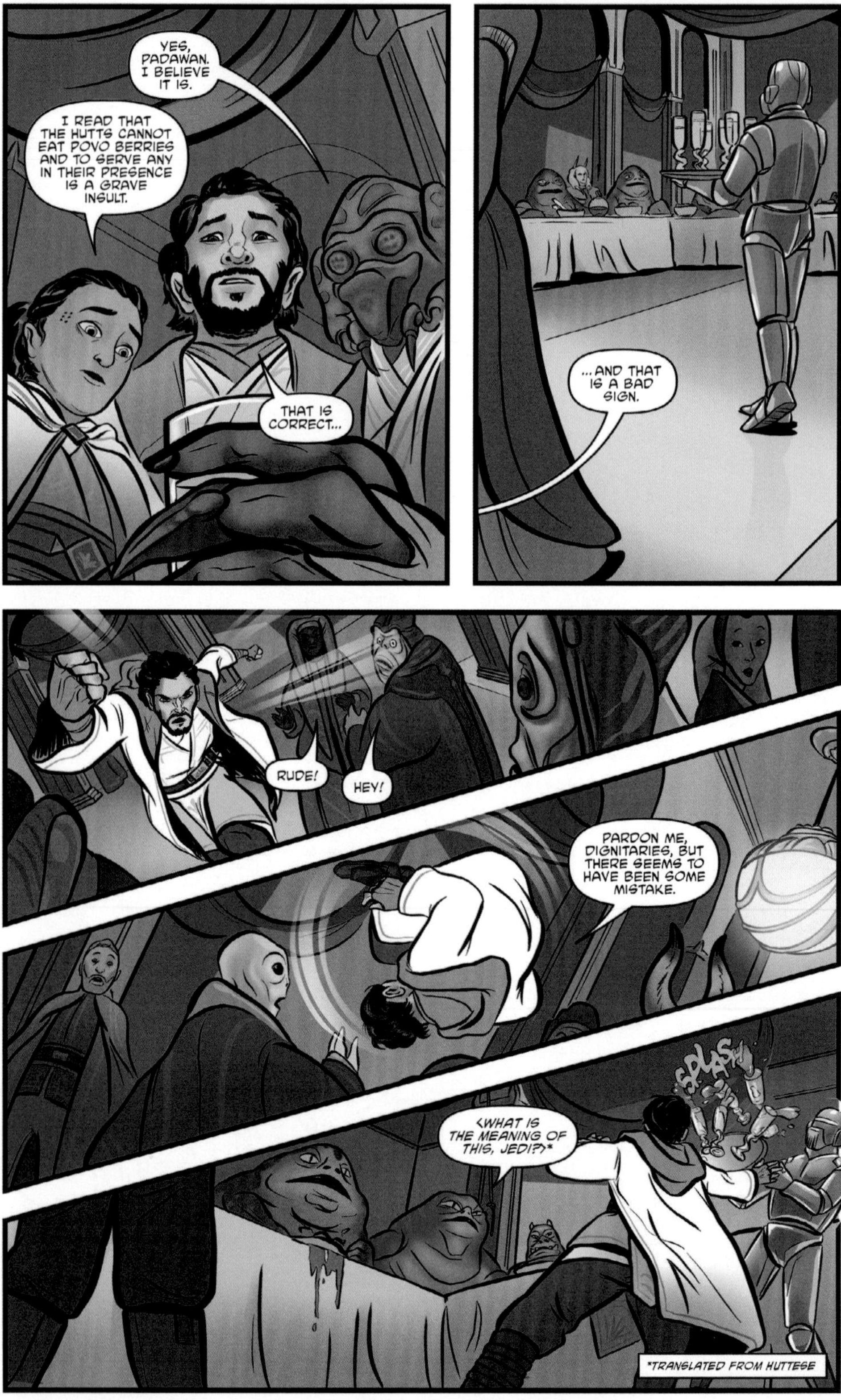
I READ THAT THE HUTTS CANNOT EAT POVO BERRIES AND TO SERVE ANY IN THEIR PRESENCE IS A GRAVE INSULT.
YES, PADAWAN. I BELIEVE IT IS.
THAT IS CORRECT...
...AND THAT IS A BAD SIGN.
RUDE!
HEY!
PARDON ME, DIGNITARIES, BUT THERE SEEMS TO HAVE BEEN SOME MISTAKE.
SPLASH
<WHAT IS THE MEANING OF THIS, JEDI!?>*
*TRANSLATED FROM HUTTESE

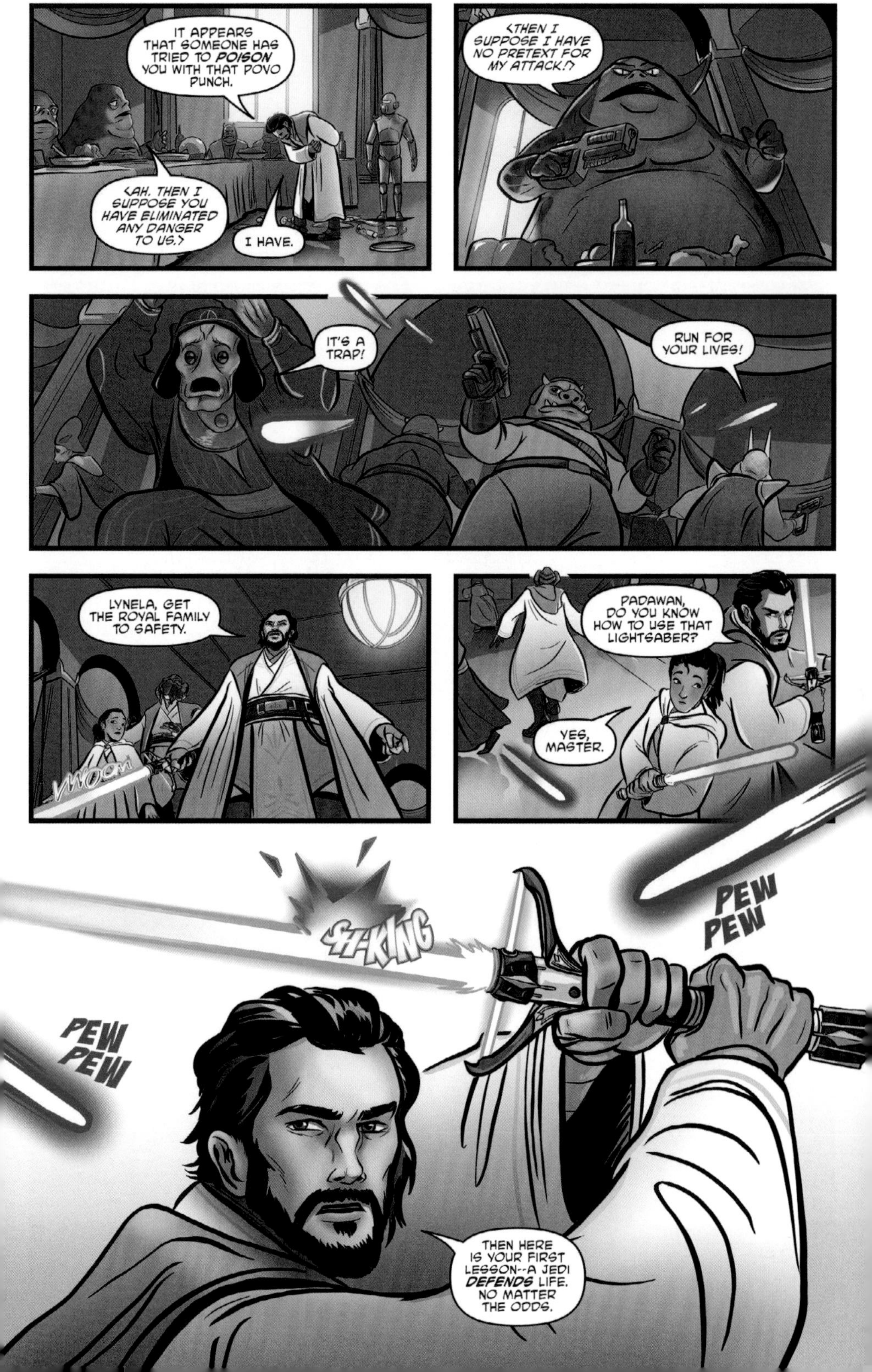
IT APPEARS THAT SOMEONE HAS TRIED TO POISON YOU WITH THAT POVO PUNCH.
<AH. THEN I SUPPOSE YOU HAVE ELIMINATED ANY DANGER TO US.>
I HAVE.
<THEN I SUPPOSE I HAVE NO PRETEXT FOR MY ATTACK.!>
IT'S A TRAP!
RUN FOR YOUR LIVES!
LYNELA, GET THE ROYAL FAMILY TO SAFETY.
VWOOM
PADAWAN, DO YOU KNOW HOW TO USE THAT LIGHTSABER?
YES, MASTER.
SH-KING
PEW PEW
PEW PEW
THEN HERE IS YOUR FIRST LESSON--A JEDI DEFENDS LIFE. NO MATTER THE ODDS.

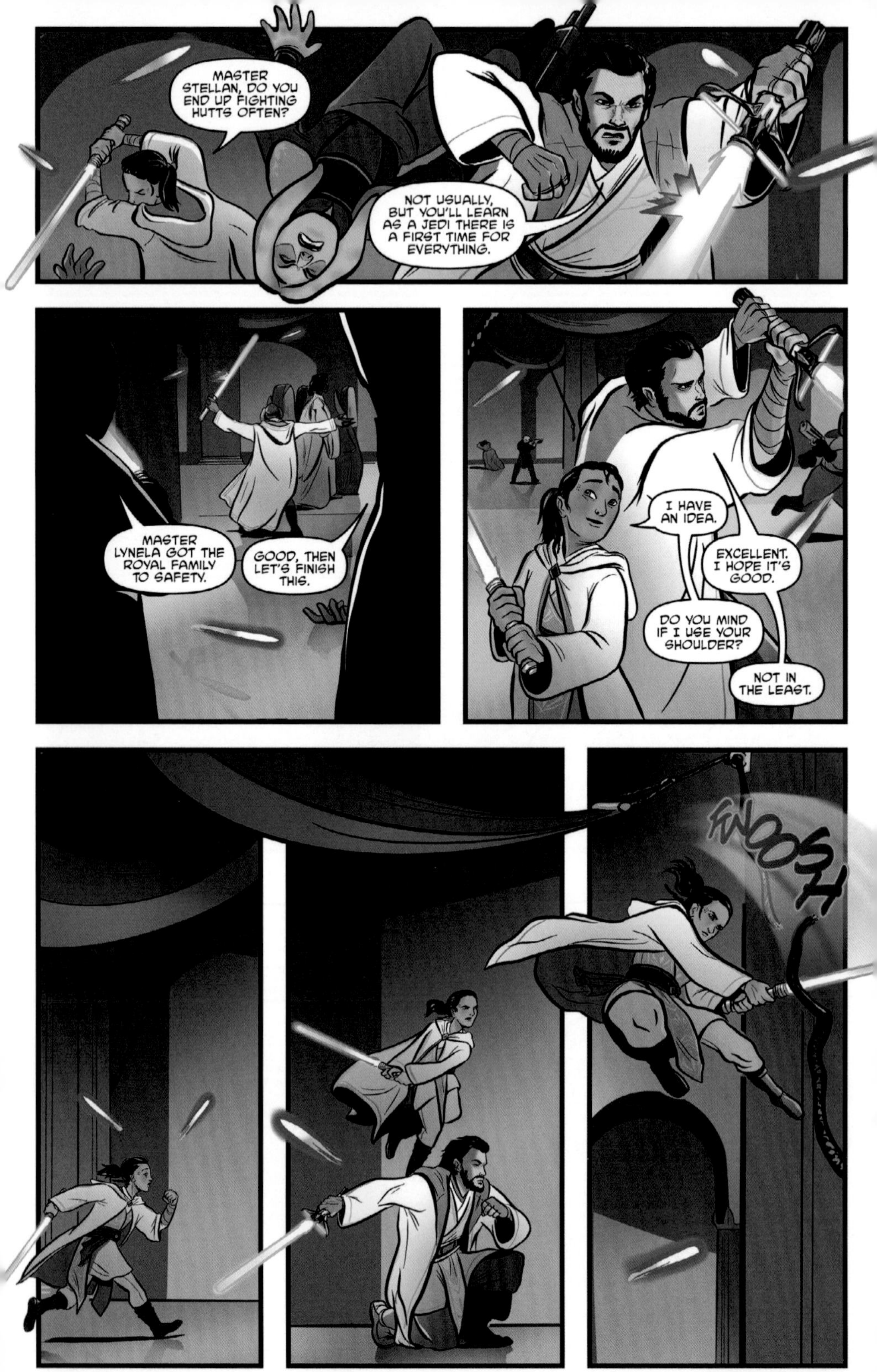
MASTER STELLAN, DO YOU END UP FIGHTING HUTTS OFTEN?
NOT USUALLY, BUT YOU'LL LEARN AS A JEDI THERE IS A FIRST TIME FOR EVERYTHING.
MASTER LYNELA GOT THE ROYAL FAMILY TO SAFETY.
GOOD, THEN LET'S FINISH THIS.
I HAVE AN IDEA.
EXCELLENT. I HOPE IT'S GOOD.
DO YOU MIND IF I USE YOUR SHOULDER?
NOT IN THE LEAST.
FWOOSH

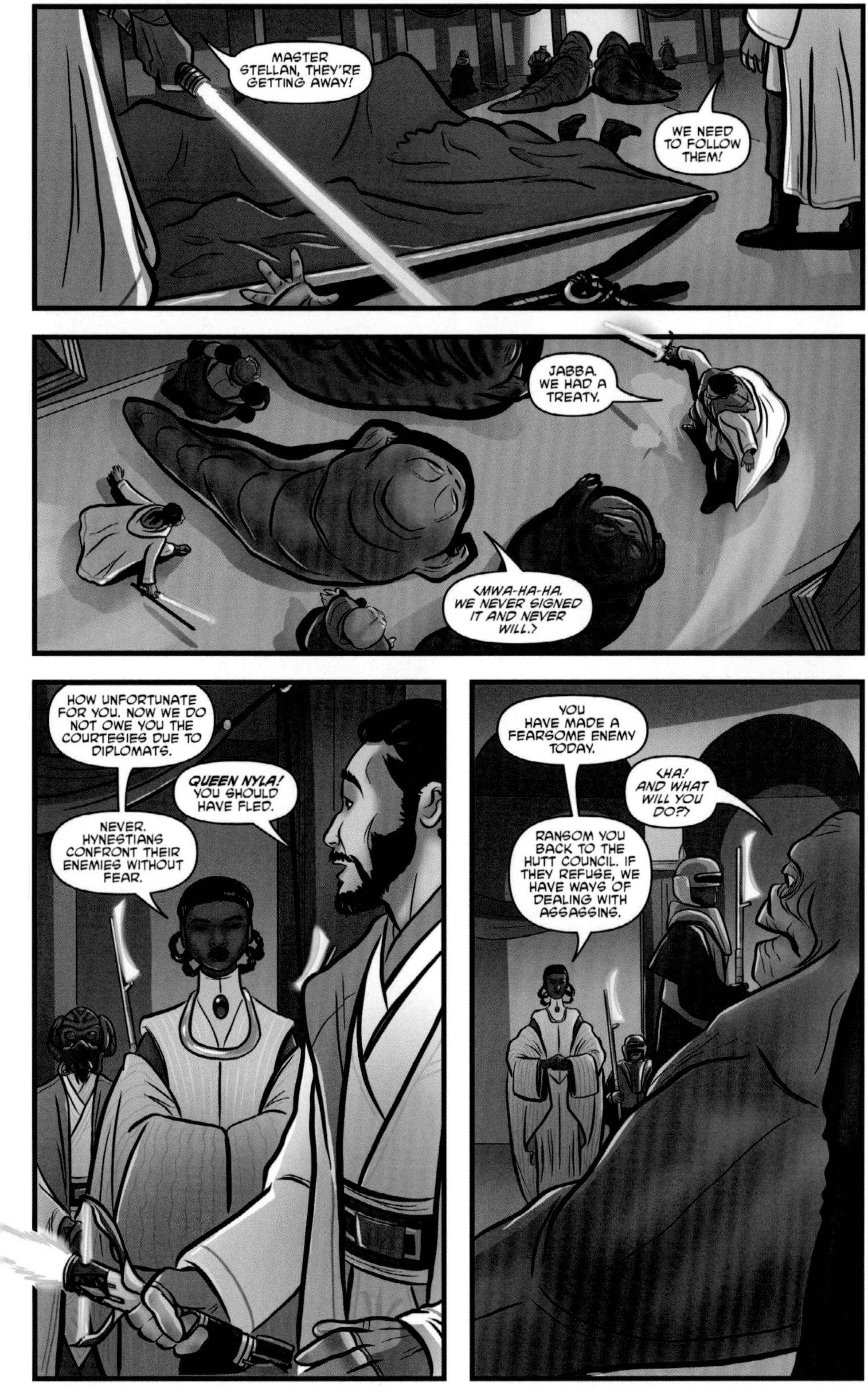
MASTER STELLAN, THEY'RE GETTING AWAY!
WE NEED TO FOLLOW THEM!
JABBA. WE HAD A TREATY.
<MWA-HA-HA. WE NEVER SIGNED IT AND NEVER WILL.>
HOW UNFORTUNATE FOR YOU. NOW WE DO NOT OWE YOU THE COURTESIES DUE TO DIPLOMATS.
QUEEN NYLA! YOU SHOULD HAVE FLED.
NEVER. HYNESTIANS CONFRONT THEIR ENEMIES WITHOUT FEAR.
YOU HAVE MADE A FEARSOME ENEMY TODAY.
<HA! AND WHAT WILL YOU DO?>
RANSOM YOU BACK TO THE HUTT COUNCIL. IF THEY REFUSE, WE HAVE WAYS OF DEALING WITH ASSASSINS.

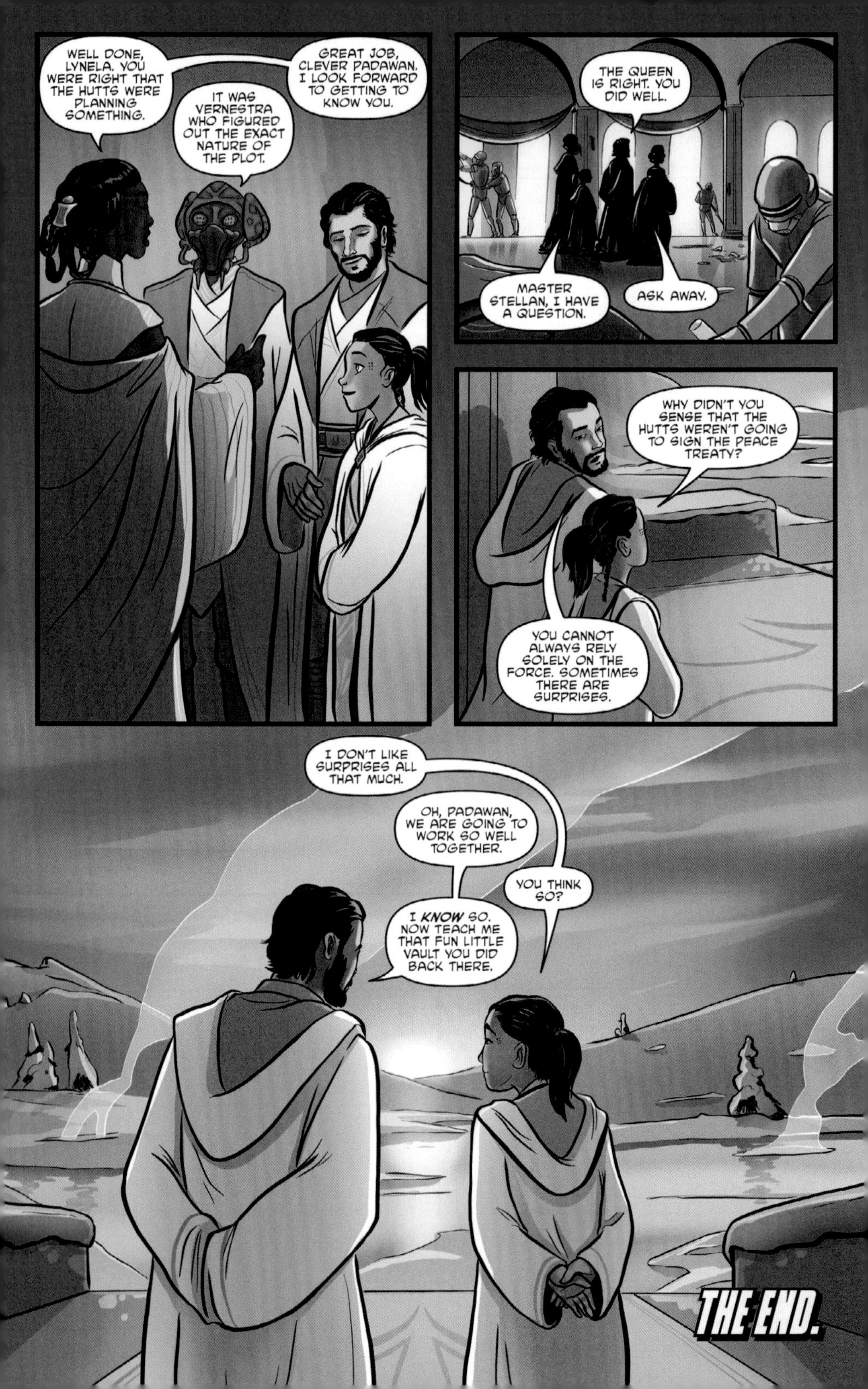
WELL DONE, LYNELA. YOU WERE RIGHT THAT THE HUTTS WERE PLANNING SOMETHING.
IT WAS VERNESTRA WHO FIGURED OUT THE EXACT NATURE OF THE PLOT.
GREAT JOB, CLEVER PADAWAN. I LOOK FORWARD TO GETTING TO KNOW YOU.
THE QUEEN IS RIGHT. YOU DID WELL.
MASTER STELLAN, I HAVE A QUESTION.
ASK AWAY.
WHY DIDN'T YOU SENSE THAT THE HUTTS WEREN'T GOING TO SIGN THE PEACE TREATY?
YOU CANNOT ALWAYS RELY SOLELY ON THE FORCE. SOMETIMES THERE ARE SURPRISES.
I DON'T LIKE SURPRISES ALL THAT MUCH.
OH, PADAWAN, WE ARE GOING TO WORK SO WELL TOGETHER.
YOU THINK SO?
I KNOW SO. NOW TEACH ME THAT FUN LITTLE VAULT YOU DID BACK THERE.
THE END.

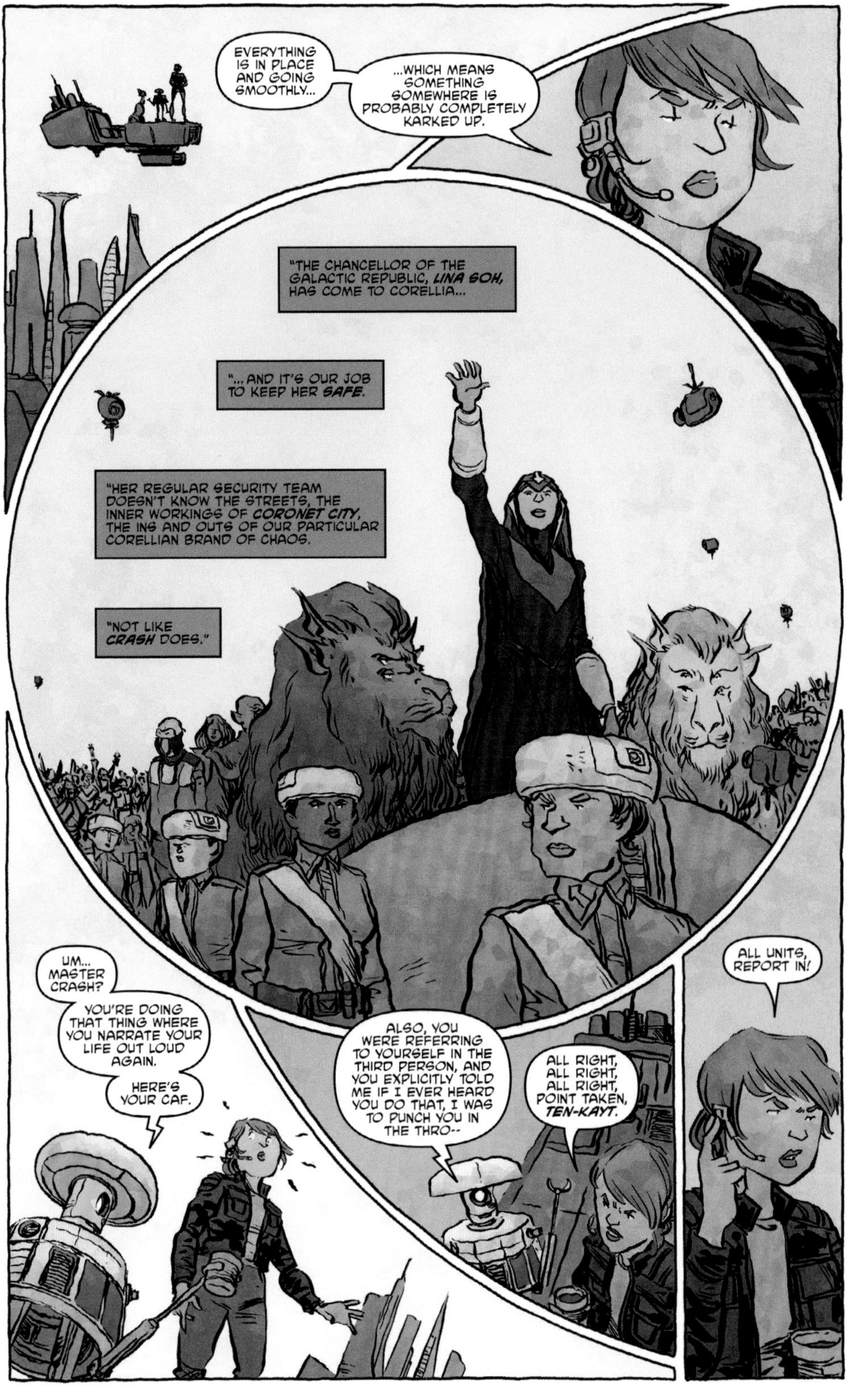
EVERYTHING IS IN PLACE AND GOING SMOOTHLY...
...WHICH MEANS SOMETHING SOMEWHERE IS PROBABLY COMPLETELY KARKED UP.
"THE CHANCELLOR OF THE GALACTIC REPUBLIC, LINA SOH, HAS COME TO CORELLIA...
"...AND IT'S OUR JOB TO KEEP HER SAFE.
"HER REGULAR SECURITY TEAM DOESN'T KNOW THE STREETS, THE INNER WORKINGS OF CORONET CITY, THE INS AND OUTS OF OUR PARTICULAR CORELLIAN BRAND OF CHAOS.
"NOT LIKE CRASH DOES."
UM... MASTER CRASH?
YOU'RE DOING THAT THING WHERE YOU NARRATE YOUR LIFE OUT LOUD AGAIN.
HERE'S YOUR CAF.
ALSO, YOU WERE REFERRING TO YOURSELF IN THE THIRD PERSON, AND YOU EXPLICITLY TOLD ME IF I EVER HEARD YOU DO THAT, I WAS TO PUNCH YOU IN THE THRO--
ALL RIGHT, ALL RIGHT, ALL RIGHT, POINT TAKEN, TEN-KAYT.
ALL UNITS, REPORT IN!

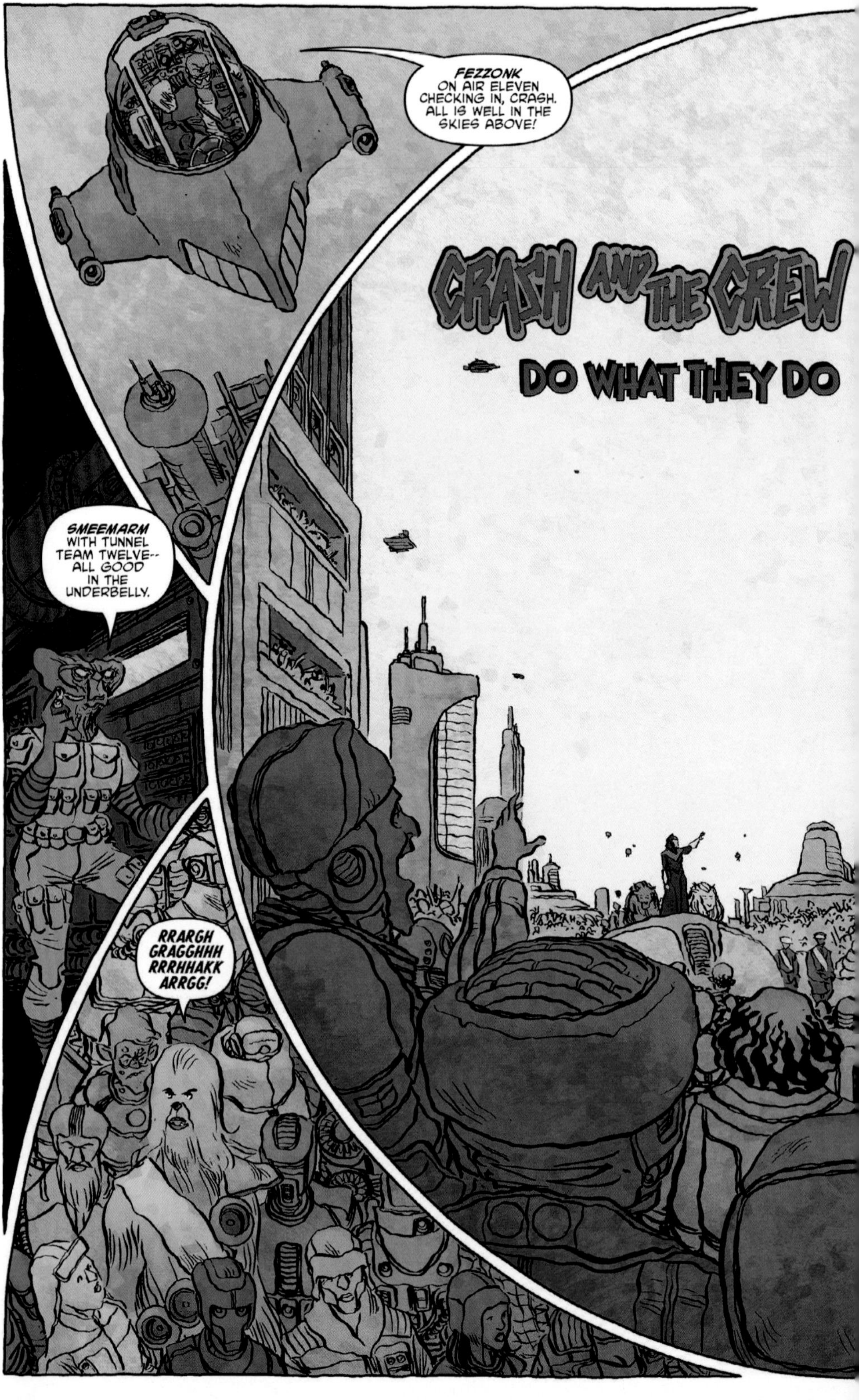

CRASH AND THE CREW
DO WHAT THEY DO
FEZZONK ON AIR ELEVEN CHECKING IN, CRASH. ALL IS WELL IN THE SKIES ABOVE!
SMEEMARM WITH TUNNEL TEAM TWELVE-- ALL GOOD IN THE UNDERBELLY.
RRARGH GRAGGHHH RRRHHAKK ARRGG!

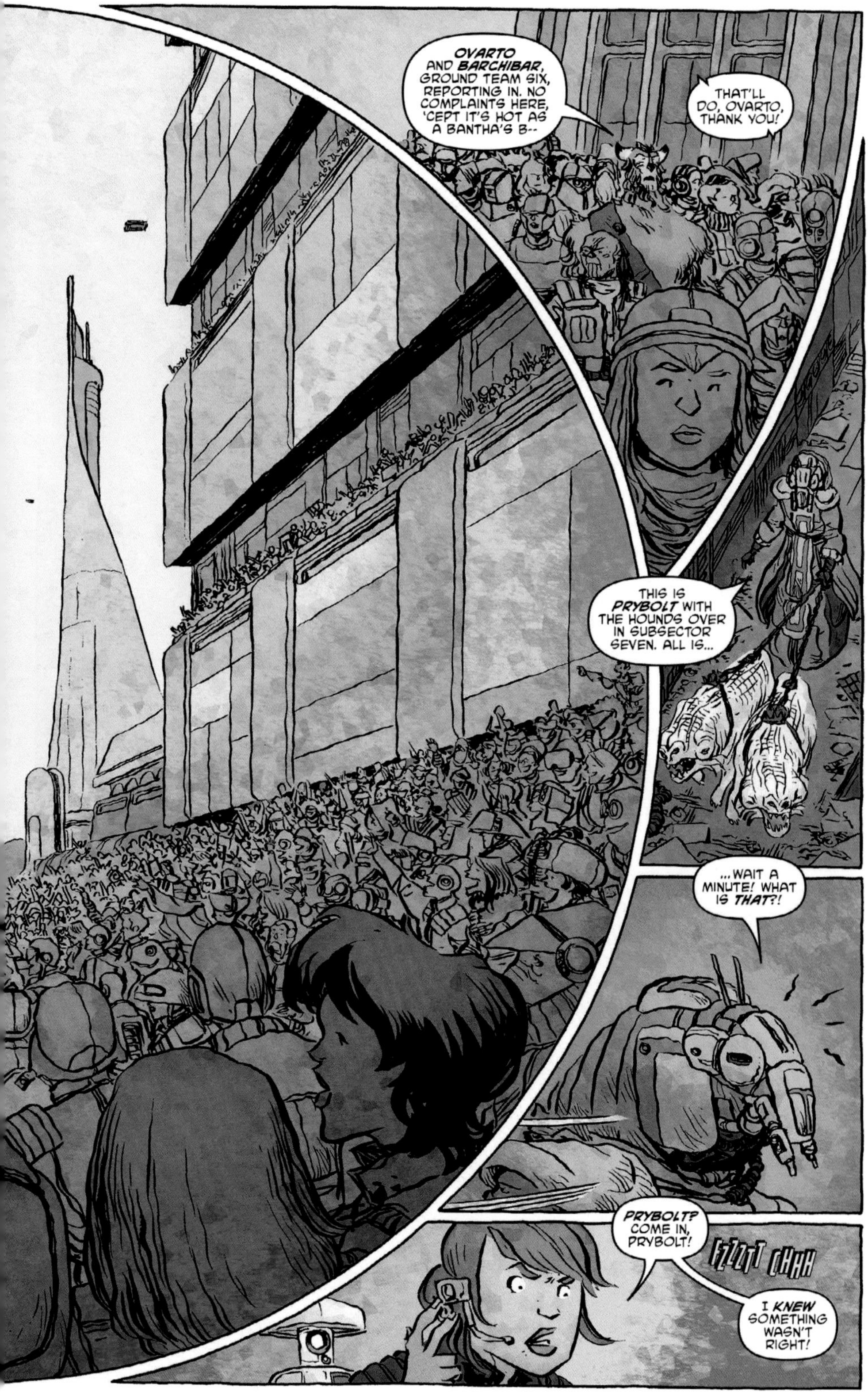

OVARTO AND BARCHIBAR, GROUND TEAM SIX, REPORTING IN. NO COMPLAINTS HERE, 'CEPT IT'S HOT AS A BANTHA'S B--
THAT'LL DO, OVARTO, THANK YOU!
THIS IS PRYBOLT WITH THE HOUNDS OVER IN SUBSECTOR SEVEN. ALL IS...
...WAIT A MINUTE! WHAT IS THAT?!
PRYBOLT? COME IN, PRYBOLT!
FZZZT CHHH
I KNEW SOMETHING WASN'T RIGHT!

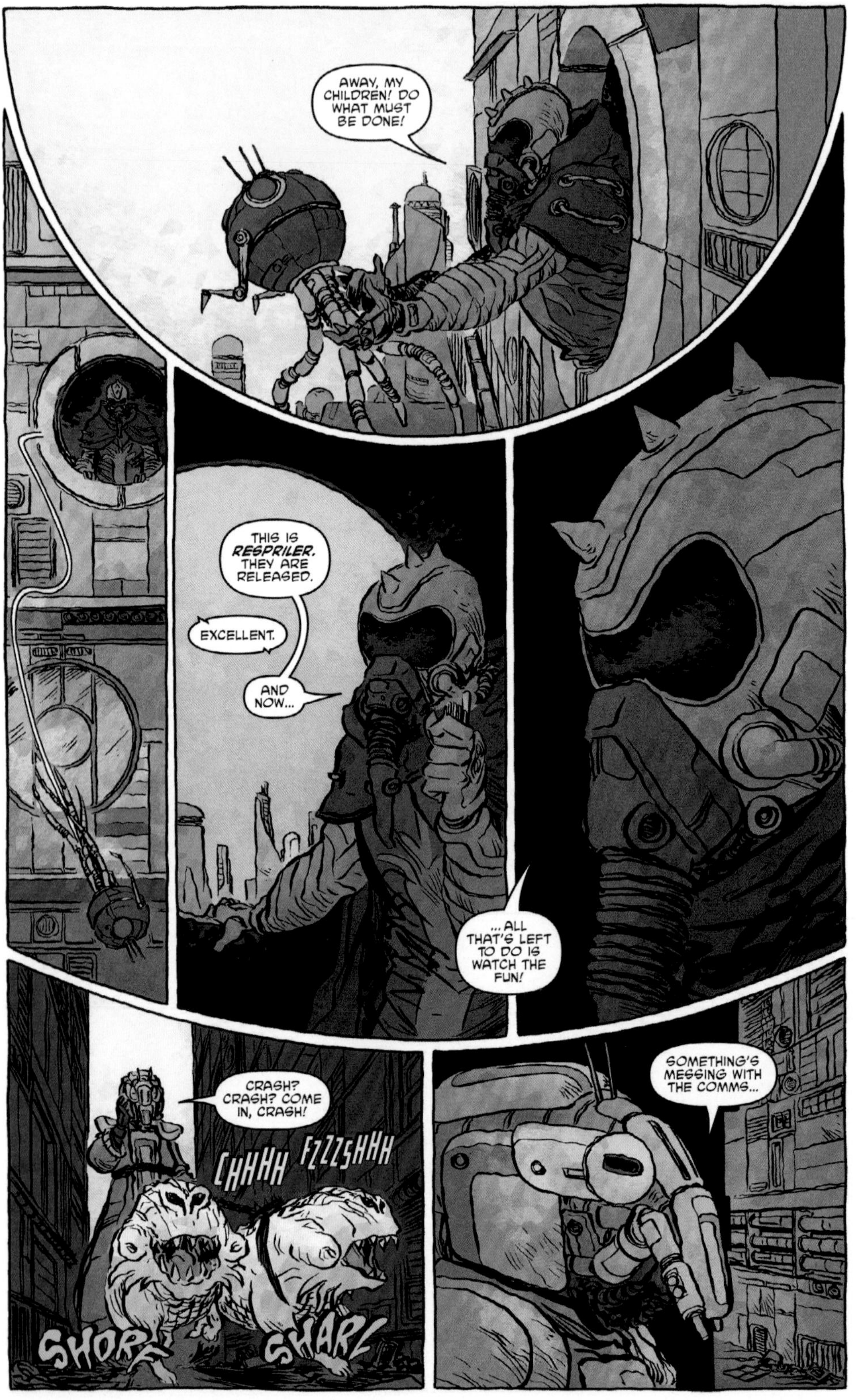
AWAY, MY CHILDREN! DO WHAT MUST BE DONE!
THIS IS *RESPRILER.* THEY ARE RELEASED.
EXCELLENT.
AND NOW...
...ALL THAT'S LEFT TO DO IS WATCH THE FUN!
CRASH? CRASH? COME IN, CRASH!
CHHHH
FZZZSHHH
SHORF
SHARL
SOMETHING'S MESSING WITH THE COMMS...

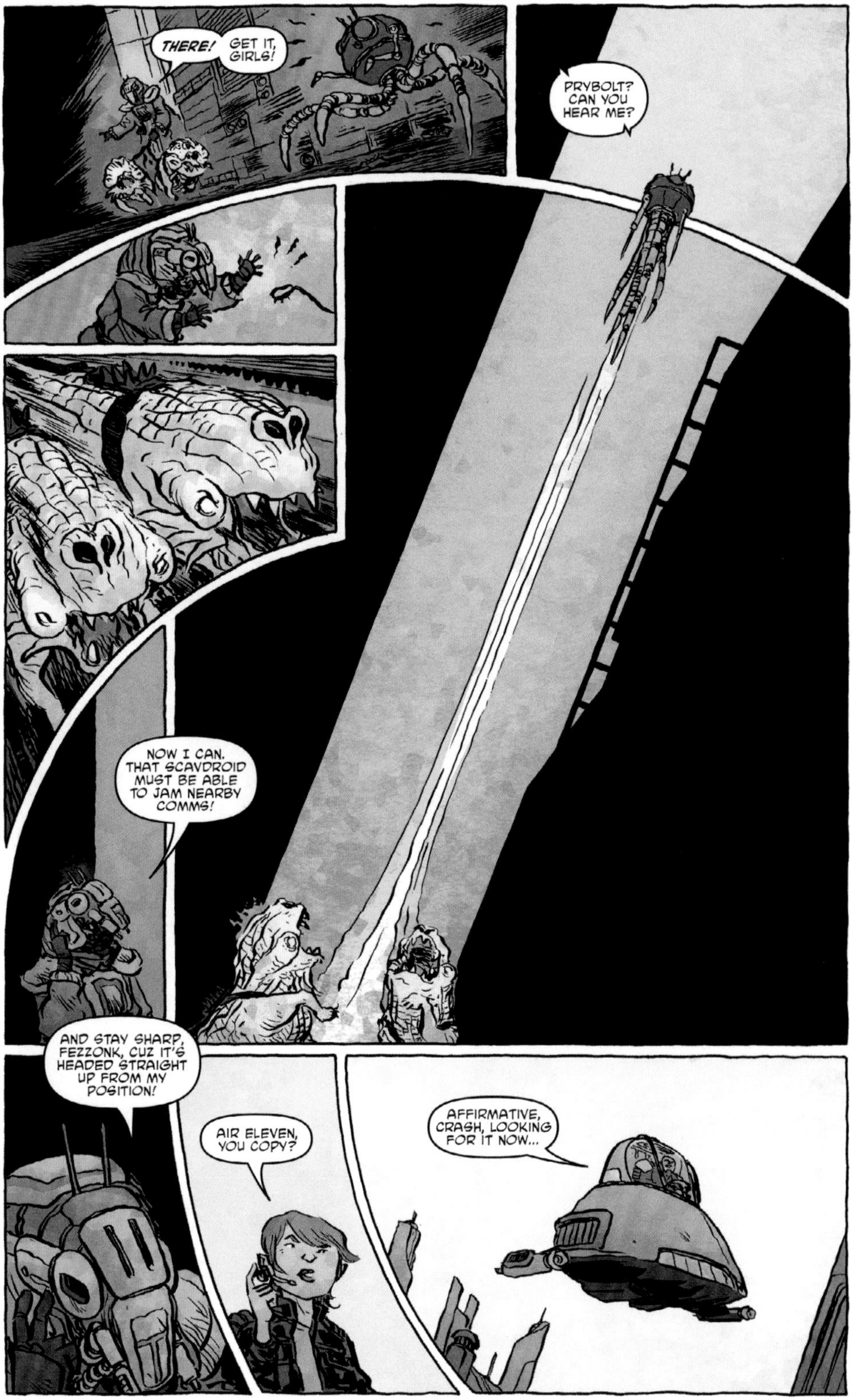
THERE!
GET IT, GIRLS!
PRYBOLT? CAN YOU HEAR ME?
NOW I CAN. THAT SCAVDROID MUST BE ABLE TO JAM NEARBY COMMS!
AND STAY SHARP, FEZZONK, CUZ IT'S HEADED STRAIGHT UP FROM MY POSITION!
AIR ELEVEN, YOU COPY?
AFFIRMATIVE, CRASH, LOOKING FOR IT NOW...

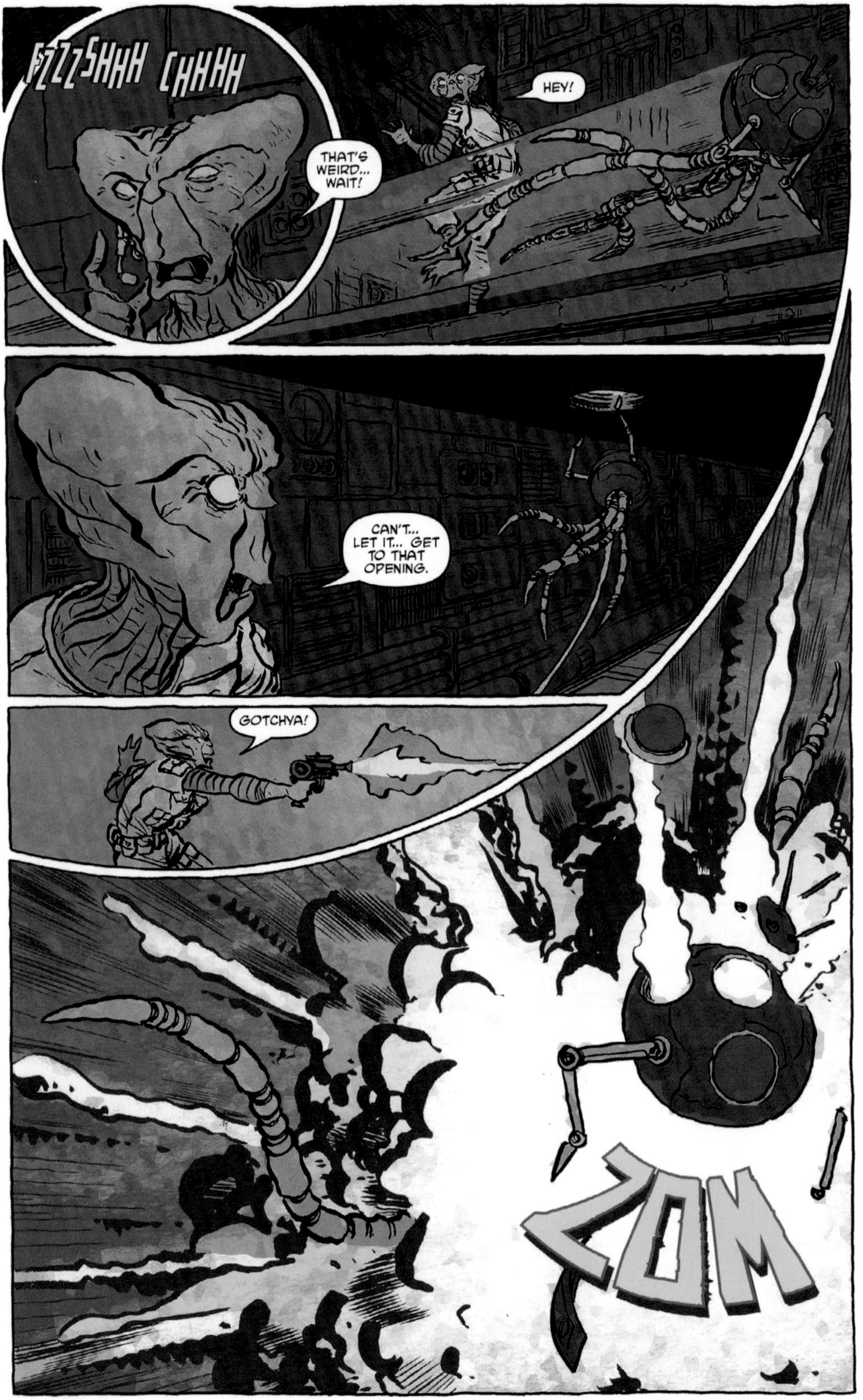
FZZZSHHH CHHHH
THAT'S WEIRD... WAIT!
HEY!
CAN'T... LET IT... GET TO THAT OPENING.
GOTCHYA!
ZOM

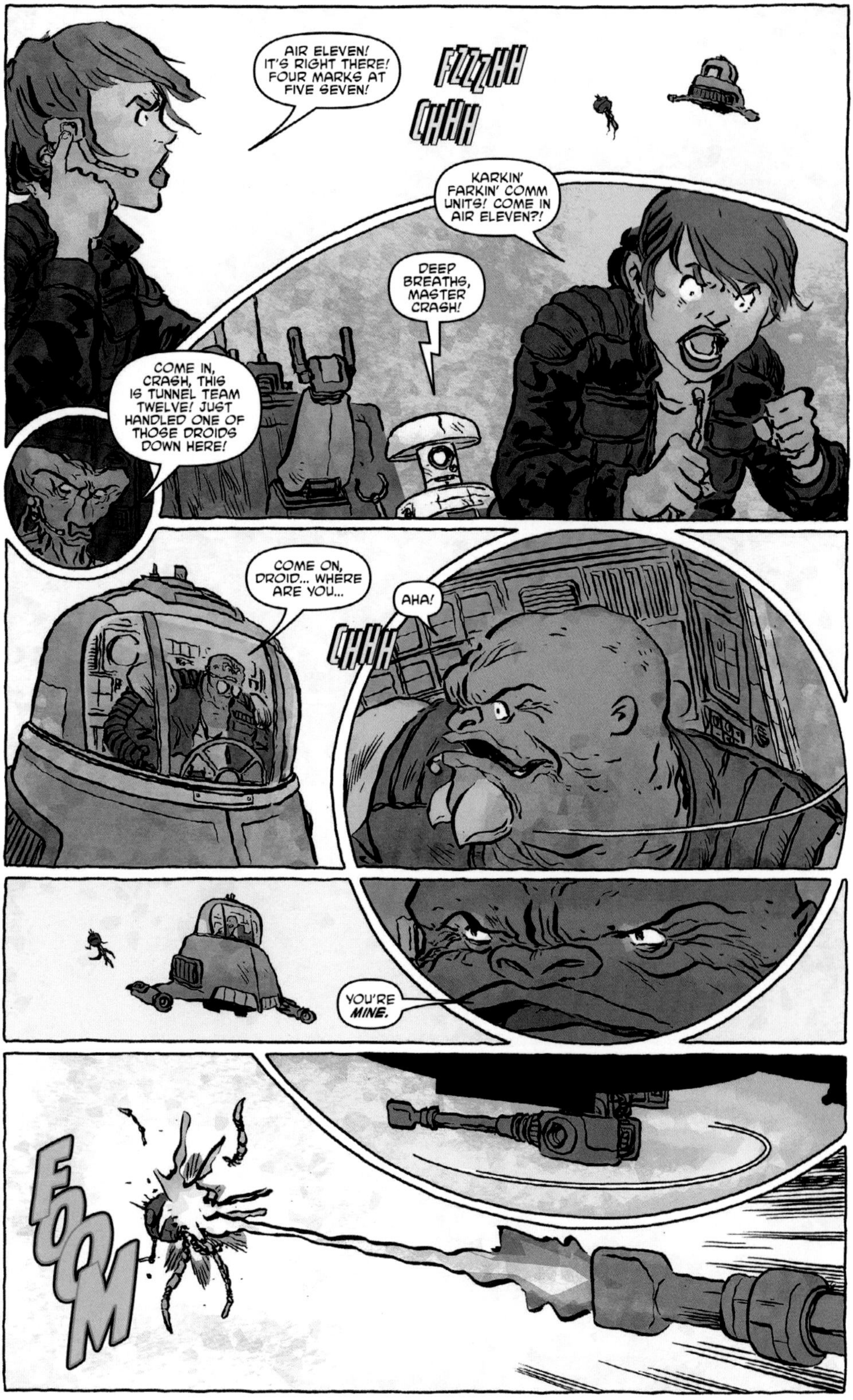

AIR ELEVEN! IT'S RIGHT THERE! FOUR MARKS AT FIVE SEVEN!
FZZZHH
CHHH
KARKIN' FARKIN' COMM UNITS! COME IN AIR ELEVEN?!
DEEP BREATHS, MASTER CRASH!
COME IN, CRASH, THIS IS TUNNEL TEAM TWELVE! JUST HANDLED ONE OF THOSE DROIDS DOWN HERE!
COME ON, DROID... WHERE ARE YOU...
AHA!
CHHH
YOU'RE *MINE.*
FOOM

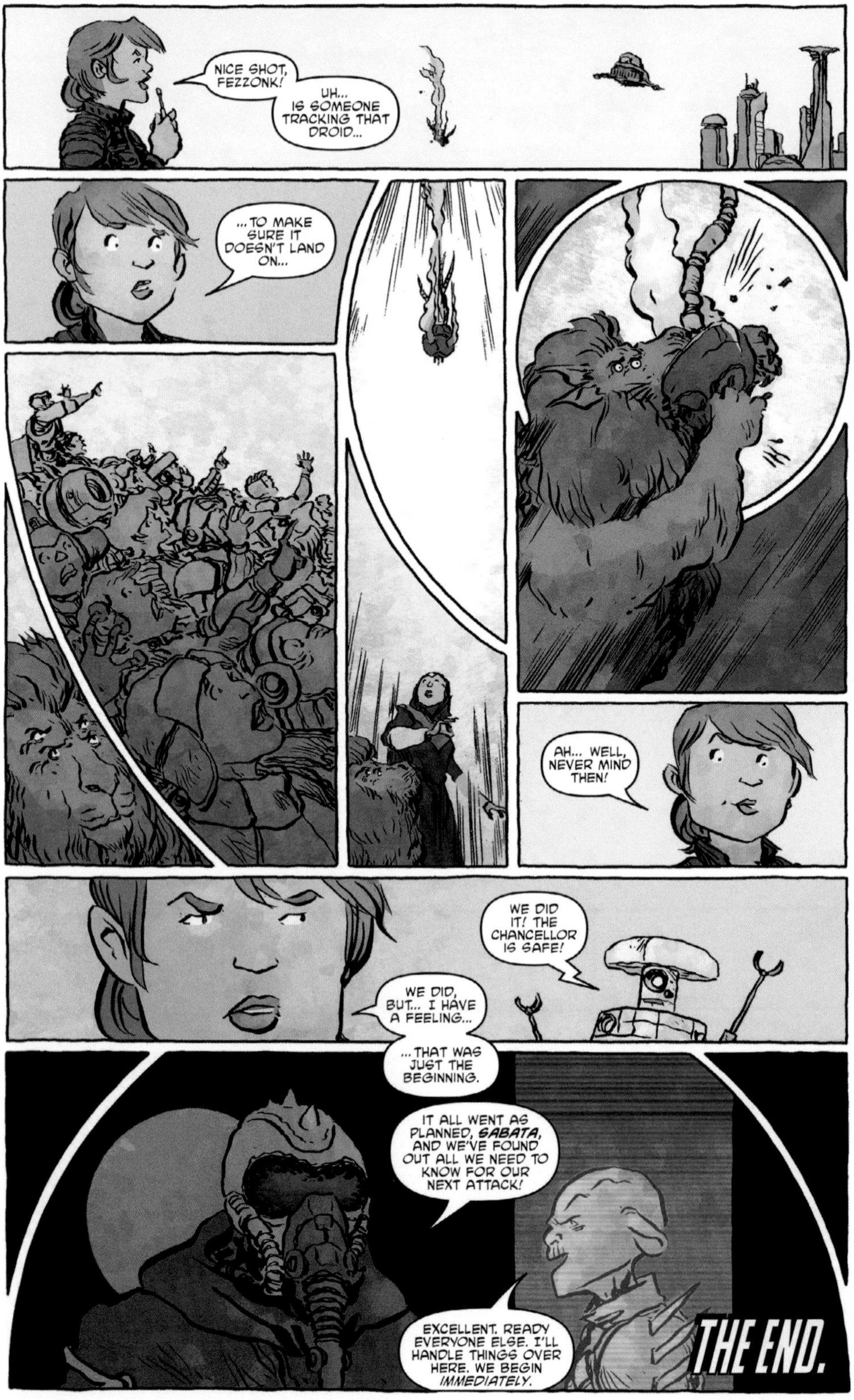
NICE SHOT, FEZZONK!
UH... IS SOMEONE TRACKING THAT DROID...
...TO MAKE SURE IT DOESN'T LAND ON...
AH... WELL, NEVER MIND THEN!
WE DID IT! THE CHANCELLOR IS SAFE!
WE DID, BUT... I HAVE A FEELING...
...THAT WAS JUST THE BEGINNING.
IT ALL WENT AS PLANNED, SABATA, AND WE'VE FOUND OUT ALL WE NEED TO KNOW FOR OUR NEXT ATTACK!
EXCELLENT. READY EVERYONE ELSE. I'LL HANDLE THINGS OVER HERE. WE BEGIN IMMEDIATELY.
THE END.

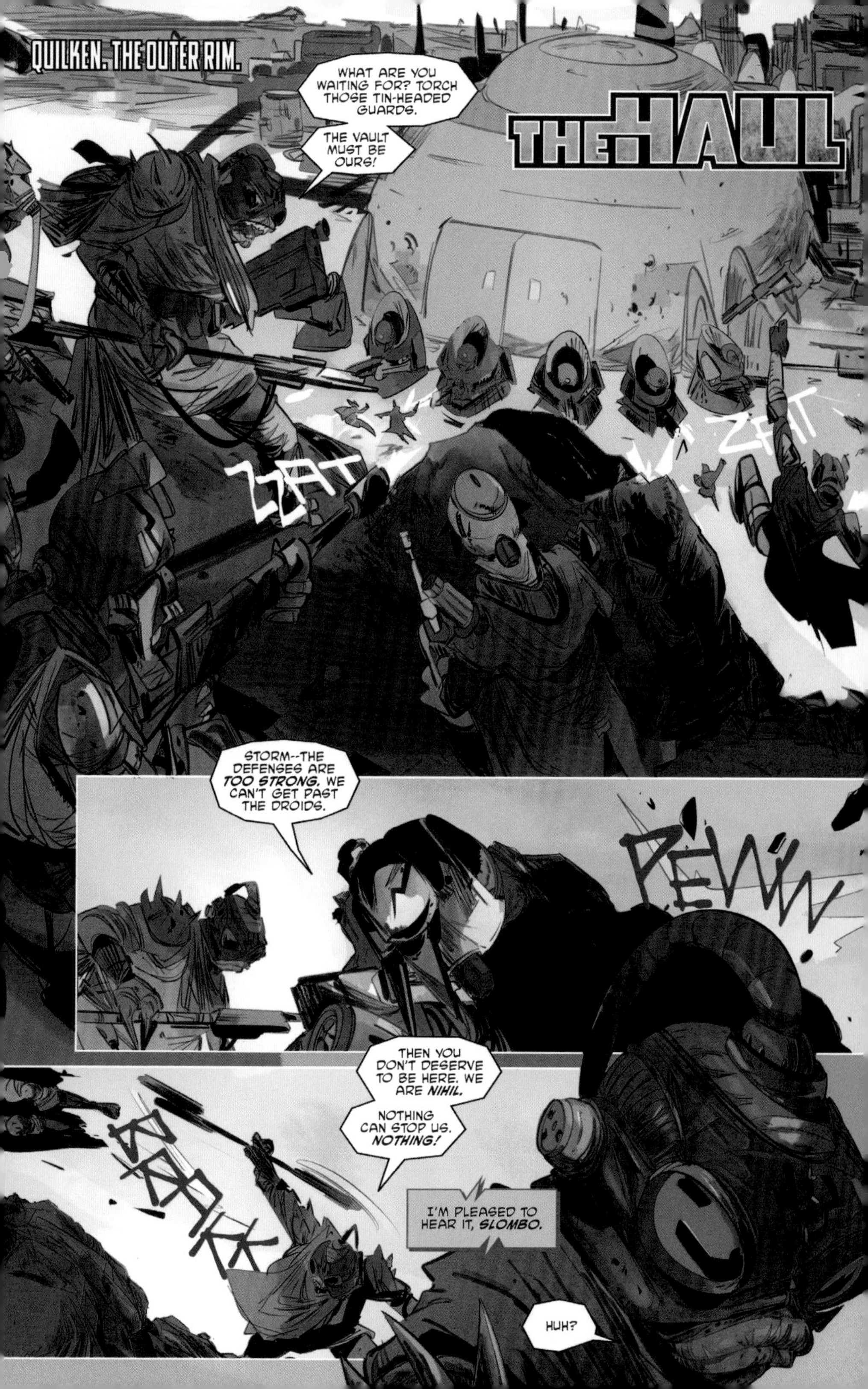
QUILKEN. THE OUTER RIM.
WHAT ARE YOU WAITING FOR? TORCH THOSE TIN-HEADED GUARDS.
THE VAULT MUST BE OURS!
THE HAUL
ZZAT
ZZAT
STORM--THE DEFENSES ARE *TOO STRONG.* WE CAN'T GET PAST THE DROIDS.
PEWW
THEN YOU DON'T DESERVE TO BE HERE. WE ARE *NIHIL.*
NOTHING CAN STOP US. *NOTHING!*
I'M PLEASED TO HEAR IT, *SLOMBO.*
HUH?

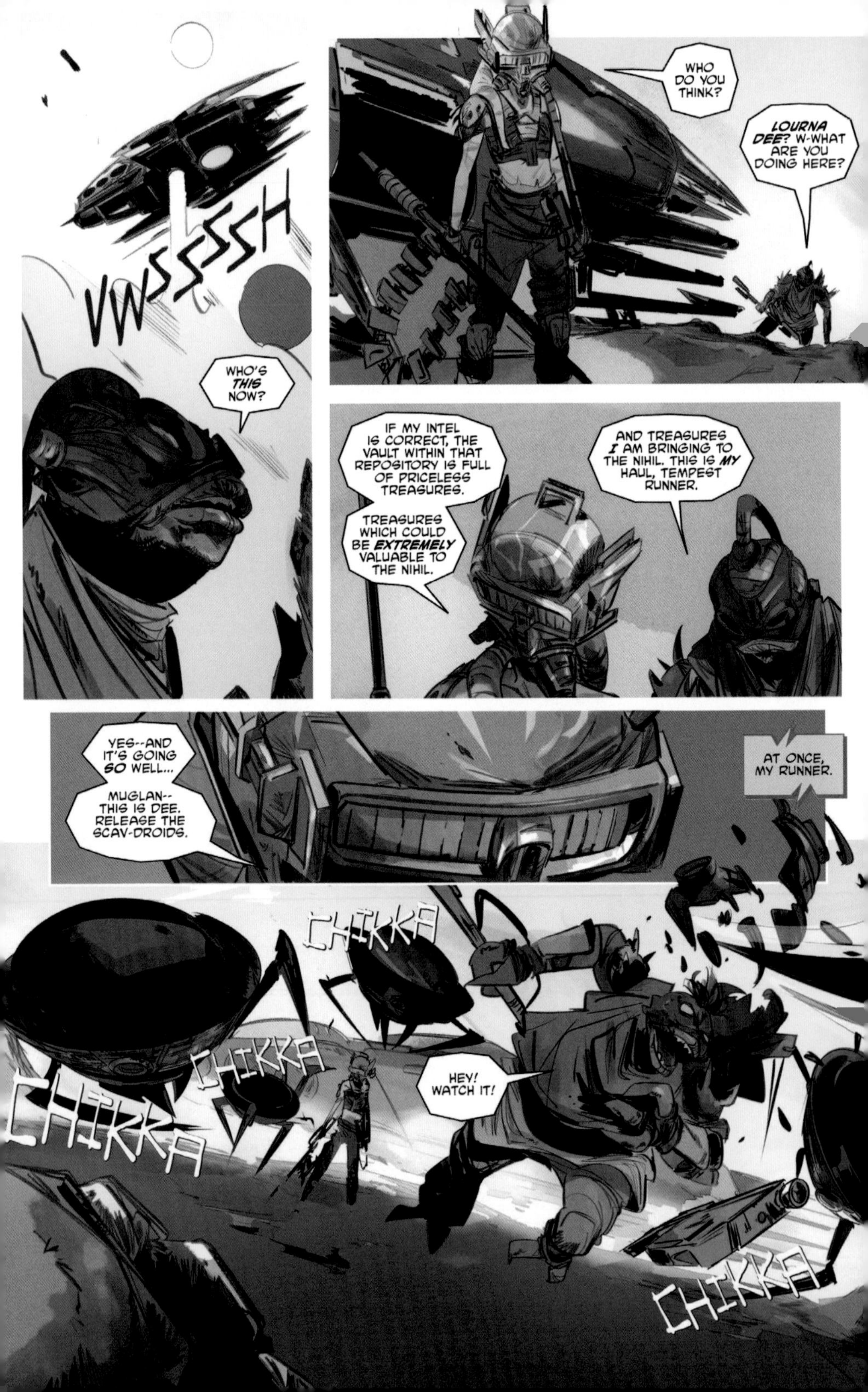
VWSSSSH
WHO'S THIS NOW?
WHO DO YOU THINK?
LOURNA DEE? W-WHAT ARE YOU DOING HERE?
IF MY INTEL IS CORRECT, THE VAULT WITHIN THAT REPOSITORY IS FULL OF PRICELESS TREASURES.
TREASURES WHICH COULD BE EXTREMELY VALUABLE TO THE NIHIL.
AND TREASURES I AM BRINGING TO THE NIHIL. THIS IS MY HAUL, TEMPEST RUNNER.
YES--AND IT'S GOING SO WELL...
MUGLAN-- THIS IS DEE. RELEASE THE SCAV-DROIDS.
AT ONCE, MY RUNNER.
CHIKKA
CHIKKA
CHIKKA
HEY! WATCH IT!
CHIKKA

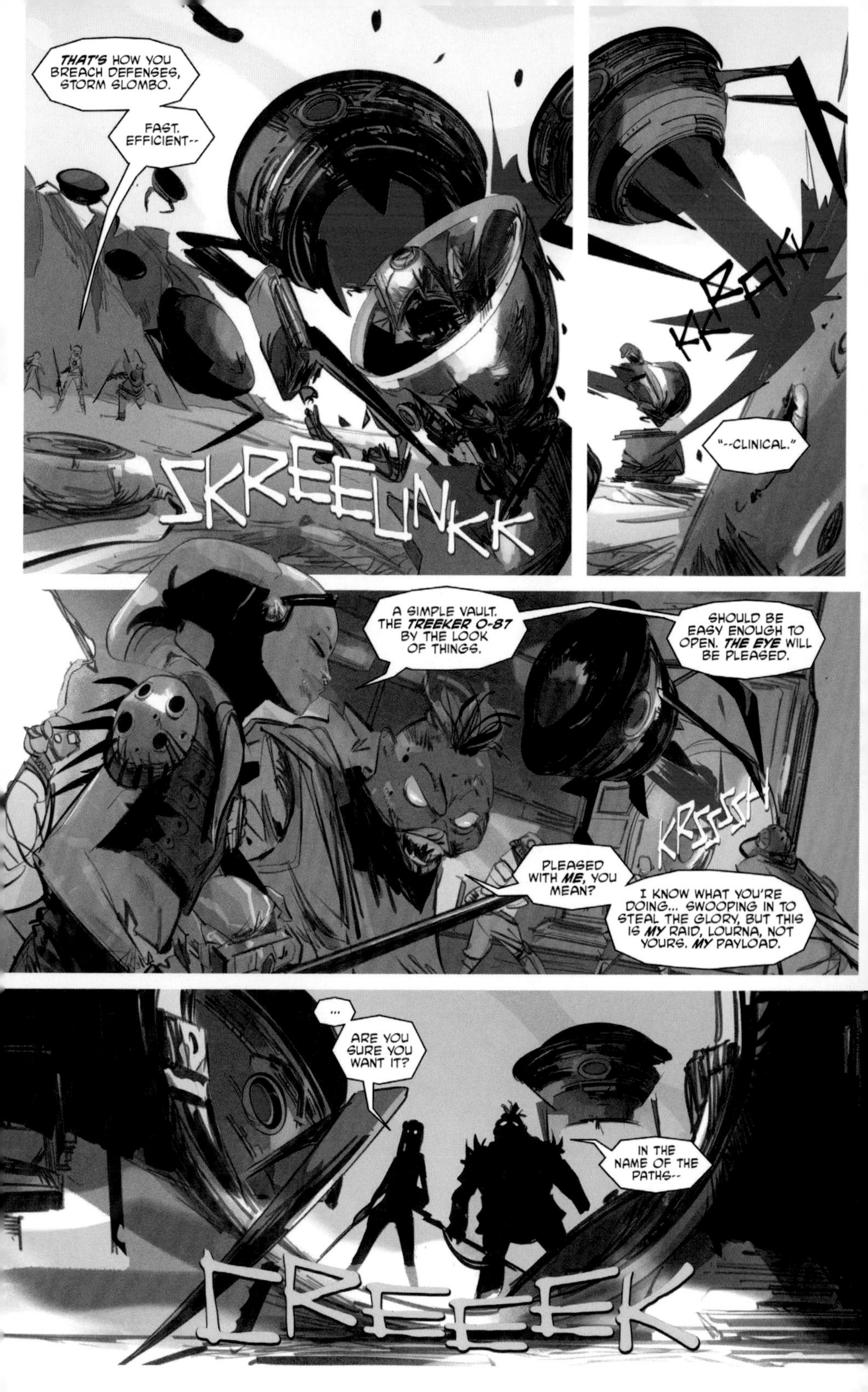

THAT'S HOW YOU BREACH DEFENSES, STORM SLOMBO.
FAST. EFFICIENT--
SKREEUNKK
KKRAKK
"--CLINICAL."
A SIMPLE VAULT. THE TREEKER O-87 BY THE LOOK OF THINGS.
SHOULD BE EASY ENOUGH TO OPEN. THE EYE WILL BE PLEASED.
KRSSSSH
PLEASED WITH ME, YOU MEAN?
I KNOW WHAT YOU'RE DOING... SWOOPING IN TO STEAL THE GLORY, BUT THIS IS MY RAID, LOURNA, NOT YOURS. MY PAYLOAD.
...
ARE YOU SURE YOU WANT IT?
IN THE NAME OF THE PATHS--
CREEEEK

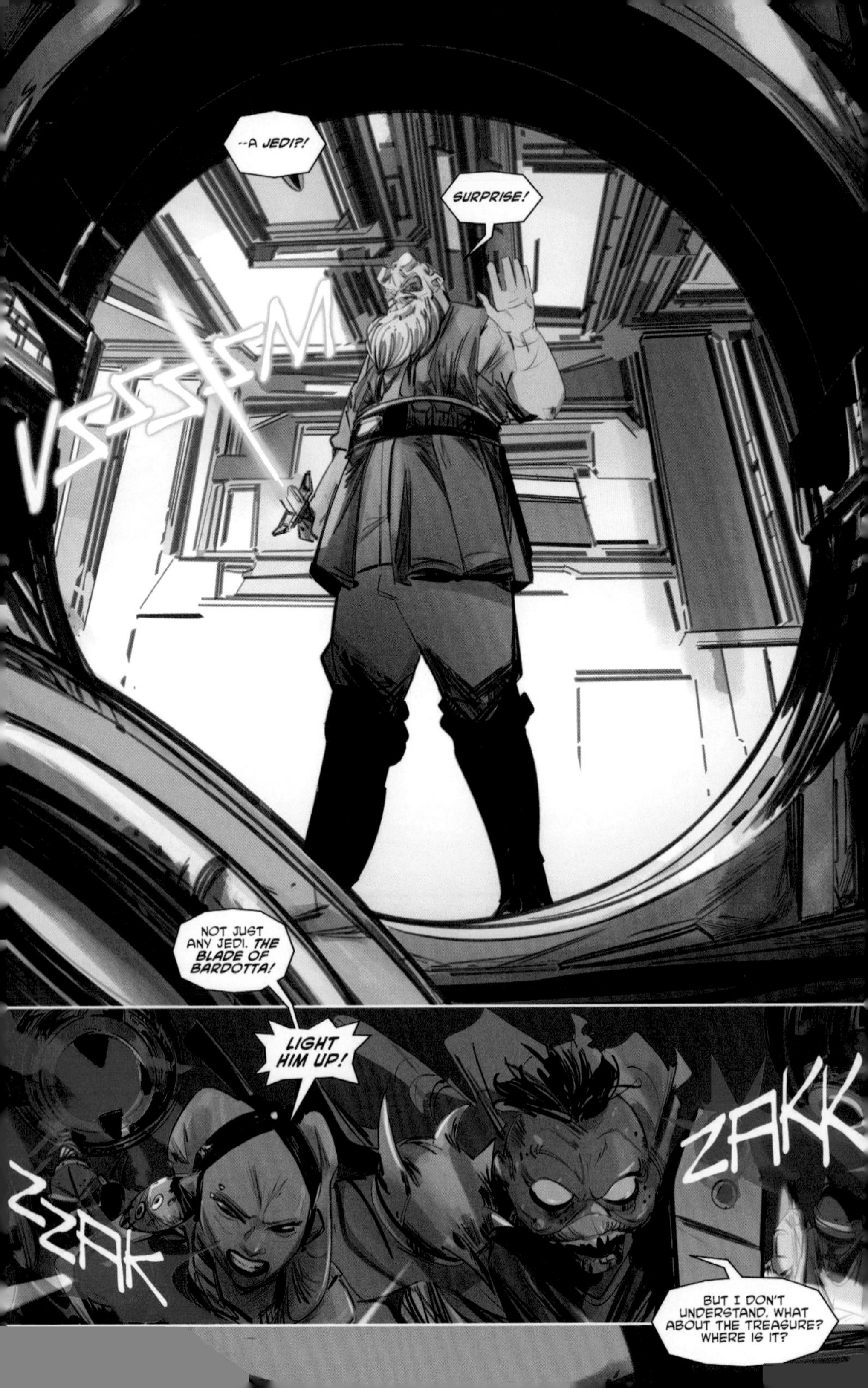
--A JEDI?!
SURPRISE!
VSSSSM
NOT JUST ANY JEDI. THE BLADE OF BARDOTTA!
LIGHT HIM UP!
ZZAK
ZAKK
BUT I DON'T UNDERSTAND. WHAT ABOUT THE TREASURE? WHERE IS IT?

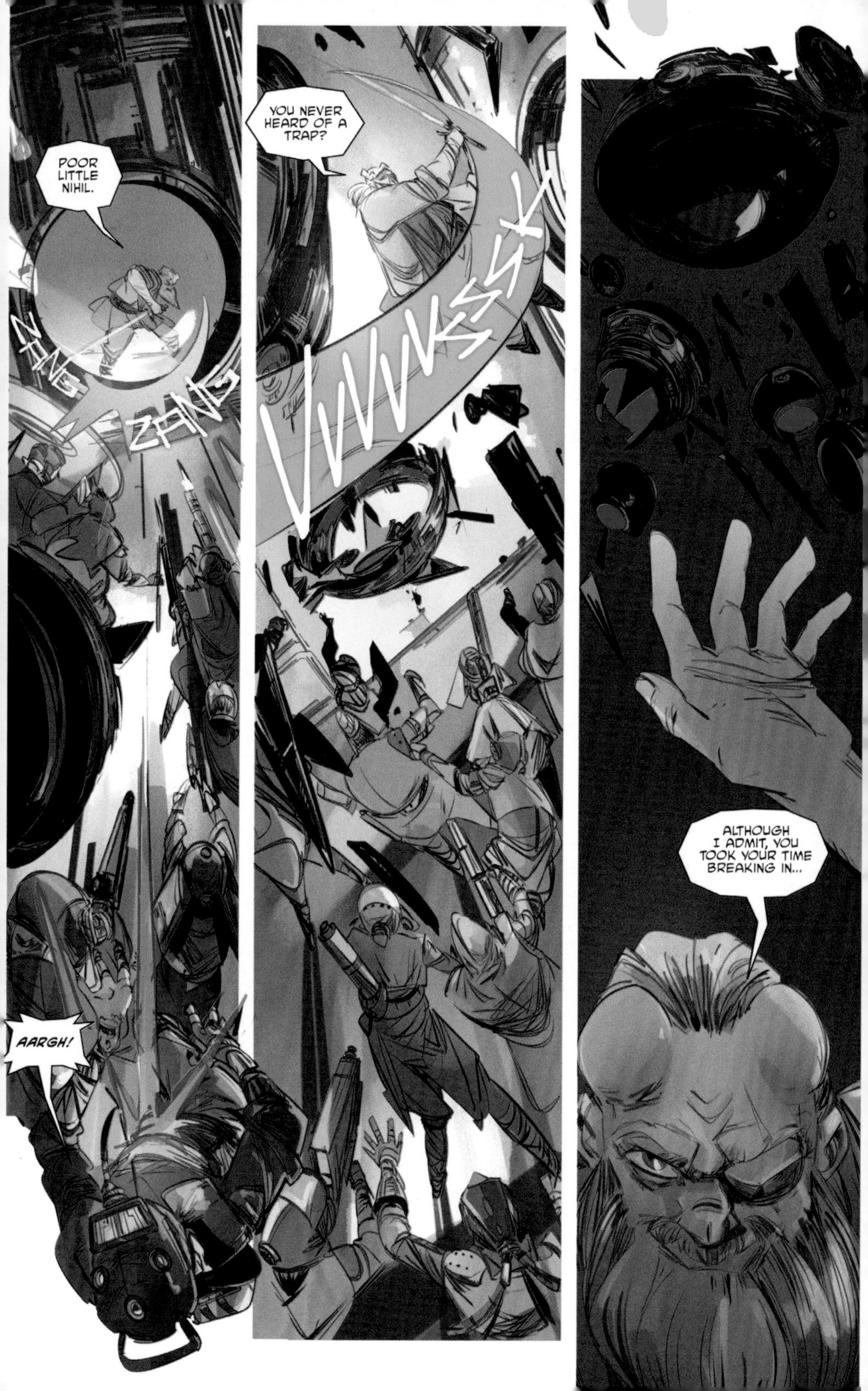
POOR LITTLE NIHIL.
ZANG
ZANG
ZANG
AARGH!
YOU NEVER HEARD OF A TRAP?
VVVVVVSSSK
ALTHOUGH I ADMIT, YOU TOOK YOUR TIME BREAKING IN...

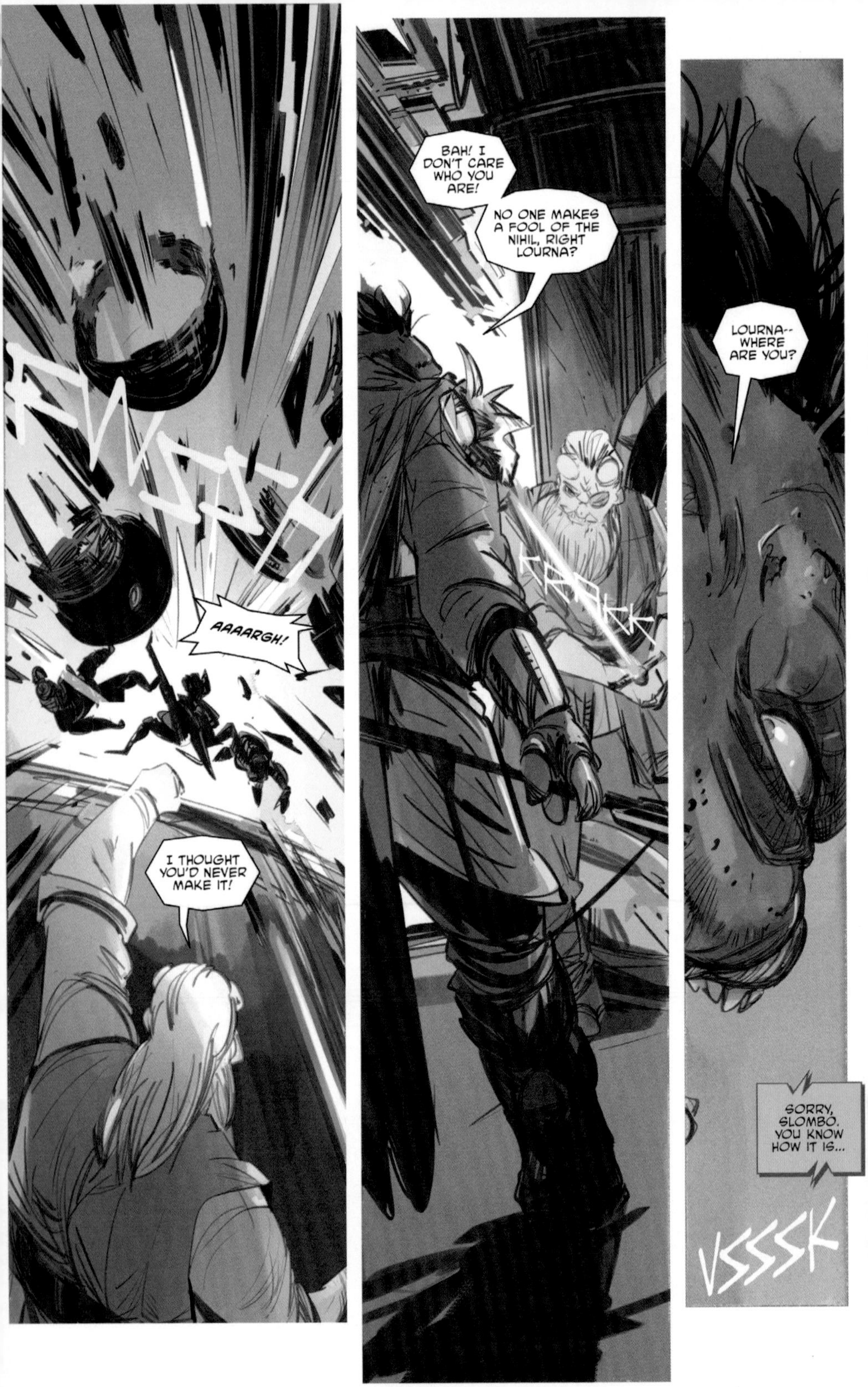
AAAARGH!
I THOUGHT YOU'D NEVER MAKE IT!
BAH! I DON'T CARE WHO YOU ARE!
NO ONE MAKES A FOOL OF THE NIHIL, RIGHT LOURNA?
KRAKK
LOURNA-- WHERE ARE YOU?
SORRY, SLOMBO. YOU KNOW HOW IT IS...
VSSSK

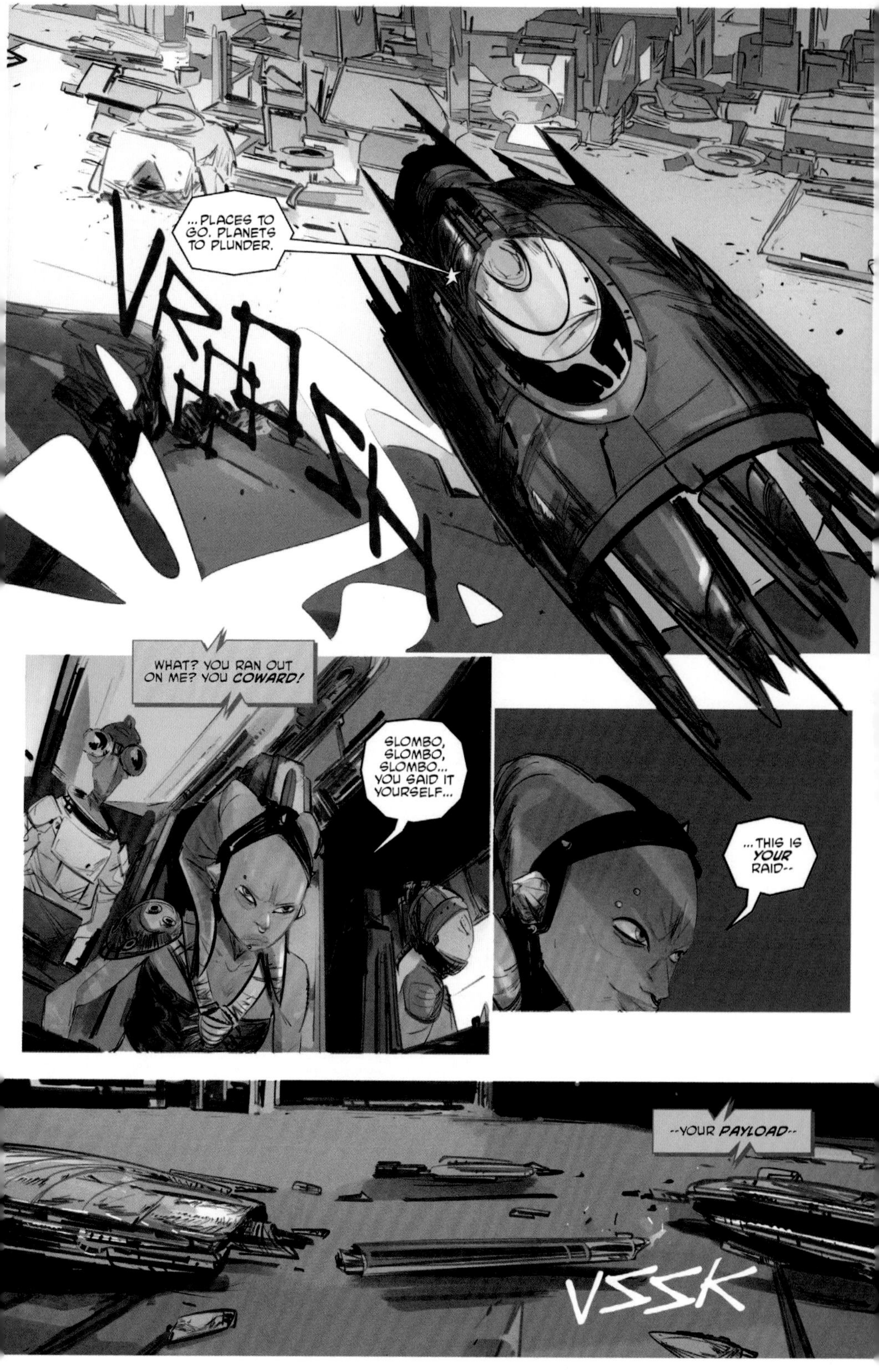
...PLACES TO GO. PLANETS TO PLUNDER.
WHAT? YOU RAN OUT ON ME? YOU COWARD!
SLOMBO, SLOMBO, SLOMBO... YOU SAID IT YOURSELF...
...THIS IS YOUR RAID--
--YOUR PAYLOAD--
VSSK

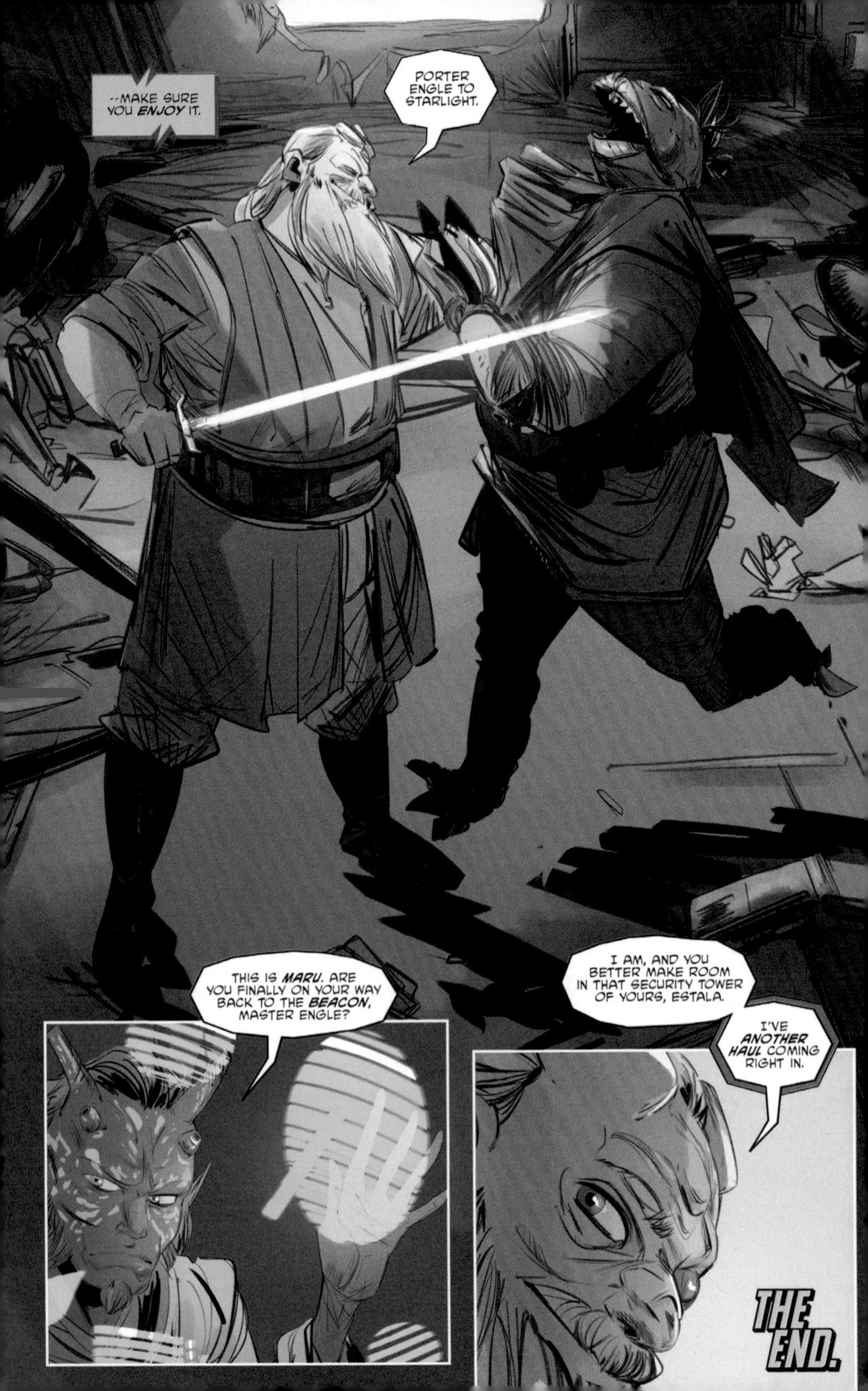
--MAKE SURE YOU *ENJOY* IT.
PORTER ENGLE TO STARLIGHT.
THIS IS *MARU*. ARE YOU FINALLY ON YOUR WAY BACK TO THE *BEACON*, MASTER ENGLE?
I AM, AND YOU BETTER MAKE ROOM IN THAT SECURITY TOWER OF YOURS, ESTALA.
I'VE *ANOTHER HAUL* COMING RIGHT IN.
THE END.

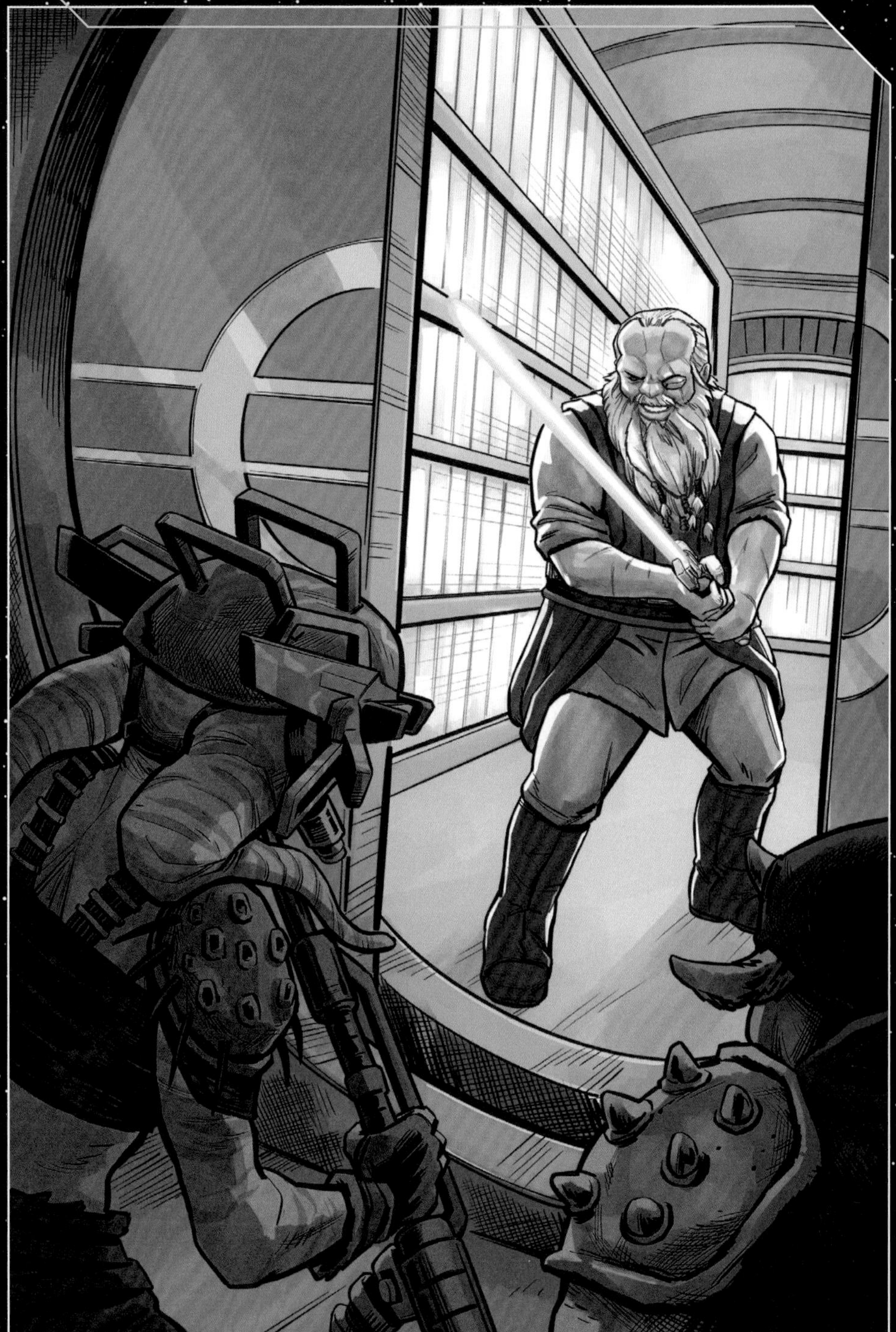

ART BY JASON LOO

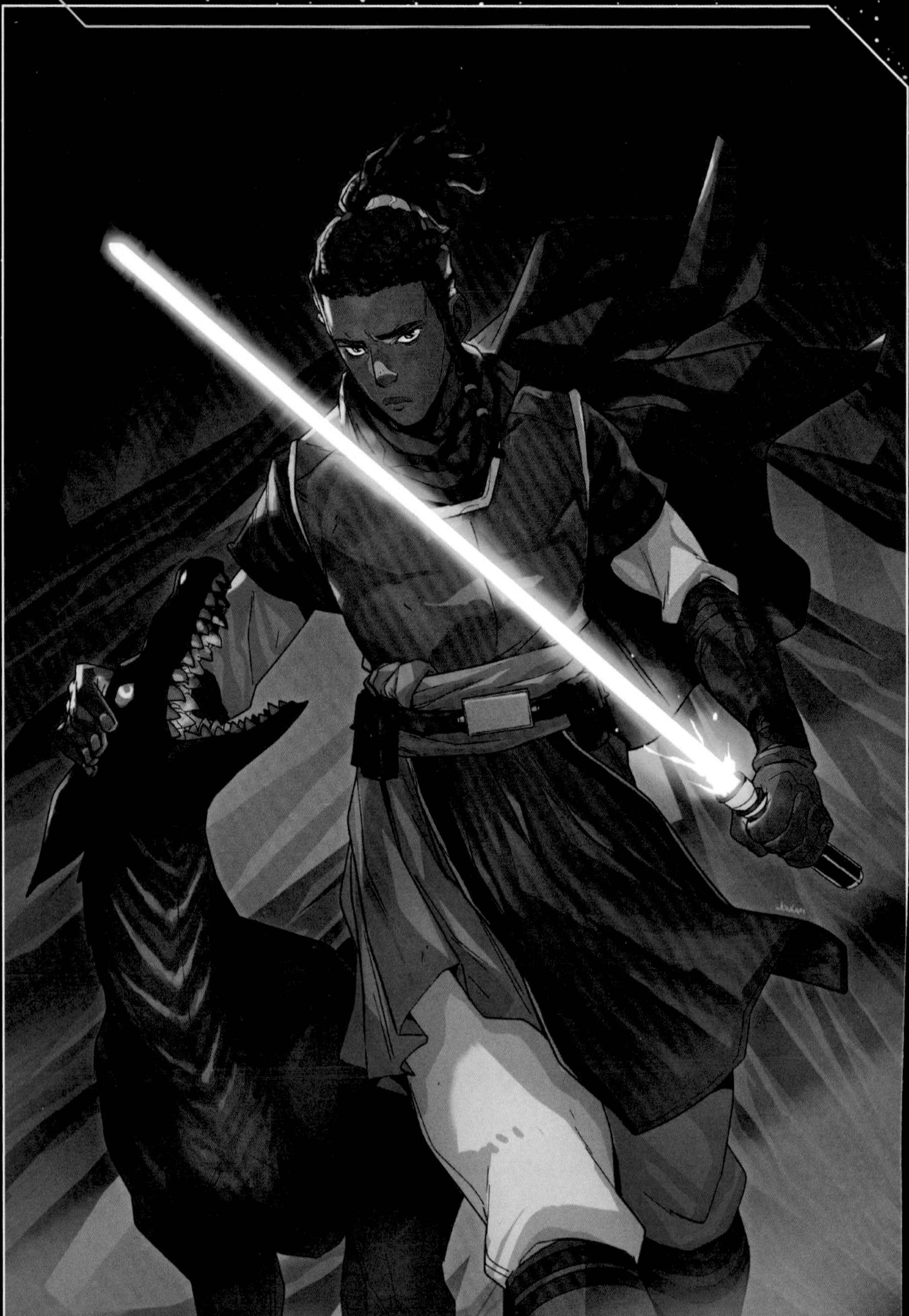

ART BY **JON LAM**